DIVINE DESTINY

An Amarah Rey, Fey Warrior Novel

Harmony A. Haun

ISBN: 978-8-9868359-0-7 Paperback
ISBN: 978-1-7363432-9-6 e-book
ISBN: 978-8-9868359-1-4 Hardback

First edition

Author Contact: harmonyhaunauthor@gmail.com

An Amarah Rey, Fey Warrior Books

AWAKEN

FEY BLOOD

DARK TEMPTATIONS

DIVINE DESTINY

DEDICATION

This book is dedicated to everyone trying to start fresh. To those that have stumbled along the way but are far from giving up. In case you need to hear this…DON'T GIVE UP! It doesn't matter where you've been or what you've done, tomorrow is always a new day, and it's never too late to do what you want and be who you want. You got this.

DIVINE DESTINY

An Amarah Rey, Fey Warrior Novel

Word Definitions

All "The Unseen" words are English words translated into Estonian. Click on each hyperlinked (ebook) word to listen to the pronunciation from Google.

Alfa: Alpha

Ammune: Old

Beeta: Beta

Esimene: First

Kaitsja: Protector

Keerutaja: Trickster

Konsiilium: Council

Lapseealine: Young

Libahunt: Werewolf

Maa Family: Earth Fey

Müstik Family: Mystic, First Fey

Õhk Family: Air Fey

Rändaja: Traveller

Sigitis: Brood

Surmajärgne Elu: Afterlife

Täiskuu: Full Moon

Täitjad: Enforcers

Tulekahju Family: Fire Fey

Ülim: Supreme

Valimine: Selection

Valmistaja: Maker/manufacturer in Finnish

Valvur: Guardian

Vanemad: Elders

Vesi Family: Water Fey

Võitleja: Warrior

Võltsimatu: Pure

Amarah Rey Series Playlist

Listen to the entire series playlist here: Spotify

Amarah: Divine Miracles

I Need A Miracle by Taylor Mosley, lost.,Pop Mage

I've never felt such overwhelming, intense, and waring emotions in my entire life. My world just ended but has also been reborn at the same time. My worst fear has come to pass. My never-ending and torturous nightmares have finally played out in real life but I'm also in the presence of an Archangel.

Logan is gone. Forever.

My soulmate is gone.

I made a deal with the Devil.

Heaven is real.

Archangel Michael is here and he's glorious.

There's finally hope for the future but there's no future I want without Logan in it.

All of my attempts at pushing Logan away to keep him safe, all of the pain I caused him, and myself, has all been for fucking nothing. NOTHING! Logan lived the last days of his life sad and angry.

Because of me.

He lived the last days of his life alone. No family. No mate. *No one.*

Because of me.

He lived the last days of his life not feeling all the love that he absolutely deserved.

Because of me.

Because I'm selfish. Because I'm weak. Because I'm the dumbest, stubborn, and most ignorant person on this entire planet.

But has this always been in our stars? I've always been a firm believer that everything happens for a reason but what reason could this possibly be for? But then, Archangel Michael is here so, how can it not be destined?

"I'm here for my son."

Michael's words hit me with the force of a lightning bolt, pulling me out of my dazed, internal turmoil. His son? Who's his son? Logan? Logan is Archangel Michael's *son*? What in Heaven is going on? There's no way I heard him right. No, that can't be what he meant. I'm grieving and not in the right head space.

"You?" Lucifer laughs deeply, "oh, how the mighty have fallen."

"You're in no position to point fingers, Luci," Michael says, defensively.

Lucifer holds up his hands, "no, no, I'm not pointing fingers, just incredibly shocked is all. I mean, I knew other Angels were fornicating with humans but I never, in a million years, would have put the mighty and honorable *Michael*, amongst that list. And a Werewolf at that," he laughs deeply again, "I think you're trying to give me a run for my money, Brother."

I'm trying to process this information. Is it true? Is Michael truly Logan's birth father? Did Michael, a freaking Angel, from Heaven, sleep with Logan's mother all those hundreds of years ago? And did Logan know? He was so shocked about *me* being half Angel,

I can't imagine he knew his own truth. I shake my head and focus on the conversation between Lucifer and Michael, desperate to learn everything I can.

"As usual, you know *nothing*," Michael spits out with malice.

Lucifer shrugs, nonchalantly, "it would have been nice to know there was another target I could have been focusing on this entire time but it doesn't matter. I got what I wanted."

Lucifer turns his attention to me. I suddenly feel extremely exposed and vulnerable under his piercing blue gaze. His smile turns devious as he rakes that gaze over me and then lands on Logan, taking in his lifeless body, and then back to me.

"Amarah, my sweet, sweet, naïve, Amarah. What can I say? It's been an absolute pleasure doing business with you," he gives me a sweeping bow, "but I'm afraid my dear brother here isn't going to let me complete my end of our bargain." He pushes out his bottom lip in an exaggerated pout. "So sorry," he says, sarcastically.

He gives his attention back to his brother, "well, I guess I'll leave you to it, whatever *it* may be. I have somewhere to be," he turns and starts walking away from us.

"Wait!" I finally find my voice, "you said you would save him! I gave you my power in exchange for Logan's life! Lucifer!" I yell at his retreating back.

He throws his hand in the air and waves as he disappears from view.

"Lucifer!" I scream, my voice hoarse from all the screaming I did as I watched Valmont's sword pierce Logan's chest.

My anger and frustration at Lucifer quickly turn into panic and desperation. I look down at Logan's cold, unmoving body. His once wonderful and bright meadow and sunshine green eyes are dull and vacant. Lifeless. Dead. I turn my head away and instead focus on my hand intertwined with his but that's not any better. His hand is cold and lifeless. His beautiful caramel skin seems to have dulled as well.

Our hands are both caked in dried, cracking blood. Even the blood is a dull red, no longer flowing with life. Everything that I used to love an adore about him is gone. Logan is gone.

A choked sob sneaks up and out of my throat. For a moment, I still had hope. For a moment, I thought Lucifer would be able to do what he promised. Bring Logan back to me. But turns out, he's exactly what everyone believes him to be.

The fucking Devil.

"Amarah," Michael's voices pierces through my grief. His voice is solid and strong. It *demands* attention.

I lift my head up and blink my tears away. His striking face comes into focus just inches away from me from where he's kneeling on the other side of Logan's body. His immaculate white wings are tucked in behind him. He's almost too beautiful to look upon but I can't seem to tear my eyes away. They're glued to his face in admiration of his Divinity, even without the glowing Heavenly light falling upon him, he's clearly an Angel. And, as I look into his golden, sunlit eyes, eyes I see now are so similar to Logan's, all I can do is apologize.

"I'm sorry," I whisper. "This is my fault. This is all my fault."

"Yes and no," Michael says, sternly but not unfriendly. "All of our actions and decisions have lasting effects and consequences, this is true. And yes, you will have to live with the decisions you've chosen to make."

I sniff and use my free hand to rub my nose. Nothing would be more embarrassing than to have snot running out of my nose in front of an Archangel.

"But," he continues, "some things are destined. Some things will always come to pass regardless of the course you take to get there. This is one of them. Death comes to all, Amarah, and it is not the end but another beginning."

I know my Bible history. I know he's talking about eternal life in Heaven, but something like that isn't exactly easy to comprehend, and it certainly does *very little* to comfort the loved ones left behind. *Me.* I've been left behind and I don't want to live another second in this bleak and utter emptiness.

"It's only a beginning for those that have passed. For me, I might as well be trapped in a coffin because this life, life without Logan," tears stream down my face and my voice gets thick with emotion, "it might as well be death. So just lock me in a coffin to wither away and wait for death to claim me. Better yet, cut out this wounded, bleeding stump of a heart I have left in my chest and stop my suffering. Please! Haven't I suffered enough?"

He sighs, not with frustration but with skilled patience and understanding. "I'm sure you've heard all the beautiful sayings about suffering. *God only gives his hardest battles to his strongest soldiers. God will never give you more than you can handle.* These are true, but I know they don't bring comfort. The only thing that can give you comfort is your Faith, Amarah. You have to believe in something bigger than yourself, bigger than your suffering, and far greater than any time you will spend on Earth. Suffering produces perseverance; perseverance character and character, hope. Why is it, that one is so quick to forget that there is a time for laughter just as there is a time for mourning? There is a time to be born and a time to die. There are times of war and times of peace. But would one know laughter, birth, and peace, if it wasn't for also knowing mourning, death, and war?"

He goes silent, waiting for me to either answer, or to let what he said sink in. I know he speaks the truth. Every word out of his mouth is a testament to life, but even being half Angel, I'm not above mistakes and selfishness. Hell, apparently neither is Archangel Michael from what I've gathered from his conversation with Lucifer.

"You need to think on this, Amarah. You need to find your Faith again. The same Faith that repelled my treacherous brother when he tried reaching you months ago, before you found out your truth. Do you remember that dream? Do you remember that unyielding Faith?"

The memory comes back to me.

Everything around me is fuzzy. All around me, people are running, screaming, scared. I can feel their fear like it's a live wire sending electricity loose in the air. I can hear them, sense them, but for some reason, I can't see them. Why can't I see them?

I don't run.

I don't scream.

I'm not scared.

I imagine myself standing in the middle of a bright glowing white light. A Heavenly light that is so pure nothing evil can stand against it and it will protect me. I know the Devil is coming, pure evil is headed straight for me, but I will stand and fight. He's coming. I could feel it. This is it. It is time to fight!

"Our Father, who art in Heaven, hallowed be thy name..."

I nod, "I do, but..." I shake my head in disbelief, "I always thought that it was a dream. Just that, a *dream*, not real. But you're saying it was real then? Lucifer was trying to reach me before I even knew what...or who, I was?"

"Yes," he says, solemnly. "And he never even stood a chance against you because your Faith was so strong. I know you've had some tough experiences since then but you need to get back to that place, Amarah."

I look down at Logan's body again. The weight of his death crushes me. It crushes everything inside of me and I don't know how I can find anything else under the weight of his death.

"I don't know if I can," I admit on a quiet whisper.

"You can and you will," his words and his tone are strong and confident in their conviction. "Perhaps you just need a little nudge in the right direction? Perhaps witnessing a divine miracle might help?"

I look up at him, the smallest sliver of hope peeking through my bleak existence, like a delicate flower fighting to reach the sunlight through suffocating and impenetrable concrete.

I look down at Logan's unmoving body once again and then back up to Michael. "Can you...?"

He nods, "I can but it will come at a great cost. We're not supposed to alter destiny but," he looks down at Logan, his face growing soft with emotion. *With love.* "He's my son," he says plainly, as if that's all the reason he needs.

He controls his emotions and his face is hard a serious when he looks at me again. "It's not his time, nor is it yours. You both have a lot left to do here on Earth. *Together.*"

He reaches over his shoulder and pulls a single white feather from his wing. He gently lays it across Logan's chest, right over his heart, over the gaping wound that took his life. The feather starts to glow, that Heavenly light that preceded Michael's arrival, pours out of this one single feather. Then, the feather sinks into Logan's chest and disappears completely.

The world around us is utterly quiet and still. There's not a single sound or even a breath coming from me or Michael. We're literally existing in a frozen moment of time. I wait on bated breath, the flower of hope pushing harder and harder through the concrete of my emotions.

It's been several minutes since the feather disappeared into Logan's chest and nothing is happening. I glance at Michael but his eyes are focused on the wound in Logan's chest so, I return my attention to it, too. That's when I finally see it. I suck in a breath as I watch the wound slowly stitch itself together and close completely. There's no scar, no sign that it was ever there at all.

I feel the twitch of Logan's hand in mine a second before his body jerks up into a sitting position. He gasps for beath and coughs furiously as his free hand clutches at his chest.

"Logan!" I want to scream his name but all I manage is

whisper around the constriction I feel in my own chest.

He's stunned and disoriented, I can see the confusion in his eyes as they search the room without really seeing anything, but they quickly find mine and focus.

"Amarah?"

That's all the confirmation I need that he's ok. I release my death grip on his hand and take his face in both of my hands and crush my lips to his. He doesn't hesitate kissing me back. His large, strong hands, now full of life again, are pulling me into his lap. I don't resist.

I kiss him fiercely. I kiss him with all the passion and love I kept from him in the past month and a half. I kiss him with all the love I have inside of me that belongs only to him. I kiss him with all the love he deserves. I kiss him with all the love I thought I'd never have a chance to give him ever again. I can taste the salt of my tears as they pour down my face in a cascade of emotions that are threatening to drown me.

Relief.

Guilt.

Love.

Regret.

Hope.

Logan pulls away from the kiss chuckling and gasping for breath but his eyes sparkle with renewed life. They're full of life, love, and…desire. Always desire. They take my breath away until I'm gasping for air right along with him. We're both bringing each other back to life. Him, physically, and me, spiritually and emotionally.

"Hi," he says, softly, a beautiful smile gracing his lips.

I manage a strangled laugh through my tears, "hi."

His hands cup my face. They're warm and alive again, and he sweeps his thumbs gently under my eyes, wiping away my tears. His eyes, so full of life, HE'S ALIVE!! His eyes are the most beautiful green and yellow I've ever seen. They've never been more beautiful than they are right now. He's never been more perfect than he is right now. He's always been my everything and I've never been more sure of it than I am now, in this moment.

I'm overwhelmed by his perfection. I'm overwhelmed by the love exploding out of my body. All of the love I tried so desperately to lock away. It's erupting inside of me like a volcano and I don't fight it. I don't want to fight it ever again but my guilt and regret are tamping it down. I don't deserve Logan's love. I don't deserve to give him my love and have it received. Not after what I've done. Not after I've hurt and betrayed him. God, he deserves so much better than me.

I close my eyes and shake my head. "I'm sorry," I say, as the tears seep through my lashes. "I'm so, so sorry."

"Shhhh, it's ok," Logan's voice is strong but soothing, his thumbs still wiping away my river of tears.

"No, it's not." I force myself to open my eyes and meet his intense gaze. He deserves the truth and he deserves to be looked in the eyes. He deserves to be seen. To be acknowledged. "I was trying to protect you. I was trying to save you. And I failed. And I was wrong. I was so wrong, Logan, about everything. And I'm sorry. I love you so much but I betrayed you. I don't deserve your forgiveness. I don't deserve your love."

"Oh, Angel," Logan gives me all of his attention, "you've definitely made some mistakes but you've never been more wrong than you are right now. If you want love then you're going to have to go through pain. Love doesn't have rules and my love for you is deeper than just the best of you, Amarah. My love for you transcends anything physical, anything in this world, and whatever comes for us in the next life, my love will transcend that too. If you love me the same way, which I think you do," he gives me one of his body-melting half smiles.

"I do, Logan, I do," I desperately promise.

9

He continues wiping away my tears, then leans in and gently kisses each of my eyelids, then kisses my lips. I feel all his love pouring into me from just a press of his lips on mine. It's so full of conviction and a promise of a lifetime of love yet to come.

When he pulls back, he's smiling the brightest smile I've ever seen. "Then that's all we need, Angel. As long as we have this love, we'll fight through anything else that comes our way. Together."

A throat clears, causing us both to jump in surprise, as we turn to acknowledge the Archangel in the room. As always, Logan is my gravity. He's the center of my entire world, and the rest of the world just falls away. Apparently, even an Archangel can't come between us.

"I'm thrilled that the two of you are reconciling but there will be time for that later. I don't have much time left before I need to get back and I'm sure you have questions," Michael reaches out and offers us each a hand.

We take them and stand. I feel small and insignificant next to Michael and it isn't just his Divinity. I mean, physically. Logan is six feet tall, packed with muscle, and he even looks small next to the Angel. He's got to be over seven feet tall and he's built like a lean football player. He's magnificent.

Logan looks from Michael to me and then back to Michael. The earlier confusion playing on his face again. "I'm sorry, who are you?"

Logan: Who I Am

Alive by Daughtry

I'm staring at this new stranger, an Angel I'm assuming, on account of the sheer size of him. Also, the wings are a pretty dead giveaway. Oh, and the fact that I'm standing here, *breathing*. But something about him bothers me. He seems...*familiar* somehow, though I'm positive I've never seen him before in my life.

The stranger sighs, I can hear the frustration in his tone, "I wish we were meeting under different circumstances. There's so much I want to say, so much time I want to spend getting to know you, but I'm afraid life doesn't always give us what we want. Archangels are no exception to the rule."

He extends his hand out to me again, this time for introductions. I take it, still trying to get my mind to catch up to my new reality. One second, I was fighting Valmont, then struggling to keep my eyes on Amarah, desperate to see her for one more second, to memorize her face, before I was pulled away by death.

I know I was dead but it didn't feel like I was. Then again, how would I know what death is supposed to feel like? But what it *did* feel like to me, was a deep, but wakeful, sleep. I couldn't feel my body, I was weightless and just...*existing*. Or maybe not existing at all. I'm not sure. I was surrounded by darkness but it wasn't ominous.

It was just dark space. There was no emotion or feeling, just...a void.

"I'm Michael and..." he hesitates. His eyes slide to Amarah's. She shrugs and shakes her head. I know I've missed some time, some important pieces of the puzzle are missing for me, and I feel left out. He returns his gaze to me and clears his throat, "I'm your father, Logan."

Of all the things I could have imagined him, an Archangel, saying, this is *not* it. I watch the Angel, Michael's, face for any signs of deception. Or humor. There's no way that he can actually be serious but he's acting like he is. I glance over to Amarah and she just nods her head in agreement with Michael.

"I'm sorry," I rub my forehead, trying to get my racing thoughts straight. "Did you say you're my *father*?"

"Yes," Michael confirms. "I know it's hard to understand but..."

"Hard to understand?" I mock with a sarcastic chuckle. "That's putting it lightly! Is this some kind of joke. Did I hit my head or something?" I look around the floor to see if I can find anything I would have knocked myself crazy with. That's when I finally notice the others. Valmont, Viveka, and Kordeuv are still here but they're frozen in place. "Are they...frozen?" I ask, skeptically. "Holy shit, I *have* lost my damn mind."

"You're not losing your mind. Yes, they're frozen in the real timeline. When I leave, and time resumes, they will pick up right where they left off. There won't be any time lag or minutes lost for them. As far as being your father, it's true. Once upon a time, Angels came down to Earth, often. We watched over people, protected them, and guided them. Then, some Angels began to cross the line between just guiding and influencing and became involved... physically, with humans. I'm amongst those that did. I never intended too," he shakes his head and then a small smile curves his lips, "but when I saw Lana, I knew she was going to destroy me in the best possible ways."

I glance over at Amarah and she's eagerly soaking up everything Michael is saying. She's so beautiful, and I know exactly what Michael felt when he saw my mother, because I felt the same way about Amarah. I even said the same thing, that she would destroy me. Perhaps Michael and I are not so different. In the realm of love and women at least.

"Of course, this was never supposed to happen. Angels were never supposed to procreate with beings on Earth," Michael continues. "For this transgression, we were forbidden to ever step foot on Earth again. Anyone who went against this *golden* rule, as Lucifer so put it, would be banished, and well, we were all witnesses to Lucifer's banishment and punishment, none of us wanted that to happen to us. So, we've been bound to Heaven ever since. Our only connection to beings on Earth has been the dream realm and, even then, we have to be invited or the host has to be open to us." He shakes his head, "I never would have left you if I had a choice."

"You *did* have a choice," I say, surprisingly calmly. "I grew up believing that my father was a good man, a *great* man, that died. My mother never told me more than vague descriptions and memories, but it was clear to see that my mother loved you. She never stopped loving you. And you just left her, left me, when you could have been with us."

"It's not that simple, Logan, I..."

"Yes, it is!" I yell.

I see Amarah jump next to me and reach out for her hand. To comfort her and reassure her that I'm ok, but really, it's to settle me. Just her simple touch alone is a balm to my soul. She's the one thing that can keep my anger buried. Hell, not even buried. When I'm with her, the anger is gone, not even hiding beneath the surface. I don't know how or why she has this effect on me but I don't question it.

I take a deep breath and run my free hand through my hair,

"we don't need to get into the details of the past, I'm sure we will just agree to disagree, besides, you said we don't have much time. What can you tell us that will help us now?"

"Alright," Michael concedes. "As you may have already realized, you and Amarah are two halves of a whole, yin and yang, soulmates, whatever you'd like to call it. She's the fire and you're the ice, literally. Your combined power is the only thing that can seal the rip between this world and the demon realm."

He says a lot in those few sentences and my mind is reeling. One thing stands out to me more than anything else, but before I can get my thoughts in order and ask my questions, Amarah is already questioning him.

"Soulmates?" She asks, her tone is dejected and her face looks defeated. I don't understand it. "The link we have…so, you're saying that we've never had a choice other than being together? So, what we feel for each other…isn't real?

"Of course it's real, Amarah, and you always have a choice. Do you not? Have you not completely blocked your connection and moved on in these past weeks?"

Amarah doesn't say anything but I can see the wheels spinning behind her eyes. She's hanging on to every word Michael says, trying to decide if he's right. If he's telling the truth because, one thing that has always been important to her about us, is that it's real.

"Freewill will never be taken away from you, Amarah. If you don't want to be with Logan, there's not a force in this universe, God included, that would make it so. However, you are destined to be together. A team. But that connection, that link, has nothing to do with love and everything to do with working together towards a common goal."

"What are you saying? The link we have doesn't include love?"

Michael shakes his head, "the two of you together has never been intended to be more than a means to an end. The link ensures a certain...*kinship*, to one another, but the fact that you both fell in love with each other is simply just a beautiful Blessing."

"So...it *is* real?" Amarah asks again. Determined to hear the Archangel say it.

"It's real, Amarah, and the love you have for each other is rare. Hold on to it. Cherish it. Fuel it. And never take it for granted."

Amarah turns her attention to me, there are tears in her eyes and I can see the relief flooding through her. It dawns on me that all I can do is *see* her emotions. I can't feel them. In fact, the place in my chest that's only for her feels...empty. Even when our connection is being blocked, I still feel it heavy and alive inside of me, waiting to be opened again. But now I feel nothing.

"Amarah, you don't need to block our connection anymore. Please, take down your walls and let me in," I plead. "I can't stand this emptiness I feel."

The relief I saw in her a second ago is now replaced by utter devastation. The tears flood down her cheeks again and I'm pulling her into me, wrapping my arms around her, without hesitation.

"It's ok, Angel. You can let me in again. I promise, whatever I feel, whatever we have to work through, we *will*. I'm not going anywhere."

She shakes her head, her voice comes out in broken sobs, "it's not that. I can't."

"What do you mean you can't?"

She shakes her head over and over again and drops her head to her chest. She crying out loud now, her sobs shaking her shoulders, and I can't wrap my mind around her sorrow. Her pain.

I cup her face in my hands and lift her head up gently to face me. My voice is soft and gentle when I tell her, "babe, it's ok. Of course you can, I'm not going to get mad at you. Whatever it is you think you need to hide from me, you don't. I promise, you don't."

She's gasping for air now, her breaths are ragged and deep, and she can't find her voice through her pain.

"She can't because she's no longer blocking the connection," Michael speaks for her.

"What does that mean?" I give the Archangel my attention as I pull Amarah into my chest and hold onto her tightly.

"When you died, she made a deal with Lucifer. She gave up her power, willingly, in order to save you."

His words hit me like a sledgehammer to the chest. She gave up her power, her Angel lifeforce, to save me. How could she do that? Why would she do that? Doubt and anger flood through me along with sadness, gratitude, and love. She gave up everything she is. *For me.* The only thing more she could have given up is her life, and as thankful as I am that she didn't, that she's still here in my arms, I'm also shattered that she gave up her power. For me.

"I got here as fast as I could," Michael is explaining. "If only I had been just a few seconds faster, I could have stopped her from doing it but..." he trails off, clearly just as shattered as I am. As we are.

"What could Lucifer possibly want with Amarah's power? I mean, he's...well the Devil, but also an Angel himself. I don't understand." I shake my head in confusion.

"Lucifer has been locked in Hell ever since he was banished. His only tie to Earth has been dreams, just like the rest of us. Amarah is both Fey and Angel. She's of Earth and Heaven. By gaining her power, he can now walk on Earth, freely."

I'm still confused but I know one thing, "that can't be good."

"No. Whatever he has planned is most definitely far from good. You need to prepare. All of you," Michael warns.

"This is all my fault," Amarah cries into my chest.

"Amarah, what I said to you earlier, is still true. All is not lost."

"How can you say that?" Her voice is muffled by the tears and being pressed against my chest. "If I don't have my power, I'm nothing. I'm no longer an Angel. I can no longer close the rip with Logan. I'm useless. I'm nothing."

"You will never be nothing, Amarah, and what is rightfully yours, will always be yours. Even though you willingly gave it to Lucifer, it does not belong to him and it never will. You are a Divine creation, God made you, Amarah. It's time to find your confidence and strength. It's time to really fight back."

"What are you saying," I ask Michael, as Amarah lifts her head off my chest, looking at the Angel too.

"I'm saying, you can get your power back, Amarah. It belongs to you and only you."

"How?" She asks, hopefully.

"That, I'm afraid, you will have to find out on your own. Regain your Faith, walk in belief in all you do, and He will guide you."

It's not an answer either of us want but it's the answer we get. Amarah steps away from me, wipes the tears from her eyes, and nods at Michael. She understands what he's saying and she understand what she needs to do. She needs to be the strong warrior she always has been, not only a warrior physically, but spiritually. The one that Lucifer doesn't stand a chance against.

"Time is running out," Michael says, urgently.

"Wait," I say, quickly, remembering my earlier thought process about what he said. "You said that Amarah is fire and I am ice." I remember the frozen imprints my fist made in the wards around Amarah's house, and the cold energy that penetrated, and almost killed, Atreya. "What does that mean? And how did Valmont never put it together? What I am, I mean. Doesn't my blood smell like Amarah's? *Different*?"

"The smell of your blood is overpowered by your Werewolf gene. To any Vampire, that's what you smell like and will always smell like. Pure Werewolf blood is potent. Now as far as your Angel power, it's the opposite of Amarah's. You've seen her white fire, well, yours is ice." He says, plainly.

"So, all this time, what I thought was a Fey power, has actually been an Angel power?" I ask, in disbelief.

Michael nods his head, "honestly, I'm surprised no one has figured that out yet. Your power has always been physical, like Amarah's. Your eyes glow when you merge your powers together, do they not?"

Amarah and I look at each other and nod together.

"It has never been a Fey life-force that you've felt inside of you Logan. Which other Fey have you ever seen do what you and Amarah can do?"

I'm baffled. I can't believe I've never seen the signs before. That I never thought to question it. We always thought that it was the Fey life-force mixed with my Werewolf side that caused it to be different. That was never the case at all.

"What the two of you can do together is beyond even my knowledge. You are *linked* together. You will be able to do more than just speak into each other's minds. Once Amarah gets her power back, you need to both explore it, train it, make it as strong and unyielding as it can possibly be. Only then will you be able to close the rip and seal evil back in Hell forever."

"But how? How do we learn to do this? Where do we even start?" Amarah is questioning him.

"I'm sorry, I must go," Michael's wings unfold. They take my breath away. They're pure white and massive but they also somehow look delicate and soft.

A radiant light pours down on him and I lift my arm to shield my eyes out of reflex but the light doesn't hurt my eyes. I reach my hand out and it passes through the light but I can feel it. It's not just air, it's heavy and thick and caresses my skin. A can almost hear a song, not made up of any specific words or instruments we know on Earth, but something Heavenly, something Divine, calling to me.

Michael's wings flap, the gust of wind snapping me out of my trance. His voice booms around us as he speaks one last time on his way back to Heaven.

"Have Faith, listen to your hearts, trust each other, and end this war."

He's gone in the blink of an eye. No more light, no more wind, no more Archangel. Or should I say, father? The only thing that's left is the reverberation of his voice echoing in my mind and everything that he shared with us. How is it that one can die and come back, minutes later, to an entirely different world?

I'm an Angel.

Holy fucking shit. I'm an Angel. Maybe I shouldn't say the word holy and fucking shit in the same sentence anymore. Is that like, blasphemy, or something?

Shit.

So much actually makes sense now. My power. How it started to reveal itself when I met Amarah. Why her and I are so drawn to each other. I'm so excited and anxious to find out what else we can do together! But first, we need to get her powers back.

"Bloody Hell," the Vampire's voice rings through my ears and pulls my attention his way immediately. "How is this possible? Amarah, is this your doing?"

"What kind of trickery is this?" A menacing voice hisses.

I turn my attention to the other woman in the room. Viveka. She's lurking in the shadows, the sunlight from the rising sun is pouring more and more light into this space. Good. I growl deep in my chest, my Wolf begging to be set free to sink its teeth into her delicate neck.

"Kordeuv," she snaps. "Bring me Amarah."

"Logan, protect her!" Valmont shouts as he stalks towards

Viveka. "It's time to settle this feud once and for all, Viveka. Let's see which one of us is more powerful. Shall we?"

3

Valmont: Divine Blood

Automatic by Deadset Society

I'm momentarily distracted by the image of Logan, alive and breathing, after I clearly watched him die. There's not a scratch or scrape anywhere on him, nor is there a whole in his chest when I know my sword pierced his heart. I felt it slide through his chest and push out of his back. There's absolutely no way that he should be alive, but then again, I shouldn't feel everything I feel with Amarah Rey's blood either. She must have brought him back to life somehow. But all I can remember is her screaming.

Oh Gods, her screams.

I know I'm going to hear that sound in my nightmares for years to come. *I* caused her that pain, and even though it seems like it was short-lived, I still caused it nonetheless. She was in excruciating pain because of me. I hate that I had to do it, but if it's a choice between saving Amarah Rey and destroying the entire fucking world well, it's no choice at all. I'll watch the world burn if it means Amarah Rey lives. But is it worth it to save her if it causes her immeasurable pain? Is it worth it, to save her, if she only ends up hating me for it? Gods, yes. Yes, it's worth it because it means she's alive and I still have a chance to love her. To let her fall in love with me. I know this makes me a selfish monster but I can't seem to find a conscious. As much emotion as Amarah Rey makes me feel, I don't feel bad about loving her, no matter the costs.

I'll worry about Amarah Rey's wrath after I've secured her safety. I shake my head, clearing my thoughts, and focus on the other monster in the room.

Viveka.

"Oh, come on, Valmont. We both know you can't defeat me. I *made* you!" She hisses from where she's hiding.

She's cowering in the darkest shadows. Lurking like a treacherous rattlesnake, coiling and waiting to strike, but I think her boisterous rattle, her feigned confidence, is all for show. I can hear the waver in her voice. Her confidence is not what it once was.

"Then why are you hiding, Viveka?" I provoke, as I slowly walk into the darker shadows, my sword resting on my shoulder.

"I'm not hiding," she seethes, "but I'm not going to stand near the sunlight so you can push me into it, either.

Amarah Rey's blood is still running through my veins. I managed to swallow down quite a bit before Viveka interrupted and just one drop of Amarah Rey's blood is enough to boost my strengths. I feel her blood singing in my veins, pulsing and thriving. I feel just as strong as I ever have, the daylight not weakening me in the slightest.

"Is daylight making you feel weak, Viveka?" I tease, as she comes into view before me.

She stands tall, shoulders pulled back, head held high, but her eyes have just an ounce of fear in them. Not much but it's enough.

"If it's affecting me then it must be devastating to you," she says, plainly. "Not to mention, you're armed and I have no weapon. It's far from a fair fight."

"Alright," I concede, as I toss my sword away. It lands in a beam of sunlight where neither one of us can reach it. "Now, it's fair."

"Why are you doing this, Valmont?" She asks, stalling. "Why are you protecting *her*? Why not just join with me again? Have power and fame and everything you want! We'll use her power to destroy the Konsiilium, together. No one will be able to stop us."

"Is that what you're after? Power to destroy the Council? I shake my head, "you were always too ambitious and power hungry, Viveka. They should have stopped you sooner but," I shrug, "I suppose I'll have to do their job for them. And when I provide them with your heart, and tell them what you had planned, I'll be congratulated. I'll be in their debt and I'll *demand* a seat on the Council. I will become even more powerful while you, well, you won't be here to see it, unfortunately."

"You're no one," she says in disgust. "Just because you became a Virtuoso doesn't mean a thing. The Council has never, and will never, pay you any mind because you're no one. You've only ever succeeded with me by your side."

"I've never realised just how delusional you are, Viveka. It's truly sad to see how pathetic you are. I can't believe I was once fooled by your charade. You need to have others tied to you because you yourself are insignificant. I see that now and it truly makes me a bit sad for you, not enough not to kill you but, sad for you nonetheless."

"I am no such thing and I don't need your pity!" She yells in anger. "I see there's no changing your mind and there's only one thing we can do to end this. So be it."

She moves quickly, just a blur, a shadow within a shadow. Even with my Master powers, I'm not sure I would have seen her move, but I'm more than just a Master now. I have Angel blood running through my veins. I see her move in to attack and I'm able step out of her grasp at the last second.

She let's out a frustrated scream as she attacks again. She's flying at me, arms waving wildly, trying to reach my chest. The only way either of us can die is if we have our hearts ripped out and our bodies burned. And, as fast as she is, I'm faster. Amarah Rey's blood makes me faster than I've ever been on my own.

I hold her off effortlessly. She growls in frustration again and continues to spin around me, trying to catch me off guard.

She finally pulls back and looks at me with a mixture of awe and hate on her face. "How?" She asks, breathlessly.

"You may think you know everything but you don't. You see, Amarah Rey is so much more than just some power she wields. She's so much more than just power to control. But you don't ever see past the power. You don't ever see the truth of a person. You never saw me, *my* potential to become a Master, to become better than you. You never saw Kordeuv's desperation to be freed of you, enough to betray you. And you never saw how special Amarah Rey is."

In the blink of an eye, I'm standing in front of Viveka, my hand wrist deep in her chest, clutching her heart in my fist. I lean in and whisper in her ear, "Amarah Rey is half Angel." I hear her gasp at the truth of my words but there's no movement from her heart. No flutter, no thump of life. We're Vampires. We lost our hearts a long time ago.

"Her blood is the true power for us, Viveka, not some weapon she has that can be used to destroy the Council. You could have had her blood in your veins and *you* would have been the weapon against the Council."

I move again, and this time when I stop, I stop with Viveka's back pushing against the sunlight streaming through the broken glass. All I have to do is rip out her heart and shove her into the light.

Here eyes are wide with fear. Tears start to build and then fall down her cheeks as she realises exactly what's about to happen.

"Valmont, please," she begs. "I'll leave. I'll do whatever you want, please!"

"Over three thousand years you've walked this Earth, destroying thousands of people's lives along the way. This has always been your fate and I'm beyond thrilled that it's my hand that you'll die by," I say, as I slowly start to push her into the light.

"Valmont, please! Don't do this! I made you! You can't do this! You can't kill me! Please!" She's frantically grabbing at my shirt, trying to pull herself out of the light.

Her skin starts to smoke immediately and then seconds later starts to blister and burn. I don't smile, I don't gloat, but I hope she feels all the pain of those she left behind, hurt, or worse, in her destructive wake.

"You know, I came to a realization recently. I never loved you, Viveka. I know what true love is now, I've experienced it, and it's sacrificing everything for someone else, even your own happiness, that's what unconditional love is," I confess. "I don't think you've ever been truly loved. You'll die knowing this harsh truth and I'll celebrate and drink a toast to your lonely and pathetic death."

Her eyes harden. She stops pleading and begging me to let her go. She wraps her hands around my forearm, her strength is incredible for her delicate size.

"You've never been loved either, Valmont. We started this together, let's finish it together," she says, with determination.

She throws herself back into the light. Her hands are fused to my arm and she drags me into the light with her.

"Valmont!" Amarah Rey's frantic voice echoes through the cavernous space.

I yank my hand free of Viveka's chest, bringing out her cold, dead heart in the process, but she's still holding me next to her. We're both flooded with sunlight. Her skin is burning and deteriorating at a rapid pace. I must be in shock because I don't feel any pain. I don't feel my skin also burning. My hand starts to smoke and I look down, terrified at what I'm going to see. I don't want to die, especially not like this. Not before I've just started living again for the first time in two thousand years! Not now that I've found Amarah Rey! Viveka's heart is what's smoking in my hand. It takes a few seconds for me to register that the smoke isn't coming from me. In fact, nothing on me is burning. I'm standing clear as day, in the sunlight, and I'm not burning. With my free hand, I pull the necklace I'm wearing out of my suit, the one that keeps me safe from fire, but it's not glowing. It's not protecting me.

Viveka's hands turn to ash and fall away from me. I instinctively step back into the shadows and watch as her body disintegrates into a pile of ash on the floor. She never screamed. She never made a sound. I can hardly believe that she's actually dead. She haunted me for so long and now…I'm free. Truly free from her.

"Valmont," I feel Amarah Rey's hand on my arm, turning me around to face her.

She reaches up and takes my face in her hands, my eyes slowly settle on her and her face comes into focus.

"Are you ok? Are you hurt?" She asks, as she studies my face. Her eyes dart quickly between mine, waiting for my response.

"I'm not hurt," I say, softly. My voice sounds far away. I think I'm in shock. Shock that Viveka is actually dead, shock that I was standing in the sunlight. Shock that, in this moment, I'm alive again. Alive, in ever sense of the word. Not just pretending to be.

Amarah Rey's eyes move to the pile of ash on the floor. The ash that used to be a walking, talking body. Ash that should also be me.

"How? How are you alive?" She asks.

I place my hand on my chest, over my heart. I close my eyes and focus on the steady thump, thump, thump I feel against my palm.

"You," I whisper. "Once again, Amarah Rey, you saved me."

"How? How did I do this? I don't understand." She asks,

confused.

"I'm not sure I fully understand everything either," I shake my head as I open my eyes and stare at the beautiful woman standing before me. The only woman that's ever owned my heart. The only woman that's actually made my heart beat again, and not just in theory. I grab her hand and place it on my chest.

"Do you feel it?"

"Do I feel what, Valmont?"

"Do you feel my heart beating?"

"Yes, of course I do. I've felt it several times. Why would I not feel your heart beating, Valmont?"

"I'm a Vampire. I'm *dead*, Amarah Rey. "My heart has not beat for centuries upon centuries. At first, I thought I was just imagining it, but now…" I shake my head. "Goosebumps, and how I *feel everything* when I'm with you. Your warmth, your body clutching mine when I'm inside of you, the cold, the snow crunching underneath my feet, everything being so incredibly sensitive, as if I'm feeling it all for the first time," I laugh, joyously.

"I don't understand. Please, Valmont, what are you saying?"

"Your blood truly allows me to live again, fully and completely."

She drops her hand from my face and lets out a heavy huff of breath, the news seeming to shock her just as much as it shocks me.

"Are you sure?" She asks, quietly.

I slowly reach my hand out and touch the light again. I close my eyes and feel the heat of it on my skin for the second time since I was turned. It's not as hot as it would be in summer, but there's no other feeling in the world like the sun on your skin.

"There's no other explanation," I smile down at her, completely and utterly enraptured.

I want to pull her to me. I want her lips, her mouth, her taste. I want to feel my heart flip inside of my chest as her tongue caresses mine. I want to slide inside of her and feel her body clinging to mine. I want to feel my body burning with my desire. I want to *feel* everything.

"Yeah, we're ok," a woman's voice says from somewhere next to me, stealing Amarah Rey's attention. "A bit worse for wear but we'll live. The ones we hadn't killed just fell to the ground. I don't know what happened but I'm not going to question it. What did we miss here?"

Amarah: One Thing At A Time

Save Me by Karl Michael, Mitchell Tenpenny

My head is spinning around so fast I feel like Beetlejuice when he's trying to seal the deal with Barbara and Adam. So much has happened in the last hour.

Lucifer has my power and can now walk on Earth.

Archangel Michael was here and he's Logan's father.

Logan died and was brought back to life *and* he's an Angel.

My blood literally brings Vampires back to life.

Viveka is dead.

Everyone else is beat to shit.

Holy guacamole, Batman! I think I'm definitely going to need to start seeing a damn shrink to deal with all this trauma that seems to come along with this new and exciting life of mine.

"Amarah," Logan's voice pulls me out of my head. "Hey," he says softly, as he reaches his hand out to hold mine. "Are you ok?"

His movement is hesitant, his eyes are wary, and it absolutely crushes me. I thought I lost him and that I was never going to have him back. The pain and the thought of him not being here anymore was beyond comprehension. The pain of losing him was beyond anything that I could ever express. It was, hands down, the worst and most terrifying moment of my life. And yet, it has been my greatest lesson and the biggest eye-opener. I will never take Logan, or anyone else, for granted again. I will live each second of each day expressing my love and appreciation for those around me. I will be present. Fuck Lucifer's advice on living for myself. We're not built to be solitary creatures. We're not meant to be alone and selfish. We're built to connect and to love and to protect those weaker than us. I will be what others expect because they only expect the *best* of me. And I'll give it to them from this day forward because it's what they deserve. It's what *I* deserve. The best of myself.

Why is it that it takes extreme circumstances and loss to shake us to our core and snap us out of our complacency? Well, I'm officially wide awake and seeing things right for the first time in a long time. I have a lot to apologize for, a lot of bridges to mend, and I'll start mending them with Logan.

I know we just had a beautiful moment together, declaring our love for one another, but nothing's ever that easy, is it? He just watched me comfort Valmont and express my concern for him. Another man. A man I slept with while Logan was fighting to get me back. The guilt and shame I feel from my actions weighs heavily on me but it's something I'll just have to work through. I can't get bogged down in my self-pity again.

I take Logan's offered hand but only to pull myself into him and wrap my arms around him. I look up into his handsome face, his peridot eyes shining with renewed life, but still cautious. I want to remove that look from his eyes and I never want to see it ever again. Not aimed at me.

I think about his question. Am I ok? I answer as honestly as I can, "I will be."

I smile up at him, giving him all of my attention, which is easy to do. Time and time again, when I'm with Logan, the entire world disappears.

He smiles back down at me. "*We* will be," he adds, as he lays a quick kiss on my forehead before easing his hold on me and raising his eyes to address the others.

I turn to face the small crowd gathered around us, but I remain in Logan's embrace, not ready to be apart from him. I need to feel him. I need to know he's here, alive, with me, right now.

It's Atreya who finally speaks up again, "well, I'm glad to see some good has come from all of this," she lifts her arms up, gesturing to the aftermath around her.

It's the first time I take in her appearance. Her hair is frizzy and pieces have come lose from her braid. She's covered in dirt and dried blood, but I can't see any open wounds on her so, she's either healed or it's not her blood. Or both.

"What happened to you guys?" I ask, as I look at Emrick, Kaedon, and Emerson's similar appearance.

Emerson seems the worst off out of the four of them. Then again, he *is* only human. I'm surprised he's even alive and standing before us. He has deep gashes running across his left cheek, as if claws were swiped at his face. His arms are covered in a mixture of cuts, gashes and…bite marks. It looks like he was attacked by a damn animal.

"The tunnels were packed with lapseealine, Hell, not even just young Vampires, these lapseealine were feral, depraved," Emerson shakes his head. "I've never seen anything like it."

"It was a trap," I say, quietly.

"Yes," Atreya sighs. "The five of us were almost not enough. We wouldn't be alive if Logan hadn't been fighting with us." She looks at him, clear respect and admiration written all over her face. "I knew you were good. I've heard stories, Hell, I've sparred with you enough to know you're a skilled fighter, but that," she shakes her head. "I've never seen anyone move so fiercely and so deadly in my entire life."

"I can't take all the credit." Logan's voice rumbles through his chest. "You four are the best I've ever seen, too. Kaedon, man, you're a beast! I've never seen anyone move so fast. Atreya, you're calculated and lethal. Your control is unmatched. Emrick, the power you have over the Earth is insane. Not to mention your skill with a blade is *damn* good. And Emerson, shit, you're better than most of the Wolves, honestly. None of us would have survived had any of us been any less."

"If I'm not mistaken," Valmont's smooth voice finally joins in the conversation. "You *didn't* survive, mate. No hard feelings, I hope? I acted only to save Amarah Rey."

"What?" I hear shocked voices and murmurs from the others as all eyes fall on Logan.

"Logan, what does he mean, you didn't survive?" Atreya questions.

"How are you standing here, alive?" Valmont continues as if she didn't speak.

Now would be a great time to be able to speak to Logan mind-to-mind. I don't know what he wants to reveal and what he doesn't. A wave of anger floods through me that I no longer have my power. I'm no longer fully connected to Logan and it's a heavy ache in my chest as I think about it. But there will be time to deal with this issue later, for now, one thing at a time.

I feel the movement of Logan's shoulders as he shrugs, his arms still wrapped around me. "I honestly don't know. I saw a light, a bright beautiful light, I was walking towards it when I was pushed, or maybe pulled, back. I don't know what happened but I woke up, alive. It must be a miracle or just not my time to die I guess," he says, nonchalantly.

Valmont cocks his eyebrow and folds his arms across his chest, not the least bit convinced. "Amarah Rey?" He questions me.

"It wasn't me," I shake my head, "but I may have an idea of what happened." I look around at all of the expectant faces, waiting to hear what I have to say, and I'm suddenly all nerves. The easiest thing to do is to tell the truth because then you never have to remember the lies. "When Logan…" I swallow hard, the word getting stuck in my throat, "when Logan…*died*," I whisper the word, "I was knocked unconscious. Well, I saw…Lucifer." I pause and look at the faces around me, I know damn well how crazy this sounds.

"Come again?" Valmont asks. "You saw, the Devil?"

I nod my head, "he came to me and offered to save Logan but…I had to give up my power in order to save him."

"Oh Gods, Amarah Rey, please tell me you didn't do what I think you did?"

I look at Valmont, tears stinging my eyes as I admit what I did. "I did it. I gave up my power to save Logan." I hold my head up high and clear my throat, "and I'd do it again in a heartbeat if I had to."

Logan's arms wrap more tightly around me, comforting me, and there's not an ounce of regret for what I did. Do I miss my power, fuck yes! Was there another option, yes, but I didn't know there was at the time. I did what I needed to in the moment and I'm confident in my decision. It's the first decision I've made since leaving Logan that I'm one thousand percent sure was the right decision.

"So, what does this mean for the rest of us? The war on the demons? You're the Võitleja, the one that's supposed to save us all. I mean, no pressure, we're all still here with you but…"

"Atreya is right," Kaedon finally speaks up. "We've been fighting and sacrificing, especially the Wolves, you were supposed to be the one that tipped the scales. We all knew it could be done after what you did at the Fire Fey's home but what happens now?"

"My power is just that. Mine. I can and I *will* get it back. I just need to talk to…oh, God." Nausea rises in my stomach and my knees give out from under me causing Logan to have to hold me up.

"Amarah!"

"Amarah Rey!"

"Amarah!"

Logan, Valmont, and Emrick call out to me at the same time.

Logan lets me slowly sink to the ground as he kneels in front of me. Valmont is next to him but he's not reaching out for me. I can see the strain on his face though. The effort it takes him to remain where he is and let Logan comfort me physically.

"What's happened?" Valmont's voice is hard and demanding. "What did you do to her?"

"I didn't do anything" Logan growls. "Amarah, what's wrong?"

"Iseta..." I try to swallow down my fear, my sorrow, but it's thick, as it fills up my chest and climbs up my throat. "Viveka..." I can't find my voice.

"Oh, bloody Hell," Valmont sighs, heavily. "Before you came in, when Viveka was making her threats, she admitted to killing Iseta."

"What?" Logan exclaims. "That can't be true. Iseta hasn't been here since Viveka showed up."

A new voice cuts through the murmur. A voice I had forgotten completely about. "It's true," Kordeuv says. She had me make the attack myself. I'm so sorry, Amarah, you know I had no other choice."

The unsettling feeling starts low in my gut and climbs and climbs and climbs until I'm wailing into the ground, clutching at my stomach and curling in on myself. How much loss is one person supposed to be allowed to handle? How can I continue to handle the people I love being killed?

"What did you do?" Logan growls, as he stands up and storms over to Kordeuv. "Tell me! Tell me what you did!" He says, as he grabs Kordeuv by his jacket and shakes him, hard.

"I didn't kill them all, like *she* wanted me to. I left some alive but...yes, I did kill the Supreme. I had no other choice," he pleads.

I barely register his words through my grief but he said,

Supreme. He said he didn't kill *everyone.* Iseta is a Gray Witch, a solitary Witch. She's not a part of a Coven and she's not a Supreme.

"What did you say?" My voice comes out stronger than I expected. I lift my head and lock eyes with Kordeuv over Logan's shoulder. "What did you say?" I demand.

"I'm sorry, Amarah, but the Supreme is dead. Your sister is dead."

"You attacked the Coven? The one in the shop Downtown?" I ask, to clarify.

"Yes," he says. The remorse is clear in his voice and in his eyes. He didn't want to kill them.

"You haven't killed anyone else outside of that Coven?" I press.

"No, no one. Viveka turned a lot of people from clubs, and homeless people, but I haven't killed anyone else. I swear."

I choke on a relieved laugh and sink into the ground. My body feels absolutely exhausted but relief floods through me again. There's a pang of sorrow for Mae and for the Coven. They were attacked, again, because of me. Because Viveka thought the Supreme was the powerful Witch I'm connected to. But I did warn Mae. I told her that this war would come knocking on their door eventually. Maybe if they had been involved with everything, an ally, they would have been more prepared and expected an attack from somewhere other than demons. But what's done is done.

"It's not Iseta," I say, quietly.

"What do you mean?" Kordeuv asks, as Logan slowly lets him go but stands next to him, ready to attack, if he needs to.

"The Supreme of the Desert Rose Coven is *not* my sister."

"Oh!" Kordeuv says, surprised. "Viveka is not often wrong in her research but, for what it's worth, I'm happy that I didn't take your sisters life, but I did take a life. Many lives." His words are heavy with sorrow. I can see how tired he is from being on Earth. From being

Viveka's slave.

"Like you said, you didn't have much of a choice, Kordeuv." I look over to the pile of ash that used to be Viveka. "Your power, your star ball…" I look back at him, the truth about his future, being stuck on Earth with no access to his Fox or power, hits too close to home. In this moment, I know exactly how he feels, because I no longer have my power either. I move to stand, my legs still feeling weak, but I'm steady enough not to fall down again. "I'm so sorry."

"There's nothing to be sorry for," Kordeuv says, as he walks towards the pile of ash and kneels next to it. He begins to dig into the pile, "quite the opposite actually." He turns towards me and he's holding a glowing golden ball between his fingers.

"It wasn't destroyed!" I exclaim, excitedly.

He shakes is head, "no, it wasn't. And now, I can finally go home. I can finally fulfill my destiny."

"Does someone want to explain all of this to the rest of us who have no clue what's going on?" Kaedon asks.

"Kordeuv is a half Kitsune and half Incubus. The ball he's holding is his source of power. Viveka got her treacherous hands on it and was controlling him with it."

"Wow, man, I've only ever heard of Kitsunes in theory. Is it true you can morph into other people?"

Right before our eyes, Kordeuv's body ripples and his face and body are replaced with a spitting image of Kaedon.

"Holy fucking shit!" Kaedon laughs, nervously. "That's hella cool but also really fucking creepy!"

Kordeuv's body ripples again and within seconds, he's back to his original form. "It's quite useful for going places unnoticed or gaining entry to guarded places. I'm not sure what you all know, but it was me, in Aralyn's form, that attacked the Fey Queen. Another, order from Viveka to draw out Amarah. But now that I'm free, I promise, I will no longer cause chaos in your lives. I'm not the enemy.

I never have been."

"What will you do now?" I ask.

"I'll finally take my place in the Heavens and be at peace."

I nod, tears filling up my eyes again with all the heavy emotions roiling through me. "Good. I'm happy for you Kordeuv, and thank you for all you did to help us. I know things could have gone a lot differently if you were truly loyal to Viveka. I know you hesitated and held back, giving us the edge we needed. Thank you."

He smiles, the first genuine smile I've seen on him, and it lights up his entire face. "My decision to trust in you and your team," he motions to everyone in the room, "was worth it. Before I leave, I did mention letting you in on a certain secret, if I remember correctly. May I have a private moment?"

For the life of me, I can't recall what secret he's speaking of, but whatever wisdom he has to share, I'll gladly take it. "Yes, of course." I move to walk towards him but Logan stops me with his hand on my arm.

"Amarah, is that safe? Are you sure you can trust him?"

"I know I can," I say, with confidence. "But you can come with me. Whatever we do from here on out, we do together. No secrets."

The smile on his face as I take his hand in mine and reassure him, again, that I'm choosing him, that I'm moving forward with him by my side, is another small step towards healing. For both of us.

Unfortunately, I have to walk by Valmont on my way to Kordeuv, and the guilt hits me like a kick in the gut. No matter which choice I made, someone was going to get hurt. Valmont is a blank slate, not even his eyes reflect a hint of emotion. He's pulling from all those centuries of control, giving the room his Master Vampire face, but I know, underneath the mask, he's hurting. I know I'm going to need to speak with him, privately, about my decision and moving forward, but that's not a conversation I'm eager to have. One thing at a time, Amarah. One thing at a time.

The three of us walk into a tunnel and out of sight and earshot of the others. Once we've stopped, Kordeuv explains his intentions.

"You asked me how to protect yourself against someone like me. Someone that can travel, spiritually, and spy on you, for lack of a better term."

"That's right, I did. I had forgotten."

"Well, I'm a man of my word. You freed me, Amarah."

"Technically, Valmont did," I grimace, not wanting to take credit for something I didn't do.

"And he wouldn't have been able to outmatch her without your blood in his veins now, would he? But, enough semantics. I can give you protection, for as long as you live, against anyone else like me."

"How?"

"A kiss from a Kitsune."

"What?" Logan, interjects. "Yeah, sorry buddy but that's not gonna happen. You are *not* kissing Amarah."

I can't help the smile that blooms on my face as Logan's possessiveness warms my soul. I've missed him so much.

Kordeuv chuckles, "calm down there, killer, it's not what you think. All I have to do is lay a kiss on you in Kitsune form. It can be a kiss on the hand, a cheek, forehead, doesn't matter where, as long as it's on your skin and only when I'm in Fox form. The kiss will imprint into your skin, not noticeably, but it will act as a shield against spiritual invasion by any other Kitsune."

I glance at Logan, he still doesn't look happy about it, but he's no longer protesting. "Alright, I think we can handle that. But I need you to also do this for Logan. We both get the protection."

"Done," Kordeuv says, quickly. "I owe you everything. That's the least I can do."

"Ok. Logan?"

He sighs, "yeah, ok."

"I won't be able to talk to you once I'm in my Fox form, and after I give you each the kiss of protection, I'm going to follow my destiny. So, this is goodbye."

Before Logan or I can say anything else, Kordeuv's body ripples again, only this time, more forcefully. His body convulses and he bends in on himself. I watched, mystified, as his skin tears apart and golden fur erupts across his body. His body changes, more quickly than I would have thought possible, and before I know it, a large Fox is standing before us. He wasn't kidding when he said he had nine tails. They spread out behind him similar to a peacock when it's showing its feather.

He looks like his fur has been dipped in gold dust, he shines and glows like a radiant star. There's absolutely no mistaking him for anything other than celestial. He's beautiful.

He takes a few steps towards us, lowers his head and licks my hand. His tongue is warm, wet, and little rough, but not unlike a dog's lick of affection. There's a small tingle of warmth that starts from the point of the lick and rushes across my body, almost like a heat flash, and then the sensation is gone. He does the same for Logan and then he steps away from us. I reach for Logan's hand and lean into him as we watch for what Kordeuv is going to do next.

The Fox opens its mouth and his star ball comes rolling out onto the ground. He then starts to rub his tails together and there's an immediate electrical current buzzing on the air. Very similar to magic but hotter, more terrifying. I instinctively take a step back, pulling Logan with me, as visible electrical currents manifest in his tails before shooting straight towards his star ball.

The star ball starts spinning and lifting into the air, gaining in size as it does. I've never in my life expected to see a portal, but I'm assuming this is what I'm seeing. I'm too entranced, not willing to

Blink, much less ask Logan if he's seeing what I'm seeing. Within seconds the marble size ball has turned into a massive sized portal.

With one last look in our direction, Kordeuv dips his head in a low bow and bounds into the portal. One second, he was here and the next, he's gone. The portal quickly starts to shrink in the same way it expanded. Twirling in the air until it's no more than the marble sized ball it once was before. Only now, its black and no longer the golden glow it was before.

I slowly sink down and tentatively reach my hands out to it. "Amarah, be careful," Logan's voice finally breaks the silence.

I pick it up and it look just like a regular old marble in my hand. I move my eyes from it and look to Logan, "what should we do with it?"

He shrugs, "I have no fucking clue," he laughs, nervously. "I've never seen anything like that in my entire life." He shakes his head.

"I feel like we should keep it. I don't know why but I feel like we should keep it safe."

"If that's what you want to do, Angel, then that's what we'll do," he says, as he pulls me into him. "Amarah, so much has happened that I can't even start to wrap my mind around, but I'm just glad that I have you back. Promise me that it's going to be different this time. That there's going to be no holding back. No hiding. No doubts about us. No *leaving*. Because I can't handle you leaving again. My Wolf about killed me from the inside out trying to get you back."

"I promise, and I'm so sorry for hurting you. For leaving you after I said that we were a family. That *I* was your family. I swear, I thought I was doing the right thing," I shake my head, tears still close to the surface and threating to fall again. "I'm so sorry I've been so stupid and so hard to deal with."

"Hey, we're gonna get past this. We have a lot to discuss and a lot of healing to do but there's one thing I know for certain. Loving you is the easiest thing I've ever done. It's easier than breathing. It's easier than being alive." He places a large hand against my cheek and I lean into it. My heart and my body responding to his simple touch in ways that both excite me and scare me.

"You take the air out of my lungs and breathe life into me at the same time. You kill me in ways I'll never survive and you're the only one who can bring me back to life. You don't even know it, but you save me, again and again. Every second of every fucking day. You save me, Amarah."

His words sink into me and add to the already overflowing emotions from the last couple of hours. The tears flood down my cheeks and he leans in and kisses them away. He lays his lips on mine and I can't help the moan that escapes me as our mouths open and I taste my tears on his lips.

Tears of hope.

Tears of love.

His large hands slide down my body and grip my ass, lifting me up easily. I wrap my legs around him and hang on for dear life. He holds me tightly as we breathe new life into each other. He's the one to move first, and he groans as he reluctantly pulls his mouth away from mine.

He leans his forehead against mine, still holding me tightly. "Fuck, I've missed you so much, Angel."

"I've missed you, too. Every second of every day. I'm not going to ever do this to you again. To us. I'll never deserve your forgiveness for my actions, but I'm prepared to spend the rest of my life earning it, and making it up to you."

"You know, death really changes things. Death is not easy to understand or accept, but it can be the light that breaks the darkness, and helps us to see reality. Whatever anger, jealousy, or doubt I felt before," he shrugs, "I dunno, it's just gone. Even though I've lived three hundred years prepared to die, the moment I met you, that all changed. Life with you is too short. Whether it's a month, a year, or another three hundred or more, it will never be enough with you. And I don't want to spend whatever time we have left, reliving the past and the past hurts. We have a second chance, something most people don't get, especially when death is involved, and I want to spend today, tomorrow, and forever loving you."

I don't have words to express my gratitude for this perfect man holding me in his arms, confessing all his love that I don't deserve, but that I'm selfish enough to take. All I can do is take his face in my hands and kiss him. Deeply. Passionately. Giving him access to my entire heart through our kiss. No more holding back. No more denying we're meant to be. We're soulmates.

Logan smiles against my lips, "God, I can't wait to make up for all of our lost time but we should probably get back to the others."

I sigh, "I suppose you're right. Business first. Besides, it's not like we can just drop down and get busy on this dirty tunnel floor."

"Says who? Don't challenge me, Amarah."

He lowers me a few inches from where he's holding me at his waist and I feel his hard length pressing against his jeans. The feeling of him hard and ready has my body thrumming with desire, my core pulsing at the thought of him pushing himself into me.

"Let's hurry and finish here so we can get home," I pant.

"Home," Logan repeats.

"Yes, home. Our home, Logan."

"Let's hurry," he agrees, as he slowly lowers me down his massive body.

We take a few seconds to regain our breaths and composure before we walk back into the open, cavernous room where the others are still waiting for us.

"Where's the other guy?" Emrick asks, as he eyes us suspiciously.

Logan answers as Emrick mouths, *oh my God,* and fans himself off. I mouth for him to, *shut up,* and we both beam at each other like silly idiots. There's definitely going to be some girl talk after all of this is said and done.

"So, what do we do now?" Atreya asks no one in particular.

"Well, one threat has been delt with," I sigh in relief at the thought that Viveka can no longer hurt anyone. "Kordeuv is gone and won't be coming back. I'll speak to the Queen, we have some unfinished business I need to handle so, I can inform her about everything we know so far. We need to plan a trip to the Air Fey and see if what the Maa Family suspects is true about Aralyn being there. I need to call my sister and figure out what we're going to do to get my power back. Once we manage that, we'll figure out how to stop Lucifer and seal the rip once and for all. In the meantime, everyone needs to be on high alert. Who knows what Lucifer has planned."

Nods and agreement go around the group.

"Someone should make a stop by the Coven, offer help, and see what can be salvaged out of that unfortunate tragedy," Emrick suggests.

"Yes, I agree," I add. "I've had dealings with them several times. I'll stop by."

"Alright, since that's all settled, let's get the Hell out of here, shall we?" Atreya urges.

"Hell yes," I agree, enthusiastically.

"Ummmm, what about you, Boss?" Emerson asks. "It's full daylight out. You'll have to stay here until we can take you back at nightfall."

Valmont has been unusually quiet since Logan and I got back. He finally looks at me but I can't decipher the look in his eyes and he looks away before I can even *try* to read him.

"That won't be necessary."

"Boss?" Emerson asks, confused.

Everyone looks around at each other, at me, and then at Valmont's retreating back as he makes his way outside to the waiting vehicle, and then back to me.

I just shrug, not knowing what to say. How does he plan on explaining his sudden ability to walk in the sunlight? He can't say it's because of *my blood*. That would give up my secret and I'm confident he's not going to do that. Not to mention, I'm not even sure if my blood has the same ability now that I no longer have my power.

One thing at a time, Amarah. One thing at a time.

5

Amarah: Facing The Music

Last Stand by Adelitas Way

The ride back to the casino was…*awkward*, to say the least. Of course, I sat next to Logan, and I was *very* aware of all of the eyes on us so, I kept it very PG-13 and just held his hand. The one set of eyes that didn't glance our way, not once, was Valmont's, and yet, I felt his attention on me as if we were having a damn staring contest.

Before the SUV even came to a complete stop in front of the casino, Valmont was out of the door faster than he's ever moved. Ok, maybe not faster than he's *ever* moved, but hot damn, he was gone without a glance or a word to anyone. My heart sank in my chest, like an anchor filled up with guilt. Seriously, first Andre and now Valmont. You think a girl would learn her lesson, but cheers to thick headed girls who continue to make the same mistakes, over and over again. What's the definition of insanity? Look it up and you'll see, Amarah Rey Andrews underneath.

I shouldn't have slept with him. Even though I *am* addicted to his bite, I should never have crossed that line with him, knowing damn well I'm in love with another man. But fuck, how was I to know he was going to develop feelings? And not even feelings, he said he's *in love* with me. Scoff. How did that even happen? I thought he was the most misogynistic, arrogant, player I've ever met. Oh, and, not to mention I did think Logan and I were done. Like, completely done, with no chance of getting back together. I'm the worst people reader, *ever*, and the worst thing about it? My power allows me to read people! Well, their energy…somewhat. Not that I have my power to help me anymore. Guess it doesn't make a bit of difference cause look at the mess I'm in. Again.

"Are you sure you want to do this now? You haven't slept in how long? We could do this tomorrow," Logan assures me.

I shake my head, "no, I'm ok. I really need to do this first and get things in motion before I can go home and sleep. Too much time has been wasted while I've been *sleeping*."

"Ok, whatever you wanna do, I'm right here with you," he rubs his thump across the back of my hand.

We haven't stopped touching since he…came back to life. I'm sure this feeling will pass eventually but I just don't want to let him go. I know it's stupid and I know it's selfish, it's more to comfort me than it is for him, but he doesn't seem to mind. Atreya's words come back to me.

He's a Werewolf, Amarah. A Võltsimatu. Werewolves are physical beings. We use touch as much, if not more, than words.

"You know, when you left me alone in the SUV with Atreya, things got…intersting," I laugh about it now, thinking about how ignorant and blind I've been.

"Oh yeah? Interesting how, exactly? Considering you both came out of the SUV unharmed. Which, I have to admit, surprised the Hell out of me."

"Oh, don't get me wrong, I was this close to murdering her," I laugh, "she's very blunt and she cares a lot about you."

He nods his head, "she's good people, Amarah."

"I know," I squeeze his hand. "I like her," I smile at him.

He shakes his head, "I swear, I'll never understand you

females, no matter how long I live. What did you guys talk about?"

"Later," I say, as I pull into a parking spot at Headquarters. "We'll talk about everything later. Right now, I need to focus on what I'm going to say to Ana," I let out a heavy sigh, thinking about the way I acted and how I threatened her in front of everyone. Not my finest moment.

Remembering Lucifer's words, that encouraged my actions, reminds me of the ring he gave me. The one that's still on my finger. I look down at it and it looks like a black ring of death now. I pull it off my finger and stare at it.

"Where did that come from?" Logan asks, his voice flat, revealing no feelings one way or another.

"Lucifer gave this to me during one of my dreams."

"Wait, you've been seeing Lucifer in your dreams?"

I nod, "yes," my voice is a hushed whipser. "Do you remember when I told you Michael was visiting me?"

"I remember."

"Well, it was never Michael," I laugh, harshly. "I was fooled from the beginning but I found out who he really was the night I..."

"The night you left?" Logan guesses.

I nod.

"You don't have to tell me anything you don't want to, Amarah."

I pull my eyes away from the ring and look at Logan. His face is open and ready to listen to whatever I have to say but he won't force me to talk. He won't demand I tell him everything. And that's why I want to. Because he needs to know, he deserves to know, but he still trusts me enough to let me make my own choices. Even after all the wrong choices I've made. Logan will not try to control me. And I absolutely love him for that.

"I want to tell you everything, Logan. Not only do you deserve to know the whole truth, but I want you by my side, my partner in every way. You can't truly be that for me, we can't be that for each other, if you don't know everything that's happened. Everything I've felt. Evertything I've done and what my reasons, as crazy and ridiculous as they may sound, were."

"I've already told you, the past is the past. I won't hold anything against you. Now, don't get me wrong, I'm not saying everything you did was ok but, technically, we weren't together. You made that clear so, it's not like you cheated on me," he lets out a heavy sigh. "I'm not giving you a green light to do whatever the Hell you please, and I'm not saying what you tell me won't take me some time to handle and process, I'm not perfect, Amarah, but I do know what we have is special. Hell, an Archangel told us as much. And I don't think you would have done any of the things you did over the past couple of months if you weren't trying to push me away."

Tears are streaming down my face for the bazillionth time today. All I can do is blink them away and shake my head in agreement as I stare at Logan's sympathetic face.

"Tell me about the ring," he says, softly as he takes my free hand in his. Patiently waiting for me to gain my voice and my strength.

"He came to me when I was at my lowest, you know this already. He offered to help me learn to manage my darkness, to control it so it wouldn't control me. I felt like I had no one else, not really. No one who could understand all the pain I was feeling," I shrug. "He visited me often. He was there for me, as a friend," I laugh, sarcastically. "A feigned friend, obviously, but I didn't want to see his canniving ways. I was willfuly blind, like I was with everything else over the past two months." I sigh, "anyway, he gave me this as a reminder to live my life for me, for myself, and no one else. It was like I had permission to do and say whatever I wanted and to Hell with what anyone else thought or the consequensces of my actions."

I take the ring and place it in a little cubby-hole in the center console. "I kissed him," I barely hear my own voice as I admit it out loud. "It was the first thing I did to try and push you further away from me. In my mind, I thought, if I do this, Logan won't want me back. If he finds out about this, it will just make the wedge between us bigger. And the further you were away from me, the further away from danger you were. That's what was in my mind as I did it."

I finally look up and meet Logan's eyes. His lips are pursed and his brows are furrowed. I can see the unhappiness on his face. But what did I expect? And if this makes him unhappy, he's going to riot when he hears about Valmont. Then again, he already knows I've slept with him, but still, that's not going to make the admition and the conversation any easier.

"I'm sorry," my voice cracks as a sob escapes my throat.

Logan caresses the back of my hand again, "I'm not going to tell you that what you did was ok. I can't say if it was wrong or right. I can only comment on how I feel and...well, obviously, it doesn't feel good."

I nod in agreement. I know. I know it doesn't feel good. I felt the same way when I saw him in that bed with Atreya believing they were sleeping together. I know the pain I caused him intimately.

"But I also felt the pain you held inside of you. That day I came home and found out I was forever locked out."

"Oh God, I'm so sorry. I'm such an idiot asshole."

He gives me a sad, half-smile, "well, you said it."

I manage a choked laugh.

"That day, you let the block down. It was just a split second, but I felt what you held inside and it dropped me to my knees, Amarah. I can't imagine living with that kind of pain and I know the choices you made were what you thought was best for the situation in the moment. I'm hurt, yes, of course I am. But I'm not angry. I told you, that all ended the second I thought I'd never get to see you, or hold you, or kiss you again. We'll get through this, like I said we would, because we both want this more than we want anything else."

"I don't deserve you," I say, as I wipe my tears away.

"And if you knew all of the things I've done in my past, you'd understand why I beg to differ."

I don't push him to open up about his past. I know he will just like I'm coming clean with all of my dirty laundry, I know he will too, but I think we've had enough truth bombs for the moment. So, I say the only thing I can in this moment.

"I love you, so much. I don't know how it happened so quickly or when or why but you're it for me. You're my last stand, Logan. And I know you're telling me that it's ok, that we're going to be fine, but I can't help but be scared," I choke out my fears as they stream down my face. "I'm so scared that you're going to hear everything and change your mind about us. That you're going to realize I'm not worth it. And if I do lose you, for real..." I sob, take in a shaky breath and try to continue, "you're my everything and I don't want to lose you, ever again. In *any* way. I won't survive without you. "

"You won't. I promise, you won't. I love you too, Angel."

"You know, you really can't call me that anymore," I say, sadly, trying to change the direction of my terrifying thoughts. Only, this is just as terrifying.

"You'll always be my Angel. And just because you don't have your power, doesn't make you less than what you are, which is a miracle. Don't forget that you are a *true* miracle. God *made* you, Angel, you're a Blessing and you'll never be anything less than that. And you'll never be anything less than the woman I love. My mate."

Again, I just nod, as I have no words. Needing to change the subject entirely, before I crumble to pieces, and to also focus on the task at hand, I bring us back to the present.

"What am I going to say to Ana?"

"She's family, Amarah, all you have to say is you're sorry. That's it."

I nod, "yeah, I hope you're right."

"Hey," he says, as he tugs on my hand, pulling me towards him. "Everything else aside, you have no idea how good this feels. To be right here, sitting next to you again. Holding your hand and being your partner." He uses his free hand to gently hold my chin and look into my eyes, "I never want to be anywhere else. Do you understand? Where you go, I go. Always."

"Always," I promise on a choked whisper. My eyes drop to his lips. God, how I've missed his beautiful, full, soft lips. I want to explore him and get to know him all over again, all the changes to his body, the new muscle. My eyes follow the veins from his hands, across his firm forearms, and up to his massive biceps. His t-shirt is stretched tight across his chest and I remember the glimpse I had of his new, rippling abs.

Sweet baby Jesus.

He's like the new rollercoaster at the theme park and I can't wait to be taken for one Hell of a ride. The heater is on low, keeping the winter chill outside at bay, but it's suddenly a sauna in here.

"Angel," he warns, "you keep looking at me like that and we're going to get arrested for public indecency as I make you sit on this," he pulls the hand he's holding into his lap, letting me feel how affected he is by me too, "right here, right now."

My mouth is watering and I have to swallow my desire down, "Jesus," I say, breathlessly, as I caress his hard cock through his jeans. I almost fogot how big he is. I look up into his beautiful eyes, heated with the same passion that's burning between my legs. "Maybe jail wouldn't be so bad?"

"It would, because then we wouldn't be together," he moves my hand off his dick then reaches inside his jeans and adjusts himself.

I groan.

"Hey, you wanted business first so, business it is. Let's go see the Queen so I can get your ass home."

"You don't have to tell me twice," I say, as I reach for my door handle. "Do you think he'll be ok in here?" I ask, as I nod my head to the backseat where Griffin is sleeping.

"Yeah, he'll be fine. We won't be that long anyways. Not if I have anything to say about it," he smirks, that damn smile he always gets when he knows damn well I'm flustered, and my stomach does somesaults. Fuck, I've missed this feeling.

"Fuck me," I whisper, as I step out of the car.

"That's the plan," he winks, as he walks to the front of the car and holds his hand out to me.

"Damn you and your Werewolf hearing," I tease, as I take his hand in mine. The warmth and the solidness of it is comforting and reassuring. It helps ground me. He's my gravity. He's home.

I feel more like myself than I have in months as we walk hand-in-hand through the Church and down into Headquarters. The throne/meeting room is empty so, we head towards the likeliest place we'll find the Queen. The library.

She's sitting on an oversized chair, next to a crackling fire, a gentle glow emenating from a lamp on the side table next to the chair. She has a blanket thrown over her legs, that are tucked underneath her, and she has a book in her hands. Her sunflower hair hangs in a loose braid over her shoulder and she looks so at ease, at peace. She looks every bit like my aunt and nothing like the authoratative Fey Queen. All I can hope for, is that she's in a good mood, and she's willing to accept my apology and forgive me.

"My Queen," Logan, speaks up as we approoch. She hadn't heard us, too engrosed in whatever story she's reading.

Her head snaps up and I'm met with piercing winter sky grey eyes. They immediately take in Logan and I, together, and linger on where our hands are joined before she looks back up and addresses us. Her eyes harden, slightly, she's guarded, but they're not cold and unwelcoming. That sliver of hope growing inside of me lengthens as it reaches for the light. Perhaps we can make amends and move forward after all.

"Logan, Amarah, it's nice to see you two together again. To what do I owe this surprise visit?" Her voice is calm, empty. Her Queen voice.

I let go of Logan's hand and step forward. This is on me. I need to do this standing on my own. I clear my throat, "I'm here to apologize for my recent actions, if you'll allow it, my Queen?"

I address her with the title she's earned. The respect she's earned. Yes, she is my aunt, but I disrespected her as a Queen first and foremost, and injured her as an aunt, second.

She places her bookmark between the pages, closes the book and places it on the table. "Have a seat," she gestures to the couch opposite her.

I quickly go to it and sit on the edge of the cushion, too filled up with nervous energy to sit at ease. Logan joins me and stays close, for support if I need it, but he doesn't reach out for me. He's giving me my own space, my own ground to stand on, and I love that he can read me so well even without our connection.

"The last couple of months have been…*difficult*," I pause with a sigh, trying to gather my thoughts and everything I need to say. It's not easy voicing your faults out loud to others.

"I thought that in order to keep people safe, I had to push them away. Hell, maybe part of it was, after Andre, I felt like I didn't deserve to be surrounded by people that loved me. That I didn't deserve any kind of goodness. I think I was pushing everyone away as a kind of punishment to myself. I let myself get dragged down into guilt and darkness. I was pulled astray by a bad influence that I let manipulate me," I run my hands down my face and sigh again. Hearing all of this out loud, doesn't feel good. "My actions and my decisions over the past couple of months truly haven't been my own but it was me, I know that. I'm not trying to make excuses, it's just...complicated, trying to describe where I was and my mindset. It was me but it wasn't me."

I hang my head in my hands, "shit, I'm not making any sense." I take a minute to breathe, the Queen is quiet, patient, giving me time to say everything I want to say. I finally lift my head up and look at her, "what I'm trying to say is, I'm sorry. I'm truly sorry for how I reacted at the last meeting. I shouldn't have challenged you like that in front of everyone, I know that. I can't say I don't have some issues with some of your actions as well, but I know that wasn't the way to handle the situation. If I had anything more to say, I should have done it with you, privately, and not the way that I did. And for that, I'm truly sorry, Ana. I don't want this to come between us any longer. I'm ready to move forward and do what I need to do for The Unseen. For you."

"I know what you've been through, Amarah, losing people you care about is never easy. I wish I could tell you that it gets easier, but it doesn't, and time isn't always an ally. I knew you were struggling and I'm mad at myself for not doing more to make sure you were ok. I didn't act like an aunt, I acted like a Queen, and that has sat heavily on my heart for some time."

"I don't think there's anything you could have said or done that would have made a difference," I shrug.

"But we'll never know now, will we?"

"I suppose not."

"As far as the meeting," it's her turn to sigh. "I'm so shocked at how you acted, Amarah, I didn't even recognize you. The way you reacted with Logan, with me...it was all just so...unexpected. Add that on top of the attack that had just happened and I have to admit, it was a lot to handle. You are correct, you handled yourself in that situation very poorly. You put my authority and position in question, in front of *all* the Leaders. It was absolutely disrespectful, and the blatant challenge to my authority, was beyond reasoning."

I nod my head, embarrassed of my actions. "I know," I whisper.

"But," she continues, "I was not completely myself either. I see that now. I was narrow minded and focused solely on finding and capturing Aralyn. The close call on my life, *in my home*, shook me more than I'd like to admit. And you were the only one to call me out on my short-sightedness, which I appreciate, but not how it was delivered." Her voice gets harder, "you will *never* defy me so blatantly in public again, is that understood?"

"Of course, I understand. It won't happen again."

The Queen moves the blanket off her legs and stands, taking the few steps to close the distance between us. She lowers herself and crouches in front of me, taking my hands in hers.

"Amarah, you're my only family, and you're a Blessing sent from Heaven to help us win this war. I appreciate and value your opinion more than you know. I want us to keep each other in line and level-headed, but we both acted out of anger and fear. In the future, when we need to talk freely, we do it in private, with only those we trust, like Logan," she nods in his direction. He nods back.

"You're *my* only family, too," I echo, tears wetting my eyes. "I never want to do anything to push you away or lose you. Going forward, we're a team. I'm on your side and I won't ever act that way again, I promise."

She leans in and wraps her arms around me, pulling me into a tight, warm embrace.

"Good, now that that's settled, we need to update you on everything we've learned in the past twenty-four hours, starting with the attack on you. It wasn't Aralyn."

"What?" Ana releases me gives Logan her full attention. "What do you mean it *wasn't* Aralyn? I saw her. It was her!"

"It wasn't." I confirm. "It was a Kitsune, in her image, trying to lure me out with an attack on you. But, the good news is, we do have a lead on where Aralyn might be."

We spend the next hour explaining everything we know to Ana. Everything that's happened with my power and who Logan really is. Unfortunately, she has no ideas on what we could possibly do to get my powers back, but we are going to plan a trip up to the Air Fey withn the next fourty-eight hours to see if the lead on Aralyn is fruitful.

One thing at a time, Amarah. One thing at a time.

Logan: Save Me

Forever and Always by Written By Wolves

We pull into the driveway and then into the garage. It's strange being back here *with* Amarah instead of begging to be able to see her, but it also sets off feelings of déjà vu, comfort and *home*. I'm not the only one excited to be back either. Griffin is whining and his tail is wagging so fast I'm worried he's going to lift off the ground as we wait for Amarah to open the front door. Griffin bounds in, not waiting for us, and Amarah crosses the threshold.

I wait.

I have to.

"Come in," Amarah invites me. "I promise, I'm going to have Iseta fix this as soon as possible. I'm so sorry."

I don't need the connection to see the remorse and shame that's clearly written on her face. It breaks my heart to see her like this. There's a lot of healing we both need but I'm hopeful because I'm *here*. I'm somehow here with her when I was almost taken from her, forever.

"Come here," I say, as I pull her to me. I wrap my arms around her, lean my cheek on the top of her head, and I breathe her in. I focus on her, tuning everything else out. All the hurt. All the pain.

She smells like home.

She feels like home.

My cock twitches just by having her this close to me. It's hard enough to control myself, my desire for her when I'm having sex with her every day, much less almost two months without it! I want her with the force of a category five hurricane. I want to take her, ravage her, consume her, destroy everything she's thought and felt over the past two months, and leave her rebuilding everything back up. With me. I want to erase any memory of *him*. And I will.

But I feel her nerves. I sense her anxiety and I know we're a long way off from where we were. She's not going to feel better until she unburdens her conscious, until she tells me everything and I decide our fate. The ball is in my court. I'll hear everything she has to confess and then I can decide if I'm going to stay or leave. I already know what I'll do but Amarah isn't convinced. Time to get this out of the way so we can move forward.

"Let's get comfortable, I think we'll need all the comfort we can get while we clear the air, hmmm."

She nods and pulls away from me. "I'd actually really like a shower first. There's no getting comfortable with dried blood, dirt and shame on me. Though there's nothing the water can do for the shame," she hangs her head.

"Alright, shower first," I agree. "Shall we have one together?" I ask, nonchalantly, but inside my Wolf and my desire are both hungry. No *starving*, for Amarah. It's been way too long since I've had sex and I'm practically bursting at the seams. The thought of her naked, water cascading down her beautiful body, soap lathered up on her skin…and, *fuck*! I'm hard, just like that.

I watch her throat bomb in a swallow, I know she's thinking the exact same thing I am. Again, I don't need a connection to read her. I know her like I know myself. Maybe even better.

She shakes her head, "I don't think that's a good idea. I

mean, don't get me wrong, I *really* want to, it's just…I don't want to cross that line with you until you know *everything*. Then, we can go from there, after you've heard the truth. The whole truth."

"Alright," I reluctantly concede. My Wolf starts pacing inside of me. I know he's not happy with that decision. This is his *mate*. He's pure animal with animal instincts, he wants to claim his mate. NOW! I clear my throat, "then you go first and I'll get in after. I'll wait out here, holler when you're out." There's no way I can chance even *a glance* at her naked body with any hope of holding on to my slim control.

I watch her walk down the hall and disappear around the corner that leads into the bedroom. I hear the faucet turn on and the water rushing out of the showerhead. I imagine her taking her clothes off and I start pacing, matching my Wolf's energy. Desire stars to pool low in my gut and low growl rumbles deep in my chest. I run my hands through my hair and grip the back of my neck as I pace.

"Fuck," I grit out. "Get it together, Logan." I chastise myself.

I hear the change in the way the water runs as her body slides underneath it. I've seen her underneath the water before, several times, and the images flood through my mind as if a dam has just been broken. My cock is hard, pressing against my jeans in an almost forceful way. I grip it, hard, trying to restrain myself.

Before I know it, I'm storming down the hallway and bursting into the bathroom. Thank fuck she didn't lock the door and I'm not forced to break it the fuck down. Two large strides later, I'm standing in the walk-in shower, the water that mists over my skin is cold but it does absolutely nothing to cool me down. My body is so hot I'm surprised the water isn't hissing on contact.

She has her face under the water, head tilted back as she runs her hands through her long, flame-red hair that ignites my fire even more. Her breasts hang perfectly, full and heavy, I want to feel her nipples harden under my touch. Her body is glistening wet but nothing compares to how wet she gets for *me*.

A frustrated growl escapes my throat.

Amarah finally opens her eyes, brushing water out of her face, and she jumps, grabbing at the walls. "Logan, Jesus! Son of a bitch, you scared the shit out of me!" She places her hand on her chest, as if that will stop her racing heart. "What are you doing?" She asks, breathlessly. She doesn't try to hide her body from me and it takes a lot of effort to pull my gaze off her body and meet her eyes.

"I know you slept with him, more than once. I know what his bite does to you. I know you're addicted to it, we already discussed that after the Air Fey attack. I know all of this and I don't give a *fuck*. You've slept with others, so have I. That's not something I'm going to dwell on. The addiction, we'll figure it out, together. I only have one question, Amarah." My voice is hard, rough, on the edge of losing all control, I almost don't recognize it as my own. I'm two seconds away from either giving into pure rage or pure desire and it all depends on how she answers my one question.

"Do you love him?"

She stares right at me, right into my fucking soul. Her beautiful hazel eyes are more green today than brown.

I feel like my heart stops in my chest. I feel like my entire world stops spinning, and the only thing keep me standing, keeping me breathing, is her. Again, she kills me and yet, she's the only who can bring me back to life.

She never blinks, never hesitates as she gently shakes her head. "No," she says, firmly. "I don't love him."

The world crashes back down around me. I take a large gasp of air, I hadn't even realized I had stopped breathing, waiting on her response. We stare at each other for another couple of beats, as my heart restarts in my chest, and then I'm crashing into her.

I come down on her with that hurricane force raging inside of me. I take her mouth with mine and push my tongue inside, desperate to taste her. She groans as she lets me in, returning the same fierce urgency I feel. Her hands are trying to pull my shirt off. It's wet and sticks to my skin. I growl as I peel it off, pulling it from the bottom over my head and discard it somewhere behind me.

Her hands explore my stomach, my abs tighten and constrict under her touch. God, I've missed her touch, but right now, I'm fucked up. I'm too close to the edge. I can't focus on foreplay, I just need my dick inside of her, now. I don't even attempt to try and take my wet jeans off. I unbutton them, unzip them and pull my aching cock out, squeezing it tightly, trying to quell some of the heat pulsing through me. Fuck, my balls ache, my dick is so hard it's almost painful.

"I need inside of you, now," I growl, as I lift her up. Her legs wrap around me eagerly. I manage to slow down, to stop long enough to give her a warning.

"Amarah, you're my mate. Mine!" I practically yell the word. "There will be no others from here on out, do you hear me?"

"Yes," she says, quickly.

"No," I lecture. "I need you to listen to what I'm fucking saying. I swear to God, if you even look in his direction or any other man's direction, in a way that suggest something I don't like, I will fucking kill him. I will rip his throat out with my teeth and lick up the blood as it flows free from its veins. You. Are. Mine. Do you. Fucking. Understand."

A part of me cringes at the words that just spilled out of my mouth. I don't want to frighten her, I don't want to threaten her, and I don't want to control her but fuck, *she's my mate!* She's mine! And I need her to understand what this role looks like. What it means to me and to my Wolf. I've held so much back with her, no more.

"Yes, Logan. Never again," she shakes her head. No hesitation, no fear from what I just shared. "I'm yours. Always and forever. I'm yours."

I position myself to enter her. She's wet, but not as wet as she would be if we had worked up to this, but I can't wait. I slip inside of her, the head of my cock forcing its way in.

"Oh, God, Logan." She moans as she clings to me.

I somehow manage to control myself enough to gradually push inside of her and not hurt her. I don't ever want to hurt her, even in this frenzied state.

"Fuck, you're so God damn tight," I grit out, as I pull out and push in again.

It takes me longer than I'd like to get her body open and able to take all of me. Once I'm fully sheathed inside of her, her pussy hugging my dick like a damn straight jacket, I finally manage to breathe. This is where I'm supposed to be. This is home. I'm so wound up, so fucking hard and horny, I'm already close to cuming just from the effort it took to push inside of her.

"This isn't going to last very long, but I promise I'm going to make it up to you afterwards," I warn, as I start pumping inside of her.

I take her mouth with mine again, drinking down her moans and whimpers, drawing in her breath to fill my lungs. To bring me back to life. To sustain me.

I take her hard and deep. It doesn't take long before I'm spilling myself inside of her. I feel like my body is being ripped in two from the power of it. I throw my head back and yell to the ceiling as I release every fucking thing I've kept pent up over the past two months.

Desperation.

Anger.

Sorrow.

More anger.

Frustration.

Hope.

I'm panting like I just ran a fucking marathon but I feel lighter than I have since all of this madness happened. I slowly slide out of her and lean my forehead against hers, my eyes closed. We stay this way for a few seconds, just breathing together. Being together. Amarah's fingers are running through my hair at he back of my head. Fuck it feels good. Her hands on me. Her body in my arms. I can't help but sigh with contented pleasure.

"Logan," she says, quietly, getting my attention. I pull back enough to look at her, but I don't move to let her down.

"This is the last time I'll say this before we move on, but I'm so sorry I did this to us. I just want you to know that I see you." She holds my face in her delicate hands. Her eyes darting back and forth between mine, almost desperately pleading, "I *see* you, Logan. I appreciate you. I fucking love you with so much more than just my heart. I love you with my body, my mind, my soul, whatever I am, whatever I have, I love you with every piece of it, and I will *never* take you for granted again. I *am* your family. I *am* your Pack."

Fuck, her words hit me deep. She's said them before but this time is different. I know she understand more now than she did in the beginning. I know she means what she's saying. She's my Pack. I'll never be alone, ever again.

"And I want you to know that I want you to be mine in every possible way," I shake my head, "but that doesn't mean I own you. You're not mine to own. You're mine to love and cherish and protect because you *allow* me to."

She nods her head, "I am yours, Logan, because I choose to be."

"I'm no saint, Amarah, being half Angel doesn't change that. I am what I am, a Werewolf, and my nature is very animalistic, very basic. I'm better when I'm with you. *You* make me better, but make no mistake about it, I will do whatever the fuck it takes to keep you. Valmont isn't the only one who's good at threats and death. I'm a *killer*, Amarah, and I'm fucking good at it. You just haven't seen that side of me and I hope you never have to."

"I don't want you to have to be a killer. Not because of me."

"You know how people say, you're never supposed to need anyone? They say that another person should never complete you, only compliment you," I shake my head. "But I do need you, Angel. I'm not whole without you. I need to know you're mine and only mine. Completely mine, from this day forward. No second guessing. No solo mission fucking bullshit, trying to be a hero. You and me, Angel, you and me, forever. Always."

"It's done. No more second guessing. No more trying to save everyone by being a dumbass, I swear to you. You and me, until my heart stops beating, and then I'll wait for you in whatever life comes next."

I press my lips to hers in a sealed promise. My earlier fervour being satiated, I intend for it to be a quick, simple kiss, but nothing is ever quick or simple with Amarah. She ignites my desires, my soul, and I just can't get enough of her.

"We need to get out of this shower because I'm not done reclaiming you yet," I say, as I let her down.

With a lot of effort and a little help from Amarah, we manage to peel the rest of my wet clothes off my body. We quickly wash up. It doesn't escape me that all of my things are still where I left them, as if I never left. I notice the same thing when we finally get into the bedroom.

"All of my things are still here, exactly where I left them," I say, out loud.

She shrugs, "I never really wanted to let you go."

She's standing next to the bed, naked, hair dripping water down her body and onto the floor. I'm suddenly parched and need to lick up every drop of water rolling down her soft skin. I stalk towards her and she's forced to sit on the bed as I tower over her. She pulls herself further on to the bed without needing to be asked. I follow. Her knees part, allowing my body to press into hers, as I lean in and take my first sip of water off her stomach.

I swear every drop I lick and slurp off her body is healing my beat-up heart and every orgasm I pull from her body is going to heal my soul. She's the fucking Holy Grail and I'm on a pilgrimage for redemption. She's my Blessing, my reprieve from a lifetime of death, pain, and loneliness.

I don't waste any time getting to my first destination. My tongue slides up her slit feeling her wetness, thick and dripping. She's already moaning her pleasure with the first pass of my tongue over her clit. Her sweetness coats my tongue and I drink it down, eager for more.

"Always so wet," a contented purr rumbles deep in my chest.

I caress her clit in languid circles, changing the pressure every so often. Hard and soft. Hard and soft. Her hips start to move in time with my rhythm of slow, steady circles, building her up to her first orgasm. I don't use my fingers, there's going to be plenty of time for that, for now, I just eat her up like the delicious dessert she is.

I can always tell when she's close to cuming. I can hear the change in her heart beats, the hitch in her breathing as she starts holding her breath in small intervals, the uncontrollable twitching of her nerves. But my favorite part, is when her hands grip my hair like she has to hold on to me for dear life and her legs start to clamp down on the sides of my head, practically suffocating me, but I've never breathed more deeply in my life.

"Oh God, Logan, fuck," she pants out.

"Mmmm," I moan, with my mouth locked onto her clit, flicking my tongue quickly, just like she likes it. The way that's going to make her cum, hard.

"Fuck, you're going to make...I'm cuming!"

Her body tries to pull away from me but I dig my fingers into her hips, holding her in place. She bucks like a wild bull, her body completely lost to her control as she releases her desire onto my tongue.

I slowly release her, as her body comes down from her high, her body still spasming in the aftershock of pleasure. I pull myself up her body, until I'm face to face with her, but I keep my cock away from her pussy. Even though I just came, I'm already rock hard, ready for round two, but not until I've completely dominated her.

"Come and taste your sweet pussy on my lips," I demand, as I lean over her, but make her come to me.

She rises up on her elbows and licks across my lips before I open my mouth and let her tongue dance inside. I move my fingers between her legs and slip two inside. I groan as they slide in, her wetness making it easy, but she's still tight. How my dick ever manages to fit inside of her is a fucking magic trick in itself.

She pulls her head back, "Logan..."

"Did I tell you to stop kissing me?" I ask, my voice deep and husky with my own desire as I pull my fingers out of her. I see it when she realizes how this is gonna go. "I'm the one in control right now, Angel. I'm calling the shots. And if you disobey me, there will be punishment." I say, as I slap her clit.

She jumps and yelps at the sudden shock of it. I see her take a hard swallow and then she lifts her head and puts her mouth back on mine. I insert my fingers back into her, pumping them and curling them up, hitting that soft spot that I know will drive her crazy.

She's moaning into my mouth as her body starts to rock. We're two bodies working in perfect harmony. She knows what she likes and I know how to give it to her. I start to pump my fingers faster, hitting that spot inside her again and again.

She's moaning and groaning deep in her chest, her lips are still locked onto mine, and she opens her mouth on a gasp as her orgasm hits. I claim her mouth as I feel her body clench around my fingers, and at the same time, her orgasm demands an outlet like I just turned on a firehose. I remove my fingers and rub them flat across her clit as her orgasm squirts out of her. Her head falls back and she screams her pleasure to the ceiling.

"Holy fuck!" She manages to finally find her words. "What the fuck was that?" She asks, eyes wide, a mixture of shock and pleasure.

I can't help but chuckle, "have you never squirted before, Angel?"

She shakes her head, her cheeks turning pink as the blush creeps in. I can't help the egotistical smile that spreads across my face. The amount of pride I feel in this moment, of making her squirt for the first time, boosts my confidence and my desire tenfold. And I don't exactly need help in either department.

"Now we just need to get you to do that on my cock." I smirk, as she blushes even more.

I make her cum five more times with my mouth and fingers, yes, I am counting, add in another squirt mixed in there, before she's begging and pleading with me to stop. She's literally soaking, drenched between her legs.

"Tell me what you want, Angel."

"I want you inside of me," she begs.

"I was thinking the same thing," I say, as I climb off the bed.

"Where are you going?"

I round the bed to where her head is almost off the side, all the bucking and moving she did as I devoured her, pushed her close to the edge. I pull her the few inches I need so that her head hangs over the side.

"You're going to take me, all of me, in that beautiful little mouth of yours."

"Logan, you know I can't. You're too big."

"You can and you will," I order. "I have faith in you, Angel."

I bring my dick to her lips and she eagerly opens up for me. Fuck, I'm so fucking hard. The earlier orgasm doing nothing to satiate my need for her. I'm making up for all of our lost time and fuck if it doesn't feel like I did die and go to Heaven.

Her warm mouth wraps around my dick as I push into her. I hit the back of her throat and give a little push. Her reflexes kick in and she chokes on me so I pull back then try again. Tears are seeping out of the corner of her eyes with her effort but she's not fighting me, not trying to stop me, but her hands are holding onto my thighs for dear life.

"Relax, Angel. Relax your jaw, relax your throat, just breathe," I instruct, as I give it another go.

I get further this time but still not all the way. I pull out and pump my hips, giving her shallow thrusts, letting her relax and get a rhythm. She's moaning her pleasure around my cock and it reverberates up through me and makes me shiver.

"Fuck."

She loves to give head as much as I do. I reach over and grab her breasts as I fuck her mouth, pinching her nipples until she yelps around me. I need her to take me, all of me, so I can finally slip inside her wet, tight pussy. "Third time's the charm, open up for me."

I push slowly down her throat. I see the bulge of my hard cock as it slides down. This time, I don't stop. I give her that last inch until I'm balls deep in her mouth.

"Good girl. I knew you could take it." I hold myself there for a few seconds, revelling in the feel of my dick fully emerged in her mouth. My pride is through the roof as I pull out of her. She gasps for air, sucking it down as fast as she can. "Now turn around. Give me that ass right here," I pat the edge of the bed.

She complies, turning around so that her head is in the middle of the bed. I wrap my hands around her calves and pull her to the end of the bed. I grip both of her ankles in one hand, holding her legs in the air as I use my other hand to guide myself to her opening.

I tease her some more, rubbing my cock over her clit.

"Logan, please, I need you inside of me," she begs.

"Is that right? You need me?"

"Yes," she pleads.

"You need my cock to fill you up completely, don't you?"

"Yes."

"Hold still," I demand, as I slip the head of my cock inside of her. She writhes underneath me. I stop pushing into her and slap the side of her ass, hard. She gasps. "I said, hold still."

I continue to push inside of her. She manages to hold herself still but she's breathing hard, moaning as I thrust into her. I finally work myself all the way in.

"God, you're so deep," she says.

A low growl rumbles through me, "this is mine." She's so wet I can hear it squish and squelch every time I push into her. The sound of it turns me on even more. *I did this to her.*

I pull her ankles apart, letting her legs rest on my shoulders. "Rub your clit," I instruct.

"What?" She asks, surprised.

I smack her clit, she yelps. "I said, rub your clit, Angel. Let me see you pleasure yourself as I fuck you." I lean down and drop spit on her clit.

She doesn't hesitate again and moves her fingers over her clit as I continue to slide in and out of her in long slow strokes.

"Fuck, you're so damn sexy, Amarah. You drive me fucking wild. *Ravenous.*"

I start to increase my speed, fucking her harder, faster. Her fingers move to match my speed. I can feel her body tightening around me. I move her leg closer to me and wrap my mouth around her calf, sucking a chunk of meat into my mouth. My teeth need something to bite. My Wolf needs something to bite.

"Fuck, Logan, I'm gonna cum."

A vicious growl leaks out of my mouth as I feel her body

spasming and sucking me in. My teeth clamp down as I follow her over the edge, spilling another huge load inside of her. Fuck, it feels like the orgasm will never stop.

I taste blood and my Wolf throws his head to the sky and howls in victory. When my body stops jerking with the waves of pleasure raking through it, I pull out and somehow manage to drag her body further onto the bed before I collapse beside her.

We're both sweating and gasping for air. I feel like a damn limp noodle. My limbs are heavy and I'm so fucking content. I find strength to pull Amarah into me. She wraps her arm around me and throws a leg over mine, resting her head on my arm as I hold her tightly to my chest.

"Jesus fucking Christ," she laughs against my chest. "That was intense. We've never…you've never been so…*dominating*, before.

"I'm an Alpha, Angel, That's just the tip of the iceberg. I want to dominate you. It turns me on to see you beg and squirm, for pleasure, that is. I didn't forget that you said you like a little pain and I want to explore *everything* with you. I want to see what else we can discover about your beautiful body besides squirting."

"Oh God," she laughs and buries her face deeper into my chest.

I pull back, "Angel, look at me."

She does, her cheeks pink again but her eyes are sparkling and there's a beautiful smile on her face.

I caress her cheek, "you really are the most beautiful woman I've ever seen."

She bites her lip and drops her eyes. I growl as I take it out from between her teeth. I want to take that lip between mine, suck on it, bite it. "You never need to be embarrassed in front of me, for any reason. I want you to feel good. I want to make you feel good. In every way, not just in the bedroom. I want to learn everything there is to know about you. I want to open myself up so you learn everything there is to know about me. I'm an Alpha but you're my mate. You're my partner, my equal, and I will bow only to you. I will always confide in you. I will always respect you, and I will never, ever hurt you."

"I know," she whispers.

"Good," I kiss her on the nose. "Now let's hydrate. I'm not nearly done with you yet.

"Logan, you can't be serious! You're going to kill me!"

"And you're going to save me."

Amarah: Flying And Falling

Don't Stop Now by Sam Riggs

The cold-water laps at my feet, drawing my attention. The water is dark, and the bubbles that linger on the sand as the gentle wave recedes, look more grey than white. I'm standing on a beautiful, deserted beach, in the soft predawn glow, but I can feel the sun waking up, close to breaking the plane of the horizon.

A quiet breeze comes in on the next wave, rustling my hair and pulling at the thin material of the golden dress that flows around my body. I know in an instant, this is another dream, but before I acknowledge my visitor, I let myself appreciate the beauty of the world waking up. Even if it's not entirely real. It's real in this moment.

Out of the corner of my eye, I see him walk up and stand next to me, on my left side. I pay him no attention as the sun finally makes its appearance. The process throws beautiful golds and oranges across the brightening blue sky. It's amazing how far the sun is away from us, and yet, it feels so close. You can feel the heat of it on your skin all of these millions of miles away.

When you stop to really think about it, about how big everything is, it's actually mind-boggling. I'm just this tiny little being in the world, in a universe, that I can't even begin to comprehend.

And it's magnificent how beautifully everything works together in perfect balance and harmony. The way the moon gives into the sun, day into night, but they both shine equally as bright in their moments on the stage. It's clear to see, when you stop to take it all in, that there's something so much bigger at play. How could I have gotten so lost?

I speak to the Devil in my dreams. He's real. Hell is real. And it's literally an arm's length away. Why did I think Heaven was so far? Why did I think that He hasn't been watching every step I take? Why did I ever lose my Faith? I've been so blind and so foolish but my eyes are open now. My heart is open again and I'm seeing and feeling so clearly.

"It's beautiful, isn't it?" Lucifer breaks the silence. "It almost looks and feels real, aye, but not quite. There's really no comparing the sensation to actually being alive and walking on Earth, underneath the glorious sun. And I have you to thank for allowing me to feel it once again."

I don't say anything. I stand still, body relaxed and full of divine confidence once more. It's ironic really, because I'm feeling more like an Angel now, now that I've rediscovered my Faith again, more than I felt like one when I had my power. But that's ok. Faith is a power of its own.

"How's our dear Logan?" He taunts.

I don't acknowledge him. I know what he's doing. He's trying to get a rise out of me but I'm done playing his games. I'm done letting him manipulate me.

"Alright, well, if you're not going to talk to me, why did you bring me here, Amarah? I must admit, I am rather surprised you called to me."

I finally pull my eyes away from the sunrise and address him. The first thing I notice, is that we're no longer matching. He's dressed in all black, black jeans, black t-shirt, but like me, he is still barefoot.

He looks like the dark demon he is against such a glorious and divine backdrop. There's no hiding who he is now. Now that I *see* him. He's nothing more than a dark bruise marring my scarred skin, but just like a bruise fades, I'll soon be rid of him.

"It's my power and I want it back. You didn't even fulfill your end of the bargain. That has to make our deal null and void."

He laughs at me. "Oh, Amarah, life isn't fair and a deal with the Devil is even less so. A bargain is whatever I say it is. You gave up your power, *willingly*, it belongs to me now."

Archangel Michael's words are embedded in brain.

You can get your power back, Amarah. It belongs to you and only you.

I know that Lucifer is lying. How do I know? Because he's fucking speaking. My power doesn't belong to him. It never has and it never will. In fact, standing here now, I can *feel* it. I can feel it like there's a rope anchored in my chest and tethered to my power inside of Lucifer. The power is vibrating down this invisible rope, calling to me, reaching out for me. Only I don't know how to reach it. I don't know how to retrieve it.

"I see you're no longer wearing my ring," Lucifer changes the subject.

"Why would I wear that ugly reminder of everything I never want to be, ever again?"

"Oh come, Amarah, do not discredit where credit is due. I gave you exactly what you needed at the time you needed it. Aye, I had my own ambitions, true, but I still provided you with what you needed along the way."

I scoff, "you're narcissistically delusional. No wonder why you were kicked out of Heaven and left in Hell to burn."

"Careful, Amarah, I don't take kindly to blatant disrespect and insults. You've seen how real these little dreams can be and well, you no longer have any power to fight me."

"Wanna bet?" I challenge. I have the one thing that he can never take away from me or ever force me to give up.

My Faith.

And my Faith is what saved me from him in the past. I have zero doubt that it will save me again, and again, and again. Being on the beach reminds me of a photo my grandmother used to have hanging up in her bedroom. It was a picture that showed a set of footprints in the sand, with a story written along side of it. The part that has always stuck with me, and is relevant to my situation now, is this…

You promised me, Lord, that if I followed you, you would walk with me always. But I have noticed that during the most trying periods of my life there have been only one set of footprints in the sand. Why, when I needed you most, you have not been there for me?

The Lord replied, my child, I would never leave you. During your times of trial, when you see only one set of footprints, it was then that I carried you.

It's so easy to see what we want to see, to believe what we want to believe. It's so easy to point the finger, lay the blame, and be the victim. But if you just have *Faith*, just look past yourself for one second, you'll see the truth. You'll see the light.

"Well, if that's the only reason you called me here, to ask for your power back, I must decline and be on my way. My new plans are revving up and I need to prepare."

"And just what are you planning now that you have my power and can walk on Earth?"

He tsks, "if I told you, that would ruin the surprise. Don't you like surprises?"

"Not when they come from a lying demon, like you" I seethe.

"I'll be seeing you, Amarah," he says, unaffected by me or my insults, as he turns and walks down the beach. "I'll be seeing you again, *real* soon."

Anger and frustration well up inside of me. I know whatever he's planning can't be good for anyone, The Unseen or the human world, and I feel so helpless about it all. But mostly, I just feel stupid. Stupid that I gave the Devil what he needed to walk on Earth. Literal Hell on Earth, yeah, that can't be good, and it's only possible because of me. Everything that comes next is on me. I need to prepare as well, and I need to get my power back, sooner rather than later.

I say a prayer as I take in the quiet beauty of this dream world one more time. I have a feeling this is the last bit of peace I'll have for a while.

"Lord, please guide me and give me strength for what comes next."

I slowly wake from my dream feeling a mixture of emotions.

Urgency.

Anxiety.

Confidence.

Happiness.

Love.

Because having my Faith again is a sure and solid thing. I know I'm not alone and I know this is my destiny, but I also know nothing is ever easy. No war, no dealing with the Devil, is ever going to come without loss and sacrifice. And I'm not entirely sure I'm ready to handle more losses.

I also can't help the overwhelming sense of peace and rightness I feel waking up in Logan's arms. He's wrapped around me like my own personal body shield. I don't think he let me go, not even once, in his sleep last night. And I'm clinging to him just as tightly. I lost him.

I.

LOST.

HIM.

He *died*. In *my* arms. Just like I feared and just like I tried to stop. But I know now that nothing is truly in my control. I may be in the driver's seat but I'm not the one navigating. I need to relinquish any feigned thoughts of control and just wake up every day determined to do my best. Because my best is all I can give, and if it's not enough, well…it has to be. It *will* be.

I snuggle in closer to Logan, pulling his arm tighter around me. Yes, he's gained more muscle, he's more solid behind me, but damn if it doesn't feel like he's a giant. I feel so small and safe in his arms. How did I ever manage to give this up? I can't imagine being anywhere else in the world. As long as I'm in his arms, I'm home.

Logan stirs behind me. I hear his content sigh as he wakes up realizing I'm in his arms. Even without the connection, I know what he's feeling, because I'm feeling the exact same way. We both lost each other and now we're found again. And it's exhilarating to be seen, to be appreciated, and to have your love be returned so deeply.

He kisses my bare shoulder, "good morning, Angel." His voice is raspy, filled with sleep, but also husky and filled with desire.

I can't help the smile that spreads across my face, "good morning you insatiable and irresistible fiend."

He chuckles and the sound sends goosebumps dancing across my skin, "only a fiend for you, Amarah. Always for you. And I'm dying for another taste."

He continues to pepper my skin with kisses, sending the butterflies in my stomach lose. I thought I had gotten over the butterflies but I don't think I ever will. Not with Logan.

I shake my head, "too soon. Not the best choice of words."

I feel him growing hard, his erection pressing against the back of my thigh. Immediately, my body reacts to him, heat pooling between my legs. My body is sore and aching from hours and hours of sex and orgasms. I swear, I've never orgasmed so much in my entire life. It was the most excruciating and exhilarating line between pleasure and pain. Not to mention, I got a glimpse of an entirely new side of Logan. A very dominate one that I can't wait to explore more.

As much as I feel like I *know* him, on a truly deep level, the reality is, we've only known each other a few months. I have a lifetime ahead of me to learn every side of him, every nook and cranny, every tiny little piece of Logan. Even the pieces he may consider inconsequential. I want to know them all. The idea of unravelling him, layer by layer, for the rest of my life, is the best gift I could ever receive.

His hand travels down my stomach, over my hip and down my thigh. His rough and calloused palm scratching across my skin makes me shiver. He reaches under my leg and lifts it up, giving his hard cock direct and easy access to my already wet and throbbing pussy.

"Then how about I'm craving you. I'm hungry for you, fucking *starving*," his voice rumbles in his chest, he gently bites at my shoulder, and rubs himself along my slit, stroking my sensitive clit.

I moan at the sensation of it all. Logan consuming me, my body and my mind. The memory of this exact moment that happened months before plays through my mind. Our very first morning waking up together, me struggling to believe that it was real and not just a dream, and every morning waking up together after. A small twinge of pain tugs at my heart as I think about all the mornings we lost because of me. I quickly push the thought away. What's important is the here and now. I need...no, I *want* to be present for every moment.

"How about you just live for me, Logan? Just live for me," I whisper, my voice heavy with emotion already.

"I do live for you, Amarah. Only you," he says, as he sinks the head of his cock inside of me.

I gasp, never prepared for how he feels inside of me. He pushes further and further in until I'm at my max. Until there's no room left for anything or anyone else.

He groans as he pulls back out, my body fighting to keep him inside of me. "Fuck, you feel so...damn...good."

He sets his rhythm, sliding in and out of me in slow but determined strokes. I'm so fucked, literally and figuratively, because I'll never get enough of him. I'm so addicted to his every word, his every moan and sigh, his every grunt and groan and rumble, his every look and every touch. Every single thing about him has me falling, falling, falling, and I don't think I'll ever stop.

Logan starts to massage my clit with his fingers and I open my legs wider, giving him more access, as he sends me flying. I'm soaring on wings of pleasure and I never want to come down.

I feel the pressure inside of me building up. It's a tsunami wave, building up, higher, higher, higher, about to crest and crash down around us.

"Oh, God, Logan...fuck," I say, breathlessly.

"That's it, give it to me. Let me feel you soak my dick as I cum deep inside of you."

Fuck if his dirty talk doesn't always pull it out of me. I love to hear him talk just as much as I love the feel of him all around me and inside of me.

I moan and buck against him as the orgasm rushes through my body from my head to my damn toes. I feel Logan grow even harder as he pumps into me again, and again, until he slams into me, so fucking deep, and holds me against him. I feel him pulse inside of me as he spills his seed. His moans and his deep growls are the most satisfying sounds I'll ever fucking hear.

After a few minutes of us both catching our beath, he starts to go soft, and finally pulls out of me. Hell, even completely soft his dick is impressive. How it ever manages to fit inside of me blows my mind but I'm not going to complain.

I turn around to face him. "Looks like we're gonna need shower number three," I laugh, happily.

"Or we can say to Hell with the shower and I can walk around with your scent on me all fucking day, and my scent on you, letting everybody know you're mine."

His words make my pussy tighten and my heart soar. I love when he's not only possessive but also proud to be mine. He wants the whole world to know it. Or, maybe he only wants one certain Master Vampire to know it.

"Mmmm, I like the way you think," I agree. "Next time you can cum on me and I'll wear your scent like perfume."

He growls, "my Wolf approves. That's definitely fucking happening next time."

He leans in and lays his lips on mine. God, I love his lips. He opens his mouth and I feel his tongue asking for mine. He kisses me slow and deep, the same way he just made love to me, and I moan into it. He echoes my moan and tugs my body underneath him as he climbs on top of me. I immediately spread my legs, wrapping them around his body. We kiss until I'm breathless and floating on the clouds once again.

He breaks the kiss and looks at me with intense green eyes from inches away. He gently traces my eyebrow, glides his fingertips down my cheek, across my jaw, and swipes his thumb across my kiss-swollen lips.

"I'll never get over how beautiful you are," he says, as he makes eye contact again. "I started falling in love with you the moment I saw you. Every time you look at me, I swear I feel it in my soul. Every touch is another step closer to the edge, and with every kiss, you pull me over it, again and again and I haven't stopped falling since."

"I swear it's like you read my mind. I was just thinking the exact same thing."

His eyes move between mine, they're so raw and honest, expressing everything he'll never find words to say. I hope that mine reflect the same thing. I hope he sees how desperately lost in him I am.

"I love you, Logan."

"I know," he smirks, that arrogant, cocky smile making my heart flutter.

I playfully punch his chest, "arrogant jerk."

He laughs, "you know I love you too, Amarah, but I don't just want my love to be heard, I want my love to be *felt*. And I am going to do everything in my power to always make sure you feel it. Feel loved. Feel *my* love."

I nod, tears stinging my eyes. "Same," I manage to whisper before he kisses me again, and he's right, he's always right.

I feel all of his love pouring out of his body into mine. It doesn't matter that I still believe I don't deserve his love, it's not up to me. It's his love to give. It's his choice. And I will never take his choice away again. So, I greedily drink down his love and let it fill me up. Let it heal me.

I break the kiss this time. "As much as I want to stay in this bed and show you just how much I love you, we can't. There's a lot of stuff that needs to be done and I'm not going to hide away or make excuses any more. It's time to go to work."

He smiles, "as long as you *do* still make time to show me you love me, at least once a day, *at least*," he insists.

I laugh, "like I could possibly keep my hands off you even if I tried."

"You have my permission to touch me in any way you'd like at any time you like. I'm yours, wholly and completely, just as much as you are mine."

"You better be, or I might be the one dolling out punishment," I tease.

"Mmmm, don't tease me with a good time," he wiggles his eyebrows up and down.

I laugh harder, "omg! You're impossible!"

He rolls off of me, gets out of bed, and walks to the dresser. My eyes follow him like a predator stalking its prey. His muscles flex and move with every step he takes, rippling beneath his skin. My eyes follow every movement as he grabs a pair of boxer briefs and pulls them up his massive thighs and over his sculpted ass. I guess he really was serious about not showering. Fine by me.

"So, what's on the agenda first?" He asks.

I close my eyes and take a deep breath, trying to slow my racing pulse. When I open my eyes again, Logan is smirking down at me and runs a hand through his dishevelled hair. He knows. He *always* knows how much he affects me. But I miss being able to share our feelings and emotions on a deeper level than just words.

"Iseta. I need to call my sister, make sure she's ok, and start working on a way to get my power back."

Amarah: United

Can't Hold Us Down by Tommee Profitt, Sam Tinnesz

The phone rings and rings on the other line. I'm getting more and more nervous as each ring passes. Maybe something *is* wrong? What if she's hurt? Or worse? Considering Viveka was on a mission to take everything and everyone I love away from me I can't help but think the worst.

"Sister, what's wrong?" Her voice is alert but edged with sleep as she finally answers.

I immediately let out a sigh of relief and feel the tension I've been holding release from my body. I knew that Kordeuv was telling the truth, that he didn't know about Iseta, but that didn't mean Viveka didn't. There was still a sliver of worry in me, that Viveka *had* gotten to Iseta, but hearing her voice washes away the rest of my worry.

"What makes you think something's wrong?" I ask, even though, in truth, there are *a lot* of things that are wrong. I just don't want to worry her, and I need to make sure that she's ok, before I can discuss *my* problems.

"It's five o'clock in the morning. You never call me this early so, what's wrong? Are you ok? Who do I need to curse?"

I can't help but laugh, which I know was her intent, but I also know she's serious. She'd curse someone in a heartbeat if I asked her to or, if they did something to hurt me.

"Besides the usual suspects, no one new needs cursing," I laugh again, "but I do need your help in other ways. Like…*a lot* of other ways," I sigh, thinking about the mountain in front of me that I need to climb. "Can you get here later today?"

"You know I can. Anything specific I need to bring? Or be prepared for?" I can hear her getting up and walking around her room, already gathering supplies.

"I need to make some adjustments to wards I had placed around my house. Mae did them so, I'm sure you can easily figure them out. You're more powerful than she ever was."

"Was? Amarah, did you…"

"What? No! No way. Their Coven was attacked. It's…a long story. In fact, I was hoping you'd go with me to talk to them and pay my respects."

She sighs, "you know I'm not a fan of Covens. And me showing up there might not be welcomed."

"I know you're not, but a lot really has happened, and I don't think they would fault you for paying your respects," I challenge.

"Alright," she sighs. "What else?"

"Well, ummmm…" I start pacing in the kitchen, my nerves needing my body to *do* something. "I sorta…kinda, maybe need your help with…" I stall.

I don't want to admit that I was tricked by the Devil himself. My sister is the one who taught me about Faith. She's the one who I've always looked up to when it comes to the Big Guy upstairs and all the unknowns that come along with Faith. She's going to be so disappointed in me, and that, that disappointment, is going to hurt worse than losing my power.

"Sister," her tone has taken on a note of authority and suspicion. "What did you do?"

"Ummmm," I clear me throat and stop my pacing. I hold myself up against the island with my free hand and hang my head as I admit my defeat. "I need your help getting my power back."

"Your power?" She questions. "As in your *Angel* power?"

"Yes," I whisper, not wanting to have to admit it out loud but needing her to know.

"And how, may I ask, did you *lose* your power?"

"Ummmm, well…that's actually a really long story. You see, there were these visitors, Valmont's Maker and a freaking Kitsune! Can you believe that?! A Kitsune! Oh, and he was half Incubus. Well, anyway, these visitors were trying to get me," I ramble, trying to avoid actually telling her what happened, "well, they were trying to get my power, and they kidnapped Valmont and we went to save him, but it was a trap, and then he ended up killing Logan…"

"What?! Logan's dead?" Her voice is shocked on the other end of the phone.

"Oh, no, no, Logan's fine. I mean, he's *more* than fine, let me tell you," I chuckle.

"Amarah!" Iseta snaps at me, trying to keep me focused.

"Yeah, right, sorry. I mean, yeah, he did die and then well, I sorta, kinda, maybe…made a deal with the Devil to save him," I spit out quickly, hoping she doesn't actually catch that last part.

I hold my breath, waiting for her response. I wait, and I wait, and I wait. She isn't saying anything and I can't hear any movement anymore. I finally pull the phone away from my ear to make sure I didn't accidentally hang up on her or drop the call.

"Sister?" I inquire.

"Let me get this straight," she finally breaks her silence. "You made a deal…with the Devil, giving up your power to save Logan. Is that right?"

"Yeah," I say, defeat heavy in my voice. "And I didn't even fucking need too," I shake my head. "Archangel Michael saved him."

"What? Wow," she says, stunned. "What the Hell has happened this past month?"

"I promise, I'll tell you everything when you get here, but just get here quickly. We also need to go back to the Air Fey. We think Aralyn may be hiding out in Revna's old house."

"I swear, Sister, you are going to drive me to the dark side."

"Don't say that! That's not even funny!"

"I'll be on my way within the hour. You better be ready to tell me every last detail as soon as I get there."

"I will, I promise. Be safe and I'll see you soon."

"Sometimes, I'm not sure why, but I love you. See you soon."

"I'm honestly not sure why either," I laugh. "Love you, too."

I end the call and put my cell phone down on the counter in front of me. I sag against the island and blow out a heavy breath. I'm relieved Iseta is ok and will be here soon and I'm relieved to have some of the weight I've been carrying off of me as well. Admitting to Iseta that I lost my power wasn't easy but she's the only person I can think of that can help me get it back.

"I got the heater turned on. Should warm up in here soon," Logan says, as he makes his way into the kitchen.

"Thank you. It's not too cold, yet, but Winter is right around the corner and I'm not a hot-blooded Werewolf like you. I hate the cold," I shiver just thinking about it.

"You won't ever be cold as long as I'm here," he leans in and gives me a swift kiss before walking over to the coffee station. "Well, that call with Iseta seemed to have gone well," Logan teases, as he starts getting coffee prepared.

He's added a pair of basketball shorts but remains shirtless and barefoot. The shorts hang dangerously, dangerously low on his hips, showing off his cut V and the new veins that have appeared below his belly button, leading south. My mouth waters as I drink up every inch of him. Sweet baby Jesus he's even larger than he was

86

before, and I'm not just talking about his body. His energy fills up the space between us causing me to fight for air.

It's like my heart is suddenly too big for my chest to hold it. I swear I can feel it swell inside of me and push against my ribcage. It's almost painful and I have to rub my chest trying to ease the sensation. I'm frozen in place, watching his muscular back flex as he moves here and there, filling up the coffee pot with water, opening a drawer to get the filter, grabbing the cannister that holds the coffee, it's like I'm watching a damn Cirque du Soleil show. It's fascinating and magnificent and I can't take my eyes off of him.

He turns and looks at me over his shoulder, "you keep thinking those thoughts and we're never going to leave this house."

I swallow, hard, "what thoughts?" I try to sound innocent but I barely even have a voice.

He smirks and decides to turn around, giving me all his attention. Every nerve in my body is firing rapidly. It's like, as his gaze rakes over me, I can feel it.

"I don't need an open connection to read you," he explains, as he slowly walks towards me.

He towers over me. I should feel intimidated but I just feel safe and fucking turned on. He reaches down and grabs me underneath my ass, lifting me up to sit on the island. Déjà vu rushes through me.

"And I sure as Hell don't need a connection to know what you're feeling. I can hear it when your heart starts to race," he says, as he leans down and kisses my chest, over my heart. He moves his head so his lips are brushing against mine as he speaks, "and I can smell your desire the second your pussy soaks for me." His tongue slips out and runs along my lips, pulling a groan from me, but he doesn't kiss me.

"You know, we did skip dinner last night," he says, contemplatively. "And I'm starving."

My mind is reeling, "W-w-hat?"

He's talking about food? How can he be thinking about food when I'm practically fainting from lack of air and my body is seconds away from melting with desire. I'm sugar quickly dissolving in hot water.

His calloused hands run up my bare thighs and slip underneath the hem of the shirt I'm wearing. His shirt. His hands find my ass and I squeal as he suddenly jerks me forward. He leans over me, his massive body pushing mine down until I'm lying flat on the island counter.

"I said, I'm starving, and it looks like I have my favorite dish already marinated and seasoned, waiting for me to dive in," he says, seriously, as he spreads my knees apart, revealing my bare pussy.

"Oh," I manage to choke out, finally understanding that he means *me*. I'm the food.

It doesn't take long before I'm writhing on the counter, moaning and losing my damn mind. The man is a fucking magician with his tongue and fingers and has me cussing and begging within minutes. He knows exactly what I like and exactly how to tease me and prolong the pleasure or go directly for the orgasm. He's wasting no time going for gold this morning, his tongue relentlessly flicking over my clit. I barely have time to register the crest of the orgasm before it washes over me.

Logan's chest rumbles with satisfaction as he licks up every last drop. He finally lifts his head up and stares at me as his tongue slides across his lips, "mmmm, fucking delicious."

I feel my cheeks burn slightly. I don't know why he still manages to fluster me. "Fucking Hell," I say, as I manage to push myself up onto my elbows.

"Would you like a taste?" He asks with a smirk.

I nod my head slightly and whisper, "yes."

He leans over me and claims my mouth with his. I can taste

my sweetness on his lips and tongue and it lights me on fire. I don't know why tasting myself on him is so fucking satisfying but it is.

"As much as I'd love to climb on this island and sink my cock into that tight, wet pussy of yours, if I give into the temptation now, I'm never going to stop," he says, as he bites my bottom lip pulling a whimper from my throat. "And we have shit to do, unfortunately," he sighs heavily. "Come on," he pulls me up with him. He's clearly ready to go, too, as he reaches inside his boxer briefs to adjust himself.

"What about you?" I ask, as I gesture towards his rock-hard erection.

"I'll be fine. Besides, it will just be that much better when I do finally get to have you," he smiles and winks at me. I swear, if my body was capable of being a puddle, I'd be a damn puddle. "But now, time for breakfast, for real. Then, we call the Queen and tell her our plans, then we wait for Iseta."

"And what exactly is our plan?" I ask.

"We get a small group together to go to the Air Fey's home, tonight. We need to see if what the Elders think is right. If Aralyn is, in fact, hiding out in Revna's old house."

I nod my head in agreement, "alright. I agree that we should go there as soon as possible so, tonight it is. I know Emrick will want to come and," I hesitate mentioning Valmont but what happened, happened. We can't walk on eggshells around the truth and we have to move past it, "I'm sure Valmont will join as well, or…send someone to join us at least. But we have a whole day available too. Once Iseta gets here, I'll fill her in on everything and we can go visit the Coven. I'd like to meet the new Supreme and see if perhaps they're ready to join forces with us. After what happened, they'd be stupid not to want more allies."

Logan doesn't seem to be put off by the mention of Valmont going with us, but I also don't have the open connection directly to his feelings. He can school his facial features and without the connection, I won't know if there was even a twinge of emotion within him. It sucks and I'm frustrated, but I try to stay positive. Logan will tell me if he's upset or uncomfortable. I just have to trust in him to be open and honest with me, and vice versa, until I get my power back. I *will* get my power back.

"The Unseen has always been this way," he shrugs, as he rummages around the kitchen, trying to find food to cook. "You're the first person to ever get the Vampires to help, if anyone can get the Witches to help too, it's you, Angel."

Four hours later, Iseta's vehicle is pulling into my driveaway, and it's barely 9:00 a.m. Damn, getting up early actually makes it feel like you have time to do things. We've been super productive already and it's not even close to mid-day yet.

Logan and I walk outside to greet her. The cold, almost-Winter air bites at me. I rub my arms up and down, trying to create some friction for added heat. Of course, it doesn't work, just a silly gesture to do something with my hands as I hug myself. Logan sees my struggle and pulls me into his arms, hugging me from behind.

Iseta gets out of her vehicle already shaking her head. "So, I see the two of you have worked things out?"

I lean my head back and Logan and I look at each other, smile, and laugh, "yeah, we did. It only takes me dying to win your sister's heart apparently."

I turn around and punch him in the chest, "that's not true!"

He chuckles, "I mean, if the shoe fits."

"You've always had my heart, you know this! And stop joking about dying," I chide. "It's too soon and it's not even close to funny."

"Alright you two, you're both going to tell me everything, but first, let's get inside. It's fucking cold out here."

Logan chuckles, "definitely sisters."

"Logan, can you help me with my bags?"

"Of course," he rushes to her side and takes everything she hands him.

Once we're all inside and somewhat settled, Logan and I began the long story of telling Iseta everything. Since we had been separated for most of the last two months, there's stuff that neither of us know either so, we take turns sharing our own stories. I have more to share since I was directly in contact with Viveka and Kordeuv, dreaming with the Devil, training with Emrick, and meeting with the Elders.

"So, the murders on the news, the bodies that were found here, just like the others, that was the Coven? And that was Kordeuv and Viveka's doing?

"I didn't know it was on the news, but yeah, that makes sense. It was Viveka and Kordeuv leaving the trail of bodies all along. At least we know there won't be any more attacks. Not from them at least," I say, somewhat relieved that one threat has been dealt with.

"You don't seem surprised about me," Logan questions.

Iseta shakes her head, "I'm not. I knew exactly what you were the minute I met you. If you recall, I said that you were special."

Logan's brows furrow, "I do remember, I just thought you were talking about me being a Werewolf."

"Nope. I could feel your energy and it's the same as Amarah's. I've never felt it on anyone else before. Honestly, I'm surprised no one else has managed to figure that out yet." She sighs, "most people, even powerful people or people in powerful positions, tend to still be ignorantly blind, only seeing what they what to see."

"Archangel Michael thought it was strange that no one else had figured it out yet either," I confirm.

"I *am* shocked that Michael is your father though. That's

definitely a piece of information I would've never guessed."

"Well, that makes two of us," Logan agrees, shaking his head.

"Three of us," I add. "And Michael didn't give us any clues as to how to get my power back. He just said that I *can* get it back. Do you have any ideas?"

"I have been thinking about this since you told me on the phone earlier. It's not going to be easy. Logan, since we know what you are now, I'll need to use your blood for the spell."

"Angel blood," he shakes his head. "I still can't quite wrap my head around it."

"Yes, Angel blood." Iseta sighs, "I have an idea in mind but there's no guarantee it will work, Amarah. And, like I said, it won't be easy."

"Since when has our life ever been easy? And when has that ever stopped us?" I say, with conviction.

"You're right, Sister. We haven't had an easy life, that's for sure. Perhaps all our past trials and struggles have led us here, exactly where we need to be and with the experience and perseverance to make it happen."

"I hope you're right."

We take a minute to contemplate all the cards on the table and the cards each of us has been dealt. I think we're all a bit overwhelmed with it all. I can't help Iseta and Logan through their thought process, but I can control mine, and I'm choosing to remain calm and positive. One thing at a time, Amarah. One thing at a time.

"When will you be ready to do the spell?" I ask, with as little emotion in my voice as possible.

I'm anxious, obviously. I want to get my power back sooner rather than later but I also don't want to put any added pressure or expectation on Iseta. This is her area of expertise, not mine, and I'll defer to her on this, completely. It's not easy to be at someone else's mercy though. Especially for someone with control issues, insert my stubborn ass here, but I'm learning. I'm learning patience and I'm learning that I can't do everything on my own nor do I want too anymore.

"Well, we need to make the visit to the Coven today and then travel to the Air Fey tonight, right?"

I nod, "yeah, that's the plan."

"So, we can attempt the spell as soon as we're done with the Aralyn situation. That could be as soon as tomorrow, depending on how tonight goes."

"Alright, that sounds good." I wish we had time to try the spell now, but I know this is the best course of action. "Oh, I'm sure you felt the magic around the house. I had some wards put up by Mae before she…" I clear my throat, "I was hoping you could alter them somehow? Allow Logan entry without me needing to invite him in?"

Iseta nods her head, "yeah, I felt them. I'll see what I can do. We can probably surpass the wards with a little of his blood in a spell. Angel blood is a powerful thing."

"I sure hope so. How about I work on getting us all some lunch while you do that and then we can head Downtown to the Coven. I'm not going on an empty stomach or any weaker than I already am without my power. I have no idea what kind of mood they're in but it can't be good."

"I'm going with you guys. There's no way I'm letting you walk into a Witch Coven without your power and without protection. No offense, Iseta. I know you're extremely powerful and will protect Amarah as much as I will, but I'm not letting her walk into potential danger without me," Logan insists. "Together. Always."

I reach across the counter and grab his hand, giving it a reassuring squeeze, "together. Always."

It's a little after 1:00 p.m. when we park in front of Nature's Magical Whispers & More. In the middle of the day, the store should be open and accepting business, but the shades are pulled down the flashing neon open sign is turned off. Even without my power, I sense the sadness and devastation around the building. Hell, maybe I'm projecting the truth I already know, but it just feels...desolate.

"The energy here is heavy," Iseta confirms my own feelings.

We're standing on the sidewalk, just below the stairs that lead to the front door, staring up at the building. "I don't know how I feel it without my power but I feel the energy too. It's heavy and full of devastation. Loss," I whisper.

"You're still sensitive to energy, that's good. Your power may have been taken but you are who you are, Amarah. You're still Fey and you're still an Angel. Don't forget that."

I nod, not trusting my voice. I'm still super emotional about everything that's happened, but especially about losing my power and accepting who I am with and without it.

I focus back on the building and the business we came to accomplish. I clear my throat, pushing the emotion back down, "ready or not, let's get this over with."

I lead the way up the stairs. They haven't been swept and the snow from the day before lingers in the cold shadows, crunching under our shoes. Once I'm on the landing, I reach out and press the doorbell. I feel Logan's hand rest on the small of my back as he stands beside me. The gesture is small and quiet but so incredibly loud at the same time. He's here with me.

Logan is here with me.

He's real.

He's alive.

He's my anchor.

He's my partner.

And the feel of him next to me reassures me and adds to my confidence. I can do this, I can face this tragedy, because he's facing it with me. And on the other side, I feel Iseta. I'm not alone.

We wait in silence for a few minutes before a pair of eyes peek through the shades. A second later, I hear the lock unlatch and the door swings open. Relief washes over me at Alisha's familiar face. She's so young, way too young to die, and I find myself saying a silent prayer of thanks to see her standing in front of me.

"Amarah," she says, hesitantly, her eyes flicking to Logan and Iseta standing next to me. "Now's really not a good time."

"I know, I heard...*vaguely*, about what happened and I'm just here to pay my respects. I know Mae and I never really saw eye to eye but I'm the reason you and your Coven were attacked. I just want to say that I'm sorry and..."

"What do you mean *you're* the reason we were attacked?" Alisha's cheeks flush with color and she narrows her eyes at me.

Every time I've been around Alisha, she's been quiet and a bit meek, but there's no mistaking the anger she has boiling just below the surface now. I can only imagine what she was forced to witness and what she survived. This Coven is her family, of course she's desperate to blame someone for this attack, for this loss, and I'm giving her a target for all that anger. Me.

"It's really a long story and I'd love to explain everything. Can we come in?" I ask, calmly.

"I don't think that's a very good idea," Alisha's voice has turned from soft and docile to laced with all the anger I feel radiating off of her.

"Alisha, please, let me at least explain..."

"I think you should go."

"Alisha," a new stern voice enters the conversation. "That is not your decision to make now, is it?"

I hear footsteps shortly before I see another familiar face in the open doorway, behind Alisha. She towers over Alisha's small stature. She's taller than Iseta and I gauge her to be around the same height as Logan. She's tall for a woman, and extremely curvy, but somehow still manages to exude soft femininity. She's the Witch that came to my house with Mae to complete the wards I asked for. She's the one who went out into the back yard and had regarded me with something other than annoyance, unlike Mae.

Her mahogany brown eyes still hold the same curiosity now, but they're also filled with sadness. I'm terrified to find out just how bad the attack on their Coven was. I know this new Witch's face but I don't know her name or anything about her. I don't know anything about the Coven at all actually and I feel bad about it.

"I'll handle it from here, Alisha, you may go," the new woman dismisses the young Witch but she throws another nasty look my way before she walks away. I don't blame her.

"Amarah, we haven't been properly introduced. My name is Brynn McIntyre, I'm the new Ülim for the Desert Rose Coven." She extends her hand and I take it.

"It's a pleasure to meet you, Brynn."

"I was hoping you would come," she says, as she drops my hand and steps aside, gesturing for me to join her inside. "Please, come in, all of you."

"Thank you," I say, as I step inside, immediately grateful for the warmth of the building. I start introductions as Iseta and Logan follow me. "Brynn, this is my sister, Iseta."

"Yes, of course, I've heard a lot about you. Please come in and be welcome," Brynn says, genuinely.

"And this is…"

"Logan Lewis," Brynn interrupts, but not rudely. "I've heard a lot about you as well. Come in, come in," Brynn ushers everyone inside and shuts the door behind her. "Please excuse the mess, we're still picking up the pieces from the attack."

At her words, I finally take a look around. The store is in even worse shape than the time I exploded in here, breaking all the glass. This looks like an actual tornado came through and destroyed everything. There are a handful of Witches cleaning up the store and I can't help but wonder if these few Witches are all that's left of the once large Coven.

"Brynn, this is awful. I'm so sorry," I say, sadly, as I look at the destruction around me. "How can we help?" I turn to face her.

She shakes her head, "we've got this handled, but I do want to speak with you about the future of this Coven, if you have time?"

"Of course, that's why we're here."

"Let's talk downstairs," she heads towards the back of the store and doesn't wait to see if we follow.

I look at Iseta for confirmation that she's ok with where this is going. She's a powerful Witch but a Gray Witch. She isn't a part of any Coven, and Witches that *are* a part of a Coven, treat her differently because of her choice to be solitary. They could also take her being here, during one of their weakest and lowest points, as a sign of aggression. Or even disrespect. I know asking her to come with me is a risk. People tend to jump to conclusions and make their assumptions based on their current feelings and circumstances. And right now, I imagine this Coven is feeling extremely scared and vulnerable.

Iseta dips her head, confirming she's ok with meeting Brynn downstairs. I exhale a heavy breath, trying to remain positive and confident in my decision to not only be here right now, but bringing Iseta with me. I lead the way across the store, Logan bringing up the rear, protecting us and watching our backs. Even without the ability to communicate privately, he seems to always know exactly what to do.

As I start descending the stairs, I feel it, the magic in the air, but it's not as strong as it once was. I don't know if it's because, without my power I can't sense it like I used to, or if their magic has been weakened that badly from the attack.

"I can still feel the magic in the air," I say out loud, hoping Iseta will understand.

"Even humans can be sensitive to magic, even if they don't know what they're feeling exactly. Again, you're not human, Amarah, you're still special. Your power is an *extension* of you, not all of you. Continue to have Faith and trust your instincts."

I nod my head as I continue down the stairs and finally reach the bottom. The basement looks as it always has. There's either been no destruction here or this was the first place they put back together.

Brynn is standing next to the table, the same table I sat at twice with Mae, and she's patiently waiting for us. When we finally arrive, she gestures for us to sit and joins us.

"It looks the same as it always has down here," I mention my observation. It's not posed as a question but I am curious about the details of everything that's happened.

Brynn seems to understand and explains, "the altar is our main concentrated power source. We protect this space with everything we have. Luckily, the attack on us seemed to be just about killing Witches, not destroying the Coven completely or our magic."

"I'm so sorry that this happened to you. Like I told Alisha, you were targeted because of me. Not because I'm your enemy or because I directed the attack here, but the people who attacked you thought that Mae was Iseta."

Brynn's brows furrow in confusion, "what do you mean?"

I sigh, "the attack was made here by mistake. The target was Iseta, not Mae, their goal was to kill Iseta and therefore weaken me. I don't have any words to express the sorrow and guilty I feel."

"Who is *they*?"

I tell Brynn everything I know about Viveka and Kordeuv and assure her that they're no longer a threat. I ask her about the attack and she confirms the way they attacked was exactly the way the bodies on the news had been found. Viveka attacking with a weapon and Kordeuv attacking with claws. Then Viveka hypnotized the survivors and made them watch as she drained almost all of the blood from the victims. Their sisters. Their family.

The Witches don't know how the human police found out about the attack but they showed up. My best guess is that Viveka wanted the Witches found out, to further weaken them. God, Valmont had been right about her. All she wanted to do was cause chaos and destruction wherever she went.

Brynn takes a moment to digest the information we shared with each other and then her eyes fall on Iseta. "And now you bring her here. Into my Coven. Why?"

"Yes, I did. I brought Iseta with me for a couple of reasons. The first reason, which I'm hesitant to share, but feel the need to start off this new relationship with you and your Coven differently than I did with Mae. After what Mae did the first time, I never trusted her. I'm taking a leap of Faith and hoping that I can trust you, Brynn. I'm giving you my trust and hoping that you don't break it."

She nods, "go on."

"The first reason, is because I need her protection. Unfortunately, I am temporarily without my specific…*power*, and I didn't want to come here unprotected. Again, not that I don't trust you, it's just my experiences with Mae were far from welcoming."

"I understand, and no offense taken. I appreciate you being this honest with me. You're basically telling me you have a weakness and trusting that I won't take advantage of the situation."

"I am," I agree.

"And what's the second reason you chose to bring Iseta into my home?"

"Because the attack is not her fault. She had no idea about anything that was happening here. Also, she's not your enemy. She's different than you, yes. She's extremely powerful, yes. But that doesn't mean she's your enemy. Neither am I or the Fey, or Logan and the Werewolves, or Valmont and the Vampires. We all live and survive in The Unseen together, and what I've learned recently, from my own damn stubbornness, is that trying to handle things alone is never the answer. It should be the last option, only when there are no other options available. I want you to be an ally. An ally to me and the Fey, to the Werewolves and to the Vampires. Of course, being an ally works both ways. We can provide you with strength, too. Especially now, in your time of need. I'm really hoping that this can be a turning point for your Coven and I'm really hoping you're the Supreme who can make this happen."

"I see," she says again.

She steeples her hands under her chin and continues to regard us. She's showing no signs of emotion on her face and I have no idea what she could possibly be thinking or deciding. I can only hope that she hears the genuine truth of my words and makes the right choice for her Coven and for all of us.

"Mae was a good many things," she finally breaks the tense silence. "She cared about this Coven, this family, more than anything else, but she wasn't perfect. I don't wish to speak ill of the departed so, all I'll add, is that her insecurities made her weak, and in turn, made this Coven weak. Not all of the Witches agreed with her decisions to remain indifferent. Including me."

I want to nod my head and agree with her because I know Mae wasn't very powerful. I know she was insecure because of it and therefore, she wanted to remain solitary in order to hide the truth from as many people as she could. Definitely a survival tactic. Don't let others find out your weaknesses in case they use them against you. However, being weak with no strong allies also puts you at risk, and unfortunately, this Coven experienced that risk. How Mae managed to become Supreme is something I never understood, and how she managed to remain Supreme, is unfathomable to me, but I remain silent and stoic, not wanting to offend the new Supreme on our first visit.

Brynn continues, "I do not wish to repeat history and I do not want to be the Supreme who ruins this Coven because of stubbornness or insecurities. I'm confident in my own power and I'm confident I can build this Coven up better than it was before. That being said, I'm not naïve to believe I can do it alone, without allies. You're here, Amarah, being open and vulnerable with me and I'll gladly reciprocate the trust. Let us move forward as allies and unite The Unseen in a way it has never known before. Let us unite and face all threats against us together, as one."

Logan's hand finds my thigh underneath the table and gives it an encouraging squeeze. I have to restrain myself from jumping up and running to Brynn, embracing her and thanking her profusely for making the right decision.

I mange to remain in my seat but the smile that spreads across my face is big and genuine. "Thank you, Brynn. I truly believe this is the best decision for all of us. It doesn't negate the fact that there are still threats to face but I can promise you one thing. You and your Cove will never have to face them alone, ever again. And being connected with the other preternatural factions of The Unseen, means we're all more informed and aware of what's going on all around us and not just what we can see on our own."

Brynn nods in agreement, "we may be weak right now. Our numbers are less than half of what they were, but we will rebuild, and we will become a strong ally."

"I have no doubt," I assure her. "Now, we can move on with

other business. Let me catch you up on everything we know and our current plans to move forward. Then, you can let us know what you need, from any of us, to get you back on your feet."

"If I may add, no big change can happen overnight," Iseta finally speaks. "But what you two are starting here today, what you've done, Amarah, with the Vampires, these are all small steps in the right direction. A powerful and bright future lays ahead for The Unseen and I hope I live long enough to see it bloom."

"One thing at a time," I say, looking around the table and seeing hope, the same hope I feel, reflected in their eyes. "One thing at a time."

Logan: My Weakness

Lost by Maroon 5

I'm in awe every damn time I watch Amarah. Whether it's watching her sleep, watching her savor food, watching her laugh, watching her cum (this one might be my favorite), or watching her speak with such passion about what she believes in. And that's what I'm doing now. I sit back, in my chair, and just watch her work her magic. No, not her power, her magic. The magic that's in every fiber of her being.

Amarah *is* magic.

And I fall in love with her more every second of every day. I still haven't quite wrapped my mind around how she came into my life and just completely flipped everything upside down. It's not as terrifying as the upside down in Stranger Things but it *is* scary. She completely flipped the narrative on everything I thought I knew about love and life. Everything I thought I knew about myself. Amarah changed everything simply by walking out onto the balcony at that club and taking the air right out of my lungs. For once, someone else was my focus and not my anger.

Amarah is magic.

She just solidified an alliance with the Desert Rose Coven. She's united the entire Unseen, something that the Queen herself has failed to do and not from a lack of trying. And I couldn't be prouder. Prouder to be a witness to another one of her triumphs. Something that she won't even acknowledge as a big deal but it is. Prouder to be by her side, her partner. Prouder to call her *mine*.

I reach over and squeeze her thigh, a small gesture to show her that I see her, that I acknowledge the good she just accomplished and fuck, I want to lay her on top of this table and show her just how proud of her I am. Maybe denying myself a release this morning wasn't such a good idea after all. Just touching her thigh, inches away from her hot, sweet center is causing my cock to twitch. I clench my jaw and remove my hand before I let it slide between her legs and rub her clit under the table.

I somehow manage to keep myself focused on business as we finish up with the new Supreme. Even though they're vulnerable now, picking up the pieces after such a devastating attack, Brynn insists on joining us tonight. I respect her more for her decision and her leadership. She's stepping up to ensure a strong alliance that she just agreed to.

"Really, Brynn, you don't have to come tonight. You've just gone through something so...tragic. I'm sure your Coven needs you here," Amarah is insisting.

Brynn shakes her head, "there's nothing much I can do at the moment other than helping to restore the store for business and they can handle that over the next day or so while I'm gone."

Amarah nods her head in acquiescence, "alright. We'll be meeting at the Fey Headquarters at 5:00 p.m. so, that gives you a couple of hours to prepare. You know where it is?"

"Of course. I'll be there," Brynn ensures us, as she holds the door open for us and we step out into the chilly and cloudy December day.

I lead the way to my truck and open the doors on the passenger side for both Amarah and Iseta. Iseta climbs into the back seat first and then I wait for Amarah to hoist herself up and slide into the front seat. I'm internally cursing that Iseta is with us because I desperately want to grab Amarah's ass as she's climbing inside. Being around her and controlling my urges to constantly touch her has never been easy but it's been even worse after our time apart. I'm going to have to get used to it though. We aren't going to have any more alone time for a while.

I sigh heavily and run my hands through my hair as I walk around to the driver side and jump in, starting the truck and turning the heater on for the ladies. I point my vents away from my already overheated body.

"We're going to stop by the Werewolf den and pickup Kaedon and Atreya, they'll be riding with us to the Air Fey, I hope that's ok with you both?" I ask, hesitantly, still unsure of how Amarah truly feels about Atreya.

We didn't exactly spend our first night together *talking*. Not that I'm complaining because it was some of the best sex we've ever had, and we always have fucking phenomenal sex, but it would have been productive to unload some baggage and get on the same page. Especially since we can't privately communicate at the moment. So, I turn to face Amarah and gage her reaction closely.

She nods her head, "yeah, that's fine with me. I'd like to get to know them both better."

I squint my eyes at her, hyper focused on all of her verbal and non-verbal clues. Her tone is calm and light, not strained in any way. Her heart remains beating calmly. I don't smell any sweat from stress or nervousness clogging her pores.

She laughs, "what? Why are you looking at me like that?"

"If you're not ok with them coming with us, I can tell them to follow us. You don't have to do anything you're not comfortable with."

"I know I don't and I wouldn't if it was truly an issue but it's not. I promise," she smiles at me and it eases some of my tension.

Nothing even close to sexual ever happened between Atreya

and me but there had been, what Amarah perceived as a very intimate moment, between us. It wasn't but I'm not entirely sure Amarah believes it wasn't. Maybe Atreya being with us will be a good thing after all. She'll see what a wonderful person Atreya is and, hopefully, she'll end up liking her as much as I do. As a friend.

"Alright," I pull my eyes away from Amarah and acknowledge Iseta. "You ok with the arrangement?"

She shrugs, "oh, I'm fine. Don't mind me, I'm just along for the ride."

Satisfied with both of their answers, I pull the truck away from the curb and drive the few blocks to Knockouts. Downtown is not the place you come to during the day, at least not for the majority of people. No, Downtown is for the party crowd, at least in Albuquerque it is. Because of this, I'm able to snag a spot directly in front of the entrance to the gentleman's club. Even though it's open twenty-fours a day, there's hardly any business at this time of the day.

Amarah scoffs, "you've got to be kidding me. You *are* joking, right? You're just using this space to park here, right?"

I can't help but chuckle at the utter astonishment and disgust on her face. "No, I'm not joking, babe."

"This is where you've been coming? To *train*," she makes air quotes around the word, train.

She's jealous. Amarah is jealous of some no name women who take their clothes off and dance in front of people for money. I can't help the swell of contentment that rises in my chest at the thought of her being jealous, over me.

"I do come here to train. You'll see," I assure her.

"You better hope I *do* see because I don't like the thought of you coming her to look at other women," she admits.

I shake my head, "I don't. It's not my cup of tea at all actually," I confess. "But you have to admit, it's a good cover. Can you think of a better front for a Werewolf Pack? A better way to keep humans blissfully distracted from what sits right under their nose?"

She huffs, still in disbelief, but I see the truth of the situation as it registers in her mind. "No, I guess not," she shakes her head. "Women, especially naked women, are a great distraction I suppose."

"You don't have to come in, but considering the fact that you are the Võitleja, it would benefit you to know the inner layout of the Werewolf den."

She sighs, "fine. But I'm not touching anything. Snail trails everywhere. No thanks," she grimaces and shudders in disgust.

"Oh my goodness, Amarah. Really? Snail trails? You had to go there?" Iseta asks, in shock.

"What?" Amarah defends. "That's exactly what it is."

I can't help but laugh at her squeamishness over the sexual details of a gentleman's club. Especially when she's a sopping wet mess for me every time we have sex.

"Really, Amarah? This surprises me considering how..."

"You better not! If you value your life, you will not even *think* about finishing that sentence in front of my sister."

I can't help but chuckle again.

"Lord, help me," Iseta mumbles from the back seat.

"Alright, alright, let's go. And don't worry, we don't have to even go through the front doors and see the stages and what not. We can go through the alley, to the back door entrance, and straight to the den."

That seems to satisfy her a small amount. She nods, "fine," opens the door and slips out of the truck.

"We won't be long," I promise Iseta, as I follow Amarah's lead and get out of the truck.

Once we're by ourselves and walking through the alleyway on the side of the building, Amarah let's me have it. "I can't believe you were about to disclose something extremely private about us in front of Iseta!"

I manage to hold in my chuckle. I forget how human Amarah still thinks. Hell, even Iseta is basically human compared to me. I've lived over three hundred years, things like being naked and talking about sex don't embarrass me. Ever.

I stop walking and grab her hand, stopping her angry stomping tantrum as well. "I'm sorry, Angel, I didn't think that all the way through. Just because I don't get embarrassed about certain things doesn't mean that you don't."

"I'm not *embarrassed*," she says, flustered.

I lift my eyebrow, looking at her with amusement, knowing full well she's lying.

She sighs and seems to deflate a bit, losing some of her frustration, "ok, fine. I do get embarrassed but she is my sister! I don't want or need her knowing about my private sex life. Or anyone for that matter."

"I understand and you don't have to worry, it won't happen again. I promise."

She nods and looks at the ground, her overall insecurity about our conversation and where we are, are speaking loud and clear.

I lift her chin up gently, forcing her head up, but she's still avoiding my eyes. "Amarah, look at me."

She slowly lifts her beautiful hazel eyes up to me. I can see her uncertainty as she looks at me, her arms protectively wrapped around herself. I hate that she's feeling like this because of me. Because she thinks that I come here to look at other women, and who knows what other false and damaging thoughts are running through her mind. I swear, I'll never understand the mind of a woman.

"I don't know what I have to do or say to comfort you right now. All I can do is tell you the truth. And without our connection, you're just going to have to trust that I'm being one hundred percent honest with you. Do you trust me to be honest with you?"

She slightly nods her head as I'm still holding her chin between my fingers.

"I've not once sat in that room and watched the girls on stage. I've not once looked at, or touched, any of the girls that work here. Not even before I met you."

I see the stiffness in her shoulders ease slightly at my admission, but I still see some worry in her eyes, and I'm not sure why she's feeling this way. I don't understand her insecurity when I've told her, more than once, how much she means to me. But if I have to remind her every fucking day, until the day I die, then I will. I will reassure her and make her feel wanted every God damn day.

"And then you came along," I smirk down at her and move my hand to caress her cheek. "No one has ever made me feel the way that you do, Amarah. You drive me fucking crazy and not always in a good way," I laugh softly and so does she. "But the way you make me feel in here," I grab her arm, pulling it away from her body, and lead her hand to my chest, covering her hand with mine, "nothing else in the entire world can compare to it. To you. Sure, I can acknowledge when another woman is attractive, just as you can acknowledge when another man is, but no one makes me feel anything here," I lead her hand down my stomach and place it on my dick.

I clench my teeth. Just the feel of her hands on me makes my blood run even hotter than it already is. That blood is now rushing to my cock and I'm quickly hardening underneath her simple touch.

"You see, this," I move her hand up and down the length of me, over my jeans, "doesn't work without this," I move her hand back up to my chest. "You control my heart, Amarah, and I only ever want to be deep inside of *you*. Inside that sopping wet, dripping, tight, beautiful fucking pussy of yours. Do you see what you do to me, Amarah? Do you understand the power you have over me? Not mystical power, this is a different kind of power. Do you know what it is?"

"What?" She whispers.

I hold her face in my hands and make sure she's seeing and hearing me. "Love, Angel. Love. And I love you so much I'll remind you every fucking day. I'll remind you on your good days, when you're laughing and smiling without a care in the world. I'll remind you on your not so good days, when you're feeling unsure and insecure, and I'll especially be there to remind you on your bad days. On the days when your guilt and regret make you hate yourself and make you feel undeserving of love. I'll be right there to make sure you *are* getting all the love you deserve. Always."

I see her throat bob in a hard swallow, her eyes are watering and without our connection, I'm not exactly sure what she's feeling right now. I'm not sure if what I said had the effect I was intending or if I just somehow made her feel worse. When she slowly nods her head, I lean in and place my lips against hers. Softly. Gently. Like I told her before, I want my love to be felt, not just heard.

She kisses me back and tiptoes, wrapping her arms around my neck, clinging to me. I pick her up and she immediately wraps her legs around me, holding onto me as if I'm a buoy anchoring her in unsteady, choppy water. The kiss turns from soft and gentle to hungry and desperate. I'm standing in the middle of a dirty alley, next to a strip club, feeling so full of love and so fucking horny, I'm close to unzipping my pants, pulling hers down and taking her right here, right now.

Amarah moans into the kiss and a growl rumbles through my chest. I kiss her deeply for a few more seconds, drinking down the taste of her mouth, savoring the feel of her tongue sliding against mine, before I finally pull back. I let her slide down my body so I can compose myself.

"Love and sex," I say, breathlessly. "One and the fucking same when it comes to you, Angel. And if we didn't have people waiting on us, I'd take you right here against this fucking dirty alley wall and not give a fuck about who might see us."

"You know, the idea of getting caught is kinda hot," it's Amarah's turn to smirk at me.

Before I even realize what the little minx is doing, she has my jeans unzipped and is pulling my aching cock out of my underwear.

"Amarah," my voice is low and deep, filled with desire and warning. I'm so close to saying fuck everyone and everything we have to do. Let the fucking world burn around us. I just need to sink inside her. That's all the matters.

I'm completely exposed in the light of midday, right smack in the middle of Downtown, but the last thing on my mind is worrying about anyone seeing us. My only thought is how fucking unbelievably good her hands feel as she strokes me. Her thumb runs over the tip of my cock, finding pre-cum already trickling out. I watch, as she wipes it off of me and then wipes it onto her wrists, rubbing them together like she's putting on fucking perfume.

"I can't smell it, but I'm sure every Werewolf in this club will be able too, and I want them *all* to smell your scent freshly on me. How's that for being embarrassed?" She asks and then sticks her thumb in her mouth and sucks, moaning around her finger, before she turns her back on me and continues walking down the alley.

I'm left standing here with my fucking dick out, harder than a fucking rock, staring after her with my jaw on the fucking ground, trying to understand everything she just said and did. Not giving myself a release earlier was definitely a bad idea. I grip my cock, hard, trying to cause a little pain to clear my fuzzy, horny fucking thoughts. It takes me longer than I'd like to admit to compose myself but I finally tuck myself back into my jeans and hurry after Amarah.

"Sorry that took so long, Sister," Amarah apologizes for our delay. "Ethan wanted to give me a tour and I didn't want to tell the Alpha no. Especially since he's been our number one ally from day one."

"It's alright, I've been using the quiet time to meditate and charge some crystals. Are the others coming?"

"Yeah, they're right behind us," I say. "Ah, there they are." I point out the window as Atreya and Kaedon approach my truck.

The back passenger door opens and Atreya slips in first so I start the introductions. "Iseta, this is Atreya, she's new to the Pack here but she's become a good friend and she's definitely someone you want to have next to you in a fight. Atreya, this is Iseta, Amarah's sister."

"Nice to meet you," Iseta shakes Atreya's hand.

"It's really nice to meet you," Atreya replies. "I'm excited to get to know you and Amarah better during this trip. I don't know what she's told you but we didn't exactly start off on the right foot."

Amarah scoffs, "that's putting it mildly."

Iseta raises her eyebrows, "I can take a guess as to why, and you better not have done anything to make me disappointed in you, Logan. I know a curse that will give you a limp dick, *permanently*."

I blanch and turn so fast in my seat that I nearly give myself whiplash. "What?! No! I swear…"

"Iseta!" Amarah scolds her sister.

Kaedon and Atreya both burst out laughing. Atreya points to me, "the look on your face!" She's laughing so hard she's wiping tears out of the corner of her eyes. "Oh man, I like you already," she tells Iseta.

"Just saying," Iseta shrugs, "you hurt my sister or disrespect her in any way and you won't like the repercussions."

"I can confirm that nothing happened between us or with
anyone else. I happen to bat for the other team," Atreya winks. "And
Logan is a down right simp for your sister."

"Just glad there's not going to be any more awkwardness or
female drama this time around," Kaedon says.

I take a minute to catch my breath. The thought of never
being able to have sex ever again was a verbal blow that took the air
right out of my lungs.

When I'm finally breathing again, I introduce Kaedon. "This is
Kaedon. He's Ethan's son, one Hell of a fighter and an even better
Wolf," I nod to him in the rear-view mirror.

"It's a pleasure to meet you, Iseta," Kaedon says, politely.
"And I promise to stay on your good side and not cross you," he
clutches at his own manhood.

Iseta smirks, "smart man."

Atreya laughs again. I'm glad some of us are having a good
time. Amarah looks at me and shakes her head but there's a smile
playing on her lips. She reaches over, silently asking me to take her
hand. I do, and now that the initial terror of Iseta's threat has
subsided, I join Atreya and laugh at the entire situation.

Inside Headquarters, we're all gathered around the dais and the large
meeting table. The last time we met here, Amarah had almost
toasted Atreya like a marshmallow over a flame and she threatened
the Queen. That was *not* a good day. But today, Amarah and I are
here, together, side by side, exactly where we're supposed to be. I
hold her hand solidly in mine, claiming her once again and letting
everyone know things are back to normal. Well, almost back to

normal.

"My Queen," Amarah respectfully addresses Ana. "Would you mind if I said a few things before we get started?"

The Queen sweeps her hand, palm up, towards the group, "the floor is yours."

"I owe you all an apology," Amarah lets go of my hand, pushes her chair back, and stands up. "Whether you were here or just heard about what happened at the last meeting, I'm extremely sorry for how I acted. I won't apologize for having my own thoughts and opinions, because I do think about what's best for us all, for The Unseen, but how I chose to handle myself in that situation was wrong. It was selfish and it was disrespectful, not just to the Queen, but to all of you," she looks around the room, making eye contact with everyone, addressing everyone personally.

"As you know or could have guessed, I was not in a good place mentally or emotionally at the time. That's no excuse, and I don't expect you to understand, but I would be forever grateful if you could accept my deepest apology and my promise that I will *never* act that way again. I am your Võitleja, and that isn't just a title for a warrior, it's a leadership role, and I haven't been the leader I initially promised to be. Well, to *try* to be. But I'm ready now and I hope you still feel confident going into battle with me."

I look around the room as Amarah is addressing them. I see varying emotions play across their faces. Some are still slightly wary, but it's to be expected after her display from the last meeting. But mixed in with the caution I also see understanding and respect. It takes a good person and a good leader to admit their faults and ask for forgiveness. Vulnerability is not always a weakness.

I return my gaze to the woman standing next to me. *My* woman. And once again, I'm beaming with pride. She's made an impact on me that has changed the course of my entire life. I know that she'll do the same for every person in this room, for The

Unseen, if she's given the chance. God, even in her vulnerable state, she's so fucking beautiful. Her heart is beautiful. Her soul is beautiful. She's my weakness in the best and worse ways. She shines so brightly, from the inside out, she's impossible to ignore.

She's my North Star.

My gravity.

The center of my entire world and I can't help but reach for her.

I take her hand and squeeze it tight, "I'm with you, Amarah."

"As am I," Prince Emrick nods his head in our direction.

"And me."

"Me too."

"I'm with you."

Agreements erupt across the Leaders gathered.

"Thank you," Amarah places both hands over her heart and takes her seat, giving the floor to the Queen.

All of their trust in Amarah is not yet repaired, but this is the first step to mending it. Amarah is going to need to work hard to prove herself to these Leaders, to this family. The Unseen is coming together in ways it never has before. It's encouraging to see, but it will take work to solidify all these new changes, and Amarah is the hub at the center of the wheel. It's only going to work and roll forward as long as she's guiding it. But I believe in her. The Queen believes in her. And she won't have to do this alone.

"Alright then, now to discuss the next steps. Who's ready to find Aralyn and bring her to justice?" The Queen asks.

Amarah: New Memories

Here For Good by Failure Anthem

On the road again. I wonder when déjà vu is going to stop happening? Logan and I are travelling back to the Air Fey, but this time we're not alone, Iseta, Atreya and Kaedon are with us. As much as I meant what I said about wanting to get to know them, I'd really love to have some alone time with Logan. Not an entire month, like we had after the Fire Fey incident, but I'd love a couple of days to really reunite. To talk about everything and to just *be* with him. To appreciate him and to make sure we're good. I mean, I know we are, or we're on our way to being ok at least.

I'm holding his hand over the center console of the truck. I'd rather be sitting next to him, wrapped up in his arms, breathing him in, but I don't think our company would appreciate the PDA. Not to mention, if I get that close to him, it will just be that much harder not to cross any private lines.

"...I had literally just woken up from a freaking frozen, scary ass nightmare, and that's when Amarah decides to come waltzing in. So yeah, I was in a bed, naked, with Logan. You can imagine how that went over," Atreya is sharing her perspective on the events over the past two months as well as filling Iseta in on the details.

"Ok, but did you really both need to be naked? I mean, I would have thought the same thing had I been in Amarah's shoes."

"Thank you!" I exclaim from the front seat.

Atreya continues to try and explain, "I know it's hard for others to understand, but we're Werewolves, Pure Blooded, and not just humans that got bitten and turned. We're brought up in a Pack, constantly surrounded by family, friends and love. Physical connections are just as strong as emotional ones for us and it encompasses *everything*, not just sex. I needed his skin contact to not only warm my body back up but to feel his kinship as a Wolf. It's a part of our healing."

"Ok, but surely you could have done that with some underwear on is all I'm saying," Iseta continues to push her point.

Atreya just laughs heartily, "yeah, I suppose we could have but it's not something we think about in the same way you do. Nakedness in Packs is normal. We don't sexualize bodies because they're built for so much more than sex."

"Trust me, Sister," I finally move my focus from Logan to the conversation, "it's hard for me to wrap my head around too."

I can't imagine anyone seeing Logan naked and *not* sexualizing his body. I mean the man is built like a Greek God, all caramel skin and chiselled muscle, like he was sculpted out of marble. And the weapon between his legs…sheesh. Just thinking about him naked is making my mouth, and other things, water.

Logan looks directly at me, rubs his nose casually with his finger and sniffs. A clue that he can smell *exactly* what's watering right now. He gives me a devious half-smile that causes my heart to race. Fuck. If he can smell me, that means Atreya and Kaedon both can too. The heat that climbs up my neck and into my face is blazing! I quickly turn my head towards the window, hopefully hiding my face from him and the others. I clench my thighs together, trying to quell the need for friction, and roll down the window, letting the cold air sweep in and cool me off.

"You ok, Sister?" Iseta asks.

I clear my throat, "yeah, just got a bit nauseous and needed a bit of fresh air," I lie, as I roll the window back up.

"So, what should we expect once we get to this house?" I'm so grateful to Kaedon for changing the subject.

"We're not really sure, honestly. We don't have much to go on other than a hunch that Aralyn is hiding out there, and with her past," I shake my head, "who knows what to expect."

"What do you mean?" He asks.

"Well, she first approached Valmont, offering him an alliance once she became Queen, and asked him to kill me. She then worked with an evil Witch to create an army of demons to attack us and try to kill me again."

"And the Queen," Logan adds.

"Yes," I sigh, "and the Queen. She's responsible for many deaths. Too many deaths," I whisper. Twenty-two total in the two attacks.

"I remember my dad briefly mentioning what happened. I'm sorry that the Wolves weren't present to help you with the fight."

"It's not your fault or your responsibility. Aralyn is Fey, it's the Fey's responsibility to bring her in or kill her."

Kaedon shakes his head, "that's not how alliances work and you know that. I'm the Alpha's son but he rarely listens to me and I'm in no Leadership position to speak my thoughts in our meetings. Half the time I'm not even allowed *in* those meeting," Kaedon huffs his frustration. "My dad is a good Alpha, a good Leader, but I've seen a change in him lately. We've suffered a lot of losses to the demon war and I think it's taking its toll on him." He shakes his head again, "still, an alliance is an alliance and it isn't something that can be followed only when it benefits *us.* That's why I've stopped asking permission to fight and have joined Logan the last two times."

"I'm embarrassed to admit that I don't know much about what it means to be a Wolf, and to be in a Pack, but from what Logan has told me, Pack Law is *life*. If you're not asking permission to fight, won't you be…punished?" I ask, suddenly worried about Kaedon.

He shrugs, "we haven't been ordered *not* to fight, and I'm a free Wolf, free to make my own choices. I haven't broken any Laws…yet."

"Kaedon is the smartest and bravest person I know. I've watched him grow up and I care for him as if he was my younger brother. I wouldn't let him join us if I thought he would be in trouble for it," Logan assures me.

"Listen, I shouldn't be sharing Pack business so openly like this. I would appreciate it if this stayed between us," Kaedon asks without *directly* asking.

"Of course," I say.

"Absolutely," Iseta agrees.

"Anyways, what do you call a Wolf that *knows* it's a Wolf?" Kaedon asks.

I look over at Logan and he laughs, shaking his head. He's so happy. I can see and feel the contentment he has from just being around Atreya and Kaedon. He misses it, I know he does, even if he never admits it out loud. He misses being with a Pack.

"I give up. What do you call it?" I ask.

"Aware Wolf," he smiles brightly and Atreya laughs and bumps him with her shoulder.

"Dude, you're an idiot," she says.

Iseta chuckles and shakes her head.

Logan laughs louder and I can't help but laugh, too. Their positive energy is contagious and I can see why Logan likes these two so much. I mentally note to invite them over to the house for lunch or dinner as soon as we get the chance.

"We're here," Logan says, as he slows the truck down and

eases off the road and onto the dirt parking lot in front of the same building we stopped at on our first visit here.

Man, it feels like a lifetime ago and yet, those memories are still vivid and strong in my mind. Vyla and little Tori and Vic, so warm and welcoming. Jon, never giving up on me as he trained me and helped me grow. Arabella, well, Arabella and I have never really had a connection but I respect her and I hope that she respects me.

One of my favorite memories was when Logan made me dinner, a playlist of nothing but songs with *Angel* in the title, and amazing sex in that jacuzzi bathtub.

Not all my memories were good ones though. Being held captive by Revna was terrifying, but I did see my mother, and that memory always makes me smile.

But, unfortunately, none of these memories compare to the one of Andre, dying in my arms. The remnants of the last battle are still visible in the burnt trees and half repaired buildings. I thought that I had healed enough to deal with it but, coming back to the place where it happened, is doing something strange to my insides. It's a mixture of pain, guilt, and sadness all fighting inside of me, and I swear I can physically feel the kicks and punches.

My door opening on its own snaps me out of my memory reel. Logan leans in and brushes hair behind my ear, "hey there, beautiful," then settles his hand on my leg, the other one on the seat behind me. He's trying his best to hide it but I see his worry. I hear it in his voice.

It's already dark outside and the light inside the cab seems brighter than usual, like it's illuminating all of my scars. I look into the backseat but no one is there. I hadn't heard anyone get out. "I'm sorry," the words are a whisper around the emotion clogging my throat.

He shakes his head, "you have nothing to be sorry about, Angel. I didn't even stop to think about what being back here would mean for you. What can I do?"

I appreciate that he doesn't ask me how I'm doing or if I'm ok. Of course I'm not ok, I zoned out to the point that I wasn't even mentally present, for who knows how long. Had they tried to talk to me too? I shake my head and focus on the worried green eyes watching me closely. I don't want him to worry about me. He's already dealt with so much because of what happened here, he doesn't need to be my caretaker, again.

"A lot of memories and feelings came flooding back," I explain. "The bad ones are pretty strong, but there are good memories here too, Logan. Really good ones," I give him a small smile and rotate my body so my legs hangover the seat.

He backs up so I can open my legs and make room for him and then he steps back into my space. I lean my forehead against his chest and close my eyes. He wraps his protective arms around me and I sigh heavily, letting my body sink further into him. His body heat is radiating off of him despite the chilly weather. It's always colder up North than it is in Albuquerque and I'm grateful for his body heat and his arms wrapped tightly around me, keeping the chill from finding me.

Logan's patience astonishes me. How he manages to be so patient with me, with all I've put him through, never ceases to amaze me. He gives me time, doesn't force me to talk or move or do anything I don't want to do. I just focus on the steady movement of his chest as he calmly breathes in and out. I drop my ear to his chest and listen to his strong heartbeat, thumping loudly in my ear. He gently places his chin on the top of my head and hugs me tighter to him. I breathe him in deeply, pulling his scent and his comfort into my body, into my bones, into my soul.

After what feels like quite a long time, I lift my head off his chest and he loosens his grip on me so I can sit back and face him.

"Thank you for just being here with me. For just letting me

take some time and for holding me. That's all I need from you Logan, just be here, be in the moments with me. Good or bad, just be present in each one alongside me. Don't leave me."

"I don't know who's left you in the past. I hope one day you'll share more of your past with me, but I'm never going to leave you, Amarah. I'll be here every step of the way. Together. Always."

All I can do is nod, "there is one more thing you can do to help me though."

"Name it. Anything. If it's within my power to give you, done."

I smile up into his handsome face, he's so incredibly giving and generous, so loving and so very fucking sexy. He takes my breath away.

"Make new memories with me. Wonderful and unforgettable memories that I can use to drown out the bad ones."

"We have a lifetime of memories to make together, Angel. I can't promise that life won't throw us more hardships and tragedies, or that you and I will have the perfect relationship, but I do know that that ninety-nine percent of them are going to be wonderful ones. And...ninety-five percent of those are going to be you cuming and screaming my name," he grins, arrogantly.

I laugh and it helps to lighten my bleak mood, "I will gladly take those odds with you any day, Logan. Can you kiss me now?"

"I thought you'd never ask."

His lips are the balm to my injured heart and soul and, knowing my luck, he's going to have a lot of injuries to heal. And I'll be here to help heal his, too.

The kiss is too short, then again, even the longest ones are. But he pulls away and caresses my cheek one more time, looking adoringly at me. I still can't believe a man like Logan is in love with me. I guess my luck isn't all that bad after all.

"How bout we start with those memories right now?" Logan asks.

"What did you have in mind?"

"Oh, a certain shy little five-year-old has been asking about you," he smiles and there's a twinkle in his eye.

"What? No way! Tori has asked about me?" I ask, in disbelief, as I jump down out of the truck. Logan takes my hand and leads me towards the building where, I'm assuming, everyone else is.

"She has. She was quite upset when I came to visit last month and you weren't with me."

My heart lurches in my chest at the thought of him being here without me. I really connected with Vyla, Jon and the kids. It hurts that I missed that trip and the chance to spend time with them. Plus, I haven't really thought about how it felt for Logan to be constantly questioned about where I was and what happened between us.

"I'm so sorry, Logan. I didn't even think…"

"Amarah, please, stop apologizing. Whatever you're trying to apologize for, I forgive you. We're moving forward, making new memories, remember?"

"'Marah!" The sweetest little squeal interrupts our conversation and I see a little blonde blur streaking towards me.

I barely make it down to my knee in time to catch her as she flings herself at me. She wraps her little arms around my neck and squeals with excitement. I'm so caught of guard, all I can do is stay kneeling, frozen, laughing at the whole wonderful moment. Last time I was here, Tori barely said two words to me and shied away from me every time I tried to talk to her. I thought she didn't like me. Shows what I know.

"Hey Tori!" I say, softly as I return her hug. "I missed you too, little one."

She unwraps herself from me and I let go, allowing her to back away. She immediately runs to Logan and lifts her arms in the air, asking to be picked up. I laugh and shake my head as I stand back up.

"Looks like *I'm* still the favorite," Logan gibes.

"You hang on to that title while you can, Mr. This girl," I point two thumbs at myself, "is making moves."

"Amarah, it's so good to see you again," Vyla's sweet and steady voice makes me turn my head in her direction.

She's making her way towards us, weaving through some tables that have been set up for our visit. She embraces me warmly, her Healer and motherly energy wrapping me up and comforting me.

"We missed you last time," she pulls away and holds me at arm's length. "You doing ok?" She asks, as her violet eyes inspecting me closely.

There are no physical marks for her to see but she's not looking for those kinds of scars anyway. She's looking in my eyes, ready to determine if I'm telling her the truth or lying.

"I'm doing ok," I nod and give her a genuine smile. "Better every day and just…moving forward."

"Good," she pats my arm. "Come, let's take a seat. We're just waiting for Emrick and Vadin."

"They should be here any minute," Logan says. "They weren't far behind us."

"And you," Vyla tickles her daughter. Tori squeals and wiggles in Logan's massive arms. "You stop pestering Logan for two minutes! Come on," she motions for Tori to let go of Logan.

"Awwww," she pouts but throws herself towards Vyla, listening to her mother without a fight.

As I stand and watch the exchange, I can't help but feel *good*. I feel myself slowly healing and growing. *Learning*. Vyla genuinely cares about me. I'm a part of their family now and it happened in such a short amount of time that it never really sank in. While I was focused on who I lost, I lost sight on who I gained. No life is ever worth more than another but every life matters and I turned my back on a lot of lives, a lot of people who care about me and were worried about me, and it never even crossed my mind in my self-inflicted solitary.

Logan takes my hand and pulls me out of my revelation. His peridot eyes rake over my face, no doubt looking for any signs of a breakdown. I smile up at him and mouth, *I'm ok.*

He dips his chin, tightens his hold on my hand, and walks us to the same table Vyla sat at. I take a few seconds to look around the room and see that everyone else is broken up into smaller groups, chatting and getting to know each other. Iseta is speaking with the Queen, Atreya and Kaedon are at a table with Arabella and another member of the Air Fey I'm familiar with, Caleb. It makes me happy to see that he seems to have made his way into Arabella's good graces even after all the bad shit Aralyn got him into. Perhaps Aralyn's treachery is what brought them together? They're both fighting to get out from under her shadow.

We reach the other table and Jon gets out of his chair, shakes Logan's hand, and offers me a hug. Unlike Vyla's, it's not quite as warm and cozy, but it's just as welcoming. Jon was a big part of my time here, training me on Air Magic and combat.

"Good to see you both," he says with a smile and returns to his seat. "Amarah, how has your Air Magic been coming along." He pierces me with his knowing violet eyes.

"I uhhhh…" I stutter as I take my seat across from him. "Ummmm…well, I uhhhh, kinda got a bit side-tracked," I wince with my admission.

"I see," he scratches at his trimmed beard as if he's deep in thought. "I guess that means a recap training session is in order before you leave."

I gulp down my guilt. And my nerves. There's no way I'm up for a training session with Jon. Granted, I have been practicing again. My training with Emrick got me motivated and going again, which included practicing what I had learned to do with air, but I haven't improved further than the last time I trained with Jon. I don't want to disappoint him. Besides, can I even do anything without my power? I haven't tried to call on the elements since I lost it.

"I don't know if that's really necessary," I say, nervously.

"I'm not asking," he says, sternly.

I nod my head. Jon is not the type of person you say *no* to. He's a big softie off of the training mat, or deck rather, but when it comes to training, *no* is not in his vocabulary.

"Jon, the poor girl literally just got here and she's been through a lot. Stop with the Drill Sergeant routine," Vyla orders.

"Honey, this is between me and my Padawan. She needs to become One with The Force. I'm just doing my civic duty for The Resistance," he says, tone utterly serious, but there's a twitch at the corner of his lips. He returns his gaze back on me but it's softened.

"Well?"

"Alright," I concede. "With your guidance and wisdom, I'll become a Jedi before you know it, Master, and we'll surely defeat The Empire."

Jon's mask finally breaks and he chuckles. "It's good to have you back, Amarah, but I am serious about the training session. Let's get together before you leave."

"We will," I agree. Looking around the room, I don't see their son. He had been the first to welcome me to the Air Fey on my first visit and is the complete opposite of his sister, Tori. He's not shy at all. "Where's Vic?"

"Oh, he's running around with other kids somewhere," Vyla says, nonchalantly.

"Emrick and Vadin are here," Logan says, as he nods his head in the direction of the door.

They take a few minutes to greet the room, Emrick winks at me and wiggles his eyebrows as he looks between me and Logan and I can't help but smile as he leaves our table to sit next to the

Queen and Iseta. Other than the little exchange between us, Emrick is back to being the respectful and professional Leader, the Prince of the Maa Family.

Vadin follows stoically behind him. Out of all the Fey Leaders, Vadin is the only one I haven't gotten to know. Emrick is completely different than I expected him to be. I wonder if it will be the same for Vadin? He's always so quiet and eerily observant. Does he have a softer side? A fun side? I suppose I'll find out soon enough as I continue my training again.

The Queen stands up and turns to address everyone, "I believe this is everyone?" She looks around the room, askingly. Everyone else looks around as well and I see head nods and shrugs all around. "Amarah, will Valmont be joining us?"

I stiffen slightly at the mention of Valmont. I haven't seen him since everything went down with Viveka and Logan. It's only been a little over twenty-four hours but *everything* has changed since then. It feels like a completely different world. A different life. Well, for me anyway. I can't say the same for Valmont. I have no idea what he's thinking or feeling, but based off of the last night we spent together, I can't imagine this past twenty-four hours has been good to him. He finally broke down and told me he loved me. He opened his heart to me. And what did I do to return this immense show of love and trust? I turned my back on him, on his love, and jumped into Logan's arms.

The guilt of this latest tragedy, that seems to just be my life, sits heavy in my chest. Although I never returned his feelings, never promised to, or even that I'd try, I'm far from innocent. I never promised to be with him but I never discouraged the possibility either. Hell, I had believed it could be a possibility! I was trying to give up Logan. I never lied or faked anything, but not speaking lies doesn't mean you're being truthful. Unspoken words and feelings will always come back to haunt you in one way or another.

"Amarah?" The Queen asks again.

I sit up straighter and clear my throat, "oh, I'm not sure. I left a message with Emerson to relay to Valmont when he woke up but I'm not sure if he'll come or not. I didn't demand it as part of the alliance."

"Very well, I don't anticipate us needing more bodies than we already have here to deal with *one* Fey. Especially since we don't even know if Aralyn is there or not. This is a recon mission first and foremost. We need to gather intel, nothing more than that. If, and that's a big if, Aralyn *is* there, we gauge the situation and move forward accordingly. If she is there, and there doesn't appear to be anyone else or any signs of a trap, we move in. *But...*if you get the feeling of *anything* amiss, anything at all, you get back here and we reconvene and approach the situation accordingly. I will *not* be losing any more people tonight. Is that understood?" The Queen demands and looks around the room, getting nods of agreement from everyone.

Arabella stands, "my sister may not be a direct fighter but we've seen first-hand the destruction her scheming causes. I don't doubt there's not a line she won't cross to get what she wants," she looks at the Queen, her insinuation clear. "Be cautious and alert out there. Be vigilant, and if you must, be brutal."

"You're not coming with us?" I ask. I was sure Arabella would be at the head of the charge, determined to bring her traitorous sister in.

She shakes her head, "as much as I'd like to go, it's not confirmed she's even there. My place is here, protecting our people. I won't leave us unprotected and unprepared like we were last time. I'm confident those of you who go will be enough and you'll do what needs to be done."

I silently acknowledge her message. If Aralyn is going to get away again, do whatever it takes to not let that happen, even if it means killing her. I dip my chin to Arabella, confirmation that I'll do what needs to be done.

"So, that leads us to discuss who will be going with me," the Queen addresses us all once more.

"No!" I shout and stand up quickly. The Queen looks at me, her eyes narrowing. I can see the wariness in her eyes, wondering what type of drama I'm going to cause this time. I take a deep breath and calm myself, speaking normally instead of shouting.

"I just mean, that you should stay here my Queen, where it's safe. Like you said, it's just a recon mission and your Kaitsja and Võitleja, along with a few others, can handle it. If she is there, we can't forget that *you're* her target. I, for one, will be more focused out there if I know that you're safe."

Logan speaks up next to me but he doesn't stand. "I agree with Amarah, my Queen. This is just a recon, to gather more intel. I understand your desire to see this through but there's no reason you should be there. We need you here, safe."

The Queen pulls her shoulders back and raises her chin slightly, "very well, but I expect updates as often as possible."

"Understood," Logan agrees.

"Alright, who will be joining Amarah and Logan?"

"We will," Prince Vadin speaks for himself and Emrick.

"And that's why we're here," Atreya motions between her and Kaedon. "I think the six of us should be more than enough."

"Then it's settled," the Queen nods. "Let's prepare."

"Good evening ladies and gentleman," Valmont's smooth British voice floats through the air as he comes strolling in, casually, through the front door.

He fusses with a button at his wrist on his black button-up shirt before sliding his hands into his matching black slacks. He's not wearing a suit but this more relaxed look is nothing less than impeccable. The top button is undone, revealing a sliver of tattooed skin and the ever-glimmering red dragon scale he wears on a chain around his neck. My eyes travel up to his full lips, impossible cupid's bow, and up into his sparkling turquoise eyes. The blood in my veins knows him, recognizes him, and the pleasure that he brings. And just like that, my craving for his bite is overwhelming my thoughts.

He holds my gaze, an arrogant smirk shaping his lips, "I would apologize for being late but it appears I've arrived right on time."

Amarah: My North Star

Moments by One Direction

I feel myself spiralling. My blood is pulsing too loudly. I can hear it pounding in my brain. My heart is beating too rapidly. I can feel it slamming against my ribcage. It feels like my entire body is vibrating with need. Need to have Valmont's fangs inside of me. *Now.*

I vaguely register pain in my hands. I glance down and see my death grip on the table, which is the only thing keeping me standing. The only thing keeping me from going to him, right here, right now. I close my eyes, suck in a deep breath, and blow it out slowly, desperately trying to get a death grip on my damn self.

Before I know it, my feet are moving. I open my eyes and sigh in relief as I register Logan's strong back in front of me, his hand is clasped tightly around mine and he's leading me out the back door, away from Valmont and away from curious, prying eyes and ears.

Once outside, the cold December air smacks me in the face, sobering me immensely. Logan gently takes my face in his hands and holds me steady.

"Look at me, Amarah. Focus on me," his voice is low but authoritative.

I focus on his eyes. They're darker than normal in the low

moonlight but the golden-yellow highlights seem to shine brighter. One of the small pieces he got from his father, I realize. His Angel eyes. I shiver, not from the Winter air surrounding us, but from the connection I have to Logan, even without our angelic link. His eyes always penetrate my senses. His scent envelopes me. My heart is racing and my blood is zooming through my veins for an entirely different reason now.

Logan.

Just like he always does, he manages to capture me completely. His eyes are my gravity, my center, my North star. He's the brightest star in the whole fucking universe. And he's mine. And I don't deserve him.

"You're my North star," I whisper, as I look up to him in awe.

He smiles brightly, only adding to the star effect, "I'll always be here to guide you back to me, Angel."

My eyes start to tear up as I think of everything I've put him through, and even now, one thousand percent invested in him, I still have a pull to Valmont. I'm addicted to him in a way that's almost uncontrollable. And I never asked for it. I never wanted it. Valmont never gave me a choice and I'm so fucking pissed at him and this entire fucked-up situation.

"This isn't fair," I struggle to speak around the emotion clogging up my throat. "Not to you. Not to me. I don't want this, Logan. It's…" I try to shake my head as the tears roll down my cheeks. "It scares me."

Logan brushes my tears away, his eyes hold a mixture of sympathy and anger, but I know the anger isn't directed towards me. Still, it doesn't make it any easier to see. I'm a part of this whether I wanted to be or not. I'm a part of what's causing his anger.

"I know," he whispers. "But it will be ok. We're going to get through this together. I'm here."

"I've never felt it this…intensely before. Yes, I've craved it since it first happened, but not like this," I shake my head. "Do you think it's because I don't have my power? Was my power protecting me from the worst of it?"

"I don't know," he shakes his head, "but that sounds plausible."

"I need it back, Logan! I need my power back! I can't live like this," my voice cracks.

"Shhhh," Logan pulls me into his chest, holding me tightly. "We're gonna get it back. If anyone can do it, it's Iseta. We'll get it back soon."

I sob into his chest. I cry for my lost power. I cry for myself and the mess I'm in. I cry for Logan who's pulled along by my freight train of hurt. I cry for Valmont never having loved before and finally loving the wrong person. *Me.*

"Babe, listen to me," Logan pulls me away from his chest, continuing to wipe away my tears with his thumbs. "You're stronger than you think. Yes, your power is an incredibly big part of you but you never even knew you had it until recently. You never used it. Your entire life, up until now, you survived on your own. Because *you're* strong, Amarah. *You.* You're heart, your mind, your soul. Don't focus on what you no longer have. Dig deep, find the strength that's always been inside of you and beat this and anything else that comes along. Fall back on your Faith, Angel. Because you *are* still an Angel, Amarah. And when you stumble, I'll be right here to catch you, ok?"

I blow out a heavy breath, focused entirely on Logan's eyes and his words, letting his belief in me wash over me. I'll wear his confidence like a shield until I can find my own. I can do this, even if I have to make this about Logan. Fuck how I feel. Fuck what it does to *me.* I can do this, I can fight this, because I love Logan and I refuse to hurt him more than I already have.

I.

WON'T.

DO.

IT.

"I love you, Logan, so much. I won't hurt you again and that's a promise."

"This isn't about me, Angel."

"For me, it is. I can and I *will* fight this, not for me, but for you. Because you don't deserve a single ounce of any more hurt. You may not agree, but I have a lot to make up for, and I will prove myself worthy of you. I will earn your love and forgiveness even if you don't require it."

He claims my mouth with his, kissing me hungrily and thoroughly, and the entire world slips away. I forget where I'm standing. I forget why we're here. I forget everything except the feeling of his tongue sliding against mine and what it does to my head, my heart, my stomach…and my vagina. There's no craving left inside of me that doesn't involve this sexy, Angel-Werewolf currently devouring me.

I moan into the kiss and he returns the feeling tenfold, growling as he picks me up and strides a few steps until my back slams into the outside of the building. He pulls away from my lips and trails desperate kisses down my neck. His grip on my thighs is bruising but I relish in the strength of his hands gripping me possessively. I gasp as his teeth bite down on my neck, right where it meets the shoulder. The memory of the last time he bit me here comes flashing across my eyes. He almost lost control of his Wolf that night. Again, pushed to claim me because of Valmont.

He forces his large hand inside of my jeans, aggressively, and manages to get a large finger inside of me. I moan louder as he pumps that finger inside of me, never letting go of my neck. He pushes his palm against my sensitive clit, rubbing it up and down as his hand moves his finger in and out of me. All I can do is grip his hair and hold on tightly with my legs as he brings the orgasm flooding through me. Right as I start to crest, right before the fall, I feel his teeth clamp down tighter, breaking skin. The pain is a quick shock before the orgasm drowns it out.

When I finally manage to come back down to Earth, Logan is watching me with amber eyes. Wolf eyes. My blood stains his beautiful lips that are pulled back in a snarl. His canines are slightly elongated and he growls, more like a Wolf than human this time.

"You're mine, Amarah," his voice is gravely and deep. I can't tell if he's on the edge of anger or passion. Maybe both.

"I've always been yours, Logan. I've never been anyone else's. Not before you and definitely not after you."

A rumble of approval vibrates through his chest and I watch as his eyes bleed back to green, his lips lower into a firm line, and he exhales deeply as he closes his eyes and rests his forehead against mine.

"If he tries anything with you tonight, I will kill him, Amarah. I'm done playing his games. You're not a chess piece to be played between us."

"I know," is all I can bring myself to say.

He lets me slowly slide down and stand on my own again. "Let's get tonight over with, I need to be inside of you as soon as fucking possible," he says, through clenched teeth, then takes my hand and leads me back inside.

Once we're back inside, I notice that the others have busied themselves getting prepared. I'm grateful that no one has made this awkward but I also notice that no one is meeting our eyes. Ok, maybe a little awkward.

I busy myself with my weapons, focusing hard on strapping on my thigh holsters, when a voice next to my ear makes me jump.

"Jesus fucking Christ, Sleeping Beauty. Is it always like that between you two?" Emrick's voice is a quiet whisper but I hear the excitement in his tone.

I can't help the blush that races into my cheeks. I clear my throat, "so, I guess everybody heard that, huh?"

He chuckles, "heard it, felt it, going to dream about it for a few damn weeks and probably jack..."

I straighten up and sock him in the arm, "don't you dare finish that line of thought."

He rubs his arm and winces, "back to hitting me, are we? Geez, a guy can never have any fun arou...Jesus, Amarah!" He whisper-yells and touches my neck, where Logan bit me.

I wince. The area is sensitive to touch.

"Sweet Mother of the Earth! Maybe I'm not jealous after all."

I can't help but chuckle, "the Prince is scared of a little love bite."

"I hate to break it you, but that ain't a little love bite, sweetie. That's a...*I'm starving and you're on the menu,* bite."

I shrug, "what girl doesn't like to be eaten?"

His mouth forms a little *O* of surprise, "oh em gee! I never knew you were so nasty!"

"Amarah," Iseta calls out to me as she approaches. "Sorry to interrupt but I think I should go with you."

"I'll leave you two to it," Emrick excuses himself.

"Absolutely not," I shake my head. "I need to know you're here, safe, with the others."

"And what about you? You don't have your power to protect you. I'm more powerful than you are right now so, how does me staying make sense? Besides, what if you need someone with magic?" She insists.

I shake my head again, "we won't. This is a recon mission, remember? Besides, I have two *very* powerful men who will both die before they let anything happen to me. Not that that's going to happen either, but trust me, I'm as safe as I can be with them."

She sighs, not at all happy with staying back. "Fine," but like the Queen said, check in as often as possible."

"We will," I promise, as I strap my sword onto my back. The weight of the weapons feels good. They're comforting. I pull out my sword, "besides, even without my power, I'm not helpless." I can feel a faint vibration of power in the handle.

Even without my own power, these are divine weapons, and they're powerful in their own right. I close my eyes and feel the tingle against my palm. It's calling to me, to my power, but I don't have anything to give it.

I sigh and slide the sword back into its sheath. "We better get going."

Iseta comes in for a hug, "be careful out there, Sister. Stay alert and stay behind Logan, ok?"

"I will," I give her a squeeze before I turn to find Logan and the others gathered near the door. I make my way to them, "everyone ready?" Nods and confirmation greet me from each of them. "Let's do this."

Amarah: Old Enemies

Madness by Ruelle

We cross the empty field, heading towards the lift that leads to the top of the mountain, where the training takes place. At the base of the mountain, we turn right, and walk for another mile before we get to the glamour barrier. Even without my power, I've discovered that I'm still sensitive to magic. I can feel the heaviness in the air as we approach. We've all been fairly at ease and calm up until now. Now, we're about to enter the forest and close in on Revna's old house.

"Alright," Logan says, taking the role of leader, "once the house comes into view, we spread out and approach it from all sides. We'll stagger, Wolf and Fey so, Emrick and Kaedon, then Vadin and so on. I'm staying close to Amarah. Valmont, you stay back and give us any details you might see from a far that we can't see up close. Any questions?"

"Amarah Rey should stay back with me. She's also been a target of Aralyn's, if that little detail has *slipped* your mind," Valmont jabs at Logan.

I scoff, "I don't need to be coddled. I can handle Aralyn if I see her."

"He's right," Logan says, irritably.

"What?!" I bark out, in shock. Never in a million years would I think I'd ever see the day Logan agreed with Valmont over *anything*.

"As much as I hate to admit it, he has a point. You're important to her, and as much as you hate to admit it, you're not as strong as you used to be."

I scoff again, "this is ridiculous, I can fight just as well as...well, I can fight and I want to fight!"

"We don't even know if it will come to that," Logan says. "Just stay back with Valmont until we know what we're getting into, if anything, and if you need to jump in then jump in." He takes a step closer to me, holding my face in one hand, "No one is going to think less of you, Angel. It's the smart thing to do." He gives me a quick kiss, distracting me. "End of discussion."

"Fine," I cross my arms over my stomach and pout, silently.

There's no use fighting him on this when I know I won't win and, reluctantly, I know he's right. Still, it's not easy being a control freak and giving up that control to someone else. I can admit that they're both right but admitting it and acting on it are two entirely different things. The stubborn part of me wants to argue, but the new me I'm trying to become, the one where I stop trying to be a one-man team, makes me shut my mouth.

We do one more comms check and send a text to the Queen before we cross the barrier and go into stealth mode. We're already staggered, Wolf to Fey, Emrick is leading the way, using his Earth magic to clear a path so we can approach silently. He raises rocks out of the river, creating a sort of rock bridge, and we all cross easily. Kaedon is behind him, then it's Vadin, Logan, me, Valmont and at the back, Atreya.

Once the house comes into view, I see Emrick circle wide to the right, rounding around towards the back of the house. Kaedon and Vadin follow suit, Logan moves to circle around the left side but remains in view of the front door. Valmont gently pulls on my arm, stopping us from going any further, then drags me behind a tree. His hand lingers on my arm like he doesn't want to let me go. Hell, being this close to him is causing my craving to spike and I don't want him to want to let go. Reluctantly, he does, and Atreya passes us and stays facing the front of the house. I shake my head, trying to remain focused on the mission and not the craving tugging at my thoughts. The house is surrounded and there's nowhere for anyone to escape.

And there is definitely someone inside. The windows are illuminated with a dim yellow light and the chimney is smoking, sending a wonderful wood burning aroma into the sky.

"All clear back here," Emrick's voice comes over the comms. "No signs of a trap or anything fishy."

"I confirm," Kaedon seconds. "I'm not picking up any strange scents but I do smell more than one around this house."

"I'm familiar with the scents," Logan's voice echoes next in my ear. "They belong to Aralyn and to Revna, the Witch who used to live here."

"It makes sense that their scents would be here then. That doesn't mean Aralyn is here, now," Atreya chimes in.

"Someone is here though," Vadin surmises.

"She's here," I whisper, to no one in particular. "It has to be her. Who else could it be?"

"I'm sure we're about to find out," Valmont says, as he takes a protective step closer to me. The slight brush of his chest against my shoulder causes me to shudder as he peers around me.

I close my eyes and take a deep, steadying breath. This only causes me to inhale his bergamot and honey scent. *Focus, Amarah!* I silently scold myself.

"I can't tell if I'm feeling more magic here because it's fresh, or if it's just residual magic from the house, but the air is thick with it," I explain out loud, giving my mind something else to focus on.

"I feel it," Valmont confirms.

His warm breath tickles my neck and I smell a familiar hint of peppermint. His scent is consuming in its own way. Where Logan's is comforting and home, Valmont's is exciting and terrifying. It calls to my darker side. It calls to my new addiction.

My heart is racing again, my blood seems to be banging like a drum against my vein, leading the Vampire home. I realize I'm breathing heavily and I've removed any distance between our bodies. My sword is keeping me from feeling Valmont's chest flush against my back so, I lean my head back against his chest.

"Amarah Rey," Valmont's voice rumbles through his chest and caresses my skin like a lover.

"Yes?" I let out a breathless whisper.

"You're not making it easy for me to stay focused," he says, calmly, as he lowers his head. "Feeling your perfect little body against mine. I can smell your need, your desperation, *for me*, and it's making me hard." I can feel his silky-smooth hair against my cheek seconds before his lips brush against my jaw.

I sigh and let myself fall back, sinking further into him, and I can feel he's speaking the truth. Yes! This is what I want. What I need! Just a small bite. Just a second. That's all I need. It won't even cause me to lose focus. Just a taste is all I need to get me through the rest of the night.

"You already know I'm not a decent man, Amarah Rey, I will give you what you want because, unlike you, I'm not conflicted. And if keeping you addicted to me is how I keep you then, that's what I'll do," his voice is deep and sexy, calm and sure, completely opposite of his aggressive, possessive words.

Wait. No! No! I don't want this! I want Logan. This isn't me thinking, this is just the addiction, and I need to fight it!

Valmont lets out a snarled hiss and takes a step away from me, his hands on my arms keep me from falling back. "Looks like someone else has already tasted you tonight," he spits out with barely controlled rage.

My hand moves up to my neck, my fingers run over the bite mark that Logan left and I wince, the pain helping to clear my clouded mind. God, how am I ever going to fight this? I've never been addicted, like physically addicted, to anything before. Is this what it's always like? I can't live like this. This is miserable. It's impossible. I manage to find my own footing and step further away from Valmont. I'm about to address the issue but I don't get the chance.

Just then, the front door opens and light floods out into the walkway. Once again, I'm struck with intense déjà vu. How could I have lived so much of this already? I just pray that this time, things turn out differently.

A small, petite figure moves into the doorway and takes slow, cautious steps outside. The lighting behind her casts the front of her body into shadow, but there's no mistaking her size and the shine of silvery-purple hair.

"I'm quite disappointed that it took this long for anyone to show up," Aralyn's deceptively sweet voice rings out over the clearing.

"You're surrounded, Aralyn, there's no place for you to go," Logan calls out. "Stop hiding and come back with us peacefully. No one else has to get hurt."

"I haven't been *hiding*," Aralyn spits out defensively. "I've been *plotting*." She raises her voice and shouts out into the clearing, "Amarah, are you out there? I thought for sure you'd be the one, front and center, ready to bring me in, like the good little Queen's pet that you are."

I immediately move to storm towards Aralyn but Valmont grabs my arm to stop me, shaking his head, "we go in only if we need to."

"Shame," she shouts. "Wish I could stay and chat but I really must be off. Amarah, dear, do come inside. There's an old friend of yours here that would really love to say hello."

I'm thrown by her words and have no time to think about them as she launches into the sky. I break away from Valmont and run towards the house.

"Logan, go! You have to go after her! We can't let her get away again!"

He's running to meet me, "no, I'm not going to leave you. Something's not right, I can feel it. We need to go."

"No!" I yell. "Stop wasting time and track her! I'll be fine here. I'm with everyone else. They'll keep me safe."

I see the conflict behind his eyes. Every time I've been hurt in the past, Logan hasn't been there to protect me. But he's said it many times, the world is dangerous no matter if we're looking for it or not. He can't always be here to protect me just like I can't always be there to protect him.

"Logan, please, you're wasting time! I'll be safe," I plead.

He pulls me to him and crushes his lips to mine for a few seconds before he pulls away. He makes eye contact with Valmont, something I've never seen him do. Something unspoken passes between them and they both just nod. Then Logan turns to Atreya, "stay with her, keep her safe."

Atreya nods and walks to my side. "Go," she says. "I'll signal you if anything goes wrong."

He nods, with one last look at me, he turns and runs. I hear him yell, "Emrick, you're with me. Use whatever Earth Magic you can to slow her down." Emrick races from the back of the house and falls in behind Logan.

I watch them rush off in the direction Aralyn went. Logan's back ripples, his t-shirt ripping, and fur emerges from his skin. In less than five seconds he went from man to Wolf. I've never seen anything like it and I don't think I'll get that image out of my mind any time soon. A howl echoes through the cold night air sending goosebumps along my skin.

"He's got her trail," Atreya says.

I vaguely hear her as I stand here, mystified, staring off into the forest where Logan and Emrick disappeared. I close my eyes, say a prayer to God, or to Michael, whoever is up there listening, to please keep them safe. Keep us all safe.

"What's the next plan?" Vadin's voice sounds quietly in my ear. "There's definitely someone else inside."

"Aralyn said there was an old friend of mine that wanted to say hello. I don't know what she means but it has to be a trap, right?"

"Let us go in, Amarah, we can scope it out and report back. You need to stay safe."

"We *all* need to stay safe," I hiss into my comm.

There's a beat of silence before Vadin's voice comes back, "Amarah, what's the call?"

I look back at the house. There's no way there's more than one more person in there. We would have seen or heard more movement. An old friend? What if someone is hurt or tied up in there? Someone I know. Someone I care about. I can't take the chance and not find out. I look at Atreya and she nods her head. Valmont does too.

"Go," I confirm.

The three of us stand as still as statues in the front yard, listening intently for any signs of a struggle. It feels like an hour has passed instead of seconds before another howl pierces the still night sky.

"Kaedon!" Atreya screams. She glances at me and then to Valmont, "I'm going in." Before I can argue or agree, she's off, disappearing into the house.

Another beat of silence, then a woman's scream, followed by growling and the sounds of a struggle. I look to Valmont and he shakes his head.

"Amarah Rey," he warns. "No. We stay here. They knew the

risks when they decided to come along. Whoever is in that house is obviously doing something to them. I feel the new magic in the air. We should go back to town and get you to safety." He reaches for me but I take a step back. A step closer to the house.

"How dare you turn your back on them when they risked their lives to save yours just a day ago!" I yell.

"Amarah Rey," he's next to me and gripping my arm tightly and I never saw him move. "I don't care about any of them," he says through clenched teeth. "It was their choice to risk their lives for me, I didn't ask them to, and I refuse to risk yours to save them. I don't care if they all die! I only care about you!" He yells.

"If you care about me at all..."

He shakes his head, "don't, Amarah Rey."

"If you truly love me, then you know that I will *never* be ok with this decision. I will never forgive you for leaving them to die."

He sighs in defeat, "I curse the Gods for ever bringing you into my life, Amarah Rey. My love for you is going to be my undoing."

I struggle to understand his words. I stare up into his turquoise eyes and try to read the meaning behind them, try to read his emotions, but he's locked everything down. He's a blank mask of boredom. I see his eyes travel down my neck, to the fresh bite on my neck, and something flashes behind his eyes. His nostrils flare and then he shuts it all down again.

He drops my arm, "bloody Hell. Stay behind me."

I nod, pushing away all the other thoughts and unknowns for another time and place. Now, I need to focus on whoever is in this house and what they're doing to my friends.

I enter the house behind Valmont, I'm trying to scan the room, but it's hard to see from behind Valmont. Once we're a few steps in, I see Atreya to my right, and immediately move to run to her, but Valmont's arm shoots out and stops me. All I can do is watch her. She's crouched down in a corner, crying hysterically, and

145

clutching at her head.

"Atreya!" I yell. "Atreya, can you hear me?"

I have no idea what she's seeing, what's tormenting her, but it's nothing in this room. She's oblivious to me shouting at her, and even though I can't see any physical damage on her body, it doesn't mean she's not in pain. She's clearly in pain and Valmont won't let me go to her!

"Valmont, let me go!" I try to yank my arm free of his vice grip but fail. "Let me help her!" I flail against him, fist punching at his back uselessly.

An evil laugh freezes me mid struggle. The coldness of that laugh seeps into my skin and encases my bones, making me shiver.

"Oh, Amarah, you always were so fun. I enjoy watching you struggle and fight, even if it is pointless."

I slowly step around Valmont and the person the voice belongs to comes into view. "How?" I ask, still frozen in shock.

"It's so rude to ask a lady her secrets, especially in front of a man, even if said main is delightfully sinful," her cold, black gaze rakes down Valmont's body. I have a second where jealousy, or maybe it's just pure hatred, rushes through my body before I focus back on the truth standing in front of me.

"Iseta killed you. I saw your body."

"Temporary setback," Revna shrugs a pale shoulder. "As you can see, I'm alive and better than ever! My Deity is an all-powerful being who rewards his loyal followers, just like he says he will."

"Stop with the nonsense. What are you saying? Lucifer brought you back to life?"

"Not just brought me back to life but gave me immortality, like he promised he would."

"Why would he do that? In case you forgot what went down, you failed, Revna."

I see the anger take hold. Anger that is no doubt masking her insecurity from the truth of my words. "He got what he wanted in the end, didn't he, Amarah? He's rewarded my loyalty and needs me by his side now more than ever. You should have joined us when you had the chance."

"I'll never join Lucifer. And if I learned anything from my experience with him, it's that he is, indeed, the Prince of Lies. You're just too blind to see it."

A howl pierces the night and my eyes frantically follow the sound. I catch a glimpse of a Wolf and Vadin through the back door. It has to be Kaedon. They're…attacking each other.

"What did you do to them?" I ask, my hands gripping the dagger handles, preparing to launch them at Revna.

"Oh them? I almost forgot they were even here," she laughs, wickedly. "Just a fun little spell. You know, magic has been so much more fun since your last little visit here. I can do so much more than I ever could before."

"My blood," I whisper.

"Good thing I got as much as I did while I could, am I right?" She laughs again. "I hear you're no longer special. Therefore, I can kill you this time." She laughs, maniacally, "isn't that delightful?"

I pull the dagger from my right thigh and throw it as quickly as I can, aiming for the Witch's cold, dead heart.

Her hand comes up in front of her body, "*prohibere*." My dagger stops in mid-air and then clatters to the floor.

"Valmont, take her!"

Before Valmont can even move, Revna raises both hands and pushes them towards us. "*Ventus dis.*"

A strong force slams into me and I'm lifted off the floor and thrown back into the wall. I see Valmont hit the wall next to me, his body crumples to the floor, but I don't. I'm suspended in the air and the breath has been knocked out of my lungs. I try to pull in a breath and a sharp, excruciating pain rushes through me.

"Amarah Rey," Valmont's voice is frantic. He's climbing to his feet, trying to get to me.

"*Morsus*," Revna's voice seems to float through the air. Valmont screams, his eyes squeeze shut as he clutches his head, dropping to his knees right in front of me.

"Valmont!" I want to scream but my voice is a strangled, wet rasp.

No! Not this again! I can't watch him die! Not again! I taste blood on my lips and finally look down at my body. There's a large hook protruding from the middle of my chest, but the immense pain I felt a moment ago, is gone. I must be in shock.

Valmont's screams ring in my ears and I watch as blood runs out of his nose and he falls completely to the floor. Revna's evil, cold laugh erupts out of nowhere. The rest of the house comes back into view in a vivid moment of clarity.

"Oh, Amarah, what a waste. You and all of your little devoted followers. I thought I'd at least have a fight, sheesh. That was so anticlimactic."

"This isn't over," I wheeze. "They will find you and they will kill you." And why did I say that sounding like Liam Neeson in my head?

"Who is they? Your precious little Wolf? Your sister? The *Queen*," she says, sarcastically. "No one is stronger than I am now, Amarah, but don't worry, they'll all be joining you in death, soon."

The room is starting to fade. My limbs are going heavy and numb. I feel cold. I don't know if it's from death rising up to claim me or from the effect Revna has on me. I'm assuming it's death's grip, finally claiming me, but I'm not scared. I know Heaven is real. I know *He* is real.

"You will lose," I choke on the blood filling my throat. "Evil never wins."

Black is inching its way into my vision. I fight to keep my eyes open as long as I can.

Black spots.

White spots.

A blur of silver.

A beat of silence.

.

.

.

A piercing howl.

Logan, I love you.

Nothing.

Logan: Loss And Chaos

Monster by Fight The Fade

Atreya's howl reaches me and stops me in my tracks. Her howl is laced with urgency and...despair. There's only one thing that would cause her to send such a message.

Amarah.

I don't hesitate or think twice about catching Aralyn or trying to inform Emrick. I launch myself back toward the house. My Wolf senses the urgency, the fact that something is wrong, very wrong, and he charges forward, running faster than we've ever ran before. As the house quickly approaches, I push my Wolf down and emerge in my naked human skin, stumbling through the back door.

"Amarah!" I shout, scanning the inside of the house, desperately trying to lay my eyes on her.

Revna is gagged and chained to the wall to my left, the same wall Amarah was chained to the last time I came charging into this house. Wait...Revna? How is this possible? It doesn't matter. I can't worry about it now. I'll find out later. Everyone else is huddled together near the wall directly across from me. The silence is eerie and my stomach flips. Something is very wrong.

Atreya breaks away from the group. "Logan, it was a trap."

"Where is she, Atreya?!" I ask, as I walk further into the room, my steps slow and unsure, the complete opposite of the chaos raging inside of me.

"I'm sorry, I..." she trails off, her eyes going back to the group.

I make my way to where the others are standing and push my way past their bodies. My knees immediately give out and I'm only kept standing by Kaedon's strong arms around my waist. I swear my heart stops at the sight in front of me. Amarah's limp body is hanging on the wall, a large hook protruding from the middle of her chest. Her shirt is soaked with blood, a large puddle of it collecting on the floor beneath her.

I somehow manage to find my strength and push my way past the others to stand next to where she hangs. I vaguely register Valmont standing on the other side of her but she's all I see. I reach out to cradle her face, her skin is ashen and cold beneath my palms. This isn't Amarah. This isn't how she's supposed to feel. She's supposed to be warm and radiant, thriving with life under my touch.

I close my eyes and will myself to focus. I call on my Wolf hearing to listen to her chest. There, painfully shallow, a heartbeat. A choked sob of relief escapes my throat. I feel like I'm in shock but it's starting to clear now that I know she's alive. Barely, but she's alive. I can't lose her.

I.

CAN'T.

The anger that lives inside of me is lifting its ugly head. I feel the heat of the beast as it rises inside of me. My Wolf rises with it, determined to enact revenge on whoever did this to his mate. A growl rumbles through my chest and out of my throat.

"Logan, man, get control of yourself," Kaedon urges. "We need to do something. This isn't the time for you..."

I snarl as I turn around and swipe a clawed hand at him. I

connect with his chest and he crashes to the floor. The others take a step away from me but I only have one face in my sights.

She lifts her chin seconds before I wrap my clawed hand around her neck, lifting her off the ground.

"You were supposed to protect her!" I scream in her face.

The intense anger has complete control of me and the only thing on my mind is my mate, my Angel, my future, hanging…almost *dead*, on the wall behind me.

"I'm sorry," Atreya's voice manages to squeak out.

"Sorry isn't going to fucking save her!" I yell, my body vibrating with rage. "And it's not going to save you either."

I slowly elongate my Wolf claws further out of my hand as it remains clasped around her neck. The urge to rip her throat out and watch her bleed and gasp for breath is the only thing I want to see after seeing Amarah drenched in her own blood. Blood for blood. It's the only thing that will satisfy my anger. My Wolf.

I vicious growl starts low in my belly and works its way up my chest and out of my throat as my hand finishes the crushing motion on her neck. I feel my claws sink deep into her flesh and then I'm hit, hard, from the side.

I stumble, my hand releases Atreya, and her limp body falls to the floor. I snarl and spin around quickly, pissed at whoever stopped me from enjoying every second of my kill.

"You," I seethe.

And then Valmont is standing before me, his hands wrapped around my wrists, keeping them locked by my side. I try to move but he's strong, stronger than normal, but I can call on my Wolf again. I can transform right here and take his throat in my teeth next.

"Logan, mate, Amarah Rey is alive and she needs you right now!"

"No! I'll kill you all! You were supposed to keep her safe! This is your fault!"

I'm not thinking clearly or logically. I challenge the Master Vampire, meeting his eyes directly with my amber ones.

His eyes start to glow and I move to look away, out of reflex, but then I remember who I am. What I am. I allow him to believe he hypnotizes me. "Logan, you're going to calm down. You're going to think clearly. Amarah Rey is alive and we need to move quickly to save her. She needs us to work together right now more than ever. Please, do this for Amarah Rey."

His words do manage to penetrate through my anger. Amarah is alive and I need to save her. The uncontrollable rage instantly seeps out of my body and I'm left standing feeling utterly spent. I blink slowly, as his words sink further into me, pushing the last of my anger out of my mind.

"Amarah," I whisper.

I look over to where she's hanging on the hook. Fuck! How much precious time did I just waste?

I storm over to her, the others all take steps away from me, clearing a path. "We need to get her to Ana right away. She's the strongest Healer and the only one capable of saving her."

"Holy shit," Emrick's out of breath voice comes from the back door. "What the fuck happened here? Amarah!" He exclaims, as he races towards where we stand. "Is she...?"

"She's alive," I confirm. "Barely. We need to take her off of this hook and get her to Ana, now."

"If you remove her off that hook, she's going to bleed out even faster. That hook is the only thing keeping her alive right now," Vadin educates us.

My mind races with what to do. "Valmont, can you use your Vampire speed to go back to the town and bring Ana back?"

"Of course," he nods without hesitation.

"I'll give you a small lead and then I'm going to lift her off this hook and run as fast as I can to meet you. We need all the time we can get."

He nods again and is just suddenly gone. I didn't see any movement, not a blur, not a gust of wind, or any sign he was ever here. Just gone. Fuck he's powerful.

"Ok, help me lift her off this hook."

"What about Revna? Vadin asks.

"She stays cuffed and gagged but she comes with us. You and Kaedon escort her back. Emrick and I will run with Amarah to meet Ana."

Everyone nods and Emrick steps up next to me. I unstrap her sword sheath from her chest. We both grab a hold of Amarah, my hands are shaking, betraying my outward calm demeanor. I'm a fucking emotional mess inside. I have no idea how I'm able to portray any sort of calmness but Amarah needs the best of me right now. We slowly and carefully begin to lift her. A whimper escapes her throat and I'm relieved and gutted at the sound. She's alive but she must be in so much pain. I'm thankful that we're not connected and I don't have to feel her pain directly. My pain and fear alone are enough to drown me.

We manage to clear her body from the hook and Emrick eases her into my hold. I hold her tightly, but as gently as I can, against my chest.

"Someone, gather her weapons. Let's go," I order, as I turn and run from the house. The image of Atreya's body laying in a pool of blood on the floor haunts me as I run.

I call on my Wolf again, using my Wolf eyes to guide me through the dark forest. I use the same clear trail Emrick created for us on our way here. Just as we're crossing the river, Valmont appears on the other side, the Queen in his arms. Hope blossoms through me at the sight of Ana, here, now, ready to save Amarah.

Valmont quickly lowers the Queen to her feet and she falls to her knees, "Logan, here, place her here in front of me." She pulls her sunflower yellow hair back and ties it securely behind her neck. She seems so out of place here. She's a light, a beacon of hope, shining brightly in this dark and dreadful forest.

I kneel down and gently lay Amarah on the cold forest floor. "Save her, Ana, please. You have to heal her," I beg.

"Tell me what happened. What's the damage?" She asks, as she closes her eyes and starts to roam her hands over Amarah's body.

"I'm not sure," I admit. "The most damage I know of is a hook through her chest."

She nods, "I can feel it."

Her hands stop right above the gaping wound in her chest, it's bleeding freely again, Vadin was right. Valmont is pacing behind the Queen and I can see the worry written all over his face. He's not even trying to hide his emotions, and instead of the sight of him pissing me off, I can't help but feel a kind of kinship to him. We both love Amarah. He's feeling everything I'm feeling in this moment. I can't fault him for falling in love with her. Who wouldn't?

"This wound is bad. It nicked her heart," the Queen tells us, as she concentrates on whatever it is Healers feel.

"Can you heal her?"

The Queen remains silent, focused on the task at hand. Her eyes are still closed and her brows are pulled together in concentration.

"Ana," I urge, my voice desperate. I need an answer. I need to hear her say the words.

She finally opens her eyes and sighs. I can see the deep sorrow in her eyes before the words leave her lips. "I believe I can but…there will be a cost."

"What's the cost?" I ask, meeting her intense gaze.

"Everything," she whispers.

I stare at her for a few seconds in disbelief. I've heard about

Healers giving too much of themselves, their auras and energy, to the person they're trying to save, essentially giving them everything they have. Their life. It hasn't happened in centuries, since Healers realized this was possible and stopped Healing to the point of death.

"No," I shake my head, refusing to sacrifice the only person who's ever been there for me in order to save the only person I can live the rest of my life with. This has to be some sort of cruel joke. "There has to be another way," I argue. "There must be something else, someone else that can…"

"There's no other way, Logan. She's special. This has to be done and I'll gladly do it, but she has to fight to come back to us, to stay here. Even with everything I have, I don't know if it will be enough," the Queen says, quietly.

She looks torn between determined and defeated. All I can do is nod as I look down at Amarah's motionless body. I'm griping her hand in mine, it's cold and limp, and I think about what she just went through with me. Our roles have been reversed and I finally understand her reason for trying to push me away. Having to see her this way, the chance of losing her, her dying in my arms, will ruin me.

"Take care of her, Logan. Guide her and support her, always. Love her like she deserves to be loved," the Queen's voice pulls my attention back to her.

Her face blurs as tears flood my eyes, "I will."

The Queen returns her focus to Amarah and all I can do is watch as she pours her Healing energy, her very life-force, into Amarah.

I lean in, whispering in Amarah's ear, "Ana is going to save you, Angel, but you need to do your part, ok? You need to fight. Please, please come back to me. Don't leave me. Not yet. We have a lifetime to spend together. I can't make new memories without you. Fight, Amarah, as hard as you can. Come back to me."

I vaguely register more bodies arriving and surrounding us.

There are whispers and directions being given, plans still being made around us, as I kneel beside Amarah and watch as her chest wound slowly starts to mend together. Ana's skin starts to pale, her sunflower hair is slowly fading, losing its vibrancy. The stories say, that once her hair turns completely white, and she gives her last breath, she will have given up everything inside of her. There will be no coming back from that. I've never seen a Fey deplete themselves before, even with Analise, it was different, but I know that's what's happening right now and it breaks my heart. I'm flooded with conflicting emotions as I watch one woman I love, like family, dying to save the other woman I love.

Did I ever even tell Ana that I loved her? Did I ever tell her how grateful I was for her? Did I ever tell her how much she meant to me? How she helped save me in ways I couldn't save myself? I can't recall those words ever leaving my lips and I vow to never let this happen again. I will always tell Amarah what she means to me. She just needs to live first.

A gust of wind, out of nowhere, rushes around me and through my hair. My chest starts to restrict, it feels like it's collapsing in on itself, and I can't breathe.

There's a quiet thud, as Aralyn drops in, behind the Queen. She moves quickly, doesn't hesitate for a second, as she takes the Queens head in her hands and twists. The crack of her spine breaking reverberates through the quiet forest like a strike of lightning touching down.

I fight the panic that's trying to climb up my throat, both at not being able to breathe and the sight of Ana's lifeless body slumping to the ground. Her hair is still the lightest shade of yellow, she didn't finish Healing Amarah. My eyes rake over Amarah's body, the hole in her chest is gone, but I have no idea if Ana was able to patch her up inside completely. What about the nick in her heart?

I try to speak, to call out to Amarah, to try to wake her up, but

I have no air in my lungs to speak. I want to shake her, to force her eyes open, but I don't know what kind of damage still lingers inside of her. All can do is silently pray and plead to my father and hope that he hears me. He saved me, maybe he will save her, too. He *has* to save her! He said we're meant to close the rip. Together! She's just as important as I am! But as I sit here, the ache in my chest growing, burning with the need to breathe, she doesn't move. She doesn't open her eyes.

The invisible hand squeezing my lungs lets up for a brief second. I gasp loudly and pull a huge breath of air into my lungs. I hear the same happening to the others around me, and then the squeezing is back, and I can't breathe again.

My eyes turn to Aralyn as the anger begins to rise again. This time, my anger is joined by that cold, frozen power inside of me. My Angel power. *I'm half Angel,* I remind myself. I focus on that fact now, as the blue shade of my power physically manifesting comes into view.

I'm on my feet and grabbing Aralyn by the throat and pulling her over both Amarah and Ana's unmoving bodies, until I'm holding her up in the air in front of me. Her wings are flapping frantically behind her as she tries to use them to escape my hold. It's a futile attempt.

I still have no breath to speak but who needs words when actions speak louder anyway? I feel that coldness that's a part of me ripple in waves down my arm. A cruel smile pulls at my lips as I watch ice spread from underneath my hand and climb up her throat. She's gasping for her own breath now. No amount of air manipulation can help you when your throat is being forced shut and ice is starting to slip inside your mouth. I'll push my ice all the way down her throat and freeze her from the inside out.

Her own Fey power falters and I feel the release of my lungs, filling them with a new wave of fresh air and a fierce growl.

"You're going to die, once and for all," I say through clenched teeth, as my ice starts to encase her face.

"Logan, no!" Vadin, yells. "You can't! By Fey Law, she's the rightful Queen now, should the throne accept her. You can't kill the Fey Queen, and leave us without a Leader, Logan."

"She's no Queen of mine," I disagree, as I squeeze her throat tighter.

"Nor mine," a weak, rasping voice speaks from behind Aralyn.

"Amarah?" I lower Aralyn's feet to the ground, my fist still wrapped around her throat, and meet Amarah's beautiful hazel eyes over the top of her head.

My power immediately withdraws inside of me, satiated and satisfied, simply because Amarah is alive. There's no room for vengeance in this moment when love and relief are flooding through me.

Amarah grabs a gasping Aralyn by the shoulder, turning her around to face her. I gladly release her. "I want you to face me," she says, as she sinks her remaining dagger into Aralyn's chest, straight through her heart, "because my face is going to be the last thing your eyes ever see. You'll never be Queen and you're going to live the rest of your eternal life burning in Hell."

Aralyn gasps, her words lost to the ice and blood flooding her chest and throat. Amarah twists her blade and then yanks it free. They both stumble, and Amarah follows Aralyn to the ground.

"Amarah!" I'm finally shaken out of my shock and fall to the ground next to her, wrapping my arms around her, and bringing her into my lap.

Her beautiful eyes lock with mine and she gives me a small smile as she reaches up to touch my face. "I guess it was finally your turn to cry for me."

I grip her hand in mine, holding it tightly to my cheek as the tears flow freely. I manage a choked laugh at her attempt to joke at a time like this, "I love you so much, Amarah. You scared the shit out of me. I thought I lost you."

"For a while, you did," she says, softly. "But your love brought me back. It's the only thing I couldn't let go of," she admits, as she looks at me with so much love and devotion in her eyes that it swells my heart. "I saw my mother again…and Ana. She said…" her voice tightens, and she tries to swallow down her emotions.

"Later," I insist. "We'll talk about it all, later." She nods and I move to stand up, her arms wrap around my shoulders and I bring her with me, holding her tightly in my arms.

I finally acknowledge the people standing around us. The utter loss and chaos that just unfolded tonight and I don't even know where to begin to address it. All I want to do is get Amarah safe and hold her in my arms forever.

Arabella is the one who finally speaks, "go. We'll take care of everything here."

I nod and turn to leave. We have over a mile to walk, to get back to the Air Fey village, but I refuse to let Amarah go for even a second.

I'll carry her every step I take.

For the rest of my life.

Amarah: No Words

A Moment Like This by Leona Lewis

I'm in and out of consciousness the entire way back to town. I feel so tired and so incredibly weak, physically. Weaker than I've ever felt before. It's an effort just to open my eyes, but I force myself to do it so I can stare at Logan, making sure he's real and I'm not still in some kind of limbo.

All we do is take turns staring at each other. We don't talk the entire way back because I think we're both too shocked and tired to even try to find the right words. His arms carry me with a newfound strength, never faltering, and never wavering.

Logan takes us to the same house we stayed in before. The front door creaks as he pushes it open, carries me inside, and then kicks the door closed behind us. We head straight to the bedroom and into the bathroom. He sits on the edge of the tub, still holding me against his chest with one arm, as he reaches out to turn the water faucet on with the other.

The memory of the last time we were here plays across my mind. "Mmmm," I hum quietly, "this tub has great memories."

"It does," Logan chuckles. "But we won't be recreating that memory tonight."

Steam is rising up from the hot water filling the tub and my body aches to sink underneath the soothing water. "That's fine with me but I'd still like to get in," I say, my way of hinting to Logan that he needs to actually let me go so that I can undress.

"We need to take these bloody clothes off of you," he agrees.

"That would require you to let me go for a minute," I lean my head back and look into his handsome face.

"I don't want to let you go, ever again."

The way he looks at me…it overwhelms me sometimes. It's so intense, so raw and beautiful. Logan feels each emotion so deeply it's actually quite mesmerizing how much he can say without ever having to use words.

"I'm not going anywhere, Braveheart."

His brows scrunch together, "Braveheart?"

I nod and smile, "it's the perfect nickname for you. You're beyond brave in the face of enemies and danger, but you're the bravest person I've ever met when it comes to matters of the heart." I place my hand on his chest, over his heart, "your heart is the most beautiful thing about you, Logan, and I'm so incredibly blown away and thankful that you've chosen to give it to me."

A shy smile I've never seen before pulls at his luscious lips before he turns it into a cocky grin. "You've officially given me a nickname, which, based on your experience with relationships, means we're *like, official, official*," he says in a feminine, mocking voice.

I laugh and slap at his chest, "I guess we are. There's no going back now."

"There was never any going back, Amarah," he says, soberly. "And there won't be an going forward without you, either."

We've tried to have this conversation before, here actually, at the Air Fey's home, where I tried to tell Logan that if anything ever happened to me, I wanted him to live and love again. I know now that it's an impossible request. For both of us.

"Oh shit," Logan, jumps and reaches for the faucet, quickly turning the water off.

I look to see that the water has reached the lip of the tub and is seconds away from spilling over. "Put me down so I can get undressed and we can finally get in," I gently order.

"Fine," he grumbles but complies.

As I stand on my own, Logan turns, reaching into the tub to unstop the drain and lower the water level so that we don't make a huge mess when we get in, and my eyes are suddenly graced by his strong, lean, *very naked*, body.

"Ummmm, you're already naked," I point out.

Logan looks down at his body as if he's just realizing it too. "Oh, ummmm, yeah. I was in Wolf form and changed back to human, and then everything just sorta spiraled out of control, and the last thing on my mind was finding a pair of pants," he shrugs.

"That's fair," I nod and laugh, then proceed to peel my blood-soaked shirt and bra off my body. There's an ache in my chest where the hook pierced through me. I rub at the new scar gracing my chest, trying to will away the sensation of the phantom hook still protruding out of me.

I lean down to remove my sneakers and I immediately get light-headed and lose my sense of balance. Logan is there, steadying me before I can fall. My rock.

"Let me help you," he says, softly. "You lost a lot of blood and..." he hesitates, "and, a lot has happened."

I nod my head and close my eyes, hoping that will help with the spinning room. I don't even know the extent of everything that happened tonight, but I do know that we suffered more loss. *I* suffered more loss. And I don't want to face it, *any* of it. Not yet. I hang on to Logan's broad shoulders as he kneels down and removes my shoes, socks, and then jeans and underwear.

His arm snakes around my back and the other sweeps under my knees and, once again, I'm being held in his wonderful embrace. He steps into the tub and lowers us down slowly. I groan as the hot water meets my skin and swallows me whole. It's really hot, but within a matter of seconds, my body adjusts to the temperature. I sigh and let my body settle, completely relaxed, and lay my head on Logan's shoulder.

We're quiet for a long time, Logan is aimlessly tracing small circles on my arm as he holds me against him. His voice startles me when he finally speaks.

"Amarah? Are you still with me?" He asks, his voice nervous and unsure.

"I'm with you, Logan," I mumble, too relaxed to try and speak louder.

"Do you promise?" He asks.

Caught completely off guard and confused by this question, I lift my head off his shoulder so I can look at him. "Do I promise what?"

"That you're not going anywhere," he clarifies.

I see the uncertainty in his eyes as he looks down at me. I feel the desperation in the way he's held onto me since I almost died. I know he's feeling like he's on rocky ground…because of me. I know that he's waiting for the other shoe to drop, for me to shut down, shut him out, and run away. He has every right to think that's how I'll respond because I did all those things last time. I've given Logan PTSD and my heart aches for him. The thoughts and feelings that must be running through his mind right now are *not* ok. And it's because of me.

I manuever myself so I'm straddling his lap and face him. I need to make sure that he sees me, sees my truth, and knows that I mean every word.

I grab his handsome face in my hands and hold his weary

peridot gaze, "I'm here, Logan, I'm here with you and I'm not going anywhere, physically or emotionally. I'm not going to shut down. I'm not going to push you away, and I'm not going to ever leave you again. Not by choice. I promise."

"I thought I lost you, for good, and that feeling…" he trails off. He takes my hands from his face and squeezes them in his, holding them against his chest.

"I know," I say, softly. "I know."

And I do. I watched him die and it was the end of me. Maybe not physically, but in every other way, I might as well have followed him into death.

"Maybe this is the price we pay for having the incredible love we have. We get to experience what few ever do. What we have is beyond special. It's quite literally, Divine love," I smile, trying to show him my strength, my stability, in us. "And maybe having something this…*impossible*, means we have to really fight for it, daily, to be reminded that what we have is glorious, and beautiful, but doesn't come without its challenges. Nothing worth having ever comes easy."

"Incredible love also means incredible destruction," he says, quietly.

"Yes," I whisper. "There are two sides to everything. But I truly don't believe that's going to be our destiny. I believe that you and I will have a beautiful, long life, filled with the type of love others only dream of. And we will appreciate it, and fight for it, every day, Braveheart."

His eyes are still uncertain as he stares back at me, "I'm just worried that the events of tonight haven't really *sunk* in yet, but when they do, I want you to know that I'm here for, Angel. In any way that you need, I'm here."

"I'm sorry that I've caused you to doubt me. I'm sorry for the hurt that I've caused you and our relationship, but losing you and almost dying tonight," I scoff, "I mean, it really shakes the shit out of you and wakes you up and puts things into perspective in ways that living just never can."

He nods in agreement and I continue, "you're right, I don't know all of the events of tonight, and I know that none of it is going to be easy to handle. I'm not perfect and I didn't just drastically change overnight. I *will* struggle. I *will* have my bad days. I will want days to just...*be*, to mourn, to feel the pain and loss, but I'll include you in the bad days too. I won't shut you out this time, Logan, and I understand if you can't just take my word for it, but I will prove it to you."

I run my hands through his silky, dark hair, scraping my nails along his scalp, causing him to flutter his eyes closed and moan, as I bring them to rest behind his neck. I lean in and place my lips against his before he has a chance to speak or comment on anything I said. There's no better time to prove that I'm here, present with Logan, than right now, because we don't know what tomorrow will bring.

He kisses me back and runs his hands up my back, stopping for a second as his fingertips trace the new scar, where the hook entered me, then he continues into my hair, grabbing fistfuls and angling my head exactly where he wants me. I can still feel the desperation in his touch, in his kiss, as if he's afraid I might vanish into thin air any second.

I feel his cock growing underneath me, the sensation causes my core to clench with anticipation and need. Need to feel him inside of me. Need to reassure him. Need to love him and let him love me. He was right, sex and love are one and the same for us, and I'm not complaining.

I push up onto my knees and reach down, amazed at how incredibly hard his cock is, as I guide him to my opening.

"Amarah, maybe we shouldn't. You lost a lot of blood and need to rest and let your body recover. You literally had a nick in your heart just an hour ago."

"Well, we don't need to have pounding, fuck the shit out of

me sex, right now. Although, that *is* going to need to happen soon."

His eyebrows arch, "oh, really?"

"Oh yeah," I nod. "You can't start this," I gesture to the bite mark still raw, and sore on my neck, "without finishing it."

"Shit, I'm so sorry, I didn't mean…"

"Logan, I'm not even close to complaining. I fucking loved it but you're right about right now. Slow and steady is going to win this race."

"Angel, we really should let your body heal."

"Logan, sex with you *is* healing for me," I say, confidently, as I sink onto him, the head of his cock pushing into me removes any more arguments from Logan's lips.

He hisses, "fuck, you're so tight without foreplay."

"Are you complaining?" I ask, already feeling breathless, as I continue to sink onto his hard length.

"Fuck no!" He exclaims. "But I've been fucking edging this release all damn day so, I don't know how long I'm going to last."

"We're allowed to have base hits, ya know. Not every swing has to be a homerun, Braveheart. Now, shut up and make love to me," I demand, as I take his mouth with mine.

A satisfied growl rumbles through his chest as he grabs my ass and guides my body up and down his impossibly hard dick in a slow and steady rhythm. I get off my knees and stand on my feet, still clinging to him for support, so I can lift myself higher and get even more of him sliding in and out of me. I break the kiss and throw my head back, moaning to the ceiling as his thick head almost comes all the way out before sliding home again.

His warm mouth descends on my breast and his tongue flicks at my nipple, causing it to peak, then he takes it between his teeth and gently bites down. I moan with pleasure and arch my back, pushing my chest further into his face. This new position allows him to slide over that very sensitive spot inside of me as he continues his controlled pace.

"Mmmm," he purrs, with his mouth still wrapped around my nipple, before he releases it and speaks, "that's the spot, right there," he groans. "I can feel you getting wetter and wetter."

"Oh, God," I manage to arch even more, his large hands moving to the middle of my back to help support me.

"I'm not going to cum until you do, Angel. Give it to me," he commands in a low, gravely voice that makes me even wetter.

My legs start to shake and I don't know if it's from the effort it takes to remain in this squatted position or if its from the intense pleasure building up inside of me. Maybe both. My whole body starts to twitch and shake as the orgasm builds. I'm panting and moaning, begging him not to stop.

"That's it," he growls, "give it to me."

And I do. My legs give out as I buckle to my knees, driving him deeper inside of me as the orgasm rushes over my body and sends shooting stars flying across my vision. When my mind surfaces and I'm back in the present again, the lip of the tub is digging into my back and Logan is on his knees in front of me, pushing deep inside of me. He's still being gentle but there's an urgency to his movements.

"God damn it, you feel so fucking good," his body is pulled tight with tension, his brows furrowed in concentration, and his beautiful, full lips are pressed into a hard line.

"Oh, fuck," he finally grits out, as he pushes every hard inch inside of me and stays there. I feel his dick pulsing as his orgasm erupts out of him.

When the pulsing finally stops, he pulls himself out of me, and we both slide back into the water, spent.

"Well, that's definitely a new memory to add to the list," I say, with a lazy, content smile.

He nods in agreement and then leans his head back against the tiled wall, closing his eyes. "How can you feel so fucking good, *every, time,*" he wonders aloud, as he tries to catch his breath.

Assuming he's not actually asking the question in hopes to get a response, I change the topic, "Logan?"

"Hmmm?" He responds, still seemingly lost in his own thoughts.

"Can you help me in the shower so we can *actually* get clean and then take me to bed?"

He lifts his head off the tile and opens his eyes to look at me. He stares at me for a few seconds, a look of raw emotions in his eyes. I don't need a connection to know what he's feeling right now.

Love.

Passion.

Reverence.

Desperation.

I feel like he's studying me, every detail, so he can remember this moment for years to come. How do I know? Because I'm doing the exact same thing.

He finally moves, pushing himself to stand, the water cascading down his muscular body, clinging to him as if it doesn't want to stop touching him either. I stare up at him as he towers over me. The sheer size and beauty of this man takes my breath away. He takes it away again and again, in new ways, every day.

He holds his hand out to me and I take it. He pulls me out of the water and helps me out of the tub, his strong arms keeping me from slipping or falling. Although, I *am* feeling more grounded than I was earlier. Sex with Logan really is a remedy for all of my ills.

He leads me over to the stand-up shower, turns the water on and then faces me as we wait for the hot water to come through. I wait for him to say whatever is on his mind. I can see thoughts swirling around in his eyes but he finally just pulls me into his chest and hugs me tightly.

He sighs as he leans his cheek on my head, "these words

never seem to be enough but, I love you, Amarah."

I nod my head in understanding. How can these three little words sum up all of the overwhelming feelings I have for this man? But then again, which words can? The answer…there are none.

"I love you too, Logan."

Amarah: It's Enough

I'll Be Ok by Nothing More

I jerk upright with a gasp, my voice choking on a scream caught in my throat. I cough to clear it and the cough quickly turns into sobs.

"Amarah, what's wrong?" Logan is instantly up, facing me.

I can barely make out the silhouette of his face with the sliver of moonlight cutting across the bed through the partially opened curtain. I'm sucking in shallows gulps of air, trying to calm my racing heart and clear my mind.

Logan is rubbing his hands up and down my arms, whispering words of comfort. "Shhhh, it's alright. You're alright. I'm here with you. You're safe. Hey," he moves his hands to my face and holds me steady. "Look at me. Focus on me."

I stare into his wide, concerned eyes, but even in their silent panic, they're still my gravity. His eyes are a force of freaking nature and, when they're focused intently on me, I'm completely at their mercy.

My rapid breathing finally slows, the rest of the room fades away, until it's just me and Logan. "A bad dream?" He guesses.

I nod my head, "nightmare." My voice is low and raspy from being unused and from the scream that was lodged in my throat a moment ago. I clear my throat and continue, "I'm sorry I woke you."

He shakes his head and leans in to kiss my forehead, dropping his hands to rest on my thighs, "you never have to apologize to me for things like this, Angel. I'm happy I'm able to be here for you. I want to be here for you. Will you let me?"

I swallow down a painful ball of emotion and just nod my head. It's the first time I haven't woken up alone after one of my nightmares and it feels good. It feels so good to know I'm not alone. That I don't have to face this alone or try to go back to sleep alone. Having Logan here doesn't make the nightmare any easier to bear but it does make it easier to face.

"Do you want to tell me about it?" His voice is soft and calm, no pressure and no expectations.

"It's the same nightmare I always have," I shrug. "Parts of it change here and there but it's always essentially the same. I watch people I love die in my arms and I'm powerless to stop it."

Logan rearranges the pillows and scoots up, leaning against the headboard but not quite sitting up, and then reaches for me, pulling me to lay on his chest. His big, protective arms encase me as I snuggle into his neck and throw my leg over his hips, getting as close to him as I can. He holds me solidly to his chest with one arm around my back and then his free hand starts to lazily trace imaginary patters in my skin. Little by little, I relax in his hold.

"How long have you been having nightmares?" He finally asks.

"Since Andre," I admit.

He sighs heavily, "I hate that I can't protect you from this."

"Me too," I whisper. "But this helps. You being here with me is enough."

We're quiet for a few minutes. I'm focusing on the rise and fall of Logan's chest. The steady beat of his heart. Taking time to be in the moment and appreciate what I have, but now that I'm awake and somewhat rested, questions are surfacing that I need answers to.

"Logan?"

"Hmmm?"

"What happened last night? Tell me everything you know that happened after you and Emrick went after Aralyn."

Another heavy sigh, "Aralyn was fast. She was weaving through the forest and somehow, she was able to manipulate her scent."

"Revna," I mutter.

I feel him nod, "she was able to mask it when she wanted to and double back in a different direction without leaving a trace, essentially sending us on a wild goose chase apparently. I think her whole purpose was just to fuck with us. Separate us and cause a distraction."

"That sounds like Aralyn," I agree.

"Luckily, Emrick's Earth Magic couldn't be manipulated and, once we caught on to her scent being masked, he started to track her instead of me. That's when I heard Atreya's howl and knew something terrible had happened. I immediately turned back and ran as fast as I could to the house."

"So, you left Emrick to find Aralyn?"

He shrugs, "I just left, Amarah. Aralyn became inconsequential to making sure you were alright, which you weren't."

I nod, the new scar on my chest itching at the memory of the hook piercing me.

"When I got back to the house, I immediately saw Revna gagged and chained to the wall. That was a new development, but again, it became inconsequential to you. At first, I couldn't see you. Everyone was standing in a tight circle around you, shielding your body from my view. Atreya stepped away and I knew…the look on her face…" he shakes his head. "I knew."

"I made my way to where the others were and that's when I finally saw you." I feel him take a hard swallow, and his arms tighten around me, as he relives the memory of what he saw. "You were hanging on the wall, your feet dangling above the floor, entire body limp and pale, blood…" he chokes on the word and then clears his throat. "There was so much blood," he whispers. "And that hook was sticking out of your chest. I thought you were dead."

I lift my head to look at him and there's barely enough light to illuminated the tears reflecting in his eyes and on his cheeks. I lean in and kiss him on the cheek and then at the corner of his mouth before I rest my forehead on his cheek.

"I'm sorry," I manage to say through my own rising tears.

"How we've both managed to end up right here, right now, with each other," he shakes his head, "is nothing less than a miracle."

I nod my head in agreement and then return to my spot, laying on his chest. "Then what happened?"

"Then…" he continues, hesitantly. "I managed to hear your heartbeat. It was almost gone, but it was there. I was relieved and terrified all at the same time, but then my dominate emotion took over. My anger. I haven't really told you much about my time after Analise but it was a dark, dark time for me. One I'm not proud of, but this…" he shakes his head again and sighs. "This was nothing like I've ever felt before. I couldn't think of anything else except getting revenge. Finding the person responsible for hurting you, and the ones responsible for allowing you to get hurt, and destroying them. Kaedon tried to talk some sense into me and I attacked him. I know I didn't kill him but I imagine I hurt him pretty badly. But…"

He goes silent. I wait, quietly but on bated breath, waiting for the next thing that's going to come after his *but*, but he doesn't continue. After I've waited for what feels like a solid five minutes, I prod him.

"But…"

"When you told me to go after Aralyn, I specifically ordered Atreya to stay by your side and to protect you. To keep you safe. She failed."

"Logan...what happened?"

"I ripped her throat out with my bare hands."

It's my turn to swallow that enormous ball of truth. The emotion so thick in my throat that it hurts to try and get down. It wasn't Atreya's fault. It was my idea to go into that house and she went in to protect Kaedon and Vadin I was left safe and sound outside with Valmont. But, trying to explain that to Logan right now doesn't seem like the best choice. Besides, would I have done any different? If given the chance, would I have craved revenge for Logan? I don't even have to think about it because I know the answer.

"Valmont tried to intervene. He attempted to hypnotize me, to calm me down, but we both know he *can't* hypnotize me because I'm half Angel. But he doesn't know that, or anyone else for that matter, and besides, his words did sober me up. He reminded me that you *were* still alive, but not for long, and we had to do something to try to save you."

"How did you manage to save me?" I ask, as I pick my head up and cradle it on my hands, looking up into his handsome, but tormented, face.

"Valmont took off to the town, to get Ana and bring her back to you, while I raced to meet them with you in my arms. We met them at the river and Ana began to assess your wounds. That's when she told me it was bad, like *real* bad. The hook had nicked your heart and she wasn't sure she would even be able to heal you but she was determined to try. She was willing to give up her life for yours, Amarah. I tried to talk her out of it though, admittedly, not very hard, because if it comes down to you or anyone else in this world, I'll choose you every time, Angel." He brushes his knuckles across my cheek.

"Same," I whisper with a sad smile.

"Ana was almost done healing you, she hadn't quite finished when Aralyn dropped in from out of the sky. I don't think anyone was expecting her, Hell, I sure didn't, and I was so focused on you, I think we all were, that no one even sensed her coming. She held us all at bay by taking the air right out of our lungs. She didn't hesitate for a second before…"

"Before killing my aunt," I finish.

He nods. "For the second time that night, I thought you were dead. I thought that Ana had failed to save you. I was about to kill Aralyn when you woke up and did it for me and, well, the rest you know."

I nod again and we're quite for a long time as I process everything he just told me.

Atreya is dead.

Ana, The Fey Queen, and my aunt, is dead.

Aralyn, the traitor to her people, is dead.

More loss. More heartache. *When* will it ever end? *Will* it ever end?

"Amarah?" Logan's voice pulls me out of my thoughts.

I blink and look up at him, "yes?"

"Not that I'm complaining, because I don't want to see you hurt in any kind of capacity but, are you sure you're ok? You're not really responding…how I thought you would with…with everything."

I nod, "I know. Don't get me wrong, I'm devastated about everything that happened, but this time is…different," I manage a shrug.

"How?"

"Killing Aralyn was a conscious choice. It wasn't like Andre. He didn't deserve to die," I whisper.

"And Ana?" He continues to interrogate me.

"Again, different. Unlike with Andre, I got to see and speak with Ana. I got to see her reunite with my mother. I saw how happy they both were," I smile, as a mix of happy and sad tears roll down my cheeks. "I got to say goodbye."

"I'm glad," he says, softly, as he brushes my hair behind my ear.

"She wanted me to tell you that it's ok. That she knows you loved her, in your way, and that it's ok. She said you would know what that means."

I see his eyes water again as he let's what I relayed sink in. This time, we're both getting closure. Closure isn't always an option, and you have to learn to heal and move on without it, which is possible but not always the easiest course.

We both lay in comfortable silence as the darkness in the room slowly starts to fade, giving way to dawn, which is fast approaching. We must have only had a couple of hours of sleep, and even though I'm exhausted, I also feel *alive*. So many things have happened in the past couple of days to really make me *see*.

See *what's* important.

Which is living every second of every day to the best of your ability. To not focus on the things you can't control, instead, focus on how you react to them.

See *who* is important.

Be there, be *present* and attentive, for others. Make others feel special. Make them feel loved and appreciated. Make them feel like a priority, because the people you love, should always be.

I must be portraying exactly how I'm feeling, because that sexy half-smile Logan is so good at, makes its appearance.

"You keep thinking those thoughts and we're not going to leave this bed," he says in a low, heated voice.

"I'm here with you, Logan. I'm here and I'm not going anywhere."

He moves too quickly for me to react. He's suddenly looming over me, taking up too much space and too much oxygen from the room. He's all I can see. He's all I can feel. He's all I need. And right now, I desperately need him to breath air into my lungs that are constricting around a heart overflowing with love.

His eyes drop to my lips, already parted and anxious for his kiss. "Together. Always," he says, as lips land on mine.

God, how can someone's lips feel so good? So soft and so powerful at the same time. Just the press of his lips on mine has me
FALLING
SINKING
SOARING
LIVING

I swear, my heart beats so fucking hard for this man I hear it like it's manifesting into the world.

BANG.

BANG.

BANG.

"Amarah! Open this damn door right now or I'm breaking it down! Do you hear me?" Iseta's voice comes crashing through my hazy, passionate thoughts.

Logan groans in frustration, "she has really bad timing."

"We better not keep her waiting, we don't want her casting any dick spells now, do we?"

I swear his face pales and there's a look of pure terror on his face as he scrambles off of me, "coming!" He yells, as he quickly throws on his underwear and stumbles into his sweats as he rushes out of the room without a second look back in my direction.

I can't help but laugh out loud at his retreating back. Despite everything I've endured in this crazy life of mine, both in the human world and The Unseen, there's one thing that stands out more than anything else. More than the loss. More than the pain.

Love.

I am so loved and have so may amazing people in my life. And as long as I have even one person who loves me, it's enough.

It's enough.

Valmont: Which One Will It Be?

Chains by Nick Jonas

Bloody fucking Hell. What the fuck even happened tonight? My mind is jumping all over the place, from seeing her again, even though it hadn't been more than a single day, it felt like an eternity, to having to hear her give her sweet moans and cries to *him*, to having her feening in my arms, to almost dying, to being fucking carried off by that Gods damned Werewolf.

I snarl at nothing, running my hands through my hair, as I pace in the small living room of the house that I'll be sharing with Emrick and Vadin. Fuck this. Why the Hell did I even come? Ally or not, I didn't need to be here tonight. I could have easily sent Pierce, Emerson, or literally anyone else.

"Why am I bloody fucking here?" I yell into the empty room.

Amarah Rey.

Amarah Rey is why I'm here. Fuck. I should have brought my mead. I need a fucking drink. I head into the kitchen and start opening and slamming cabinets, looking for something to toss down my throat and hopefully numb me a little. I finally find a half empty bottle of Crown Royal *Apple* in the freezer.

"Who bloody chooses to drink fruit flavored alcohol?" I ask

myself in disgust. "Way to ruin perfectly good whisky," I mumble, as I unscrew the lid and toss it back.

The whisky burns my throat as I chug, the apple flavor leaving an unpleasantly sweet aftertaste. I definitely prefer the taste and texture that honey provides in alcohol. I cough as I come up for air and the whisky settles in a warm pool in my belly. Alcohol hasn't had this much effect on me since I was human. I feel the heat blooming up my chest as goosebumps race down my arms. I have to lean against the counter, closing my eyes, as the rush of roughly four shots of whisky tingles through me. There can only be one caused to my reaction.

"Amarah Rey," I whisper her name like a forbidden secret.

Revna had me completely immobilized by mind crushing pain when I fell to the floor next to Amarah Rey. Her blood was running profusely down her body, puddling on the floor, and I managed to slide underneath the drip and drink it down.

Gods it was glorious.

Not the same as taking it straight from her veins, with my dick being squeezed by her pulsing pussy, but it was still warm and sweet, its thickness coating my tongue and sliding down my throat. Her blood is still every bit as potent as it's always been. Losing her power hasn't changed *everything* about her. She's still an Angel, always will be, with Angel blood.

Does *she* know this?

I'm pulled out of my thoughts by the feeling of dread that's tugged at my stomach for centuries.

Dawn is approaching.

I can feel it with my entire being. It's like, once I became a Vampire, became a slave to the night, I was also intimately mated to the sun. I'm bound to it. To sense it as it rises from the night sky every day and yet, never able to feel it on my skin, ever again. A life of torment to be drawn to the very thing that will kill you. Until Amarah

Rey came and changed fucking everything. I scoff at a perilous new thought crossing my mind.

I reach for the bottle again, determined to drown my depressing thoughts, but hesitate as I feel the clutches of the alcohol in my system reaching into my head. Good. This is good. This is what I wanted. Isn't it?

The vibrating buzz of my phone in my front pocket jolts me out of my trance. I've been sitting on the couch in front of the window, curtains pulled wide, watching the world wake up and brighten as the sun climbs over the horizon and into the sky. I'm not sitting in direct sunlight, but I should be feeling extremely weak and my skin should be tingling and itching with just the rays filtering in.

But...it's not.

I pull the phone out of my pocket and swipe the screen open. My heart soars at the sight of Amarah Rey's name on the notification at the top of the screen. I open the message.

Amarah Rey: Hey, we're calling a meeting to debrief everything that happened last night. I'll fill you in on everything when you wake up tonight. I just wanted you to know.

Of course they'd have a debrief meeting and of course, I'd miss it. My slavery to the night causes me to miss out on everything. Ok, perhaps not everything, but so much happens in the day. That's when everyone else is awake and living. That's when Amarah Rey is awake and living.

But you know what? At the moment, so am I. How long will her blood in my veins last? How long will her blood protect me from the sunlight?

"Guess I'll find out," I say to myself, as I get up off the couch.

I walk over to the mirror hanging over the fireplace and give myself a once over. This won't do. I'm a bloody mess, quite literally. They'll just have to suffer a while without my presence while I get cleaned up. I head into the small bathroom that's just off the living room. Small is an understatement. I pull back the shower curtain and stare at the shower and tub combo and grimace.

"Gods, this is bloody awful," I say aloud, as I bend over to turn on the water.

I'm not even going to fit under the showerhead. I'll have to bed over to get underneath it. Again, I find myself wondering what the Hell I'm doing here. The same reason why I'm about to torture myself in this inadequate, poor excuse of a shower.

Amarah Rey.

Thirty minutes later, I'm clean and presentable. I look in the mirror as I finish rolling up the sleeves of my button-up. My tattoos are a stark contrast to the crisp white of the shirt. I don't normally roll the sleeves up, like some thug, but I know Amarah Rey likes my ink. I've also left the top two buttons open, revealing a nice amount of my muscular, also fully tattooed chest. I stand back, slide my hands into the pockets of my black slacks, my silver belt buckle gleams, asking for attention. My lips are a beautiful shade of pink I haven't seen on them in centuries, my eyes are brighter than they've ever been, and my hair gleams as if I'm being staged for a damn shampoo commercial. I can't help but smirk because I know I look good. Better than a simple t-shirt and jeans ever will.

I head out of the bathroom and towards the front door. I can feel the heat of the sun, even behind the gloomy December sky, and I can't help but hesitate. What if this doesn't work? What if last time was just a fluke? What if her blood was more powerful when she had her power? So many doubts are creeping in that I almost convince myself to say fuck it, turn around, and hide away in my coffin.

I take a deep breath and let it out as I reach for the handle. I open the door slowly, one inch at a time, until I'm standing in the open doorway.

When nothing happens, not even a slight tingle or itch, I take a step out onto the porch. The porch is covered so I'm still not standing in any direct sunlight or rays. I cautiously move across it and down the three small steps until I'm standing on the ground, under an unobstructed blueish-grey sky. I feel the sun like a magnet as it slowly slips out from behind a cloud. I feel...so many things. I'm overwhelmed by my senses and I'm trying to soak it all in. The cold winter air finds my exposed skin and makes my shiver. I can feel it. I can feel the cold. I let out a nervous laugh as I shake my head and proceed towards the townhall meeting place.

I hear Amarah Rey speaking, detailing what happened from when we got to the house, as I approach the door. I push the door open and close it quietly behind me before I stroll inside. Amarah Rey immediately makes eye contact with me as I step into the room. She's stops talking and all eyes immediately follow her gaze and land on me. There are dozens of eyes all trained on me but I only see one beautiful hazel set.

"What in the..." I hear someone blurt out but my attention is on Amarah Rey.

I watch as her eyes take in my appearance and slowly travel down my body. I see her throat bob on a hard swallow and I can't help the pride that rises inside of my chest. Pride at her appreciation of the way I look. Appreciation of *my* body. There's no way anyone in this room can deny the hunger in her eyes as she stares at me, lips parted, heartbeat racing. And I don't believe it's all because of her addiction to my bite. She was eyeing me with curiosity and appreciation long before I ever slipped my fangs inside of her.

Amarah Rey blinks and the spell is broken. She reaches for Logan and he's there. Comforting her. *Distracting* her. Her eyes lock with his and I can't deny what is so clear to see. I clench my jaw against the jealousy threatening to expose just how much I care.

The awkward silence is finally filled with whispers and murmurs, as everyone discusses the fact that I'm standing here. In daylight.

Finally, the Fey Princess speaks up, "Valmont, as nice as it is that you've been able to join us today..." she trails off, the confusion written clearly on her face.

I walk over to the nearest wall and lean my back against it, crossing my ankles and sliding my hands into my pockets, a picture of casual boredom. All eyes are on me except for the ones I *want* on me. It's incredibly hard to stand here and seem unassuming, waiting for the Princess to continue.

"Ummmm...exactly *how* are you joining us during the day?" She finally gets out.

"I *am* a Master Vampire, older than everyone here put together. Did you truly believe you know everything I'm capable of?" I say, condescendingly, looking directly at the arrogant little Princess. I've never cared for her, *chip on the shoulder*, routine. I try to catch her eyes but she looks away. Smart girl. I'm feeling rather... *murderous*, and well, since I can't murder anyone here, I'm a bit put off and grouchy.

"Alright," she pulls her shoulders back, trying to regain her confidence. "Keep your secrets as you wish. You're an ally and not a threat so, I don't see..."

"I am *always* a threat, Princess," I say slowly, annunciating every word.

"Valmont," Amarah Rey's voice grabs my attention. "Please," she pleads.

I pull my hands out of my pocket and raise them up in mock surrender, "by all means, don't mind me, continue."

The room's a bit on edge, and it takes a few minutes for the focus to return to the events of the past night, but eventually it does.

"So that brings us to Revna," Princess Arabella says. "What

shall we do with her?"

"Kill her," Amarah Rey practically yells.

I fight the smile that wants to pull at my lips. Amarah Rey has grown and come a long way since I first met her at the Fire Fey's home. She's finding her confidence and her voice. She's making the hard decisions but they are also the *right* decisions. She's making the choice to sacrifice one, very evil life, to save countless others. Not to mention, her anger and need for revenge excites me. I'd love to kill Revna with her and then sink my fangs and cock into her while she's covered in Revna's blood.

"Amarah," Iseta scolds her. "You don't mean that."

"I love you very much, Sister, but please don't tell me what I mean and don't mean, especially when it comes to Revna. She needs to die, period."

"Why don't we just keep her locked up? Contained?" Iseta argues.

Amarah Rey scoffs, "have you never seen any movie, ever? What happens every single time the good guys try to lock away the bad guys? Huh? I'll tell you. The bad guys always manage to escape and cause more death, more chaos."

"This isn't a movie, Amarah."

She shakes her head, "no, its real life, which means, real lives lost. I won't lose anyone else to Revna. I won't risk her escaping or being saved somehow by Lucifer. We kill her. If it can even be done but we have to try."

"What do you mean *if* it can be done?" Emrick speaks up.

"Well, you know she died once already. Iseta killed her." She looks pointedly at her sister, "and according to Revna, Lucifer not only brought her back, but gave her immortality. I highly doubt he'd do that. He doesn't exactly do as he says he will but there's only one way to find out."

"I agree with Amarah," Logan joins in.

"Well, you would," Emrick smirks, his insinuation clear.

Chuckles erupt around the room. It adds to my murder-y thoughts.

"Who else agrees with Amarah?" Arabella asks the group.

Hands shoot up, mine included, the majority of us outnumbering the few.

"I appreciate everyone's opinion. I understand the want to save lives and not take them. Lord knows, we've had too much death," she sighs, "but I also agree with Amarah on this decision. She's too dangerous to keep alive."

"I'd like to be the one to do, if you'll let me," Amarah Rey offers.

"Very well," she agrees. "And that leads us to the very last topic of discussion today. Our Queen has been murdered and taken from us entirely too soon. Her body is being taken back to Headquarters where it will be cleaned and prepared for Surmajärgne Elu, the Afterlife. We will have her ceremony in one week's time."

Solemn faces nod at the announcement.

"And, we need to discuss the way the events of this tragedy unfolded, and what it means for the Fey." She sighs heavily, "I am personally mortified and…*livid*, that it was my own flesh and blood, my sister, that killed the Queen. This black mark will never leave our family line and I am forever regretful." She clears her throat, "however, Aralyn did kill the Queen, which means, had the throne accepted her, she would have been the next Fey Queen. That potential title now falls to Amarah, should the throne accept her."

"What?!" Amarah Rey's shocked voice echoes loudly through the muted room. She turns to Logan, "did you know about this?"

"I know the custom in theory, yes," he admits.

"Why didn't you tell me? Or *warn* me at least?" She seethes at Logan and then addresses the room, "I'm nowhere *close* to Queen material! There has to be another way! Let all of the Leaders vote and decide who the next rightful Queen should be!"

"It doesn't work that way," Vadin shakes his head. "Even though we are Fey, we're not above faulty logic and emotions. We're not above petty grievances, revenge, or wanting power, as we've seen first hand with Aralyn. We cannot be given the power to elect a new Queen. The power of the throne, the essence of who we are, the very reason we exist, is the only source pure enough to determine the Queen. The Selection Ceremony must take place. All of the Fey thrones possess this power and select each Fey Leader. It's how it's done."

"See! I don't even know the ways of the Fey!" Amarah Rey argues. "I'm the worst possible choice, please," she pleads, "there has to be another way."

Vadin shakes his head again, "the throne will decide, and if you are found unfit, then we will put forth another candidate to be tested."

Amarah scoffs and crosses her arms. She looks to Logan but he only shakes his head. There will be no avoiding this and, honestly, there's not a better candidate out there to be Queen. Yes, Amarah Rey is young and inexperienced compared to the rest of us, yes, she has a lot to learn, but her character and her heart are both rooted in *good*. With the right people by her side, guiding her, she will blossom into a wonderful Queen, not only for her people, but for The Unseen as a whole.

"Then it's settled, we will prepare for the Valimine after the Surmajärgne Elu," Arabella confirms. "You're all dismissed."

I push off of the wall, intent to head back outside, to enjoy as much of the sun and daylight as I can before this ability wears off, when Amarah Rey's voice stops me.

"Valmont!" She calls out. I turn to see her walking toward me, Logan is engrossed in a conversation with Iseta. "Can we talk?"

"Amarah Rey, I've already told you once before, whatever

you need from me is yours."

She clears her throat and nods, "somewhere private."

I smirk, "I'm liking the sound of this more and more. Come on," I lead the way out the front door.

The sun is still playing hide and seek behind storm clouds, and despite the Winter air, I can feel it's heat on my skin. I close my eyes for a brief second, savoring the feeling, before I lead us away from the townhall and around the side of the next building so we can have our privacy.

Once we're hidden from view, I turn to Amarah Rey, "alright, what would you like to talk about?"

"I think you know what I want to talk about," she implies.

"I don't think you wish to talk at all," I grip her arm, pulling her in against my body and then push her up against the outside of the building. She gasps and looks at me with wide, surprised eyes. I lean my body into hers, letting her feel my excitement, as I whisper against her neck, "you want to feel my hard cock push deep inside of you, while my fangs pierce your vein, and I fuck you into oblivion." I push my hips into her, grinding my hard length against her.

A shiver runs through her body and I know damn well it isn't because of the cold air. I scrape my fangs along her neck and she groans, arching her back and pushing her chest into me as she fists her hands into my shirt, pulling me harder against her.

"Gods, your body is so quick to respond to me, Amarah Rey. I want to take you, right here, right now," I declare. The urge to rip her clothes off has me clenching my hands in fists in her shirt as well.

"Amarah!"

"Logan," Amarah Rey whispers his name and pulls away from me, lighting a fuse in my head.

I manage to take a step away from her before Logan rounds the corner and slams into me. I land hard on the ground, Logans body on top of me, Wolf eyes and teeth snarling in my face. I give a fierce push against his chest with all of my strength and he launches into the air, back slamming against the building before he lands solidly on his feet. I'm on mine, mirroring his fighting stance in an instant.

We're both about to launch forward when Amarah Rey runs in between us, hands out to each side, as if she could hope to hold us off.

"Stop!" She yells. "Both of you, stop!"

"I already told you what I'd do if he crossed a line with you, Amarah. I wasn't lying," Logan says, in a voice that's low and choppy. His Wolf is close to breaking through.

"I know! And I believe you but this is not happening right now. Not because of me. So stop, please, both of you."

Logan growls but stands up straighter, his hands lowering to rest at his sides. I follow his lead, only because it's Amarah Rey that's begging us to stop.

She turns to me, "Valmont, I'm sorry." Her eyes tear up and that sobers me more than anything else. "I'm sorry for letting things get out of hand. Things went too far with us, and I won't say I regret it," she looks at Logan, "because I don't." She looks back at me and I see the sadness in her eyes. All I want to do is pull her into my arms and take that sadness away. "Valmont," she almost whispers, "it's no secret that I crave you, your bite. I'm addicted and it's not something I asked for." Tears roll down her cheeks, "I have to live with it and I'm trying to do my best, but you can't continue to take advantage of my addiction. I've made my choice so, please, stop putting me in these impossible situations. Please."

Her words are like a stake to my heart. I can feel it, physically, my heart being stabbed and crushed beneath my ribs. The sensation is so intense, I grab at my chest and look down, expecting to see a stake sticking out of my chest.

She claims to have made her choice but what about my

choice? I've also made my choice. I chose Amarah Rey. Am I supposed to just give her up so easily? Without a fight? What kind of love would that be?

"I'm sorry," Amarah Rey's voice cracks against her tears. They're flowing like a raging river down her cheeks. "I'm sorry," she repeats, "I'm so sorry."

Logan reaches for her hand, she takes it, and turns around to bury her face in his chest. Her entire body convulses with the emotion running through her body. Her sobs seep into my chest and add further damage my heart.

Once again, I'm a cause of her pain. My love is the cause of her pain and I'm momentarily stunned and confused. Love isn't supposed to cause pain. It's supposed to set us free from pain. But all my love has managed to do is wound us both.

My earlier unspoken thought rises to the surface. Amarah Rey is my sun. I'm cursed to live a life drawn to her, loving her, and never being able to feel the benefits of a requited love. The sun can, and will, destroy me. The question is, which one will it be in the end?

"I'm sorry, too, Amarah Rey," I say, before I turn and leave her in the arms of the man she chose.

Amarah: A Warning

A Storm Is Coming by Tommee Profit, Liv Ash

I'm so fucking exhausted and overwhelmed and it's not even ten o'clock on a brand-new day. Since that night at the club, when my power decided to make an appearance, my life has been a whirlwind.

A whole new world.

Demons.

Magic.

Love.

Pain.

Found family.

Lost family.

And just overall, immense and all-consuming events and emotions. Even with all of the sleeping I've done recently, when I locked myself away from the world and slowly withered away, I still manage to feel like I haven't actually rested in months. I guess I truly haven't. Not with the nightmares invading my sleep.

When the tears and the sobs have finally stopped, I loosen my grip on Logan and look up at him, "I'm sorry."

"Hey," he gently jostles me, his arms hooked around me. "We're going to get through this and it will be easier and easier every day. I'm not scared and I'm not running away."

I nod and he leans in, pressing his lips to my forehead. "Iseta said she'll be ready for the summoning tonight."

I sigh, already dreading this next step I have to take on this obstacle course that is my life. "I feel like I'm training for Ninja Warrior and I'm currently getting beat to shit and thrown off the obstacles into the water."

"It's not always going to be like this, Angel."

"Promise?"

"I promise."

"I hope you're right, but right now I just want to go lie down. I'm exhausted and I have a feeling tonight is going to require a lot more energy. I need to try and sleep."

He nods, "whatever you need, but first, let's get some food in you."

At the mention of food, my stomach grumbles loudly. We both laugh softly, any remaining tension slipping away, as he takes my hand and leads me back to our house.

I'd like to say that I'm waiting patiently and calmly for Iseta to finish setting up for what we're about to attempt but I'd be lying. I'm pacing back and forth, chewing on my fingernails, in front of where Iseta is sitting on the floor, completing the summoning circle with blood from a chicken she just sacrificed. The couch, chairs, and coffee table have all been pushed to the sides of the room, leaving the living room a nice open and spacious work space.

"Amarah, I swear, I'm about to tackle you and bop you on your forehead repeatedly with a spoon, like I used to do when you were little and annoying me."

Logan let's out a strangled, amused laugh, "wait, you used to do what? I'd pay good money to see this."

I stop my pacing to glare at him, which only causes him to laugh harder, before I return my attention to Iseta.

"I'm sorry," I say, sarcastically. "It's not like I'm waiting around for you to set up and read my tarot cards while I enjoy a glass of wine, you're literally about to summon the devil."

Iseta stops, looks up at me with a dead serious look on her face, "yes, I know, and if you haven't caught on by now, I am *not* happy about it. This isn't shit anyone should mess with, ever."

"I know," I say, humiliated and completely defeated. "I'm sorry that you're having to do this for me. I knew better, I just..." my eyes fall on Logan. No words are needed.

Iseta sighs, "I know. Look, what's done is done. We can't change what happened or dwell on it. Let's focus on getting through this unscathed."

I nod my head, "ok."

"But again, not happy and you owe me big time. Like, you're going to owe me for the rest of your life."

"That's fair," I agree.

"Bring me those black candles and the yellow one with the sigil carved into it, and the bell."

I walk over to the coffee table where her supplies have been laid out and I grab the requested items. I notice that the black candles have peacock feathers tied to them as well. I find it odd, but then again, I'm not the Witch. I hand them over to Iseta and watch as she places the five black candles at each point of the upside-down pentagram and sets the yellow candle and bell off to the side, on the outside of the circle.

"Now grab me that canister," she orders.

I oblige, handing it to her. She unhooks the lid and grabs a handful of a pale-yellow powder and starts to spread it around each of the black candles.

"What's that?" I ask.

"Sulphur," she says, without any further explanation.

Once she's done, she stands and dusts her hands on a rag she has hanging from her belt. "Alright, well, that's everything. Now, I just need to do a protection spell for the three of us, just in case. Logan," she gestures him to come closer.

"Time for my blood?" He assumes.

"Time for your blood," Iseta confirms.

"You know, my blood is still Angel blood too. We could use mine," I suggest, feeling bad that Logan has to open a vein for my mistake.

"How do you know?" Iseta narrows her eyes at me.

"Valmont," I shrug. "That's the only piece of the puzzle that I didn't have about last night. How did Revna end up gagged and chained to a wall when she had us all beat? Valmont fell to the floor right beneath me. I bet he drank my blood, which made him strong enough to beat Revna, and, if that wasn't enough proof, he was literally walking around in the sun today."

"Shit," Iseta says, a look of shock on her face. "So it's your blood that allowed him to walk in the sun? God, Amarah, no one can find out about this, especially other Vampires. They'll all come for you."

I shrug, "I don't even know if it would work on Vampires in general or if it's just because Valmont is a strong Master Vampire," I shrug. "I have no idea how it all works, but yes, it's a side-effect of my blood. Well, *our* blood. For all we know, Logan's blood may even be *more* potent because he's a direct descendant from Michael."

"Geeze," Iseta rubs her forehead. "Ok, one thing at a time here. We're going to use Logan's blood because we know for sure that it *is* Angel blood. Let's hope it's more potent too. That definitely can't hurt."

Iseta grabs a small bowl and knife from the coffee table and walks back to where Logan is standing beside me. He holds his forearm out to her willingly, then hesitates.

"That blade's not silver, right?"

"This isn't my first rodeo, cowboy."

He extends his arm again, she gives it a quick slice, and he turns it over to let his blood pour into the bowl. The blood pours out of the cut for a few seconds before it trickles off and comes to a stop.

"Do you need more?" Logan asks, offering up his now completely healed arm.

"No, this is enough, thank you," Iseta assures him.

I shake my head, "I still can't believe how fast you heal."

"Perks of being Võltsimatu."

I return my attention to Iseta. She's just tossed in a pinch of salt into the bowl with the blood and is now pouring in a light green liquid. It has a strong alcohol base scent but a hint of mint and something…floral, maybe? It's different but not at all unpleasant. She reaches for a large crystal and proceeds to mix the new blood concoction with it.

She approaches us, bowl in hand, "pull your shirts aside so I can reach the skin above your heart."

Logan and I both comply. She proceeds to repeat the spell as she uses the crystal to paint crosses on our foreheads and above our hearts.

With blood of your blood
I pray to you now
Protect your son and daughter
From that which evil would allow
For nothing is greater than you, O' Lord
With your protection we stand stronger
With blood of your blood

I pray to you now

"That will protect both your mind and heart from any nefarious acts the devil may try to play with them."

"What about you?" I ask, voice full of concern.

If I hadn't already known Lucifer, I'd be shitting bricks right now with what we're about to do. Even still, all of this is making me extremely nervous. I have no idea how Lucifer is going to react to be summoned or what he may try and do. After all, it's not like he has to pretend anymore. He got what he wanted. What use am I now? I'm nothing. I'm expendable. Even worse, I'm a threat to him now because I'm trying to take what's rightfully mine back.

"I'm protected, don't worry about me," Iseta says, confidently.

"Shit," I breathe out on a shaky breath. "I'm suddenly really nervous and, honestly, a little scared."

"Don't be. Use your Faith like I taught you. Surround yourself in the Heavenly light and be the fighter you've always been. You too, Logan."

I nod my head a bit frantically and take a deep breath in, settling myself. I've done this before I can do it again. Logan grabs my hand and I squeeze it, comforted by his presence.

"I'm here, Angel," he says, softly.

Iseta has finished lighting the black candles, "hit the lights, please."

I can't seem to bring my feet to unglue from the floor so, Logan moves to turn the lights off and quickly returns to his spot beside me, slipping his hand back in mine. I can't help but wonder if he might be a little bit scared too.

Iseta is safely outside the summoning when she starts chanting in a language I can't understand. It sounds like the same language Revna was using earlier.

tenebris dominus

gehennae

i praesentiam vestram requiramus

Exite et videte me

Once she's done chanting the spell, she reaches for the yellow candle and lights it, then picks up the bell and rings it five times.

I feel the magic expand from the circle and engulf me in its heaviness. Goosebumps erupt across my skin, a cold shiver slithers down my spine, and my heart is hammering so hard in my chest that it feels like it's going to crack my ribcage.

A breeze sweeps through the room, flickering the candle flames, but they don't go out. The sulphur starts to smoke and I'm immediately gagging on its pungent smell. I hear Logan choking and coughing as well. The taste of rotten eggs climbs thickly down my throat and I double over, coughing and gagging. I have to close my eyes and concentrate all my effort on not throwing up. As quickly as the smell appeared, it's just suddenly gone, as a familiar voice fills the room.

"Amarah, Amarah, Amarah," he tsks. "I didn't think you had it in you."

Lucifer is standing in the center of the summoning circle, he's once again dressed in all black, as if he's one with the darkness that's pressing in against the weak candle light. He looks exactly like he did in my dream when he convinced me to take his treacherous hand. The memory, and my stupid decision...make that, *decisions*, has me mentally kicking myself.

I push my regrets aside and focus on the buzzing energy I feel immediately. My power. I feel it calling to me. Reaching out through the invisible link that seems to connect my physical body to it. My chest aches with the need to have my power back, settled inside of me, making me whole once again.

"I'm not the weak girl you think I am. You just happened to meet me, and take advantage of me, at the absolute lowest point in my life," I seethe, instantly angry and the mere sight of him looking all smug and arrogant.

Lucifer walks to the edge of the summoning circle but doesn't cross over it. My heart is still slamming in my chest, but seeing him stop at that boundary line, boosts my confidence. Until this moment, I really wasn't sure if all of this would work or if it would contain him.

"Weak or not, you're no match for me, no matter what my ridiculous brother, or anyone, tries to tell you."

"I don't need anyone to tell me what I am and what I'm not. I may not be everything I'm meant to be just yet, but I'm closer to becoming her every day, and I'm capable of more than you think I am."

Lucifer laughs, his quick dismissal of me only adds fuel to my growing fire. "Oh, Amarah, just as naïve as you've always been."

"You talk a big game, but I know how powerful my Faith is, and as much as you try to make me believe otherwise, I know you fear it, and *Him*."

"Well, that's a cute theory, Amarah, but I'm rather bored with this conversation. That's enough talking."

"I agree." I close my eyes and focus on the sensation of my power down this invisible rope.

I follow it with my mind, with a feeling, and find my power swirling and restless inside of Lucifer. It feels like a caged animal, anxious and pacing in front of the bars, eagerly waiting for any chance of escape.

"Well now, that's enough of that," Lucifer states. I can hear the slight nervousness in his voice. He knows, just as well as I do, that my power is just as desperate to get back to me as I am at taking it back. "I answered your summons, as I must, but I'm afraid you're just not strong enough to keep me here."

I try to ignore him, squeezing my eyes shut and focusing on my power, trying to figure out how to connect with it. How to free it from Lucifer. I just need a little more time to figure it out.

"As much I'd love to stay and watch you fail, I'm afraid I'm on a tight schedule and I must be off. The curtain is about to open on my best show yet! I assure you, you don't want to miss this," he winks, and then the wind and stench of sulphur whirls around us again.

And then he's gone.

Taking my power with him.

Amarah: No Time To Waste

The Show Must Go On by Queen

The three of us stand in silence for a few minutes, the only movement in the room coming from the candles still flickering, fighting against the shadows. Finally, Logan walks over to the wall and hits the switch, flooding the room with light and illuminating my failure.

"Well, that was…" Iseta hesitates.

I stomp over to the couch and throw myself on it, "that was an epic fucking fail is what that was!" I exclaim, as I hang my head in my hands.

"I'm sorry, he's right. I wasn't strong enough to hold him here, I tried," Iseta's voice sounds tired, defeated.

"It's not your fault, sister, it's mine. All of this is my fault," I let out my own defeated sigh, the hope inside of me slowly burning out. "Thank you for trying though. I know this wasn't something you wanted to do."

"I'll do whatever it takes to help you get your power back, you know that."

"What would we need to make it work? He said we weren't strong enough. Do we just need more Witches? I mean, Amarah did just ally with the Coven," Logan suggests.

Iseta considers it for a moment, "the additional power from a Coven could intensify the strength of the spell but," she sighs, "I'm not sure it would be enough. We need something to hold him here, something to anchor him, or else he may just be able to leave again. I mean, he *is* the devil. He's powerful."

The hope inside of me sparks. Ok, the Coven may just be able to help. I can't lose my Faith, not yet, Hell, not ever again! We have to keep trying. *I* have to keep trying.

"I'll reach out Brynn. Maybe she'll have an idea of how to anchor him," I suggest.

"It's worth a shot," Logan sits down next to me and grabs my hand. "We're not giving up. We're going to figure this out and get your power back."

I smile weakly at him. I seriously wouldn't be as hopeful or brave if I didn't have these amazing people around me. And as long as I fight, I know they will fight right alongside me.

The front door slams open, causing me to jump, and Emrick comes charging in, "there's been an attack on the Vesi Family!"

Logan and I both jump up.

"What?"

"When?"

"I just got a call from my mom, it just happened! Oh man, guys, it's bad. It's so bad. Vadin and I are leaving, like *now*! He hasn't heard from *any* of his family. No one," Emrick's eyes are wide, his hands are shaking, and he's overall frantic.

"Emrick, please tell me everything you know," I walk up to him and grab his hands, willing him to calm down and focus.

"We don't know details. One of the Watchers of the rip managed to get a call to my mother. He said that demons were flooding out of the rip in a force he's never seen before. That's all he managed to tell my mother before..."

"Oh my God," I turn around and face Iseta and Logan. "This is what Lucifer was talking about. This is why he wanted my power and why he kept mentioning he had things to do. That's why the demons haven't been attacking. He's been amassing them at the rip, waiting for this moment, waiting to freely and forceful attack. He's been planning this all along."

"This isn't your fault, Amarah," Logan says. "There's no way anyone could have seen this coming."

"I should have! I knew something was happening. The demons just stopped attacking out of the blue? And Lucifer took my power, which allows him to walk on Earth? It was all there! I just didn't see it! He's literally unleashed Hell on Earth and he's leading the charge all thanks to me."

"Amarah…" Logan starts to try and comfort me but Iseta interrupts him.

"It doesn't matter. None of it matters. What matters now is how we're going to stop this. You all need to get down to the Water Fey's home as soon as possible. Assess the damage, save anyone you can, and start killing demons. We need to stop this before it bleeds into the human world."

Logan nods and turns to Emrick, "tell Vadin we're right behind you. Let's get everything packed up and go."

We all move quickly. Whatever fatigue and defeat we felt minutes ago have disappeared in the light of this news. I can feel the adrenaline pumping through my body, helping me move quickly, but I'm dreading the long drive we have in front of us. Two hours back to Albuquerque and then another four hours or so to get to the Water Fey's home. Hopefully a lot less if we haul ass.

We're packing up the truck when her voice stops me in my tracks, "don't forget about us."

I turn around quickly and see Atreya walking up to us with Kaedon. I quickly glance at Logan who seems frozen, eyes locked on

Atreya.

"I know I'm a show stopper but we really don't have time for an intermission, I'm afraid. The show must go on and quickly from what I hear."

Logan finally moves, he slowly walk towards her, I follow. I'm also just as confused as Logan. He said he killed her but yet, here she stands, alive and well. Well, I think she's well. I watch as Logan's hand reaches out towards her throat.

"How?" He asks, his voice barely above a whisper.

Atreya shrugs, "Hell if I know. Apparently, Valmont stopped you just in time, before you ripped out my throat completely, and while everyone was distracted with Amarah and the Queen, Kaedon brought Vyla to me. She was able to save me."

Logan stands in front of her, frozen again, as he just stares at her. A long, silent minute passes. Both Kaedon and I are on alert, watching for any signs of anger from Logan. He tried to kill her for allowing me to get hurt. I'm not sure he's gotten over seeing me hanging on that wall. I don't think he ever will because I'll never get over seeing Valmont's sword pushed through his chest.

Atreya breaks the tense silence, "thank God for being a Werewolf, our own healing abilities, and being damn hard to kill, am I right?" She gives a nervous laugh.

Logan suddenly closes the gap between them, Kaedon and I both jump forward, prepared to pull him off of her, when he throws his arms around her and pulls her into a tight hug. Kaedon and I both look at them and then each other with shocked and confused expressions.

"God, I'm so sorry, Atreya. I wasn't thinking. I wasn't in control. I…"

"It's ok," Atreya laughs against his chest, this time it's a relieved sound. "I understand why you did it and I know I would have reacted the same way. We're Wolves, Logan. It's the nature of who we are. I'm sorry I didn't keep her safe."

Logan releases her from his hold and steps back. Both of their faces show their immense relief as Atreya dabs at the corner of her eyes.

"Enough of that sappy ass shit," she tries to play off her emotion, a lifetime of having to be strong and show no weakness is a hard trait to break.

I know how much they both mean to each other. Logan would have never admitted it, well, maybe only to me, but he would have deeply regretted killing Atreya the way he did. In a rage. Even if it was to avenge me.

"To be fair," I intrude on their moment, hoping to take the focus off of their emotions, "I didn't keep you safe either, Atreya. But we're all still here, still alive, and there's no one to blame. No fingers to point. We survived a battle when others haven't been as fortunate. Let's focus on that and let's focus on this new threat."

"Are you going to be ready to fight? Both of you," he asks Kaedon and Atreya.

They both nod and say they are, determination clear in their eyes and body language. They're ready to fight against this new threat. This new evil.

"Good, because we're gonna need you," I admit.

"You're going to need all the help you can get," Valmont's voice joins in the conversation.

He's leaning up against the truck, literally a few feet away from us, and I don't think any of us noticed him. I sure as Hell didn't. It's still so damn unnerving how he moves and can literally stand so still that he goes unnoticed.

"Yes, we will," I agree.

"I'll meet you there, tomorrow night," he says, plainly, and then he's gone. Just gone. All I can do is stand here, staring at the spot where he was literally *just* standing, and pick my jaw up off the ground.

"Amarah," Arabella now joins our growing group. "We'll be sending people behind you all as well. Jon is gathering them now."

I nod, "thank you."

"I know you wanted the pleasure of ending Revna's life, but..."

I shake my head, "no, it's ok. We can't stay here any longer, we need to get to the Vesi Family immediately. That's what's important. I trust you to handle Revna. Don't wait," I urge her. "Do it as soon as possible and please let me know once it's done."

"I will," she assures.

"If you need help with any type of magic, ask Iseta or reach out to Brynn with the Desert Rose Coven. She'll help if she can."

"Is that everything?" Logan interjects. "We really need to go."

I wrack my brain, trying to go through everything that's happened in the last twenty-four hours. The Queen has already been taken to Headquarters. Her body is safe. Aralyn is dead. Arabella will do what she must with her sister's body. Revna is captured and will be killed, *if* she can be. We summoned Lucifer, and I failed to get my power back, giving him the ability to walk on Earth and lead his demon army from the front line. Oh, and then there's the possibility that I may become the Fey Queen and take on that unfathomable responsibility that I don't want.

I shake my head. That's the last thing I want to think about right now. "Let's go," I order.

Everyone moves. We pile into the truck and Logan peels out of the gravel driveway as we race towards the unknown.

Amarah: Pay Attention To The Signs

The Resistance by Skillet

We make it back to Albuquerque in one hour flat. We drop Atreya and Kaedon off at the Den, they'll drive separately to join us with more Wolves at the Water Fey's home, then we rush home to gather what we need and drop Iseta off with her vehicle.

Everything is happening so quickly, literally just minutes of rushed conversation, and hoping we can all react before too much damage is done. Time is ticking by too quickly, and yet, I feel like it's been five days. How can time rush by so quickly while I feel absolutely stuck in place, helpless, with no way to control a damn thing that's happening?

On the way into town, I texted Mariah, asking if she could, once again, house sit and watch Griffin for me. We'll be leaving for the Vesi Family's home right away and I have no idea how long we'll be gone. I'm starting to see how The Unseen is just not a pet friendly place. At least, not for me, but the thought of not having that sweet little soul crushes me. He's been my steady and loyal companion, getting me through some of my darkest days. We really don't deserve dogs and their unconditional love. I push that depressing thought out of my head as we finish packing up my car for the next leg of the trip. There's no way I can sit idle in the passenger seat for the next three or four hours. I need to be in control of *something*.

Iseta wraps me in a hug as we stand next to her vehicle, "I know you're anxious, we all are, but please drive safely, ok? No crazy fast speeding. We don't need this turning into Grand Theft Auto. Unless you see a demon, then run his ass over, but no running over hookers."

I can't help the smile that spreads across my face. Iseta always has a way of calming me down, making me feel like everything is going to be ok, and...by easing my worry, even momentarily, with her silly jokes and wit.

"I promise I'll be safe and won't run over any hookers," I laugh, softly.

"I'm just going to regroup and gather some more supplies. I'll meet you there, ok?"

"You know how to get there?" I ask. That would make one of us.

"Yes, Amarah, I know how to get there. Unlike you, The Unseen has always been my home. I know everything I need to know."

"I don't know why I even asked. That doesn't surprise me."

"I'll see you both soon," she says, confidently, as she climbs into the driver seat, shuts the door, and slowly backs out of the driveaway.

Once again, I'm left standing here watching her taillights fade. Logan stands behind me and wraps me in his arms as I watch her go. All this déjà vu is seriously starting to make me feel like I have a parallel life. Another timeline running alongside this one.

I sigh and sink into Logan's hold. It's the first time I've had a second to just breathe. I can't believe all of this is happening. We've had some big wins but it feels like we're worse off than ever before. Like we keep taking one step forward and three steps back.

"I really need to get my power back and we need to figure out

How to close the rip. We need to end this, once and for all."

Logan kisses the top of my head, "we will, Angel. We will."

We're still standing in the same spot when Mariah's jeep pulls into the driveway. I lift up my arm and shield my eyes from the bright headlights. She manuever the jeep so that it's parked out of the way of our vehicles being pulled in and out of the garage. She hops out of the driver side and then comes rushing over. Logan releases me from his arms as Mariah approaches and throws her arms, full force, around me.

"Oh, Amarah, I'm so, so sorry for your loss," she squeezes me tightly.

"I'm sorry for your loss, too," I say, as I hug her back.

I can't help but feel a little bit ashamed of the fact that Mariah knew Ana way better than I did. They probably had more of the aunt/niece relationship than we did. She was my only family, my true blood family, and I never took the time to get to know her. I never made the effort to see her other than when The Unseen demanded action. And now it's too late. I lost any chance I had.

Mariah finally pulls back, wiping tears off her cheeks, "I'm here for whatever you need as long as you need."

"Thank you, Mariah, I really appreciate that," I say with a smile. "We really do need to be going though, do you have everything you need?"

"Yes, go, go, I'll be fine," she reassures me.

I nod, "thank you, again. I'll be in touch when I can."

"Okay. Don't worry, we'll be fine here."

I nod once again and then walk to my car, get in, and start the engine. It roars to life, the engine purring with excitement. It's almost as if my car can sense my urgency and knows I'm about to unleash all four hundred and twenty-six horsepower.

My phone connects to the Bluetooth and *The Resistance* by Skillet comes on loud and clear through the speakers. It's so on point and accurate of this moment that I can't help but think of one thing.

Destiny.

And not just destiny.

Divine Destiny.

I am exactly where I need to be right now. I am on the right path, and as long as I keep my Faith, I'll get where I need to. I just need to remind myself that I may be in the driver's seat but I'm not the one navigating this life of mine.

I toss my phone to Logan, "you should probably hang on to that so I'm not distracted any more than I already am."

"You mean you're going to let me control the music?"

"Well, technically, it's all the music on *my* phone so, I mean, not really," I shrug. "But you can pretend," I wink at him.

Just as I'm reaching to put the car into reverse, something glints in the garage light and catches my attention. I keep the car in park and reach for it, holding it up to the light. Logan and I both stare at it and I suddenly know what we need to do. It's like a flashing neon sign just went off in my head.

"I know what we need to do," I whisper, a bit shaken and in awe of my revelation. The song, the ring. Everything is speaking loud and clear and I'm so thankful I'm listening.

"What do you mean?" Logan asks, looking between me and the ring.

"This belongs to Lucifer," I explain. "This is what we can use to anchor him here, to this plane, so that I can have enough time to take my power back."

"How do you know this will work?"

"I don't. I mean, not based on any type of experience or knowledge of magic, but... I just do. As sure as I know that I love you with everything I have, I know that this will work."

I know this will work to anchor Lucifer here, but what I don't tell Logan, what I don't want to admit out loud, is that I still don't know how to get my power back. I can sense it, I can feel it calling to me, but I have no idea how to actually reach it. How to claim it. But... one thing at a time.

Logan reaches up and takes the ring from between my fingers. He holds my hand and then slides the ring securely onto my middle finger.

"We don't want to lose it," he explains. He leans over and kisses me, a sweet, soft kiss. "I love you too, Angel. Now let's go and get your power back."

I head in the general direction of where we're going. I know that the Water Fey live in or around Bottomless Lakes, but I have no idea how to actually find them. Logan continues to give me directions as we get close.

"So, what exactly do you know about this place?" Logan asks.

I shrug, "honestly, not much. Emrick mentioned that the rip is located in a cave somewhere underneath the lake which, now that I'm thinking about it, how exactly is that possible?"

He lifts an eyebrow and looks at me like, *really, Amarah?* But he tells me anyway. "Well, the lake is over land, obviously. There are tunnels into the cave where the rip is being hidden. That's one reason why it can't truly be guarded completely. There are too many tunnels to manage, just like Headquarters.

"Oh," is all I can manage to say, still reeling from it all.

"There's only the one lake that's accessible to the public and used for swimming but there are actually nine lakes total, all surrounded by high cliffs, and eight of them are a part of the State

Park." He continues to educate me.

"Wow, I didn't know that. I grew up around here and I never knew that," I say, baffled.

Logan pulls up a photo on his phone and shows me an aerial view picture of the lakes.

"Huh," I mutter. "It looks like a poke cake."

"A what?"

My eyes widen in shock as I look over to Logan, "you don't know what a poke cake is?"

He chuckles, "no, Angel, I don't know what a poke cake is."

"Wow, ok, well, we are definitely going to have to remedy *that* situation as soon possible, but what I mean is, the Earth looks like a freshly baked cake and someone came along and poked holes right down the middle of it, and then filled the holes with water. That's what that looks like," I gesture to the picture.

Logan tilts his head slightly, studying the picture, "huh. Yeah, I guess it does."

"Anyway, you said only eight of the nine lakes are a part of the State Park so, what about the ninth one?"

"The ninth one belongs to the Fey. The Queen purchased it under the guise of an environmentalist group called, The Fin and Feather Club. Of course, it's actually the home of the Vesi. It also happens to be the lake that sits furthest South, away from prying eyes, which is beneficial."

"All of the Fey homes are so well positioned and thought out. Actually, all of The Unseen is. It's crazy."

Logan just nods his head in agreement, "take this next right and follow this road all the way to the end."

I do as I'm told and slow the car down to take a right onto a narrow, paved road. The sky is starting to brighten as dawn approaches. I can see some small patches of snow that are clinging to shadowy areas, but mostly the weather is clear. The further South we drive from Albuquerque, the hotter or, at least milder, the weather gets. I'm thankful for it since my car isn't the best vehicle to have in icy conditions. Something I didn't quite think through when I demanded that I drive. No need to fuss about that now that we're here.

As I come out of a bend in the road, I notice smoke billowing up from ahead. "Logan? Do you see the smoke?"

"Yes," his says, his voice hard and eyes locked on the smoke up ahead.

I park where he tells me to and we get out of the car. The smell of smoke immediately clings to me and pushes up my nose and down my throat. I turn in a slow circle, taking in my surroundings. My heart starts to race and there's a sinking feeling in my stomach as I take in the damage. There's evidence of a fire, or several fires, having just been put out. The Earth is scorched and trees and bushes have been burnt down completely, smoke still rising from their hot remains. It reminds me of how the Fire Fey's home looked after the demon attack.

As I look more closely, I see that the ground is also covered in a mixture of the dark, thick substances that comes from demons, and blood. Regular, red, Fey blood. But where are they? Where are the ones who have been injured? Have they been taken inside? I hate to think about the worst, but what about dead bodies? I can only imagine some Fey did not survive this attack. I can only imagine what these grounds would look like if demon bodies didn't disintegrate and get sent back to Hell. I shudder.

"Logan," my voice is gripped tight with dread, "this doesn't look good."

He doesn't comment on the destruction we see. Instead, he holds his hand out for me, "c'mon, let's go inside and see how we can help."

I quickly take his offered hand and wrap my other arm

around his, clinging tightly to him as he leads us inside. I walk into what would normally look like any business's front office. A waiting area with a few chairs, a table, and some magazines. The front desk is high, reaching up to my chest and would be successful in hiding anyone sitting behind it. Except, a simple, clean, white space is not at all what I see.

The front desk has chunks missing out of it, scorch marks and deep claw marks marring its entirety. The table and chairs are tossed around the room in burnt, broken pieces. Blood, both dark black thickness and red liquid, are splattered across the walls like someone came in here and just started throwing buckets of paint at the walls. There's too much blood. There's way too much.

Logan leads me to the opening behind the desk. The door that once hid the opening from view is lying broken on the floor and we carefully pick our way over the jagged wooden pieces sticking out here and there. Then, before I know it, I'm being guided down a dark, narrow staircase. The walls turn into hard packed Earth the deeper we go.

Once again, I'm in a labyrinth of underground tunnels just like Headquarters has. I'm disoriented and have no idea where we are or how I'd even get back. We still haven't passed anyone and that worries me.

We finally emerge into a huge open cavern and we're both immediately struck with absolute devastation. The ground is strewn with bodies, all lined up next to each other, covering the entire cavern floor. Hundreds of bodies.

Dead bodies.

Men.

Women.

Children.

My hands come to my mouth and I run back in the direction we just came from. I make it a few steps before I double over and throw up all the contents, which is not much thankfully, from my stomach. I squeeze my eyes closed against the horror, praying that what I just saw isn't real. Praying that I don't have to turn around and go back in there. Praying that this is all a terrible, terrible nightmare, and that Lucifer didn't just destroy the entire Vesi Family.

I finally manage to stand up straight, using the wall to keep me on my feet. I look over my shoulder and Logan is standing in the spot that I left him in, staring blankly out over the room. I can't imagine what he must be feeling. He knew some, if not all, of these people. I didn't know them personally and the sight of it is the worst thing I've ever seen in my life. I'm gutted. My heart hurts in my chest. I've never seen anything like this and, honestly, I think I'm in shock.

I finally get my legs steady enough to carry me back to Logan's side but I hesitate. I don't want to look into that room again. I don't want to see it, to face this God awful, ugly reality. This unnecessary evil. I want to be anywhere else in the world than right here, right now. But I can't run away from this. This is my life, these are people, whether I knew them or not. They've sacrificed everything trying to keep the rest of us safe. They deserve to be seen.

So, I slowly walk back to Logan's side, shoulders pushed back and held head high. I look into the room again and let my eyes scan over each body closest to me. I look at their faces, one by one, each hero that died trying to stop Hell on Earth. Their glamour has been stripped away in death. Each body is adorned with beautiful, iridescent scales, but their beauty has been disfigured by burns and gashes. Blood, ash, and dirt cover their bodies in varying amounts, but there's not one body that has been spared.

Movement on the other side of the room draws my attention. I see Emrick and Theo carrying another limp body between them. They lay the body down next to another one, their faces are distraught and portray everything I feel. I know we need to move, to help in any way that we can. I look up at Logan and he's still staring out over the room, unmoving, but his eyes are glossed over. I don't think he's here with me right now. I mean, physically he is, but he's seeing something beyond this room. I've never seen Logan like this. I've never seen him react this way. He's always been my rock, my strength, the one to face everything with a brave face and reassuring words.

I move to stand in front of him and take his face in my hands. I gently pull his face down, towards me, and speak loudly but softly. "Logan, hey, I need you to look at me."

He blinks, his eyes focus and land on mine. We stand like this, just staring at each other for a while. I can't say what he's thinking or feeling, but I'm memorizing his handsome face, I'm thanking God for bringing him into my life and for the miracle of both of us standing here alive when so many others have paid the ultimate sacrifice.

"I'm here for you," I say, as I look into his haunted eyes. "Whatever you need, I'm here. You're not alone anymore, Logan. Just like everything that's happened before, and everything that will happen in the future, we're going to get through this, together." I repeat the words that he's said to me so many times.

He finally moves. He reaches up and caresses my cheek with his thumb, grabbing my face gently. "Together. Always."

"Always," I smile up at him. "Now, I need Braveheart to make an appearance because I definitely can't handle this alone."

I see his throat roll on a hard swallow but he nods his head. "I'm here."

He reaches for my hand and we both turn and walk down the narrow pathway that's been left between bodies and leads to the back of the room. Emrick and Theo are still standing there, waiting for us. They must have seen us when we were talking.

As we approach them, I realize I don't even know what to

say. I have no words inside of me for this moment. For what I've seen. For what I'm feeling. I can't even imagine how they're feeling, and how they've managed to remain moving and sane, I can't even fathom. And what about Vadin? These are his people, his family.

"Vadin?" I ask, once we're finally in front of them.

That's' the only thing I can manage to ask. I can't string together a proper sentence. I can't ask, how is he doing? Of course he's not ok. None of us are ok.

Emrick sighs, "he's holding it together. For the survivors."

My heart aches in my chest at the news, "there are survivors?"

"Not many," Emrick shakes his head. "Some managed to hide and some are alive but wounded badly. The Healer managed to hide in time, with a handful of others, mostly kids. She can use all the help she can get, Amarah, if you can try to heal as much as you can. I know you don't have your power and not much experience but..."

"I'll do whatever I can," I interrupt him. "Take me to them."

Emrick nods and we follow him and Theo through an archway, down a short hallway, until we emerge into a smaller cavern. It's bustling with quiet, urgent energy. I see a group of kids huddled together, eyes wide in shock and fear. Some of the older kids are helping the Healer. I see them hurrying back and forth with clean cloths, removing blood-stained clothes and replacing bandages, giving survivors water, and holding their hands.

My eyes find Vadin. He's kneeling next to one of the survivors, holding his hand and providing whatever comfort he can. He's Leading what's left of his people, during one of the most devastating situations, when I'm sure he'd rather be grieving all the lives lost. But he's not. He's standing strong. He's showing no fear, no sorrow, no weakness. And my resect for him grows immensely. He's the only Leader I don't know, but in this moment, I know everything I need to about him.

I tear my eyes away from him and walk to the nearest survivor. I kneel down beside her. She looks like she's no older than nineteen or twenty. Her blue eyes are wide with fear and pain. Her dark brown hair is plastered to her head and side of her face by blood and sweat. It's hard to see her injuries because she's covered in blood, dirt, and grime.

"I need clean water and cloth," I say out loud to anyone who's listening." I hear Theo say he's on it. I manage to keep my face neutral as I hold her terrified gaze, "my name is Amarah Rey Andrews, niece of the Queen and descendant of the Müstik Family. I'm going to do everything I can to help you."

I see the first signs of hope filter through the fear in her eyes as she slowly nods her head. I may no longer have my Angel power, but I am still an Angel, and I am still Fey. I still have power within me and I just need to access it and use it. I close my eyes and open myself up completely to my Faith. Just as I'm not in control of my destiny, I know I'm not in control of this situation either.

I pray. I pray to God. I pray to Michael. I pray to my mother and to Ana. I ask for them to guide me. To help me in this moment to save this girl's life. To show me how. To show me what to do. And then I feel it. I feel hands slide on top of my own. I feel something deep inside of myself unlock. A whole new part of me that I didn't even know existed until now. My Fey essence.

I've been so focused on my Angel power that I didn't even realize there was more inside of me. More to who I am than just half of what makes me, me. The other half is here now, showing itself to me and helping to fill that void that was left when I gave up my power to Lucifer.

This new Fey essence slowly unravels inside of me, flooding out from the center of my body and into my limbs. It tingles all the way down my arms and into my very fingertips. The hands that are laid on top of mine began to move, guiding me, leading me to where I need to be, and then that tingling sensation is pushing past my fingertips and into this young girl's broken body. And once my Fey power settles within me, within this girl, I know what I need to do.

I start to heal her.

Logan: Past, Present & Future

Yours by Russell Dickerson

I swear, there's not a minute that goes by that Amarah doesn't cease to amazing me in the best possible ways. I don't know how she managed to do it, but she was healing people like she's been healing people her entire life. For once, I felt so useless, as I stood back, completely enamored, and watched her work.

She healed people for hours, took time to help clean their wounds, and just talked to them. She asked them questions about themselves, to help distract them from their current situation, and to get to know them. I remember just thinking one thing.

God, she's beautiful.

And not just her face, not just her body, but who she is. She's beautiful from the inside out. She's far from perfect, no one on this Earth is, but she's perfect to me. She's perfect in the way she's selfless and helps others. She's perfect in the way she cares so much about this world, and protecting it, even though she doesn't even know it. She's perfect in the way she admits her mistakes. She's perfect in the way she looks at me. She's perfect in the way she fits against my body. She's perfect in the way I fit inside of her. She's perfect in so many ways I'll never be able to explain them all with words.

"Why are you staring at me like that?" She asks, as she blushes slightly and gives me a shy smile.

I'm leaning against the bathroom door jam, right where her beauty stopped me in my tracks, watching her lovingly. She's sitting on the end of the bed, wrapped in a towel, brushing out her long, wet hair.

"I was just momentarily stunned by your beauty," I admit.

Her blush depends but she doesn't look away from me. I love that I still have this effect on her. I hope I always will. I smirk as I stalk towards her, her eyes finally leave mine and travel down my body. Her throat bobs and her lips part. I can hear the change in the rhythm of her heart beats.

My smirk turns into a cocky grin, fuck, she's bad for my ego, but I fucking love the way she looks at me and responds to me. I come to a stop in front of her, she has to lean her head back to continue looking at me.

"Logan, did you...*see* anything...when I was healing those people?"

I cock my head to the side, studying her, "what do you mean?"

"I mean like, did you see anything weird or suspicious? Did you maybe see any other auras around me or...anything, really?"

"No, Angel, I only saw you doing something extremely amazing. Why do you ask? What happened?"

"I felt another set of hands on mine, guiding me and showing me what to do. I just had this sensation that Ana was there with me, helping me. Is that...strange?"

"Not at all, Angel. I believe she was with you and will always be there to help you."

She nods and smiles sadly.

I grab her cheek and she leans into my touch, "please don't

take this the wrong way," I warn her, "but you look tired. You healed people for hours today, not to mention the emotional toll of what you've seen. You need to rest."

She lets out a heavy sigh and her shoulders slump into the motion. "I am tired. I'm exhausted. But I don't think I'll be able to sleep after what I've seen today."

"Let me help you relax."

Her eyes narrow on mine and then drop to my lips, where they stay, "what did you have in mind?" Her voice is lower, desire taking its hold.

I chuckle, "not *that*."

She looks back up, her brows drawn together in confusion.

"I'm going to give you a massage. Take the towel off and lie down on your stomach," I not to the bed.

I expect her to argue but she doesn't. She opens the towel and scoots up, further onto the bed. Once she's in the middle, she pulls her hair over her shoulder, turns around, and lays on her stomach, her face turned to the side, and her arms relaxed next to her.

I walk back into the bathroom to grab some lotion. We don't have any kind of oil but lotion will work. I drop my own towel to the floor and climb onto the bed, straddling her thighs. The scar where the hook entered her back is still pink and healing compared to the jagged white scars slicing across her back from a demon attack. The scars don't bother me. They're just another sign of her strength and perseverance.

I squeeze a large amount of lotion into my palm and rub my hands together, warming it, and then I lean over place my hands on her body. Both of my hands span the width of her back. How can someone so small be larger than life? I start low on her back and slide my hands slowly up to her shoulders, giving her back a nice coating of lotion before I start to knead my hands into her tired muscles. I start with her shoulders and she immediately starts to moan her pleasure into the comforter.

Fuck.

I realize this wasn't the best idea. My hands gliding across her slick skin, squeezing her and rubbing her, her moans of pleasure, all have me hard within seconds. I maintain my control and work my way down each of her arms, massaging her palms and each individual finger, then I start to make my way down her back. Once I reach her ass and the tops of her thighs, her moans begin to change. They go from, completely relaxed and enjoying the massage to, I love the way your hands feel on my body.

I move my hands between her thighs, getting incredible close to her core, but not touching it. I move her legs so I can kneel between them and keep the massage going down each of her legs, but having her legs spread, leaves me with a view of her beautiful fucking pussy. My mouth is watering to taste her, my fingers itching to sink into her folds, my cock twitches at the need to push inside of her. I still manage to hold onto my control until I've massaged all the way down to her toes and am working my way back up. Once I'm done, I focus once again on her ass. I knead and rub her ass, sliding my hands closer and closer to her center.

Her moans are louder now, her breathing heavy and I can smell her desire. I can't hold myself back any longer and finally slide my finger over her pussy. My finger sinks into the wetness already pooling there. She groans and lifts her hips up higher, giving me better access.

I slide my finger over her clit and she moans my name into the mattress, her arms no longer relaxed by her sides but clenching the comforter in her fists.

"Fuck, Amarah, you drive me so fucking crazy," I say, as I continue to rub her clit. "I want you so fucking bad."

"I want you too," she breathes. "No foreplay, just give it to me."

Most of the time, I live for the foreplay. I love to make her feel good. Sometimes I enjoy the tease and drawing out her pleasure, but right now, I just need to be inside of her.

I push her legs back together and straddle her again. This time I grab my cock and rub it up and down between her cheeks, amazed at how big I look against her and how her body manages to take all of me inside of her.

"Logan, please," she begs.

"Hold yourself open for me," I demand.

She reaches back and spreads her cheeks, allowing me to see everything. I reach between her legs and soak my fingers with her desire, then rub them over the head of my cock, lubricating it so I can slide in easier. I guide myself to her opening and start to push into her. She gasps as the head of my cock stretches her open. I can see every centimeter of my dick disappearing inside of her from this position.

"Fuck," I groan. "I really wish you could see this, Amarah. It's so fucking sexy the way your body takes me."

I move her hands and let mine take their place, holding her open as I push further inside of her and then back out. I'm only giving her the first couple of inches of my dick, letting my thick head push into her again and again, savoring her gasp every time my tip sinks into her.

I can always feel when she's close to cuming. Her pussy gets so fucking wet as she builds up to her release. I can feel it happening now and she's panting and gripping the comforter, desperately holding on to something physical as her body starts to soar.

"Fuck, I love how even just the tip of my dick can make you cum. Are you going to cum all over my dick, Amarah?"

"Yes, don't stop, Logan. Don't stop," she says through heavy breaths. He body starts to shake and I feel the orgasm release inside of her. "Oh, fuck," she groans.

I lift her hips higher and finally push all the way inside of her. I grip her ass and drive my dick into her again and again, all the way in and all the way out. Her body seems to fight me every time I try to pull out, hugging me and refusing to let me go. Fuck, she's so fucking tight.

I growl as I try to fight off my orgasm. I want to draw out this feeling for as long as I can. She feels so good and I never want this pleasure to end. I want to slide in and out of her pussy for the rest of my fucking life.

"Damn, you're so hard. I can feel how hard you are."

"This is all you, Amarah, you make me this fucking hard."

"Let me feel all of it. Fuck me harder, Logan," she demands.

God damn it! Her words almost make me cum, but I bite it back and pull her to her knees, determined to give her everything she asks for.

I reach forward and wrap her hair around my fist. I pull her head back, arching her back, and it's so fucking sexy, as I slam my length into her. She moans louder and louder, panting, "yes, yes, yes," every time I'm balls deep inside of her.

"You're going to make me cum again," her voice comes out strangled through her strained neck.

I keep her head pulled back and I spank her, the smack cracks loudly through the room and she screams in pleasure. I do it again as I fuck her, hard, my hips coming into contact with her ass with every thrust. I feel her pussy spasm around me, coating my dick with her pleasure. I spank her one more time before I let go of her hair and grip her hips tightly as I pump inside of her again and again and again, until I feel like I'm breaking apart inside of her.

"Oh, Shiiiiiit," I groan, as the orgasm explodes out of me.

I swear I fucking cum for ten Goddamn minutes before I'm finally spent. I somehow manage to walk to the bathroom to hang up

Our wet towels and to get a towel to clean myself and Amarah up with. Once I'm done, I climb onto the bed and hug Amarah close to me. Cuddling with her after sex is one of the best things I've ever felt in my life. Love and sex. One and the same with her and I love every minute of it.

We also tend to have some of our deepest conversation while we're cuddled up, satiated, and relaxed together. It's like all of the walls come down and it's just raw, open, and honest. Today's no different. Amarah is so relaxed in my arms that I think she must be asleep, but her low, sexy voice finally breaks our silence.

"Logan?"

"Hmmm?"

"Today," she starts, but then seems to hesitate.

"What about today, Angel?" I try to reassure her, let her know that there's not anything she can't ever say to me or ask me. I don't ever want her afraid to speak what's on her mind.

"When we walked in and saw those bodies…" she hesitates again, I'm sure she's replaying that awful moment in her mind and I wish I could take it from her so she never has to see it ever again. "I've never seen you respond like that to anything. Why did it effect you the way it?"

I heave a sigh, "it brought back a lot of memories and none of them are good."

"Your past?" She asks, softly.

"Yes, Angel, someone I never want to be again."

"Will you please tell me about it?"

I brush my fingers against her temple, smoothing her hair in a short, repeated stroke. Sometimes just this small act of touching her, comforting her, is actually more beneficial for me. It comforts me. Having her close and being able to be someone with her that I've never been with anyone else. Someone vulnerable and someone who can show their emotions so freely. It's such a drastic change from the man I was. The man I'm scared I still am.

"I'll tell you anything you want to know, Angel, always. All you have to do is ask, and if it's in my power to give you, it's yours. So, yes, I'll tell you." I let out another heavy sigh, preparing myself for a trip down memory lane that's not going to be easy to face. No matter how much time passes, it's never easy to face.

"I won't get into too much detail but you'll get the overall idea."

"Ok, whatever you want to share, I'm ready to listen."

"You know what happened with Analise." I feel her nod her head, "well, after she died the way that she did, in front of me, and after my Pack decided I was no longer Pure and could not remain a part of the Pack and exiled me, I was completely lost. Lost and angry. Everything I had ever known and loved was taken from me within a couple of months. With nowhere to go, nowhere to call home, I wandered. I travelled all over the world but nowhere I visited ever felt like it could be a home for me. I met other Packs along the way too but none would take me in. Everyone was too afraid of how strong I was and what I could do. I was too different."

"I'm so sorry, Logan," she whispers against my chest.

"This left me with a lot of time to myself. A lot of time with no one but my Wolf. I think that's why he and I are so connected and I have such good control over him. Because we've always only had each other. But, after a while, we both became restless. Again, the anger of being cast out and rejected again, and again, and again, finally caught up to us."

"The first war I ever become a part of was a small war called, King Phillip's War, around 1675. I didn't even know the reason for the war. I didn't care who was right or who was wrong. I didn't care which side I was even fighting on. All I wanted to do was fight and release my pent-up anger. If I couldn't kill my Pack or the Packs that continued to reject me, then I'd kill aimlessly as part of a war that was going to be slaughtering people anyways, whether I was a part of it or not."

"The next war effort I joined was the Pueblo Revolt, in 1680, then The Great Turkish War, War of the Spanish Succession, and on and on and on. I just kept moving after wars were done. I couldn't exactly stay in one place for too long, not when I don't age, and not when some men saw some thing they weren't supposed to see. So, I just kept moving. Moving and killing. Those battlefields, Amarah," I shake my head as I remember the screams of agony and the stench of blood, shit, and piss.

"I haven't just killed, Amarah, I've *slaughtered*. Thousands, upon thousands, I've taken countless lives, all because I was lonely and angry at the unfairness of the world. I haven't seen anything like that for a long time. The last war I was a part of was World War I, so it's been over a hundred years since I've seen death like that, but today…" I sigh again. "I wish I could take that vision away from you so that you never have to be haunted by it ever again."

She moves to rest her chin on her hands, on top of my chest, and looks up at me with her beautiful, sad hazel eyes. "I don't think anything could have ever prepared me for what I saw today, and I don't think there will ever be a time when it doesn't haunt me, but you can't protect me from this world, Logan. You can't protect me from the cruelties of life."

"I know that," I brush her hair back behind her ear, "but I would if I could."

"Thank you for sharing your past with me. I'm so sorry that you've been alone, Logan."

"I would take another thousand years of it if it meant I still got you in the end, Angel. You've changed me in ways that no one ever could, not even myself. I'm forever grateful and indebted to you, and I plan to make it up to you for hundreds of years to come, by loving you as fiercely as I possible can."

She smiles and I swear it both cracks my heart and heals it all at the same time. "You don't owe me anything more than I owe you, but I'll take hundreds of years of you loving me... and fucking me," her smile widens, "any day."

I growl and spin her around, causing her to let out a little yip of surprise before she laughs brightly. I'm on top of her now, looking down into her beautiful, smiling face. Her eyes, although still showing a hint of sadness, are also full of life and love. God, how did she become my entire world over night?

"How did I get so lucky?" I ask, as I stare into her eyes from inches away.

"I keep asking myself that same question," she replies.

"I love you, Angel."

"I love you too, Braveheart."

And then there are no more words as my mouth falls onto hers and I push myself inside of her.

Valmont: Never Enough

You & Me by Memphis May Fire

If I had known how many boring meetings I'd have to attend becoming an ally to the Fey I'd have never agreed to it. Ok, perhaps that's a lie, I think I would have agreed to anything just to get closer to Amarah Rey. Nothing's changed since then, and yet, everything's changed.

But this meeting is far from boring. It's sad. And I'd take boring over sad any day. As a Leader for the Vampires in my Territory, I understand the immense responsibility to not only do what's best for those who depend on you, but also to keep them safe. Although this particular situation is one that no Leader, no matter how spectacular, could have seen coming or prevented. Still, I know that doesn't matter. I know Vadin is taking each and every single loss personally, and honestly, I don't know how he's managing to remain in such control of his emotions. Had this happened to my people I'd be on a rampage.

Nevertheless, here we are once again. Meeting and discussing our next steps. Our plan of action, which honestly, is always a plan of *reaction*. Then again, how could anyone have predicted this attack?

This time, everyone is here. Ethan has finally maned up and joined us along with Kaedon and Atreya, Princess Hallana is here with a handful of her people. More Fey from the Maa Family have come to provide support alongside Emrick, and Jon has come with some Air Fey, along with myself and some of my best Vampires, and a handful of Witches lead by their new Ülim, whom is speaking right now.

"I will reach out to the other Covens in the area and we will spread the word to not only be on the lookout for demons, but to hunt them down, if they can."

"Thank you, Brynn," Amarah Rey says, gratefully. "Any help we can get to spread the word as far and wide as possible, the better. I highly doubt Lucifer's plan is to remain in our area, though, we will be the center of the attacks no doubt. Are there other Fey, Werewolf, and Vampire regions we can contact to spread the word?" Amarah Rey looks around the room expectantly.

Ethan nods, "I can reach out to neighboring Packs."

"The Queen did keep communications open with other Fey Queens in the United States and even some abroad. I'm sure her information can be found at Headquarters," Hallana informs us.

I've been half-ass listening to plans being made, too busy staring at Amarah Rey...and Logan. Of course, they're sitting next to each other, his hand is draped around the back of her chair and his fingertips are making light circles on the back of her shoulder. I absolutely despise the fact that he gets to touch her whenever he wishes, however he wishes. I want to bite every single one of his fingers off and spit them back out in his smug face.

"Valmont?" Her attention falls to me, "what about the Vampires?"

"I can make some calls but don't expect too much excitement from Vampires of other regions. Remember, fire can kill us so, we aren't too keen on seeking demons out," I shrug, nonchalantly, as if nothing in the world is bothering me. "But I'll make the calls."

"Okay," she sighs. "There's really not much we can do other than post a good amount of protection here, at the rip, and go out and hunt the demons that have already crossed. Hopefully, we can make a big enough impact and not see too much damage."

"There's already been incidents pouring in on the news," Iseta shares with the group. "I've been monitoring it closely and the chaos has already started. Mass shootings, and stabbings, fights and vandalism. It's like everyone is acting on their worst urges and the evil is escalating at an increasingly fast rate. We need to do all we can to intervene as much and as soon as possible before it truly does become, Hell on Earth."

"Vadin, I'm going to leave the logistics up to you and the other Leaders," Amarah Rey says. "I'm going to work with Iseta, Brynn and a few Witches to try getting my power back again. Once I have that, I can finally work on figuring out how to close the rip once and for all."

"We'll take care of it," Vadin nods.

Everyone seems to start talking all at once but my eyes remain on Amarah Rey. She immediately turns to Logan and I fucking hate everything about it. How she looks at him. How she touches him. How she smiles at him. How she listens to him. Everything about her with him, I fucking hate.

As everyone starts to disburse, I turn my attention to Alistair, "I need a minute. Handle the rest for me."

"Of course, Boss."

I approach Amarah Rey before she can disappear. "Amarah Rey, may I have a few moments?"

She looks up at me, a bit wide eyed and startled. A part of me, a very small part, feels bad for how I acted last time she asked to talk. Again, if I was a better man...

"Oh, ummmm," she hesitates and looks at Logan, who is

glued to her side, possessively.

"If you have something to say, you say it in front of both of us," Logan speaks for her.

I sigh, annoyed at the entire situation but seeing no way around it. I mean, I could insist but, what I'm about to say, he should probably hear anyway. "I need just a small amount of privacy, but you can stay close, with your eyes and ears on everything I have to say if that makes you feel better."

"I don't think so," he insists.

"Logan," Amarah Rey chides him. "I appreciate your need to keep me safe but I think what Valmont is requesting is fair. It won't really be private when you can see and hear what's going on."

"Fine," he concedes, angrily.

That makes two of us.

Logan leads us down a couple of hallways until he stops in front of a door. "This is the most privacy you'll be able to get with everyone walking around here. I'll be right here, just on the other side of the door and if I hear *anything* I don't like, you will not like the outcome."

"Logan, please," Amarah Rey puts her hand on his arm in an attempt to quell his irritation. "Enough people have died and he's just asking to talk, with you right outside the door. Please, trust me."

He's glaring at me, his eyes burning with hatred. I know I'm giving him nothing but a blank slate in return which, I'm sure, is only making him angrier. He finally looks down at her and his eyes soften immediately. It's like he's two entirely different Logans within the span of three seconds.

"Alright, Angel. I do trust you. I'll be right here," he leans down and kisses her.

Of course, she kisses him back, and my heart feels like it's going to rupture inside my chest. I clear my throat and open the door, holding it for Amarah Rey to enter, still hoping that I'm giving none of my emotions away but not entirely sure it's possible at this point.

She steps away from him and he grabs her hand, "I'll be right here."

She nods and walks into the room, slowly letting go of his hand, as if it's the hardest thing in the world for her to do. Just another shot to my already wounded heart.

I follow her into the room and shut the door behind me. The illusion of privacy isn't at all comforting, knowing what I have planned, and having Logan hear every damn word but... I'll take what I can get.

Amarah Rey has stopped a few steps into the room and turns to face me, arms crossed over her stomach. She looks so unsure and nervous and I hate that I've made her feel this way. Yet another reason why I'm here.

I take my time admiring her. I roam my eyes over every inch of her beautiful face, down her delicate neck, and onto her shoulders and chest, dipping lower until I've made it all the way down to her feet and back up again. Gods, I wish she was naked and I could look at her perfect body one more time.

She clears her throat, "so, what did you want to talk about?"

I meet her eyes and I see the change in them. I see the need mirroring my own. But no, that's not right, is it? It's a craving for something I can give her. Not for me.

I slowly approach her and stop right in front of her, too close to be considered just friendly. "I promise you, I'm not going to do what I did last time. I'm not going to put you, as you put it, in an impossible situation."

"Okay," she breathes out, still hugging herself tightly.

"To be honest, I don't even know where to start," I smile sadly down at her.

"Valmont, what is it?" She asks, genuinely concerned. "What's wrong?"

"If you really have to ask, then you didn't believe a word I said."

"I did believe you, Valmont. I *do* believe you."

"Then you know that I'm in love with you. That you're the best thing that's ever happened to me since I became a Vampire. Bloody Hell, maybe even before then, because I don't recall ever loving *anyone* as a human."

"Valmont..."

"Please, Amarah Rey, let me finish."

I see the roll of her throat as she swallows down her argument, probably even whatever craving she's starting to fight being this close to me.

"The way you've made me feel these past weeks has been truly amazing. A gift. I've literally been brought back to life and felt and experienced things that I haven't for over two thousand years. Although, it's temporary, and I can only ever feel these things again with your blood in my veins, I'm still incredible grateful to you for allowing me the chance to live again, even briefly."

Amarah Rey's eyes have started to water and, like always, her tears crush me. I hate to see her in any type of pain or discomfort. But I need to cause her just a little bit of pain, so she can feel a small amount of what I feel, before I take it away.

I sigh, "although, I must admit, it is a double-edged sword, that's for certain. I've tasted what it feels like to love, I've felt the sun on my skin, and my heart beating in my chest, only to have to let it go all over again, for a second time. It's just as torturous as it is invigorating."

"I didn't mean..."

I finally reach up and touch her. I caress her cheek and she relaxes just the slightest bit at my touch. "Amarah Rey, I'm not telling you this to make you feel badly. I just want you to understand, that's all."

"Okay," she repeats, her voice a soft whisper.

"I thought, perhaps, that you and I would have a chance, a *real* chance to see what might happen between us. I know that you don't love me the way that I love you, but is it so impossible to think that maybe one day you could? Maybe one day, if things were different, I truly believe you could."

A lone tear falls down her cheek and I let it run over my finger. I don't wipe it away. "It's not impossible to believe, Valmont, if things were different."

I sigh, "I see the way you look at him, Amarah Rey. I see the way you give him everything, without hesitation. I see the way you look at him and I know, just by one simple look, just how much you love him because… it's the same way I look at you."

Her tears are falling freely now.

"As much as it pains me to say this, Logan is a good man, and he's incredible lucky to be the recipient of your love. Of your heart. I also see the way he looks at you, Amarah Rey, and I know that he truly loves you in return." I grab her face with both of my hands now, "and I'm not a good man, Amarah Rey, but bloody Hell I'm trying to be. I'm only going to attempt this to see if it works so, please, mate, don't break the door down and come barging in like a wild animal. I promise, when I'm done, you'll thank me," I say to the Werewolf eavesdropping but my attention hasn't drifted from Amarah Rey's stunningly beautiful hazel eyes.

I hold her gaze and let my eyes start to glow. I call on my power of hypnosis. "You want to kiss me," I instruct her.

She immediately unhooks her arm from around her body and traces them up my chest as she stands on her tiptoes, trying to reach me. I close my eyes at the sensation of her hands on me, one last time. And if I was a better man, I'd stop it now, but of course, I'm no such thing.

I lean down and I meet her for the kiss. Gods, her lips are a drug. I could stay locked up forever, taking hit after hit, surviving off of her kiss forever. I open my mouth and invite her to make the kiss more, but I let her take the lead. She doesn't let me down and slips her tongue into my mouth. I can't help the groan that escapes from the ache in my chest. I kiss her softly, gently, dragging out each movement, each long caress of her tongue on mine, each press of her lips against mine. I hug her body tightly to mine, feeling it pressed against me with such want, such desire. I can feel it in the way she's kissing me back. I never want to let her go but that's exactly what I'm about to do.

Forever.

I reluctantly pull away from the kiss and she lowers herself back to the floor but she's still looking up at me with need in her eyes. Craving more.

"You're so utterly devastating, Amarah Rey, just like I knew you would be."

She scrunches her eyebrows together, "I don't understand."

"I know," I say, as I continue to hold her face in my hands. As I continue to try and memorize every single little detail about her in this moment. "I'm prepared to spend the rest of my life, however long that may be, a hundred years, a thousand, loving you, but we both know it would be in vain. I can give you everything I have, all of my love, all of my attention, all of my laughs," I smile sadly. "I would happily empty myself to fill you up, and we both know, it would never be enough. *I* will never be enough. I will never hold the love you crave. The love that you so desperately love back."

"Valmont, you are enough, you..."

I don't let her finish. I don't want to hear anything she might say to make me lose my nerve. To make me believe that maybe, just maybe, there's a chance. Because I know in my heart, there never will be.

My eyes start to glow again, "Amarah Rey, we had one night

of pleasure in my office. It was after you thought Logan was sleeping with Atreya. It meant nothing to either of us. You no longer crave my bite or any Vampire's bite. You're not addicted to it even a little. You will forget the night in the Penthouse and you will forget every word I ever spoke to you of feelings. We are allies, nothing more. You trust me with your life, you know I would never do anything to hurt you, and if you ever need to give me your blood again, for any reason, you will refuse to let me take it from your vein. The mere thought of a Vampire biting you repulses you. People will say that I'm not a good person, I may do or say things that aren't good, but deep down in your heart, you'll know that I am."

I release my old on her and step away. I see the confusion in her eyes as the power of my hypnosis fades and she comes back to reality.

She wipes at her cheeks and laughs nervously, "why am I crying? And why are you and I alone in my room?"

"You just needed a breather after the meeting, everything you've been through has been hard to handle. I brought you here for some privacy but Logan should be here in any second." My voice is strained, it feels like my heart is clogging my throat and I can't breathe, but somehow, I manage to push through it.

The door opens and Logan steps inside. "Logan!" Amarah runs to him, wraps her arms around him and buries her face in his chest. He embraces her but he never takes his eyes off of me.

"I wasn't sure if it would work, and I'm not sure if it will hold once she gets her powers back," I admit.

"I understand," he says, voice calm. "Thank you."

"I didn't do it for you. I did it for her." I look at her one more time, wrapped in Logan's arms, and then I head for the door. Right before I leave, I stop in the doorway, but don't turn around as I speak. "If you *ever* hurt her, in any way, I will kill you and cut out your heart so there's no coming back."

I don't wait for a response and storm off to find Alistair. I need something to kill.

Amarah: Teamwork

Revival by Fight The Fade

Vadin has allowed us to use the common room space to attempt another summoning. It has the room we need and no one is going to be using it until this is all over. Until we hunt down all the demons, every single last one of them, and send them back to Hell for good.

"Thank you, Brynn, for coming on such short notice and for assisting in...well, everything."

"I meant what I said, Amarah, The Unseen needs to be united and I'm happy to do my part. We all are," she motions to the three other Witches she brought with her.

Iseta has still taken the lead on the spell, having been successful in it before, it makes sense to me. It doesn't seem to be bothering Brynn or the others. I like that about Brynn and her leadership. She's not insecure like Mae was.

"Alright," Iseta says, as she stands up from adding the final touches to the summoning circle. "Everything is ready."

"Amarah, can I see the ring, please?"

I slip it off my finger and hand it to her. "Do you really think it's going to work? To anchor him here?"

"I sure hope so," she sighs.

"It will work," Brynn says, confidently.

Iseta drops the ring into the bowl of blood, my blood for the anchoring spell, Logan's blood still being used for protection. I'm not sure why she's doing it this way, but again, I don't ask. She's the expert and I trust her entirely.

Iseta and Brynn begin to chant in unison over the bowl, adding this and that, and doing what Witches do best. Spell casting. Once they've completed the spell, Iseta returns the ring to me.

"Now, when we light the yellow candle with Lucifer's sigil, we need to pour the wax over the ring, ok? That's going to complete the binding and anchor him here, to that ring."

I nod, "got it."

"Ok, well, are we all ready?" Iseta asks, looking around the room and everyone nods and gives their confirmation.

"Ready or not," I sigh.

I move to stand next to the yellow candle on the outside of the summoning circle. Logan joins me, refusing to let me do this alone, and I appreciate him for it. Having him at my side while I face Lucifer makes me feel a hundred times better. Iseta and the others form a circle around us, the last Witch hits the lights, leaving us in a low glow from the five black candles in the summoning circle, and then she joins the circle and they all clasp hands.

This time, when Iseta starts the summoning chant, she's not alone. Five voices ring out, loud and clear, and I can't help but wonder what the significance of the number five is? Shouldn't it be six?

tenebris dominus
gehennae
i praesentiam vestram requiramus
Exite et videte me

"Now, Logan," Iseta instructs.

Logan reaches down for the yellow candle. He lights it and waits a few seconds for the wax to melt, and then he pours it onto the ring. I wince as the hot wax drips onto my skin, but the pain only lasts for a moment before the wax cools off and hardens. Logan returns the candle to the floor and then picks up the bell and rings it five times.

The wind is almost immediate, and the stench of sulphur rises up from the summoning circle. This time, I'm more prepared for it and don't have to bend over, gagging. I keep my head held high as Lucifer manifests inside of the summoning circle.

Lucifer sighs, "again, with the theatrics, Amarah? Have you learned nothing from our time together and our last meeting?"

"Actually, no. There's nothing that I can learn from you."

He raises an eyebrow, slides his hands into his pockets, and his voice is full of amusement when he says, "that's not at all what you said when you were practically begging me for guidance with all that wonderful darkness that lives inside of you. And don't try to deny it, Amarah. It's still there. You can't get rid of it."

"You're right, it is, and it always will be, but you're mistaken if you think that I want to get rid of it. It's a part of me, it helps make me who I am, but that's not all there is to me, and I don't have to be a slave to it."

"Who said anything about being a slave to it? You can *rule* it," Lucifer smiles, maniacally.

"Enough distraction, I didn't call you here to have a chat and you know that."

"What did you think of my opening number, Amarah? It was a beautiful thing, wasn't it?" He gloats.

The image of all those innocent people, dead, flashes behind my eyes. All of their mangled and destroyed bodies, people killed for absolutely no reason, taken from this Earth well before their time, just...*because*. Because this is *fun* to Lucifer. This is the type of senseless evil he lives for. The evil gleam in his eyes ignites the fire within me. He needs to be stopped, and Lord help me, I *will be* the one to do it.

"You're going to pay for what you did to the Water Fey, to everyone you've hurt or killed along the way, and your punishment is going to start by being locked back in Hell."

"Oh, here we go again," Lucifer rolls his eyes. "I thought I told you last time, you can't keep me here."

"Then leave," I challenge him.

I know that the ring will keep him here. I don't know how or why I know it will, I just do. Plus, I have my Faith. I know what my destiny is, and it doesn't end in me failing. This will work, and it's passed time for me to take my power back.

I close my eyes and start to focus on that pull I feel to my power. This time, the pull is stronger. I can feel it even more deeply rooted inside of me. I can feel the emptiness where it needs to go, right next to my newly released Fey power. I'm yearning to be whole, to be complete, I just need to make it happen.

I start to reach down that invisible rope, inching my way towards Lucifer, until I feel my power again, locked and restless inside of him.

"What kind of magic is this?" I hear Lucifer's angry voice. "How are you keeping me here?" He snarls.

I can feel him pacing inside the summoning circle. I can feel his agitation through the link of my power. My power is agitated, too. Even more so by his new fury of emotions. But how do I get to it? How do I free it?

Logan. A voice seems to whisper in my head. I have the same sensation of someone helping me the same way they did when I started healing people. My mother and Ana, they're here with me, guiding me.

I turn to Logan, "I need your help."

"Anything, what can I do?" He doesn't hesitate.

"Take my hand and call on your power, too. Let me use our link to call my power home."

"Ok, Angel."

He takes my hand and I immediately feel that gentle, cool breeze of his power on my skin. I shiver as his power caresses my skin and I'm suddenly brought back to the night we met. Standing in my backyard, my hand outstretched to meet his. His words come back to me now...

Let go of your fear and doubt, Amarah, and concentrate on yourself. Feel the power inside of you. You can't run from it or ignore it. You are *the power. Concentrate.*

His power now, is coaxing that part inside of me open. That part that I can block off, shutting off the connection we have to each other, I hadn't realized it was being blocked until now. Until Logan's power tried to reach inside of me and couldn't.

I open myself up to him and I'm suddenly flooding with the tingling sensation of *my* power down this invisible rope. Once again, I feel hands guiding me, showing me what to do. But this time, it's not Ana I sense, it's my mother. She's guiding my hands down the invisible tether until I've reached the very end, the place where my power resides, but is seemingly locked away.

I sense a hand reaching out, her hand or mine, at this point I can't tell the difference. I push through the barrier that holds my power captive. It feels like the ward around my house. Like a magical wall that I can feel and push my hand through, clear to the other side. But this wall is thicker and stronger. I keep pushing and fighting to get through. The resistance I feel is sooooo strong.

I fall to my knees with the effort of pushing so hard

metaphysically. I push and I push and I push. Somewhere in the back of my mind I hear someone yelling, screaming. I feel Logan's hands on my shoulders, his power enveloping me, comforting me. I pull on his power for strength. I don't know how I manage to do it, but I take a hold of *his* power. I feel it like I can feel my dagger in my hand. I use his power to slice through whatever is left of Lucifer's barrier and then I feel it.

My power.

I feel it's warm tingling sensation envelope my fingers, and then my hand, and then my wrist, as it's trying to climb up out of this cage and back into me, where it belongs, and so…I pull. I take a hold of my power in my hand and I pull with everything I have. I can feel Lucifer fighting against me. It's almost like a mystical and metaphysical tug of war. It would be one Hell of a fight but I have my mother, my Faith, Logan, and my power all fighting with me.

I feel it the moment my power breaks free from Lucifer's hold. It floods through my body. I feel it sinking into every single inch of my skin. I feel it happily mingling with Logan's power.

Yin and yang.

Hot and cold.

Fire and ice.

And then I feel it settle, content, inside of my chest where it belongs. Inside of me. A part of me and who I am. And once again, I'm brought back to the first night Logan and I mingled our powers together. It fills up every lonely nook and cranny of my soul.

Every missing piece made whole.

Every broken piece healed.

Two halves of one whole.

Complete.

My body falls spent and content from my knees to my butt. Logan's is there, kneeling next to me and holding me upright. I let out a giddy laugh, half delirious with exhaustion, and half elated.

Angel, did it work? Can you hear me? Logan's voice comes through loud and clear in my mind.

I smile up at him, *hi, Braveheart.*

A huge grin splits across his face, matching mine, and then he grabs my face tightly and his lips are crashing onto mine. It's a mixture of kissing and laughing and crying. I don't think I've ever been happier than I am in this moment. After everything I've gone through, everything we've gone through, to be here now, together, back to where we should have been all along.

Back to being together.

Back to being whole.

And maybe it's all of the hardships, trials, and heartbreak that we've gone through, but this moment just feels that much more special because of it all. You can't truly enjoy happiness without having experienced pain, too. And this moment, in Logan's arms, is the purest form of happiness I've ever felt.

And then it's interrupted by the loudest, demonic sound I've ever heard in my life. I slam my hands over my ears and glance up at Lucifer. He's screaming, but it's more than that, it's terrifying. It sounds more like a beast than a human or even an animal, and it's so loud, I'm scared it's going to make my eardrums rupture and bleed, causing permanent damage. It's unlike anything I've ever heard before. It seems to be coming from every direction, assaulting us from all sides. The room even feels like it's shaking.

I feel like the scream lasts forever, but once it finally stops, Logan manages to stand and helps me to my feet with him. Lucifer is glaring at me, chest heaving, and I swear I see the fires of Hell reflected in his eyes.

"This isn't over, Amarah. Not even close," his voice is

dripping with anger.

"Actually, it is over, Lucifer. You could never touch me before and you're never going to be able to again. You lose."

"You're not the only one I can target anymore, are you," his eyes cut to Logan.

I laugh, "you can try, but I'll fight and protect him with just as much force, if not more, than for myself. You'll never get close to either of us, ever again."

"I don't know who you think you are, Amarah, but I'm Lord of Darkness, and I'm going to…"

"I've heard enough." I cut him off. "Iseta, send this piece of shit back to Hell."

> *evocatio concluditur*
> *Hic es non receperint*
> *abiit satanas*
> *ad foveas igneas inferni*
> *ubi manebis in aeternum*

The wind kicks up, more powerful this time, as if he's fighting against it. The sulphur smokes, making a couple of the Witches gag, and then it's gone. The wind. The smell. The silence is deafening in the wake of the devil's angry screams. I think we're all suspended in a state of shock at what just happened here tonight.

Lucifer was summoned.

Lucifer was defeated.

Maybe not permanently, he will be back again at some point, in some new devious way, but this win belongs to us.

"Amarah?" Iseta's voice breaks the silence. "Did it work?"

I turn to her, nod, and without a word I walk straight into her arms. She hugs be so tightly I swear all of my broken pieces are being pushed back together by her arms. I'm crying against her shoulder, and I'm not even sure what the tears are for. Tears of joy for having my power back, tears of gratitude for having her and all of these amazing people in my life, tears of regret for all the decisions I've made that have affected people badly, tears of sorrow for all of the lives lost because of me and all the lives just...lost.

"Hey, it's ok," she whispers into my ear as she hugs me tighter. "Nothing in this life is ever perfect, but it's ok. Everything is gonna be ok."

I cling to her. I cling to her words. Because even though I know we just succeeded, even though I know we're one step closer to victory, I also know that the fight is far from over.

Amarah: The Rip

Awaken by League of Legends

Once again, I'm exhausted. Physically, mentally, emotionally, spiritually. Any kind of tired that I can be, I feel it deeply, but I know this is no time to rest. So, I push through it. I put my big girl panties on and I do what I need to do.

It's also invigorating to feel my power inside of me again. I finally feel like I'm back to being myself after so long of fighting it, blocking it and then, losing it. So, even though I'm two seconds away from collapsing with exhaustion, I'm also looking forward to the future in a way I haven't in a long time.

With excitement!

After the summoning, I found out that the Witches were going to be paired off with some Vampire groups, and go out to hunt the demons that came through the rip and managed to escape. Which, based on the absolute devastation here, is a lot.

Apparently, Witches have a spell that will allow a person to see a being's *true* self. This will help the Vampires to locate any demons hiding inside of human bodies that they've possessed. Werewolves can smell the demons, and the Fey can sense or even see their auras, so they don't need the added assistance of the

Witches.

I've never really tried to get in tune with auras on a deeper level other than having a gut instinct about someone. Looks like I have another task on my plate to work on but that one isn't nearly as important as working on my connection with Logan. He and I are the only ones capable of closing the rip, and how we're supposed to do that...well, I have no idea. I do know, however, that I connected with him in a way I've never done before when I was fighting Lucifer.

I'm contemplating this while we're sitting in the common room, finishing a quick meal I'm not even hungry for, but I know I need to eat.

"What's that serious look all about?" Logan asks, as he studies me. He always sees me.

"When I was fighting against Lucifer, there was a point where it felt like I actually took a hold of your power and used it, as if it were my own. Did you feel anything different on your end?"

He nods, "oh yeah, I definitely felt that."

"What did it feel like on your end?" I ask, curiously.

He shrugs, "it's hard to explain. You know our power is very physical." I nod. "Well, it felt like you were literally taking a piece of me and using it. Like if you were to take my hand in yours and use my fist to punch something, to guide it. It felt like that but, obviously, you didn't actually use my body, just my power."

I nod again, "I can make sense of that. Did it hurt? Or was it uncomfortable?"

He shakes his head and reaches for my hand, entwining our fingers, "it felt just like this. Just like I was sharing a piece of myself with you. It was as easy as breathing."

I take a moment to feel his hand in mine, to really *feel* it. To savor his big, strong hand, rough against my own. The way his hand dwarfs mine but also seems to fit it perfectly. I almost lost this.

"Maybe this new ability is something we'll need to use to

close the rip. We need to explore it more and practice using our powers together."

"We can practice whenever you'd like. I don't think there will be much for us to do here at the moment. Vadin and his people are preparing the lost Fey for their Surmajärgne Elu, their journey to the Afterlife, and the rip is being monitored as much as it can be, which honestly, is not much. But unless you want to go out and hunt demons, there's nothing more we can do."

"This sucks, I've been so useless without my power and now that I have it back, I feel just as useless not doing anything."

Logan scoots closer to me and brings my hand, still in his, up to his lips in a soft kiss. "Angel, our job is to close the rip. No one else can do it and that's how we're gonna help The Unseen. We're going to stop demons from *ever* coming through again, and that's going to change our world *entirely*. Let the others focus on hunting demons, what we need to focus on is so much more important."

"I know you're right. I just hope we can figure out how to do this sooner rather than later."

"Me too."

"Can you take me to go see it?"

"The rip?" He asks.

I nod. I see the hesitation in his face, in his delay of responding to me. Now that I have my power back, and our link is back in place, I can feel his fear and I want to do anything I can to take it away for him.

"I've only been there once," he admits. "It…" he licks his lips, his eyes are seeing past me and back into a different time, "it affected me more than I'd like to admit. It's almost like it reached inside of me and pulled out my anger. It has a way of," he shakes his head, "I don't know exactly just…it brings the worst out in anyone who gets near it."

"Hey," I squeeze his hand in mine. "We'll be ok. We can

protect ourselves better than anyone else with the power that's inside of us. With *who* we are. This is what we're destined for, Braveheart. If we can't do this, no one can. We don't have a choice."

He seems to contemplate my words. I pour as much belief and confidence as I can down our link. He finally nods, "alright, come on," he helps me up and we head out of the common room.

He leads me towards a part of the compound I haven't been to yet. It's on the complete opposite side of the Fey living spaces. I hang on tightly to his hand as he leads me down tunnel after tunnel. There's no electricity down here, like in the rest of the compound, and we're making our way with an old fashion torch that Logan picked up at the entrance to the tunnels. I guess it makes sense to keep these tunnels in the dark and make it that much harder for demons to make it through. Although, I doubt a little darkness does much to deter them.

I'm thoroughly lost within seconds of being in the labyrinth of tunnels and have no clue which way is out and which way is further in.

"These tunnel systems are all insane," I whisper. "I don't know how anyone ever figures them out."

He chuckles, "they've all been mapped out and studied, plus years and years of travelling them, and a good sense of direction always helps."

"It's warmer down here than I thought it would be considering it's Winter."

"This far underground, the Earth isn't affected by what's happening on the surface. This is the temperature it remains year-round. Although, the rip does add more heat than normal. I'm sure that will affect the climate down here once it's been sealed off."

Just as he mentions it, I feel the temperature increase. It's getting warmer. Either that, or I'm only thinking it is because of the new information I have. It's crazy how influenceable we can actually be by our surroundings, what we see and hear, without even realizing it most of the time.

Just when I'm about to mention this to Logan, I see a glow up ahead. As we approach, I realize that it's an antechamber that opens up to a larger chamber beyond. There are torches everywhere, both here and in the chamber ahead, lighting it up like the Griswold's house on Christmas. There are several Fey, all with weapons, and all on high alert.

"Any activity?" Logan asks as we enter.

"None," one of the Fey shakes his head.

I slowly walk to the other side of the antechamber and look out into the larger chamber. It's the size of a football field, maybe even bigger, and in the middle, I can see a black, gaping hole.

"Is that it?" I ask, as I stare out towards the rip.

Logan walks up beside me and nods, "that's it. The Fey have to remain this far back or risk being corrupted by the energy that surrounds it, like I mentioned. That's why it's so hard to guard. The demons can come up the rip and escape down a number of tunnels that then branch off into other tunnels. It's impossible to guard every exit and so, we guard the tunnels that leads to the Water Fey and do our best to keep the demons that do get through, to a minimum."

"We can usually manage well enough," a young male Fey speaks up. "But when hundreds came through at once," he shakes his head. "That's never happened before and it was a slaughter."

"What's your name?" I ask, turning to face him, giving him my full attention.

"Steven, Ma'am," he dips his head in greeting.

"Please, call me Amarah," I insist. With my power back, I can sense his aura, his Fey energy. Not to mention, his sapphire eyes give him away easily enough. "And you're Vesi?"

"I am."

"Why are you not with the others? Preparing for the ceremony for your fallen family?"

"I was helping some of the woman and children get to safety when others were fighting. I know what I did saved lives but..."

"But you feel like you need to fight," I finish for him.

I understand him completely. I feel the need to fight too, to make difference, to put my life in the same dangerous situations as others do. How can you ever ask, or expect, others to do something you're not willing to do yourself? Even worse, how can you move on knowing that you were safe while others fought and died? The survivor's guilt would eat me alive. It practically has once before.

He nods.

"I understand, Steven. Hopefully, you won't have to fight much longer. Well, demons at least." I turn to Logan, "I need to see it."

He nods and offers his hand again. Before I can take it, Steven's hand touches my arm tentatively, but it still stops me.

"Be careful," he warns. "That rip is pure evil. I don't know how, but it has the ability to get inside of your head. It calls to any and all darkness or evil thought you have inside of you, no matter how small or insignificant. It makes you want to act on them, to do..." he swallows hard, his eyes are wide with fear from what he's no doubt experienced for himself. "It makes you want to do bad things," he continues. "The longer you stay in that energy, the more insistent those thoughts become."

"Thank you for the warning," I say, genuinely. "We'll be ok."

I turn, taking Logan's hand in mine. "Let's use our power as shields," I suggest, as I pull my power out and securely around myself. I feel Logan's cool breeze rush against me shortly after.

I turn my attention towards the gaping hole in front of us. I close my eyes, take a deep breath in, imagine myself and Logan surrounded by Heavenly light, exhale, and open my eyes. I take the first step out of the antechamber and one step closer to the source of all this evil. I immediately feel the energy pushing against my shield. It's thick and heavy, like walking into the humid weather of San Antonio, Texas, in late July.

Logan follows my lead, taking a step up next to me. Then we take another, and another, clinging to each other for strength. It feels like it takes us forever to approach the rip, as if it's trying to repel us, push us away. We have to fight for every step we take against this evil, invisible force that's pushing against us. It's almost as if the energy is alive and knows that Logan and I, together, will be its undoing.

I'm finally standing at the edge of the rip, staring into its black depths. Black doesn't even seem to describe it. It's void of anything else. Just a gaping, empty and evil hole, cut raggedly into the Earth. I can't see more than a few feet down into it but I can feel...everything. I feel the heat radiating up from its deep, Hellish depths, causing me to break out in a sweat. I feel its evil, corrupt, and damning energy. It's so strong and so alive, its like it's almost whispering to me. As if I can hear it, calling to me, reaching out to me, just like Lucifer reached his hand out to me not so long ago.

There's a part of me that wants to listen more clearly, to drop my shield and hear what this evil energy has to say to me. There's that dark part of me that wants to be let out, that wants to be selfish and say, *screw everyone else. I don't owe them anything.*

I let go of Logan's hand and kneel, placing my palms flat against the Earth. Immediately, I feel it's pain. If the Earth could scream and cry in a way that we could hear it and see it, it would be excruciating to witness. I feel it's pain as if it was a part of me. I feel my heart breaking for the pain the Earth is in and has been in for how long? How many decades upon decades has the Earth suffered this way? Even one day of this evilness is too much.

I feel the energy of the Earth responding to me and I try to heal it. I've always had a strong connection to the Earth, able to command it easily. I use that connection now and try to pull the Earth together, but it's no use. It's being held open by something so much stronger than I'd expected. To be honest, I was holding out hope that I would get here and that my connection to Earth would allow me to close it. I should have known better if even the strongest Maa can't close it. I have to find a way to defeat this. I have to find a way to close this rip, to contain the evil beneath, and heal the Earth.

I open my eyes and stare at my hands, blurry through the tears that flood my eyes. I blink them back, trying to gain control of myself and my emotions again. That's when I notice it.

I stand up, letting the pain I felt from the Earth settle deep in my bones, fuelling me to fight. Motivating me to set this all right. Once I've gained my composure, I remove Lucifer's ring, that I'm still wearing, and hold it up between my fingers. The flames etched into the sides start to glow red and I can feel the evil energy vibrating through it. But just as this evil energy is a strong, influenceable and almost tangible essence, so too, is Faith.

"I know now what this ring was all along," I speak into the pit, my words intended for Lucifer, and I'm confident he can hear me. "It wasn't a generous gift to help remind me of who I am. It was nothing more than a way for you to have more control over me. To use your evil energy to continue to influence me to *your* purpose. But you never intended for me to use it against you, did you? Everything happens for a reason," I laugh, finally seeing it all fall into place, "I needed to experience the darkness to see that it's *not* the answer. I needed to experience the darkness to know that I'm *not* a slave to it, that I *can* overcome whatever is thrown my way and, had I not turned to you, I wouldn't have received this," I twist the ring in my hand, "the key to holding you hostage and allowing me to defeat you. Well, I'm not done *yet*."

I look over to Logan, he's watching and listening to me

intently. I feel his support through our link, along with his own boost of confidence, and always, his love.

"*We're* not done yet," I amend, as I take Logan's hand back in mine. Because one of the hardest lessons I learned through all of this, is that I can't, and don't want to, do this alone. I turn my attention back on the pit. "You're influence over me ends here," I declare, as I throw the ring into the pit. I swear I can feel the Earth rumble under my feet as Lucifer unleashes his anger.

"No, we're not done yet, Angel," it's Logan's turn to squeeze my hand. "Come on," he turns and leads me away from the rip.

We don't speak as we traverse the tunnels back to the living quarters. Once we're alone, back in our room, I finally break our contemplative silence.

"How was that for you? How did it feel?" I ask, as we settle into seated positions in front of each other on the bed.

"I could definitely still feel the darkness, the evil, trying to push its way in to my head, but it didn't get through. It was no more than an inaudible whisper, but...it was still there. I know it will attack the second it has an opening."

I nod my head, "yeah, I felt that too. There's a heaviness and an evilness to the energy in that room. I don't know how anyone would be able to fight its grip once it gets a hold of you."

"They don't," Logan says, plainly.

I sigh, "did you see their faces though? The Fey that were there, watching us. There are going to be questions as to how you and I were able to stay in that room and remain completely unaffected."

"I know," Logan agrees and runs his hands down his face with a heavy sigh. For once, I can see his own exhaustion pushing through his carefully crafted mask. I can feel it, heavy and weighted down our link.

"We're both exhausted. Maybe we should try to get a few

hours of sleep while we can. Like you said, there's not a whole lot we can do at the moment, and I don't know about you, but I'm not going to be much good to anyone if I don't get some sleep."

"Yeah," he says, the exhaustion clear in his voice. "Let's try and get some rest."

Logan walks over to the light switch and turns it off, sending the room into its own pit of darkness. I feel the bed dip as he climbs back on it, then settles in behind me, and pulls me in close. I let out a contented sigh as my body sinks into the mattress and into his protective hold.

"Logan," I whisper into the darkness.

"Hmmmm?"

"I don't like lying to everyone. I don't like keeping this secret of who I am. Who you are."

"I don't either, Angel. Let's tackle one thing at a time though. Let's close this rip and then, I promise, we'll figure out the best way to tell everyone."

"One thing at a time," I echo, as I let sleep pull me under.

Perhaps Michael, my mom, or Ana, will come to me in a dream and tell me how Logan and I are supposed to close this rip because I don't have a fucking clue.

Amarah: Give Everything You Have

Never Surrender by Liv Ash

I'm forced out of my dreamless sleep by Logan shaking me, urgently. "Amarah, get up! Get your weapons! We have to go!"

My heart is immediately pounding inside of my chest, practically jumping out of my throat, with the adrenaline rushing through my veins.

"What is it? What's happened?" I ask, as I pull my hair into a ponytail and start strapping on my weapons.

"I don't know," he says, jaw clenched tightly as he helps me get my sword over my head. "I can just hear the screams and yells. It has to be another attack of some kind. We need to hurry," he says, as he strides for the door.

I'm shoving my feet into my boots as I hurry after him, still unable to hear whatever it is that his Wolf hearing is picking up. Logan runs down the tunnels, barely slowing down enough that I can keep up with him in a full out sprint. Once we reach the darkened tunnels, that lead to the rip, I hear the screams and roars. I've heard it enough now to know exactly what the sounds are. Battle.

Logan doesn't stop for a torch as he hurls himself down the tunnels. I pull my power out and into a white, glowing ball of light in my palm, and continue racing after him. We pass more Fey running through the tunnels, heading to help in the new fight, as we run for our lives toward the screams and shouts.

Logan unleashes a vicious growl as he barges into the antechamber, claws already out, making contact with a General demon. My sword is free a second later as I come in behind him, I pull my power around me and down into my sword, lighting up the crosses etched into the blade, and quickly finish off the stunned demon Logan just attacked. He bursts into flames as I continue past him and on to the next one.

I have a moment to survey the world around me. There's no way we can all stay in this small antechamber. It's too small for this many bodies trying to manuever and fight off the demons without the possibility of hurting one of our own.

"Logan!" I yell, "we need to move into the larger room! We can't all fight in here!"

"I'll go with you," Steven yells from across the room where he's just killed a demon, black mist temporarily blocking him from view.

"It's too dangerous for anyone else," Logan says.

"I can handle it," Steven argues, as he comes to stand next to us.

I look into the larger room and it's being flooded with another wave of demons climbing out of the rip.

"We don't have much of a choice," I admit. "We're about to be overrun! We need to attack them head on, out here."

We don't have time to think, only to act. Logan leads the way and I follow. I know others will be joining us, and all I can hope for, is that the evil energy allows them to be even more fierce in their fighting. I can only hope that the evil fuels them to kill more demons. We can figure out the consequences once we're all safe.

Logan, use your power· I remind him.

I feel his cool breeze erupt out of him as he protects himself. *Be safe, Amarah· Stay close to me·*

I do my best to stay as close to him as I can, but when you're in the midst of battle, your world narrows down to the few feet around you. I move in a steady circle, making sure no demon sneaks up on me, as I swing my sword and dive and roll to avoid massive claws and brutal tail hits.

As I'm rolling, coming up to my knee, I focus my attention and my power out in front of me. Instead of blindly sending it out in a bomb like explosion, where there's a possibility of innocent casualties, I concentrate my power and push it out, straight in front of me, demolishing a handful of demons at once. They burst into flames as my power engulfs them and then I turn back around and continue fighting with my sword. I'll only use my power when I know there are no Fey or innocent bystanders in the way. I refuse to take any chances.

A tail comes swinging at me. I step out of its way, but not fast enough. It connects with my shoulder and throws me back. I stumble but manage to catch myself before I fall completely. The demon that attacked me doesn't hesitate for a second as I'm struggling to regain my balance. He's on me, slashing at my shield with his claws. I can't get my sword positioned to strike so, I reach for a dagger and slice as hard as I can. I'm sprayed in the face by black demon sludge as its hand is cut clean off its arm.

Another demon is suddenly at my back, pushing against my weakening shield. I slam my dagger behind me and hear the demon roar as my dagger sinks into its stomach, but it's not enough to kill it. They're both coming at me with nothing but animalistic rage. They're predators and nothing else. They don't feel pain. They don't get tired.

They just keep on coming and coming, like fucking zombies, until they're dead. Or...dead again, I suppose.

I can't see who's around me. I don't want to use my power and potentially hurt someone. Instead, I focus on the air. I feel the particles hanging everywhere in the air around us. I open up another compartment inside of me. One I didn't even realize I had closed until recently.

My Fey power.

Because I'm both.

Fey.

Angel.

I use my Fey power to feel the particles in the air more strongly than I ever have before. I use the air now, to surround the demons, pick them up and throw them as far away from me as possible.

Angel, you ok? Logan's voice echoes through my mind.

Never better, Braveheart. I smile, as I race towards the demon I just threw, sprawled and stunned on the ground. I sink my sword into his chest and am gone and on to the next before his body is ash on the ground.

I see another Fey close to me, struggling with a demon, and I run to help her. Her weapon has just been knocked out of her hand the demon swept his tail at her feet, knocking her to the ground. Its leaning over her, teeth inches away from her throat, when I sink my dagger into its back, pushing with all of my strength to get the dagger into its heart. I manage to push the demon off of her as its body bursts into flames next to her.

The blade she was using begins to soften and lose its shape underneath the demon's Hell fire flames. The girl places her palm to the ground and calls a wave of water from the water in the ground beneath us, quenching the flame. The hot metal hisses as the water flows over it, essentially hardening it once again into a new, mangled shape. I stare at the weapon in awe. At the way the heat manipulated the steel and the cool water then set the metal against any further warping.

It's exactly the same way they quench blades in *Forged in Fire*. My human hobby of TV watching has definitely come in handy. The blacksmiths use the forge to heat the metal to a point where they can work it. They can mold it and shape it into anything they'd like. Then, once they have the metal where they want it, they heat it up once again, and then immediately thrust the hot metal into a cold barrel of water, essentially sealing the metal into that design.

Hot and cold.

Fire and ice.

I know how to close the rip! Meet me there!

I make sure they Fey is ok before I race towards the rip. Once again, I see fire, smoke, and scorched Earth all around me. I see a few Air Fey in the air, attacking with bows and arrows, essentially like snipers in the sky. There are waves of water that seemingly come out of nowhere causing the ground to become muddy as I run towards the rip, but there are no more demons coming through. We're winning.

Logan runs towards me, the fighting taking place now closer to the antechamber than the rip. He practically collides with me as he takes me in his arms for a quick embrace before he's scanning my body for injuries.

"Are you ok? Are you hurt anywhere?" His voice is urgent and scared.

"I'm ok, I promise, I'm not hurt any more than you are."

He takes my face in his hands and crushes his lips to mine. The force of his kiss is almost painful but he pulls away just as quickly as he kissed me.

"Logan, I'm fine. Listen to me," I insist, grabbing his hands from my face and squeezing them. "I know how to close this rip. I'm the fire and you're the ice."

His brows furrow together in confusion, "I don't understand."

"You know how blades are made, right?" I continue before he can answer, "you heat up the metal to move it and mold it where you want it and then you drop it into cold water to harden it. I will use my Angel fire to mold the Earth back together and once I'm done, you will use your Angel ice to seal it," I'm beaming up at him, waiting for my words to sink.

I see the light in his eyes once he finally understands what I'm suggesting. "What do we have to do?" He asks.

I shake my head, "honestly, other than the *idea* of what do to, I don't know how it will actually work in reality. I need you to stand over me, protect me from any attacks, as I focus all of my energy on closing the rip. Then, when I'm done, I'll do the same for you as you focus on sealing it."

Logan looks over his shoulder and I follow his gaze. The fighting is still intense but it's no closer to us than it was before. It seems to keep moving further and further away from us.

"Ok, but what about in there," he gestures towards the black hole, "what if more demons come as we're weakened and trying to close it?"

"That's just a chance we're going to have to take. I think Lucifer sent his last wave of demons all at once. I don't see why he'd be holding back a few more? Now is our best chance."

"Ok, Angel. I'll follow your lead." He leans down and kisses me again, more gently this time, but its just as quick. "Let's hurry."

I nod and turn to face the rip, dropping to my knees once again. I don't waste any time placing my palms against the Earth and connecting with it. I feel that immense pain shoots up my hands, up my arms, and grips my heart. It's so strong, I immediately start to cry again, but I don't let the pain hinder me. I use it to motivate me. To guide me.

This time, instead of just asking the Earth to do my biding, I pour my Angel power into it. I feel the heat of my power as it rushes out of my body and down into the Earth. I focus on heating my power even more. I imagine myself as a forge. Forges can reach up to thirty-five hundred degrees Fahrenheit. I can't even begin to imagine what that feels like, but I try. I try to send my power into he Earth as hot and forceful as I can. I imagine the Earth like that blade I just saw, softening and giving in to the heat.

I pour and I pour and I pour, until I feel my power completely surrounding the rip, and then...I start to forge.

And I feel the Earth move under my power.

Amarah, it's working. Logan's voice is full of awe and I feel him sending strength and love down our bond. Cheering me on.

The Earth is moving at my command. I open my eyes so I can see exactly what needs to be molded and where. I watch as the rip closes, achingly slowly, but just like a sword being shaped from a hunk of metal, I know each push, each strike, is one step closer to a finished product.

Angel, are you ok? Your eyes are solid white. You're scaring me.

I'm ok. It's working! My voice in my head sounds tired and strained, even to me. I can feel my energy draining, my power depleting, but I have to do this. I wouldn't have been given the power to do this but not the strength to see it through.

Amarah, Logan's voice is strained now too, but also laced with fear. *You have to stop. You're doing exactly like what Ana did to save you. This is killing you, please, you have to stop!*

Trust me, Logan. Have Faith.

I keep my power pushing and pulling the Earth closed. It's so close now, only a few feet away from being closed completely, but I know Logan is right. I feel my power fading. *Myself* fading. I say a silent prayer. I pray to God, to Michael, to my mother, and to Ana. I pray for them all to give me the strength I need to make this happen. I can't fail or my mother's and Ana's lives will have been lost in vain. They gave up their lives for me. Because they believed in me. This is what I was created for. A miracle baby.

This is my divine destiny.

Amarah, please! That's enough! Logan's voice begs and I can feel his hands on me, shaking me, trying to get me to stop.

I give one last push and feel the Earth sigh in relief as it finally closes completely. I open my eyes and I'm met with intense, worried green ones, spilling tears down his cheeks.

"You need to seal it," I try to order him, but my voice is weak, barely above a whisper, but he nods. He knows he needs to see this done.

"You stay right here," his voice is the hard command mine wasn't. "You stay right here beside me, you hear me?"

"I'm ok," I say, wearily. "Hurry."

He reluctantly pulls away from me and follows my lead. He places his palms down on the Earth and chills run up my arms as his normally cool breeze rushes out like the freezing depths of the Antarctic Sea. I'm in and out of consciousness. I lose track of time and how long Logan has been working on the seal.

"It's done," he says, a smile spreading across his face as he stares out over where the rip used to be. It feels like only a second has gone by before he finishes, unlike the extensive amount of time it took me to pull the Earth back together.

"It's done," I echo before the Earth rushes up to meet my face and I'm once again plunged into total and utter nothingness.

Amarah: No More Fear

You & I (Nobody In The World) by John Legend

I'm suspended between sleep and wakefulness. It's that weird middle ground where you feel heavy and deep in sleep and oddly alert all at the same time. I can hear voices murmuring but I can't make out any words. Am I dreaming or waking? I can't tell.

"Amarah?" Logan's voice sounds loudly next to me. "Amarah, can you hear me?" He asks and I feel his fingers gently caress across my forehead and down my cheek.

My eyes flutter open and his distressed green eyes slowly come into focus. They're bloodshot and dark circles have started to form below them. I watch as his eyes water and single tear escapes before he blinks the rest away. My heart soars and sinks at the same time with that look and show of emotion. A genuine smile spreads across his face as he lifts my hand to his lips and kisses my knuckles. His smile is contagious and I find myself smiling back at him although, it feels weak, like the rest of me.

"Oh, Angel, thank God you're awake. I've been so worried. I didn't know what to do. No one knew what to do. I swear I've never prayed so much in my damn life."

"I'm ok," my voice comes out raspy, my vocal cords tight and cold from unuse. I clear my throat, "water."

"Yeah, of course," Logan shakes his head, as if he's clearing his mind, and reaches for a bottle of water sitting on the nightstand. He uncaps it and hands it to me.

I take it from him and the small bottle feels heavier than it should. I bring it to my lips, hand shaking slightly, and drink deeply, almost finishing it all in one go.

I clear my throat once more, "thank you. That feels much better. How long have I been out?"

I watch Logan's throat roll in a deep swallow, "two days. We've been so worried."

I'm shocked by his words. "Two days?" I ask, incredulously. "What's happened? Is everyone ok? The demons! The rip!" My memories come flooding back to me and I try to sit up.

Logan's there, helping me into a higher position but not letting me get up. "Everyone's ok, Angel. There were more wounded but everyone's been healed. No more lives have been lost. It's over. It's done," he sits on the side of the bed, next to me and cups my cheek, a look of pure love and adoration on his face. He leans in and presses his warm lips to mine for a brief second before he pulls away again. "You did it. The rip is closed."

I let out a heavy sigh and sink into the pillows, letting my head fall back against the headboard and close my eyes in another silent prayer. "Thank God," I whisper aloud, as I open my eyes and reach for his hand on my cheek. "*We* did it."

He shakes his head, "no, Amarah, *you* did. That was ninety-nine percent you're doing. I swear, it was no effort at all on my end to seal the rip but you, what you did," he stares at me, appraising me, "you're such a God damn miracle." He leans in and places his forehead against mine, closing his eyes and sighing heavily. "I almost lost you, *again*. I thought you were gone. Spent. I thought you gave up all of your power to close the rip. I honestly don't know how you survived."

"I'm here, Logan. I'm ok," I reassure him. "A little tired and…actually, *really* hungry," I chuckle, trying to lighten the mood.

He pulls back so he can see me. The smile on his face is a mixture of relief and sadness. I try to focus my attention on our link but I feel too weak to really concentrate on it and Logan's emotions are too complex to try and decipher.

"Logan, talk to me. I'm here. What's going on?"

"I just…" he runs a hand through his hair in frustration, "I'm always so damn helpless when it comes to you. To protecting you. To saving you. It's always something that's so far out of my hands I can't even grasp a single strand to try and make a difference."

"You should know better," I scold him. "We're not in control, Logan, none of us are. This is all so much bigger than any of us, but this is nothing new, what has you so shook this time?" My brows are furrowed as I study his face, his demeanor, trying desperately to understand where his thoughts are at so I can try to settle them.

"You know how Fey Healers can use up all of their power to save someone? They can give up every single ounce of their magic, their essence and, essentially, deplete themselves to the point where there's nothing left for themselves." He looks at me, staring fiercely into my eyes, making sure that I'm hearing him. "They give up too much of themselves and they *die*, Amarah. *They die*."

"Yes," I slowly nod my head, still confused. "I know that, Logan. What does that have to do with me?"

He reaches over and pulls a chunk of my hair from behind me and brings it up in front of my face.

I gasp, my hand raising to cover my mouth, as I stare at the hair laying against his palm. I tentatively reach out and slowly take it between my fingers. It's mine. It feels the same as it always has, but it's now white as snow.

"I watched you deplete yourself to close the rip, Amarah.

Once a Fey's hair has gone completely white, it's too late. There's nothing left to save."

I finally look up from my hair and into his tortured and love filled eyes. "You should be dead," he whispers. "I'm so fucking relieved that you're not but," he shakes his head again. "I didn't know if you would ever wake up. It was a miracle that you were still breathing and your heart was still beating but…no one knew if you'd ever wake up. God, these past two days have been more Hell on Earth than a million demons could ever create."

"I'm so sorry," I whisper, my eyes tearing up as I look at the utter devastation on his face. "I always seem to cause you the most pain and I'm so sorry."

"Shhhh, Angel," he wraps his big arms around me and pulls me into his chest, holding me firmly but gently. I wrap my arms around him, fisting his shirt in my hands, holding onto him as tight as I can. His scent invades my nose and I breathe in deeply, sucking it down into my chest, wishing I could hold it there forever.

"It's not your fault," he whispers against the side of my head as he strokes my hair. "I'm just so glad you're ok. I love you so much, Amarah, so fucking much."

"Even though I have old lady hair now?" I sniffle into his chest.

He chuckles, "you know, some people dye their hair white on purpose, it's not old lady hair and, even if it was," he pulls me away from his chest so he can look at me, "I would love it, like I love everything about you. I would love you with wrinkled skin and missing teeth."

I snort-laugh through my tears and he smiles brightly as he wipes the remaining tears away.

"There's not one single reality this world can conjure that would ever effect the way I love you, Amarah, not one."

His beautiful peridot eyes move back and forth intensely

between mine and there's no denying the truth of his words. They're clear in the way he looks at me. They're clear in the way he holds me and comforts me. They're clear in the way he believes in me and always allows me to choose my own path, make my own decisions. They're clear in the way he touches me, with the slightest touch of his fingertips across my skin, to the possessive grip he has when he pushes himself inside of me and claims me.

Love.

Deep and fathomless.

Unconditional.

All-consuming.

I've always craved all-consuming love but I've always feared it more. For once in my life, I'm not afraid of love. Of giving everything I have inside of me and of opening myself up completely to receiving it. Because I'm confident in the man sitting next to me in a way I've never been before. And it's the most freeing feeling I've ever experienced.

I've known that Logan is my soulmate since day one. Since the night he wandered into my backyard and stole my heart with nothing more than a simple touch. A simple kiss. I've known he's my whole world in the way that he draws me in and nothing else matters. And yet, I don't think I've completely let go of my past hurts, my past traumas, until right this moment.

I try to exude everything I'm thinking and feeling into my eyes and down our link because I know there are no words I can say that will sufficiently explain or define this moment. There are never any words deep enough or beautiful enough to convey what's inside of a person's heart.

"I don't know what I did in this life, or a past one, to deserve you, Logan Lewis," I shake my head. "In fact, I *know* I don't deserve you but fuck if I'm not selfish enough to have you. Because I'm all yours, Braveheart. In a way I've *never* been to anyone else. If I could cut out my heart and give it to you to hold in your hand, I would. Because it's no longer mine, not one tiny piece of it."

I lean in and claim his mouth with mine before he can say anything else. I kiss him in a way I've never kissed him before. Without an ounce of fear of getting hurt. Without the faintest whisper of doubt in my mind. I finally give in, all the way, one hundred percent.

His lips are so soft and warm, devouring mine. His tongue is expertly pressing and twirling around mine, sending my body into overdrive, my pussy throbbing. His breath is hot and heavy against my face and his hands are strong and possessive, holding me to him, but it's not enough. I need to feel more of him. More of him on more of me. I'm practically crawling and clawing my way up his body and manage to straddle his lap, rocking my hips to grind against the hardness I feel between my legs. He groans into my mouth and I swallow it down, savoring the tase of his desire.

I return the desperate groan with so much need and desire built up inside of me that I don't think I'll ever be satiated. I *need* this. I need to feel him this way, now that I've completely let go and given in to the truth. I want to kiss and touch and explore every fucking inch of his body all over again with this new sense of abandon and appreciation.

I feel the power inside of me waking up. It's weak and frail, it needs time to rebuild and restore itself, but I want to make love to Logan with everything I have. Everything inside of me is his for the taking and I'm going to offer it up on a God damn divine platter. One he's worthy of. One he deserves.

Logan is the one to pull back and push out a heavy breath, "Jesus." He groans again, as he tugs my bottom lip out from under me teeth and nips it himself, causing me to moan and grind against him harder. "If you hadn't just woken up from a fucking coma I swear to…" he clenches his jaw and tightens his grip on my waist. "I've never in my life had a kiss drive me this fucking crazy before. Jesus," he repeats. "That was…"

"Everything I feel for you, Logan. That's what that was," I interrupt. "And I very much want to continue this, like…I would almost sell my damn soul again to make love to you right now."

"No! No way," Logan shakes his head adamantly. "No more selling souls."

"I said, *almost*," I smile up at him, completely and utterly entranced. Completely and utterly fucking gone. So far past head over heels. I'm fucking Alice down the rabbit hole. "But, like usual, you're right. I don't have the energy I would need to do all the things I want to do to you right now."

"Oh, don't worry, there's plenty of time to make this happen and I'm not going anywhere, Angel."

"Neither am I, Braveheart," I lean in to kiss him softly without taking my eyes off of his. I see the heat spark behind his beautiful green eyes with the promise of things to come. "Now, can you please take me to get something to eat before I pass out?"

"Whatever your heart desires, it shall have," he stands up easily with me still wrapped around him.

I hang on tighter to his shoulders as he proceeds to carry me out of our room and down the tunnels, seemingly content to let me cling to him like a monkey, and so, I do. Without a care in the world to what others may see or think. There's no one in this world but us.

And just as if he's reading my mind he sings, "ain't nobody in the world but…"

"You and I," I whisper on smile.

Amarah: Spread Light & Love

Where Is The Love by Black Eyed Peas

I almost missed the ceremony for the fallen Water Fey. Turns out, Logan wasn't going to bring it up because he said I needed to rest. I mean, he's not wrong. You would think that two days in a damn coma would be all the rest one needed, but how I manage to still be so exhausted and weak, frustrates me immensely. It's been one full day since I woke up and I barely have energy to get up and eat.

I'm getting my strength back slowly but surely and I have to remind myself that it's only been one day since I woke up. I need to be patient with myself after almost dying. Again. I gain a little more strength every time I eat and every time I manage to nap for an hour or so. Which, sadly, are the *only* two activities I've been doing for the past twenty-four hours.

But I *am* gaining my strength back and argued stubbornly and *insisted* on being present for the Surmajärgne Elu. So, here I am, getting dressed in a deep blue, flowing dress that was provided to me by Vadin. It's beautiful in its simplicity with flowing, sleeves and a small train that drags along the floor behind me. I slip on the matching blue flats and then sit on the small chair that's been brought in. I was told that one of the Water Fey would be in to help me prepare for the ceremony. What that means exactly? I have no clue, but I'm here for it, eager to learn more about them and their customs.

There's a knock on the door. "Come in," I yell from my chair.

A familiar face walks in and stops in front of me. I watch as her eyes linger on my hair before she kneels before me and bows her head, "Võitleja, I owe you a debt for saving my life. I'd like to start by saying thank you. I know that saying those words doesn't really…"

I gently pull on her arms, urging her to stand up. She hesitates for a moment but then stands, head still bowed in my direction. "What's your name?" I ask.

"Fi Quinn, but everyone calls me Quinn, my Lady."

"Quinn, please, you don't owe me any kind of debt, do you hear me? We all fought equally. You may have very well killed a demon that could have killed me. Perhaps I owe you a debt and don't even realise it?" I shake my head, "no, there are no debts to settle in battle, only lives to mourn and lives to celebrate, and we need to do both tonight for those that have fallen."

Quinn nods her head in reluctant agreement. She lifts a bag that's clutched in her hands, "may I?"

"Please," I smile up at her, wanting her to feel as welcome and as comfortable as possible.

She moves to stand behind me, I hear her rummaging through the bag and then her hands are in my hair. She starts on one side, just behind my ear, twisting and pulling and pinning with a gentleness that has me closing my eyes, relishing in the way her fingers scrape against my scalp. It feels so good, I barely manage to keep from moaning. Her fingers make quick work of whatever she's doing as she makes her way across to the other side.

She moves to stand in front of me, "I'm going to do your eyes now."

I nod and close my eyes, letting her work. I can feel a small brush making its way across my eyelids, off to the side and then over the bridge of my nose. This process takes a bit longer than the hair did, but I'm completely relaxed under her gentle touch and in no hurry.

It still feels like it comes too quickly when she says, "you're all done, my Lady."

"Please, call me Amarah," I say, as I push out of the chair and walk into the bathroom to appraise myself in the mirror.

I'm left speechless as I take in my appearance. The makeup covers from just above my eyebrows, down to the middle of my cheeks. Different shades of blues, greens and white, shimmer in the light, resembling the natural skin of the Water Fey. Scales.

My hair has been adorned with the same shades of flowers woven into my hair. They're constructed in a way that makes me look like I'm wearing a crown. A crown of the most beautiful blue and green flowers that seem to glow against my white hair.

I look like a Fey Queen and it finally dawns on me why Quinn has been calling me, *my Lady,* and bowing to me. I actually may become their next Queen. A small little detail I had forgotten until this moment. One that I'm still not ready to face, but based on the women I see in the mirror, one that I'm going to have to face sooner rather than later.

I walk out of the bathroom and Quinn is watching me with a worried look on her face. She's nervously twisting her hands in front of her as she looks me over once more and then averts her eyes again.

"Do you like it?" She asks, voice a bit shaky.

I walk up to her and take her hands in mine. She raises her deep midnight blue eyes to meet mine. "It's all so beautiful. *I* look beautiful, and I'm honored to represent you and the Vesi in this way." I gently push a small amount of my power into our joined hands, willing Quinn's glamour away. She gasps and is suddenly standing in front of me in her true Fey form. "*You're* beautiful," I say with a genuine smile as I squeeze her hands in mine. "Thank you."

She squeezes my hands back before she drops them and backs away, "I'm glad you like it, my…Amarah," she corrects herself. "I'll send Logan in."

I don't have to wait long before Logan walks in. He's also been dressed in a deep blue ceremonial style robe. It's sleeveless and hugs his massive chest tightly before it ties at the waist and hangs all the way to the ground where the same style of shoe I'm wearing peeks out from underneath.

His eyes meet mine the second he steps into the room and he stops as if he's hit a wall. I watch his eyes travel over my body, taking it all in, before he moves again, quickly closing the distance between us.

His eyes take in the makeup, his fingertips linger over it, but not touching. "This is a huge honor," he informs me. "they've painted you as one of them. They consider you to be Vesi, *Family*, and the crown of flowers," he smiles brightly, "well, that speaks for itself, doesn't it?"

"Don't get me wrong, I'm definitely honored to be considered one of them, to be taken into their Family…"

"But…?"

I shake my head, "but I'm no *Queen*," I emphasize. "I mean, they're making this assumption because of what their law states but what if the throne *doesn't* acknowledge me as Queen?"

"Then it doesn't and they elect someone else," Logan says, matter-of-factly. "And you will remain Võitleja, right by my side and by the side of the new Queen."

"And what if the throne *does* recognize me as Queen?" I whisper. This thought scares me more than the former.

"Oh, Angel, how quick you are to lecture me but then forget your own words when it comes to yourself. We are not in control, remember? Everything happens for a reason and you and I both know you'd make a wonderful, strong, and fair Queen."

"I *don't* know that, Logan!" I say, with desperation.

"Well, *I* do," he says with conviction as he lifts my chin and stares lovingly into my eyes. "And obviously, so do the Vesi. Let us be your conviction and your support until you find your own belief and confidence. Whatever the throne decides, I'm going to be right here beside you. You aren't going to face anything alone, ok?"

I swallow down my doubts and fears and nod, "ok."

He leans down and brushes his lips against mine in a soft, chaste kiss. "Now," he says as he pulls back and holds his arm out to me. "May I escort you to the Surmajärgne Elu, my Queen?"

"Logan!" I slap at his arm, "I'm not the Queen!"

"Amarah Rey Andrews, you've always been my Queen and always will be."

I can't help the smile, or the blush, that spreads across my face as I beam up at him. I wrap my arm around his, lean into him for added support, and let him escort me to the ceremony.

We're back topside, but in a different place than where we entered. This looks extremely private and cut-off from the rest of the world. However, the tingling I feel against my skin let's me know there's glamour in place. The sun is setting, throwing beautiful shades of pinks and oranges across the crisp blue sky. The creations of this Earth never cease to amaze me when I stop to appreciate them. Which, sadly, is not often enough. A breeze kicks up and the chill of the Winter air makes me pull my cloak around me tighter and I'm thankful Logan insisted that I wear it.

I'm too busy gazing up into the sky to notice the two forms waiting patiently on the trail for us.

"Amarah, you look absolutely stunning," the familiar, soft voice pulls my attention forward.

The smile that greats me is warm and genuine and pulls a matching smile out of me easily. "Vyla! Jon!" I unhook myself from Logan's arm and embrace them one at a time with all the strength I can muster. "I'm so glad you're here. Did the kids come with you?"

"Yes, they're with the others at the lake," Vyla informs me. "We heard about what you did, Amarah," she says, softly, as she runs a piece of my hair through her fingers. "It's an absolute miracle. You're a miracle."

"The student has surpassed the Master it seems," Jon says, with a smile and a wink.

I scoff, "hardly. What I did was because of the power that's inside of me. My power. I still have a long way to go before I surpass you, Jon, which I highly doubt is even possible."

"Nothing is impossible, Amarah, you're showing us all that."

"We better hurry. We've kept them waiting long enough," Logan announces. "Jon and Vyla are going to fly us the rest of the way. It's a bit of a trek and you need to save your energy."

For once, I don't even try to argue. It never even crosses my mind because I know I don't have the energy for more walking much less a hike.

"Alright," I say, looking around at them. "What are we waiting for then?"

Vyla moves to my side. She secures one arm around my back and leans down to scoop my legs up in the other. She lifts me easily as her wings appear behind her in a shimmering flutter. The strength of the preternatural still astonishes me. I guess I need a few more years of really immersing myself in The Unseen to stop being so damn mystified all the time. Not that I'm complaining.

Jon does the same for Logan and I can't help but chuckle at the sight of a massive Logan cradled in Jon's arms.

"I don't even want to hear it," Logan grumbles.

Jon bites back his laugh and launches into the air with Logan in his arms. Once safe from his verbal onslaught, Vyla and I erupt in shared laughter.

"Oh my, I don't think I'm ever going to get that picture out of my head," Vyla says.

"I only wish I had taken a damn picture," I laugh. "But I'm never going to let him forget this."

Vyla laughs again, "hang on."

I hold on tightly to her neck, careful not to get in the way of her wings. They look so dainty and fragile but they lift us both into the air effortlessly. We glide smoothy across the evening sky as the sunset starts to fade and the darkness is making its way in. Vyla flies us up and towards the top of a decent size mountain however, once we get to the top and make our way over, I realize it's not really a mountain. It's one of the cliffs that surrounds the lake. There are torches lit across the grounds, lighting the edge of the lake where a small group awaits us.

Too small of a group, I mentally note. The Water Fey almost lost their entire line. It's going to take centuries to rebuild into what they once were. Life is cruel in ways I just can't understand sometimes. The pure evil that exists in the world, and not just demons, but in the hearts of some people. I've seen it in the human world time and time again. Some people just hate and hate for no apparent reason. I've seen the value of life decrease in people's minds as people become no more than names behind a screen. More and more innocent lives being taken by senseless evil.

And those of us that are left standing on the sidelines, witnesses to the tragedy and loss, have no other choice but to endure. We have no other choice but to continue moving forward with life, pushing through our own trauma to try and *do* better. To try and *be* better and make the world a better place. But if my short human life has taught me anything, it's that being a survivor is the *hardest* thing to be. The ones who get taken from us are lucky in their own way. They don't have to continue to live in such an ugly and hateful world, trying desperately to hang on to the light. To shed the light on others that need it. But as survivors, we owe it to those who have paid the ultimate sacrifice, to honor them with nothing less than a life lived through love and light. And so, I shall continue to be and fight for that light. I shall continue to live my own life beautifully and bring as much beauty and harmony to this world as I can.

Vyla touches down and gently sets me on my feet. Logan is there immediately to steady me and offer his solid and unwavering support. He leads me towards the water's edge, and everyone steps aside, making room for us. I hear murmurs of praise and thanks as those we pass all bow their heads at us. No, at *me*. Some even reach out and touch my arm as I pass by. I try to acknowledge all of those that do, smiling and offering a touch of comfort of my own. It should unsettle me but I feel oddly at peace.

We make our way to the front of the group and Vadin is standing alone by the edge of the lake. He's wearing a similar style robe to the one Logan and the other men are wearing, but Vadin's is far more elaborate and the sapphires sewn into his robe glint off the torch lights. A crown in the shape of waves sits atop his wavy brown hair. Large sapphires gleam at the peak of each wave, and even though I know the crown must be worth a fortune, its beauty comes from its simplicity.

"Welcome, Amarah," Vadin opens his arms and bows slightly at the waist. "We owe you a great honor for what you've done for the Vesi and all of the lives that reside in The Unseen."

"It's what I was meant to do, Vadin. You don't owe me anything. This is my world now too, and I will always do everything in my power to protect it, and its people."

"Even so, I would be honored if you'd be a part of this

ceremony with me?"

"Of course," I say, enthusiastically. "Whatever you need, I'd be honored to assist."

He dips his chin in acknowledgment before he turns to face the small crowd. Most are Vesi but there are a few others from the other Families as well. I spot Princess Hallana and Nicholas, Prince Emrick and Theo...holding hands, which makes me smile. I also see Princess Arabella and Caleb. They seem to always be together now and I suppose that makes me happy as well.

Towards the back, I finally spot my sister, Iseta. I haven't had a chance to see her much since I've been in and out of sleep for the past day and completely unconscious before that. All I know is that her and Logan have been at my side day and night, barely taking the time to eat and sleep themselves. I make eye contact with Iseta and we share a loving smile before she nods her head, understanding that my attention needs to be elsewhere, and that we'll get our time together soon enough.

Vadin's voice is ringing out, loud and clear, "...and so, let us remember and honor our fallen, as we send them into the Afterlife." He turns back towards the lake and gestures for me to follow him. We take a few steps until our toes are inches away from the water. "I'm going to say the Fey prayer and once I'm finished, I need you to reach down and send a flame out into the water."

I'm a little taken aback by his words. How am I going to set a flame out upon the water? I look out, over the lake, but all I can see is a few feet in front of me from the torch lights. Pass the circle of light, the lake is enshrouded in the darkness of the night. I turn back to him and nod my understanding, even though I don't actually understand anything at all. I have Faith that everything is as it should be and will all work out.

Vadin raises his arms over his head and speaks out towards the lake.

elu pole kunagi kadunud

sest keegi pole kunagi päriselt kadunud

võib-olla olete maksnud lõpliku kulu

aga meis sa elad edasi

kuni me kohtume taas

elagu teie hing rahus ja harmoonias

Vadin drops his arms and gives me a nod. I sink down until I'm crouching over the edge of the water. I place my palm on top of the surface, feeling the cold, fresh water lap at my hand. I call on my power, even stronger than it was an hour ago, and I feel the warm tingle of it rush down my arm, as a white flame emerges from my palm. The instant it touches the water, it lights up and rushes out across the lake. They must have used some kind of flammable substance.

I stand up and Logans hand finds my elbow as he helps me step away from the lake. The flames have separated and rush across the entirety of the lake in precises rows. That's when I finally notice the blue-clad bodies. All of the fallen Fey have been wrapped in their Vesi color of deep, sapphire blue, and placed on individual wooden rafts with the same flowers that adorn my hair decorating them as well.

It's breathtaking.

It's heart wrenching.

The sound of a lighter pulls my attention over to Logan. He's holding a lighter to a piece of paper. Once it's caught the flame, he releases it, and it floats high up into the air. That's when I notice more of them. I glance over my shoulder and see everyone lighting pieces of paper and sending them to float up into the night sky over the lake.

Leaning in to Logan, I whisper, "what's everyone doing?"

"Sending memories into the Afterlife with their loved ones."

"I feel bad that I didn't know any Vesi to join in."

"You had the highest honor tonight, you set he fire that will cleanse them and free their souls to travel to the Afterlife."

"Oh," is all I can muster, as I turn back to look at the beautiful show that's happening on and over the lake.

I had no idea I had been given such an honor. I don't know all of the customs of the Fey or if each Fey Family has a different tradition to send their fallen to the Afterlife, but I do have my own beliefs and so, I bow my head and say a prayer of my own.

Lord, please see these souls through the gates of Heaven and into your arms. Let there be no more pain and no more suffering. Until their loved ones can meet them once again in eternal life. In Jesus' name I pray, Amen.

We stand by the lake until all of the fires have completely gone out. The only light we have now are from the torches lighting up the area we're standing in, but out over the lake, it's pitch black. It's also peacefully quiet. The only sounds are the quiet crackles of the flames on the torches. No one is moving or speaking or Hell, even breathing. It adds to the overall feeling and atmosphere of the dark lake. It could very well be a tunnel into the Afterlife. Dark and silent. A place I've visited before. But what's on the other side? I have an idea of what Heaven will be like but no one truly knows.

"Amarah," Logan's soft voice by my ear makes me jump. "Come on, Vyla is read to fly you back."

I blink, coming back into my senses, and look around us. Everyone else has gone. It's just Logan, Jon, Vyla and I standing by the lake.

"Oh, I'm sorry. How long have I been staring out at the lake?" I ask no one in particular.

"A while," Logan says as he cups my cheek. "Are you

alright?"

I nod, "yes, I'm alright," I give him a small smile. "The Fey prayer that Vadin said. What are the words?"

"A life is never lost, for no one is ever truly gone. You may have paid the ultimate cost but in us you will live on. Until we meet again, may your soul live in peace and harmony," Logan translates the prayer.

I smile at how similar the words I said were to their prayer. "It's beautiful. I hope that each soul does make it to the Afterlife. Thank you for bringing me and letting me be a part of this."

"This is your life now, Amarah. You're one of us," Vyla says, sweetly, as she moves to my side, ready to carry me back.

"Yes," I agree. "Yes, I am."

Amarah: The Way You Love Me

What's Mine Is Yours by Kane Brown

I wanted to spend more time with Vadin and the Vesi, getting to know them and helping them rebuild, but we're back at Headquarters to attend the ceremony for the Queen. And then, after that, I'll have to go through the Valimine to find out if I'm going to be the next Fey Queen or not.

My strength is coming back faster and stronger now but I don't think any amount of my power or strength will be enough to prepare me for this. I honestly don't know if I'll make a good Queen and I sure as Hell know I'm not ready to be a Queen, but I also am desperate to be found worthy. I don't want the throne to reject me but I'm terrified of what it means if it doesn't. My mind and emotions are a mix of my uncertainty. I really don't know what I want.

"Amarah," Logan's deep voice pulls me from my reeling thoughts.

I stop my pacing and take a minute to appreciate Logan's beautiful body. He's stretched out on my bed in my room at Headquarters. My eyes start at his bare feet, ankles crossed, up his grey sweatpant clad legs, over a rippling stomach and muscular chest. His arms are up, hands clasped behind his head, giving me a drool worthy view of his biceps, before I take in his full lips, pulled up into a sexy, confident smirk, and then finally, I lock onto his heated peridot gaze.

"That's better."

"What's better?" I ask, already feeling breathless with just looking at him.

"Your attention focused on *me*."

I walk to the edge of the bed and climb on, sitting back on my heels directly in front of him. The bed is huge and even his large body doesn't come close to filling it.

"Is that the only thing of mine that you want on you?" I keep eye contact as I start to lift the bottom of his shirt I'm wearing.

It hangs down to my thighs so, I give him a slow show of revealing my naked skin, inch by slow inch. I lift the shirt over my hips but leave it hanging in front of me, between my legs, so he can't actually see anything.

"Or maybe you'd like my hands on you?" I suggest, as I trail my own fingertips up my exposed thighs. I keep one hand traveling up, over my breast and to my lips. "Or maybe you want my lips on you," I trace my lips with a single finger. "Orrrr...maybe it's my mouth you want on you," I say, as I swirl my tongue around my finger before I slide it into my mouth and suck on it.

His eyes darken with desire and his nostrils flare. I see his cock twitch under his sweatpants and it's my turn to smirk. "So, my mouth then."

"I want all of you, Amarah," his voice is a low growl, caressing my skin along with those intense eyes, making me shiver.

"What about this?" I ask, as I let go of my power, sending its warmth to caress Logan's body.

I watch as goosebumps spread across his exposed skin and his cock stiffens. "Fuck, I forgot how good your power feels in the bedroom."

A second later I feel the cool breeze of his power on my thighs and then it slithers up the shirt and my breasts peek at the sensation. I close my eyes and sigh against the feel of his power on me, teasing me as if it were his own hands.

"Amarah," his voice once again frees me from my mind. "Come here," he commands.

I crawl to him, stopping to trace my tongue against his hard length through the sweatpants. He groans, but still hasn't moved. I crawl until I'm straddling his waist, looking down at all of his perfection, still in awe as if it's the first time I'm seeing him, standing shirtless in my kitchen.

"I want that kiss," he orders. "The one you gave me when you woke up. It's all I've been fucking thinking about. I fucking crave it. Whatever it is that made you kiss me like that, I want it again. I *need* it again."

I lean down and press my lips to the star that's scarred on his chest. "I think we need to add another star here," I say, with my lips still against his skin. I kiss my way up his chest, up his neck and jaw until I'm hoovering right above his lips. "Because you're no longer a Lone Wolf, Braveheart. I'm yours. For better or for worse, I'm wholly yours."

I press my lips to his and his hands finally move, sliding underneath my hair, holding me against him. I kiss him with everything I have. The same way I did before. No holding back, no doubts, and no fears. No jaded thoughts of him potentially hurting me. Hurting my heart. I pour all of my love and confidence into the kiss and down our bond.

His moans let me know I'm giving him exactly what he needed and I live for them. His moans are life to me. The sexiest fucking sound I've ever heard. They're better than any song or any lyric in the entire world. I could make a playlist of Logan's moans, groans, and growls, and listen to it on repeat for the rest of my life.

His kiss becomes more urgent and his hands leave my hair to remove the shirt from my body. I'm left straddling him completely naked and I couldn't be more comfortable. I've never been more comfortable in my skin and it's all because of Logan. The way he looks at me, the way he touches me and damn near worships me. He makes me feel beautiful and perfect.

Again, as if he can read my mind he says, "God, you're perfect."

"Perfect for you," I clarify.

"I'm starving again," he says, with a wicked grin.

My pussy throbs at his words, understanding his meaning completely. He scoots lower on the bed and lays back. I'm confused for a moment because I thought I was going to be the one lying down.

"I want you to ride my face, Amarah. I want to see that beautiful body above me while you take what you need from my mouth and tongue."

Oh, sweet baby Jesus. Had I been standing I would have collapsed. My knees are weak just by those words, my pussy already soaking, and I haven't even started to cum yet. Had he asked me to do this any other time before now, I don't think I could have done it. I would have been too self-conscious and embarrassed, but I'm not any more. Not with Logan.

"You don't have to tell me twice," I say, as I climb up his sexy body until I'm right above his face.

His hands wrap around my thighs and hold onto my legs. He slips his tongue out and licks me right up the center, parting my lips, and gliding across my already sensitive clit. That one simple stroke has me throwing my head back, moaning, already lost in the pleasure of his warm, wet tongue on me. He keeps working his tongue against me, building me up and up and up, like a sky scraper. He always knows how to work me up to a release so quickly. I'm already close and it's only been a quick minute. Then he stops. I look down with a frustrated groan.

"I want you to take it, Amarah," he says, as he sticks his tongue out but doesn't move it.

"Fuck," I huff out, but I don't argue.

I start to rock my hips against him, moving my clit over his tongue instead of his tongue moving over my clit. Fuck, I'm so sensitive already. I spread my knees a little wider and press harder into his tongue, giving my clit more pressure as I roll my hips in a counter clockwise circle.

"I'm close," I pant above him.

His proud growl reverberates off his tongue and lips and rumbles through me. It's all I need to fall over the edge. I grab onto the headboard for support as I buck against him, his hands on my thighs holding me steadier as he eagerly licks up all of my juices.

My legs are shaking against the sides of his face as I try and catch my breath, "holy shit."

"That was the sexiest thing I think I've ever seen," Logan's voice is low and husky, sending more waves of pleasure through my hot, weak body.

I move off of him and finally look at him. "Oh my God," my face heats even more as the blush explodes. "I made a mess!" I exclaim, as I reach to wipe his face clean.

He grabs my wrist and tsks, "lick it off me and kiss me. I want every last drop."

"Fuck," I breathe out. "Why is everything you say so fucking hot? And the things you want...and do..."

"Are you complaining?"

"Hell no! It's just...it's sexy and I love it. I love you," I say, as I lean in and lick my desire off his chin before kissing him, letting him taste me off my my own tongue.

He finally sits up and slides off the side of the bed. He drops his sweats, kicking free of them, and stands completely naked in front of me. His hard length pressed against his flat stomach. The thick veins engorged with blood pumping through them reaching towards his slick, soft head. I've never thought penises could be beautiful but fuck, everything about this man is perfection to look at.

"Come here," he demands again.

I do. I crawl to him for the second time tonight, and I'll crawl to him for the rest of my damn life. I'd crawl on my hands and knees for miles for this man. He puts me on my back and steps between my legs.

"Do you remember when you took a hold of my power to fight Lucifer?"

My brows furrow, confused at where his train of thought is going at a time like this. "Yes, why?"

"It gave me an idea and I want to try something. Using our connection."

"Ok," I whisper, still not sure what he's getting at.

I need you completely open to me, Angel. His voice floats through my mind.

I'm yours, Logan. Take what you want. I trust you.

Close your eyes and focus on our power. On our connection. He tells me.

I do, easily. I can feel our power mingling together and, just like with Lucifer, I can feel his power as if it's mine. As if it's another extension of myself. Then, I feel him taking my power, controlling it,

292

just like I did with his. And he's right, it feels normal, just like we're sharing a hug or a kiss. Then, an image floods my mind. I gasp as I realize what's happening.

"Do you remember when I told you that I wish you could see what I see? That I wish you could see the way your body takes me?"

"Yes," I whisper, all the air in my lungs seems to have disappeared. I open my eyes, I can see Logan standing above me, but I can also see myself, laying on the bed in front of Logan, through *his* eyes.

"I think this is just one more thing we're capable of sharing with our bond," he says, excitedly. "And now, I want you to watch as I take you. As I slide my big cock into your little body, and you get to see how beautiful it is when I disappear inside of you."

My heart is racing in a whole new way. This is exciting in a way that I've never felt with anyone else. I mean, how could I? I'm going to watch him fuck me from his own view point. The thought alone has me getting slick and pulsing with need again.

He fists his hard cock, pumping it a few times, letting me get a good view of what it looks like when he jerks off. Fuck it's hot. Then he finally slides the tip of his cock through my lips, gathering my wetness so the head gleams with is. He runs the length of his cock against me, back and forth, coating himself with the only lubricant we'll ever need.

Me.

I'm so fucking hot for this man it's unreal. My body will always and forever give up everything for him. I watch, from his eyes, as he holds his cock to my entrance and starts to push inside of me. I gasp, both from the intense visual and the intense pressure of his massive head stretching me to fit him. The tip slowly slips inside of me and then he pulls it back out, before pushing inside again, this time with another inch of his length.

He does this over and over again, so incredibly slowly, and

I'm so fucking gone. It's the hottest thing I've ever seen, as I watch his dick push inside of me. My eyes are locked on the visual and I don't even want to blink. I don't want to miss a second of watching him take me, fill me. He still hasn't given me everything and I'm already on the verge of another orgasm. The visual is adding to the sensation and I'm fucking coming undone.

I watch as he finally pushes the last thick inch inside of me and then he starts making love to me in long, slow strokes.

"Holy fuck, that's the sexiest thing I've ever seen," I echo his words from earlier. "You're going to make me cum, Logan."

He finally moves his eyes up to the rest of my body, letting me see myself through his eyes, as I lose all control of my body and the desire rocks through me.

"Fuck," I hear him groan.

But he holds the image solid as he continues to push into me. When I finally manage to open my eyes and look at him, I can't help the tears that are running down the sides of my head. Logan sees them and stops immediately. The image cuts off, he slides out of me and climbs on top of me, moving us both to the center of the bed.

He wipes at my wet eyes, "Amarah, what's wrong? What did I do?"

I shake my head, "nothing!" My voice is thick with tears and emotion, I'm having a hard time speaking. "The way you look at me, the way you see me..."

"What, babe, tell me. Please don't cry, I didn't mean to make you cry." His eyes have lost all the heat and desire they held a minute ago as they turn to concern.

"You see me in a way I've never seen myself," I manage to get a hold of my emotions and my voice. "It's...beautiful," I choke out. Maybe I don't have control of my emotions. I push against his chest until he's lying on his back and I'm looking down at him. "Thank you,"

294

I whisper. "Thank you for loving me the way you do."

I take his mouth with mine again, and if he thought I kissed him with everything I had before, it's nothing compared to how I kiss him now. I climb on top of him while I kiss him, never once breaking the kiss, as I slide back onto his hard cock. He groans and I gasp as he pushes back inside of me. I finally pull away from the kiss so I can breathe and get more of his length inside of me. I arch my back and throw my head back. Logan's hands slide up my sides and squeeze my breasts as I ride him with abandon.

"Amarah," He once again pulls my attention back to him. "Look at me," he commands.

And I do. I see him. I see him the way he sees me. There's never been anyone else before him and there will never be anyone after him.

"You're mine," he says, eyes never wavering from mine.

"And you're mine."

Amarah: Every Ending Has A New Beginning

Drive by Incubus

Needless to say, I didn't get much sleep again last night. The ache between my legs is a pleasant reminder of exactly *how* I spent my time instead and I'm not complaining. We managed to spend a little bit of time in the natural healing hot spring/tub in my bathroom and I'm honestly feeling better than I have in a long time.

My power is back.

My strength is back

Aralyn and Revna are both dead.

The rip has been closed.

Other than having to attend a ceremony for Queen Anaxo, my aunt and last family member, and the hundreds of lives lost in this war, things are actually finally looking up. I finally feel like we're taking more steps forward than we are backward.

I've come to realize, and with the education of Logan, that all of the Fey Surmajärgne Elu ceremonies are basically the same. There are, of course, a few differences for each Family and how they choose honor their fallen and send them into the Afterlife.

The Headquarters throne room as been filled to the brim with chairs, and they're *all* taken, with more people standing around in every available space. It seems like every single person in The Unseen is here to honor the Queen and pay their last respects. She really was a great Queen and this turn out is proof of that. Not that I had any doubt.

The Queen has been prepped and is up on the dais in a beautiful gold casket. Well, I say casket because I don't know any other word for it, but it's a large, elaborate golden…case. The Queen has been dressed in the same golden dress I met her in. Her hair, once a vibrant sun-yellow, is almost white, with just a hint of the yellow it once had been. Still, even in death, she looks beautiful and regal.

This ceremony is more like the human funerals I'm familiar with. The loved one is displayed and you can walk up to the dais and say any last words or a goodbye. I was fortunate enough to have alone time with her before everyone else was allowed entry into the throne room. I'm not nearly as sad as I thought I would be but it's because I still feel her with me. She was there with me when I healed the Water Fey and again when I closed the rip.

She'll always be with me.

She'll always guide me.

As her last blood relative, I've been asked to say the Fey prayer, to send her off into the Afterlife. So, I stand from my seat in the front row, gathering my own golden dress around me, and climb the stairs of the dais. Once I'm on the platform, I turn to take in the massive crowd gathered around me. All the Families are dressed in their colors, blue for the Vesi, White for the Õhk, green for the Maa and red for the Tulekahju. There are only a handful of the Müstik bloodline wearing gold, like me, but none of them are from our direct family line. Still, there's a bond there that I want to develop and explore. The other preternatural factions are not present though. This is a Fey only ceremony for the Queen.

I clear my throat and a quiet hush feels the room and my voice echoes throughout easily. "I'm not exactly sure the right way to do all of this so please, bear with me. Before I say the prayer, I just wanted to say thank you, to all of you who have come here today. I knew that Anaxo was a great Queen the very first time I met her, and you being here," I gesture to the entire room, "says more than any words ever can. I'm proud to be an Andrews, proud to be Müstik, and proud to be amongst all of you. No matter what happens next, let us be united together, because united, we can overcome anything thrown our way."

There's applause and some shouts of agreement, from Emrick, if I'm not mistaken, which makes me smile. Once the room is quiet again, I continue.

"Now, let us put Queen Anaxo at peace and send her into a beautiful Afterlife." I turn to face Ana and open my arms like Vadin did when he spoke the prayer.

elu pole kunagi kadunud
sest keegi pole kunagi päriselt kadunud
võib-olla olete maksnud lõpliku kulu
aga meis sa elad edasi
kuni me kohtume taas
elagu teie hing rahus ja harmoonias

Once I'm done with the prayer, and another silent one of my own, I walk up to the large casket and drop in my paper of memories I wrote on it. As I turn to leave, Logan is standing just behind me, a line forming behind him. Everyone will drop in their own memories before she's taken away and buried in the crypt.

Logan is also wearing gold since he served as Kaitsja, protecting the Queen and the Fey. The gold of his robe brings out the golden yellow of his eyes, his father's eyes, his Angel eyes, drawing me in like they always do. God, he's so beautiful and he's my rock. I wouldn't be able to do any of this without him by my side.

You did everything perfectly, he says directly to me.

I love you, is the only response appropriate for what's in my heart.

I step off the dais and return to my seat. Logan is back at my side within seconds, reaching for my hand. We sit, side by side, in perfect contentment, as we wait for the large group of Fey to make their way onto the dais and leave Ana with their beloved memories.

Once everyone is finished, the Leaders of each family, plus Logan and I, make our way back up the dais. Logan takes one side, I stand next to him, and Emrick comes in behind me. Then, Vadin takes the other side, across from Logan, Hallana across from me, and Arabella across from Emrick. We each take a hold of the handle and lift it up. To say it's heavy would be an understatement, but none of us are human. Hell, Logan could have probably carried it on his own, but we all walk in unison, down the dais steps and off into the tunnels.

Once, again, I have no idea where we're headed, but Logan and Vadin are leading us. We walk for a solid five minutes, twisting and turning down tunnels, until we come to a fairly large cavernous room. There's a hole that's been carved into one of the walls, big enough for the casket, and we slide it inside. The bottom of the casket has a removable bottom that Logan slides out. This allows Ana's body to fall into the shallow grave that was dug inside of the hole.

The Müstik Fey are more one with the Earth, like the Maa

Family, than the other Fey. We will return Ana's body to the ground where her body can give back to the Earth and her soul can travel to the peace and harmony of Afterlife. Once Ana's casket is secure inside and the false bottom removed, Emrick moves the Earth and seals it shut. He then uses rocks and roots to mark Ana's resting place like a headstone would a grave. I watch as fresh flowers are pulled out of the Earth and bloom right before our eyes.

"They're beautiful, Emrick," I say, smiling, as I watch them bloom.

"This room is where you will also be laid to rest, if you choose," Logan informs me.

"As long as I'm next to you in life and in death, I don't really care where they lay my body," I say, matter-of-factly. "But here would be perfect."

We all stand together for another moment of silence before we head back to the throne room. In another couple of hours, once everyone has had a chance to mourn Ana and celebrate her life, we will start the Valimine, the selection of the new Fey Queen, because they cannot be without a Leader for any longer than they already have. And even though I'm still trying to focus on the Queen we just laid to rest, I can't help that my thoughts are swirling around what this next step might mean for me. The next couple of hours can drastically change my life. I'll either be a Queen to an entire race and world, or I'll be in the service of a Queen, and I'm not sure which option makes me more nervous.

Amarah: Divine Destiny

Biblical by Calum Scott

I'm standing on the dais looking out into the packed room, even more crowded than it was for the Queen's ceremony, if that's even possible. Everyone is here. In addition to all of the Fey, Valmont is here, along with Iseta, Brynn, Ethan, Kaedon and Atreya. Everyone in The Unseen has come to see who the new Queen is going to be. Because this decision affects everyone, every single being in The Unseen, whether Fey or otherwise.

As I stand here, looking out over the many faces I now know and some I even love and care for, I can't help but reminisce about the first time I stood here looking out over only five unfamiliar faces. I was in complete awe and shock, and so incredibly scared at what all of this meant. I was scared to learn who I really was and who I might become. I've definitely had some bright moments along the way and some very hard and embarrassing stumbles, too.

But through it all, I've survived, and now I'm standing here, stronger and more confident and surer of myself than I've ever been before. There's no uneasiness in my heart or soul.

There's no more wondering about what's missing.

Wondering if this is all there is to life.

Wondering what my purpose is.

Wondering who I am.

For the very first time in my life, I know exactly who I am and what my purpose is.

I'm half Angel.

I'm half Fey.

I belong to this world, to The Unseen, with all of its beauty, Magic, and danger. This is where I belong. These are my people. This is my family, even though we may not share blood. No matter what the future holds, I'm home.

Logan's voice is a whisper next to my ear as he leans in, "you did this, Angel. You brought The Unseen together like this, when no one else could. Take a good look at this moment and remember it. Cherish it."

I listen to his advice and look out over the crowd one more time, really soaking it in. I did do this, didn't I? No matter what happens next, I did accomplish something good in my time here and I *can* continue to do good here, in any capacity.

"Now kneel," he instructs.

I take in a deep, shaky breath and expel it as I drop to a knee. I keep my head up, looking out over the crowd as Logan's voice booms from behind me.

"Amarah Rey Andrews, of the Müstik Family, you have been brought forth for Selection to become Queen of the Fey and the throne *has* deemed you pure of heart and worthy of this title. Do you swear to honor the throne and to not only do what's best for the Fey, but for all of The Unseen, at all costs? Even if that cost is your life?"

"I do," I state loudly and with conviction.

Logan places the crown on my head, and even though it's not as heavy as it looks, I feel the weight of it on my shoulders. The weight of what it means to be responsible for so many others. Again, I say a silent prayer of my own as I accept a new role, a new life, and ask that I truly be worthy. That I continue to be guided down the right path.

"Then rise, Amarah Rey Andrews, Queen of the Fey, Queen of the Unseen."

I feel two sets of hands, one on each of my arms, as I rise, and I know in that moment, I will never, ever be truly alone. Ana and my mother will be with me every step of the way, to lead me and to pick me up when I stumble.

The crowd erupts in cheers and applause, people are shouting and whistling, I even hear a couple of howls, and I can't help the huge, genuine smile that spreads across my face as the happy tears stream down my cheeks in floods. I couldn't be happier or prouder than I am in this moment.

Until the crowd stops yelling and gasps erupt instead.

I blink back my tears and look out over the crowd, trying to gauge their reaction. Trying to understand what's happened. When I lock eyes with Emrick. His face is stubbornly blank, but he points behind me. I turn around and a small gasp of my own fills the suddenly silent room before my hand clamps down over my lips.

Logan is on one knee, with a beautiful diamond ring held up between his big fingers. His green eyes are shining with tears of their own, and the smile that spreads across his face is about to make me melt into a puddle, right here on the dais.

"Amarah, my life before you is irrelevant. All of it. I didn't start living until you found me. You not only saved me, but you showed me the type of man I want to be, the type of man you bring out of me. I never knew a love like this could even exist and I'll do whatever it takes to keep it, to cherish it, and to never disrespect it. Or you. You're so much more than my mate, my Angel, or my Queen, you're my entire fucking world. Will you continue to save me, every single day, for the rest of our lives? Will you be my wife?"

My heart is pounding out of my chest harder than when I was

up here being tested for Queen. And if I thought that moment, on stage, was the happiest and proudest moment of my life…I was wrong.

This is it.

I fall to my knees in front of him, taking his face in my hands, tears blurring his handsome face, as I say, "yes, Braveheart, together, always. Yes!"

I crush my lips to his as the crowd erupt in cheers again. This time there are way more whistles and jeers and definitely more howls. Our kiss a mixture of smiles, laughter, and tears, from both of us.

He finally pulls back and lifts up the ring between us. "You didn't even look at the ring," he chuckles.

"The ring is just a bonus. You're the only thing I need," and I want him to know that I *mean* it, but I look down at the ring and gasp again. "Oh. My. God. Logan! It's beautiful," I say, as more tears stream down my face as he slides it onto my finger.

It's a diamond, a very *large* diamond, in the shape of a star, with smaller diamonds framing it but slightly underneath the raised larger center. So, it resembles two stars.

"Logan, this is…"

"I got worried when you kissed my scar and mentioned I should get another one. I thought you knew."

I raise my eyes to look up at him, "no, I swear! I didn't know!"

He chuckles again, "I can see that." He touches my chin with his fingers, bringing my eyes back to him because they fell back to the giant ring on my finger. "Amarah, you are my other half, my North Star, my mate, my *everything*. I know that I'll never be alone again, and as long as you wear this ring proudly on your finger, I'll never be a Lone Wolf, ever again."

I shake my head, "I'm never taking it off. In fact, I'm going to have Iseta put a spell on it so that it can't ever come off or get damaged. It's too beautiful. It's perfect. *You're* perfect."

He kisses me again and the sound of the crowd cheering again finally reminds me that we're on the dais, in front of hundred and hundreds of people. Once again, Logan has completely consumed me and nothing or no one else mattered. Not even being crowned Queen.

I blush as Logan helps me stand and we face the crowd, hands clasped together. He raises my hand and yells, "she said yes!" As if they didn't already know that.

The crowd erupts for a third time and I can't help but laugh and beam like a fucking idiot as people start to make their way up the dais stairs to congratulate us. I'm lost in a sea of people, words, and hugs. People demanding to see the ring and ooing and awing over it. I feel like the *Grinch*, my heart swelling to an immense size inside of my chest, practically suffocating me. Logan and I manage to make eye contact through the throng of people and his voice sings in my mind.

So, do you believe that this is your destiny? He asks.

I do. Do you?

He only nods. *Together, Fiancé.*

Always.

Epilogue: Amarah

I Get To Love You by Ruelle

The July summer heat filters in through the open sliding glass door. It's no use trying to keep the house cool, not with people constantly coming in and out, but I don't mind. In fact, the scene in my backyard is giving me life. I take a quiet moment to lookout into the back yard and observe everyone.

"Hey!" Emrick shouts across the cornhole game to Jon. "You better not be cheating! I felt that push of air!

"What?!" Jon exclaims, "I would never stoop to cheating! We can beat you fair and square, ain't that right honey?"

"With our eyes closed and one hand tied behind our backs," Vyla agrees, taunting Emrick and Theo.

Theo leans in and kisses Emrick on the cheek with words of encouragement, "come on, Babe, you got this!"

Little Vic is playing fetch with Griffin, who's tail is wagging so fast, I'm worried he may fly away.

Logan's laugh pulls my attention away from the cornhole game and over to the BBQ grill. His head is thrown back on a laugh, so is Atreya's, more than likely at something Kaedon said. Logan takes a swig of his beer as he flips burgers. His tank top pulled tight across his chest and his massive arms on full display. The sight of him laughing and at ease with friends, no…*family*, has my heart clenching and eyes watering. I think if you had told either of us a year ago, that this is where we would be today, we would have laughed in your face.

I pull my eyes away from him and to the table on the patio, right in front of me. Iseta is entertaining Paula and Cristi, doing a tarot card reading on Cristi, who's leaned in completely focused on what she's revealing.

I had finally broken down and told my friends the truth about me and The Unseen. Surprisingly, they took it all extremely well. Paula didn't even bat an eye and Cristi has been enthralled completely wanting to know everything about me and my new world. I think she has eyes for Kaedon and…I think he's equally interested. Iseta says that she's sensitive to magic and has promised to teach her more about crystals, cards, and magic.

I'm relieved that all of the people I love are finally connected and I no longer have to keep them separate. I no longer have to be someone I'm not. A lost, human girl, trying to find the missing piece in the wrong world. Now, standing here, looking out at my new life, my new normal, I'm so incredibly blown away and grateful.

I have a family.

A beautiful and wonderful family, filled with the best people, which is so much more than any girl could ask for.

"Marah! Marah!" Tori's little voice screeches up at me as she comes plowing into my legs. "Can I help?" Her sparkling, violet eyes gaze up at me.

"You sure can, sweet girl," I say, as I smile down at her. I reach onto the counter and hand her an empty serving platter. "You can take this to Logan for me."

She beams up at me, "ok!" She takes it and rushes off to her favorite person without another question.

I pull the baking sheet of jalapeno poppers out of the oven, these things are always a hit and a *must* for every get together, and follow little Tori outside to the man of my dreams who, coincidentally, is also *my* favorite person. I see Logan bend down to his knee, taking the tray from Tori and then kissing her on her cheek, making her giggle before she runs off towards her mom. The interaction tugs at my heart strings even more. I have to clear my throat from the knot of emotion starting to build up.

"I come bearing gifts!" I announce, as I place the tray on the small island counter in front of the grill, and then move to stand beside Logan. He pulls me into his side and I wrap my arms around him as he places a kiss on my forehead.

"I swear," Atreya moans as she takes a bite of a popper, "you guys seriously have the *best* food here. Amarah, please promise to invite me over for every get together."

I laugh, "a party without you isn't a party at all."

"Amarah, those hands are too empty and you've been working too hard on all of this. It's time for you to sit back and enjoy it with us," Kaedon says, as he offers me a cold Dos Equis. My favorite beer.

God, it would be the perfect thing to beat the summer heat but I decline. "None for me, thanks," I say, as my hand subconsciously moves to my belly.

Kaedon's eyes immediately go wide, staring at my hand, then up to my eyes, then to Logan and back to my hand. He's pointing with the beer in his outstretched hand, his mouth opening and closing as he tries to get his words out past his shock.

"You...you're...you and Logan..."

I laugh and nod. "Yes," I say, as I look up at Logan. His eyes are already on me, a huge smile on his face and he's beaming down at me. The love and pride so clear you'd be able to see it from outer space.

"My man," Kaedon says, setting the beer down on the island and moving in to congratulate Logan.

I step out of the way so he can give Logan a thorough bro hug before he turns his attention on me. He wraps me up in a big, tight hug and whispers into my ear, "you're the best damn thing that ever happened to him, Amarah. You've always been his family, the only one he ever needed but this," he pulls back, tears in his eyes as he looks at my stomach. I'm not even showing yet, but it's like he can already see an eight-month belly. "This," he says again, a huge smile breaking across his face, "this is everything."

"What'd I just miss?" Atreya says through a mouth full of food.

Logan pulls me back into his arms, this time, wrapping both of his arms around me, looking down on me with those damn, irresistible fucking eyes. "I," he says, never taking his eyes off of me, "am going to be a dad."

"What?" I hear Atreya exclaim somewhere behind me. "Oh my, God! This is the best news!"

I hear the others yelling across the yard, asking what's going on. There's commotion behind me as everyone reacts to the news and I can feel the presence of the others as they're all gathering around us but all I see is Logan. All I feel is Logan.

Hi, Wife, he smirks as he stares at me from inches away but slips into my mind for a private conversation.

Hi, Husband, I beam up at him.

You are so fucking beautiful. More beautiful than you've ever been. And you're only going to grow more and more beautiful every day as my wife, and as the mother of my child, and I cannot wait to spend every fucking day of the rest of my life with you and this family.

Our family, Logan. Mine and yours and no one is ever going to take that away from us. Our own little Pack. And I will love you and this family more and more every fucking day.

Our Pack, a beautiful smile spreads across his face. *God, I love the sound of that with you. It's always been you, Amarah, always and only you. For the rest of my life.*

I love you, Braveheart.

I love you, Amarah Rey Lewis. Together. Always, he says, as he takes my mouth with his.

It's a small, soft kiss, because even though he's all I see, I know that that can't be said for those eagerly standing around, watching us, waiting for us to address them and celebrate. But they can all wait for one more second as I show my husband how much I love him.

And as I stare up into Logan's handsome face, his green eyes locked on mine.

My gravity.

My center.

My whole fucking world.

I can't help but let all of the emotion and love pour down my cheeks as I stand here, surround by love, by family, and I look into the eyes of my future.

I'm home.

I'm found.

And for the first time in my life, I can't wait for tomorrow. And the day after that. And the day after that.

<u>Author's Note & Acknowledgements</u>

This is the end of the Amarah Rey Series. It's so bittersweet and surreal that I'm sitting here typing this. When I sat down to write this story two years ago, it was mainly an outlet, a way for me to become someone else, to dream up a world that was better than reality, and I never in a million years thought it would become one of my greatest and proudest achievements. It's with a full, but heavy heart, that I say goodbye to Amarah and all of the beautiful characters I created along the way. You are so loved. You will forever hold a special place in my heart. You will be cherished. You will be missed.

As always, if you're reading this, I ask that you please leave your thoughts in a review on Amazon, Goodreads, and any other social media platform you have. It's extremely hard being noticed as an unknown indie author and my greatest source of marketing is YOU, the reader. So please, share, share, share! But always be kind.

This may be the end of Amarah and the Fey Warrior Series, but it is just the begging for me, as a writer. I can't wait to bring you even more stories, more variety and more genres, as I explore my own story and bring my dreams to life! Let's do this!

I want to take this time to also thank some amazing people in my life. People who have been on this journey with me, believing in me, supporting me, and encouraging me along the way. Of course, first and foremost, is my husband, Luis. The one who gets to see the good, the bad, and the ugly. He sees all of my triumphs and wins and all of my defeats, struggles and tears. He is, by far, my biggest cheerleader and believes in me when I don't even believe in myself. My sisters, Danelle and Kizzy, who encourage, love, and support me every day. My mom, Lucy, who eagerly asks when the next book is going be ready, even though I'm slightly embarrassed about the spicy scenes I write knowing she's reading the lol!

And to my bookstagram family. I am seriously blown away by the amount of love and support I receive from strangers over the internet! But some of these beautiful souls have become the best of friends, people I love and adore. I'm going to name a few that have been with me from the start. Lindsay D, Sarah F, Ada A, Sasha D, Shelley, Gabby L, Stephanie K, Leigh R, Moira D.

And a huge shoutout to my new Street Team! Abigail, Gabby, Ashley, Janelle, Veronique, Diana, Emily. Kriti, Ashley, Mega, Leigh, Lyssa, Moira, Cristy, Rose, Sarah, Stephanie, Ada, Sara, Jodena, Jenny, and Effie! You ladies are the best team a girl could ask for and I'm looking forward to such a beautiful future and partnership with you all!

And I cannot forget my amazingly talented and wonderful artist, Nora! @adamszkiart for bringing to life Amarah and all of my characters so beautifully! I am looking forward to a beautiful future and partnership with you as well!

If I missed anyone, I am so sorry! It is not my intent to leave ANYONE out. Thank you to everyone who takes the time to find me on social media and give me a follow, who engages on my posts, and support each small step towards my dream of becoming a full-time author. My DMs are always open! With so much love and a full heart xoxo, Harmony.

Made in the USA
Middletown, DE
30 May 2023

31754682R00191